STAR

QUADRANT

OMEGA

STEPHEN J

Our Universe…
So many worlds in an ocean of stars.

Copyright @ 2019 by Stephen Joseph Gerli
All rights reserved. This book or any portion thereof may not be reproduced or used in any manner whatsoever without the express written permission of the publisher, except for the use of brief quotations in a book review.
print ISBN: 9798330451166
ebook ISBN: 979834821787

CONTENTS

Chapter 1: Britannia 410 AD — 1

Chapter 2: Andromeda 2217 — 18

Chapter 3: The Android Doctor — 40

Chapter 4: The Solarist — 60

Chapter 5: The Academic Experience — 88

Chapter 6: Trikan — 99

Chapter 7: The Rain Forest — 114

Chapter 8: Escape Across the Desert — 134

Chapter 9: The Old City — 169

Chapter 10: The Northern Fortress — 201

Chapter 11: Revelations — 223

Chapter 12: Emissary — 254

Chapter 13: Destination: Sports Arena — 278

Chapter 14: The War Games — 303

Chapter 15: The Safehouse — 343

Chapter 16: The Holographic Code — 372

Chapter 17: Therapeutic Prognosis — 390

Chapter 18: Central Detention — 414

Chapter 19: Shields of Destruction — 451

Chapter 20: Star Voyage — 475

Chapter 1:
Britannia 410 AD

In the early morning hours, the fog of the damp fields begins to lift, and the silence of the night gives way to the sounds of nature's creations of innocence. The pleasant moments of daybreak in this wild forest of Britannia are suddenly disrupted by the hard gallop of horses and their mounted warriors.

The lead cavalry centurion continuously shouts to the camp guards who protect the Legion Base Camp's outer perimeter that he carries an important message for the tribune. As he approaches the camp of this rural outpost in the unsettled Highland Territory, he throws out a cylinder-type canister wrapped in embroidered leather with the emperor's seal on it. He shouts in a loud, harsh voice, "Take this to your tribune! A proclamation from the emperor!"

As he pulls his horse back abruptly in front of the centurion guard, he stops momentarily before turning his mount. Without further explanation, the rider hurriedly retreats down the muddy forest road from where he came, followed by several of his cohorts.

The officer in charge of the main gate immediately picks up the cylinder-type canister and, for a moment, stares down the path as the riders disappear into the morning mist. He cleans off the dirt on the canister with his tunic, and with an expression of disgust, he spits on the ground where the lead horseman turned and failed to salute him.

Turning to one of his subordinates, he speaks in a low, calm voice, "Take this to the tribune's messenger immediately!"

The centurion gate guard abruptly mounts his horse and is about to ride off, but instead, he turns his mount to the centurion officer and salutes him. With his expression changing from anger to one of appreciation, the officer of the guard gives the rider a respectful nod in return, as the centurion then rides down the main path of the camp complex, shouting out the name of the Tribune's messenger.

This is a striking contrast to an early morning roll call to assemble, where moments ago, the troop personnel were sleeping in their tents and are now abruptly awakened. Most personnel will not inquire about what has just occurred within their tent compound; they automatically revert to their routine of discipline, free from personal thoughts that might intrude on their actions. They immediately dress and hastily gather their gear, putting on their armaments without the familiar sounds of assembly trumpets. There will be no disciplined line of assembly outside their tents.

The disarray and personal inquiries become spontaneous throughout the camp as the cavalrymen attend to their horses and prepare them for the chariots that will carry the Roman army to another victory. Their movements are spontaneous as they go about what their military training has equipped them for. Spears and pickaxes are placed where they belong inside the personnel chariot carriages, while other infantrymen attach the brave animals that will carry the first attack against the enemy. The troops stand ready outside their tents with everything in place, awaiting the final orders from their unit captains to assemble.

The call of his name awakens the tribune's messenger as he throws aside the opening of his tent. The early morning sunlight momentarily blinds and disorients him. Holding up his hand to block the sun, he shouts to the centurion dismounting from his horse, "You have orders for the tribune?"

The centurion replies as he hands the sealed scroll to the tribune's messenger, "Yes, it has just arrived moments ago from the emperor."

Trying to clear his mind after an early morning awakening, he looks down and realizes he is still wearing his nightclothes. "Wait here for a moment, centurion."

As the tribune's messenger quickly leaves for his tent, he returns and is now wearing his field rank authority, which he has thrown over his night garments, identifying him as the tribune's messenger. He says, "Centurion, ride me up to the tribune's tent!"

The two men mount the centurion's horse and ride to the far end of the camp, an elevated plateau offering a panoramic view of the entire base. This well-protected compound is manned by the imperial emperor guards, who have sworn allegiance and would sacrifice their very existence to the emperor and his tribunes.

After receiving the messenger, the imperial guard's captain enters the tent, respectfully excuses his intrusion, and then salutes. The tribune and his two generals are studying a map on a large oak table, inscribed with the legion symbol of Roman authority, the *Golden Eagle*. They quickly look up at the centurion captain, and the tribune says, "Just a moment, captain."

He then turns his attention to the table and addresses the generals while marking the map with a stylus. He allows the captain to hear what confidential instructions would typically be shared with his generals.

"This is where we will meet the noblemen of the highlands to begin the peace treaty process... Do you agree?"

The two generals nodded in acceptance, and the tribune looked up to the captain and asked, "Yes, captain, what is it?"

"Your messenger has arrived; may he enter the tent, your excellency?"

"Yes." As the captain pushes aside the canvas entrance, he addresses the nervous young messenger and says, "You may enter."

Upon entering, the young messenger does not salute and offers the message scroll with extended arms. Clearing his throat and looking for the right words, he addresses the tribune without acknowledging his title. With a slight smile, one of the generals responds to the young messenger, "Are you at a loss for words, young man?"

Nervously, the messenger responds, "No, Sir! I never expected to be carrying a message from the emperor."

The tribune replies, "I will give you a well done if you release your grip on the scroll."

Tribune Verlairius takes the canister from the messenger's hand. Looking at the disarray of the young envoy, adorned in his nightclothes and war armament, he smiles and says, "I'm sure you will someday be a fine centurion." You may go, young man, and tell the captain to enter my tent."

The messenger quickly leaves the tent and addresses the centurion captain. "Sir, the tribune wishes to see you."

Putting down a hot goblet of broth and a share of hard bread, the captain enters the tent, salutes, and remains silent. The tribune takes the canister, breaks the seal, and pulls out the message scroll. He then unrolls it and places it on the table, over the map, in front of the two generals.

The three men study it for a few moments, and then the Tribune reads the message from the emperor to the centurion captain,

"Hear the emperor's words, Captain! Greetings to my champions! Tribune Verlairius and all that follow in his command.

Heroes of the people, the Senate, and Rome, I stand with you in the sunlight of Peace! My sincerest wishes that you all remain safe; Rome needs you! By command, all legions must leave Britannia by the fourth night.

The two generals step back from the large table, allowing the centurion captain to view the document as Tribune Verlairius continues to read the rest of the emperor's message aloud:

Salvage whatever you can! War transports are awaiting your arrival, as well as eight hundred barges for supplies and the cavalry livestock. All legions must follow this decree by the fourth night, or all will be lost."

The tribune then hastily signs the two documents and presses his ring, which makes his mark alongside the emperor's wax seal. He then hands only the top scroll to the captain and advises, "Centurion, take this message to every man in every squad in your legion and prepare for withdrawal!"

Before the captain can leave to announce the proclamation, a disturbance occurs outside the tent. Two centurions enter while restraining a large man dressed in expensive robes and wearing gold bracelets. For a moment, the Tribune is startled by the intrusion. General Pontus then yells out to the two guards, "Who is this man?"

In a loud, angry voice, the tribune commands the guards, "Release him!"

The two centurions immediately obey; however, this does not satisfy Diplomat Claudius Demetrice's temper, as he insists on a last physical attempt to push the two centurions away from him. Brushing his garments off with his hands, he responds to the tribune, "I order you,

Tribune Verlairius, to tell your scoundrel troops to keep their distance from my person! Don't you teach them how to treat the emperor's ambassador properly? I simply asked for an audience with you, and I was denied and questioned by senseless legionnaires who would not believe my illustrious title!"

Raising his hand, Tribune Verlairius says, "Claudius Demetrice, calm down... Reserve your temper! I'm sure my centurion guards will shed tears of anguish when they think about how badly you were treated."

"Well, Tribune Verlairius, you must appreciate the important work I do here; sent by our glorious emperor, I have endured much hardship to bring peace to this province."

Tribune Verlairius grins. "I do appreciate your work, Claudius, but I am sure none of my centurions recognized you. If I may introduce you to my generals, I would like to present General Pontius and General Cassius.

He then asks his two generals, "Do you recognize this man?" The two generals stay silent as Tribune Verlairius adds, "Let me explain who he is; for almost a year, he has supplied our camp with fresh produce, and was not allowed to speak a word, because of his secret mission. You must recall seeing him at the supply camp with his three servants unloading his wagons full of produce. He was allowed, along with his servants, to enter and leave the camp several times when our fresh produce supply required his services. His disguise was perfect for his mission."

Turning his attention away from the generals, the tribune looks towards the ambassador. Do you have the peace treaty agreement so I can sign it?"

The ambassador replies, "Why, yes, of course, tribune. I travel day and night with it, and it's never out of sight!"

Pointing, Tribune Verlairius says, "Then lay it down on my table so that I may sign it."

The diplomat immediately unzips his large carry case, resembling an animal feed bag, and places the emperor's peace treaty before the tribune. The tribune takes a moment to read the agreement, already familiar with its conditions; he speaks out as he signs the document, "I, Tribune Verlairius, in charge of all legions in the Province of Britannia, agree to all the words and conditions in this peace document. There will be no further reasons or conditions that will deny this agreement. I sign on behalf of the Emperor and the Roman authorities of the Senate."

Pressing a wax seal of his ring to the document, he places it before the two generals. The two generals confirm it with their signatures and press their wax seals from their rings onto the document. "Claudius, I will assign several of my guards to escort you and your servants to Nobleman Jameous Shawnwood; when he signs, there will be peace in this great land!"

Acknowledging, Claudius asks, "Verlairius, am I to understand that you will not ride with me and attend the peace agreement with Nobleman Shawnwood? You trust in this man, yet you insult him with your absence?"

"These are bad times, my good friend Claudius! Moments ago, before your entrance into my tent, I was instructed by our emperor by decree to have all my legions abandon Britannia. We must cross the channel with as much as we can take with us?"

As he unfolds the emperor's decree, he allows Ambassador Claudius Demetrice to read it. Claudius looks up at the tribune in question. "Does this mean everything is lost?"

"No, Claudius, but we are in difficult times! We must move to avoid a complete disaster. You must complete your mission! Nobleman Shawnwood is our only hope for creating the balance we need at this time. The legions will sail across the channel to put down the uprisings in Gaul. I will provide you with my fastest chariots, and upon completion of your mission, you must graciously withdraw and make haste to the port city of Julius. A long boat and crew shall await you and your party there. Hasten and let providence guide you! By this time tomorrow, you should be on your way to the shores of Gaul, where you will be reunited with one of my legions. General Pontus will accompany you with his captain of the cavalry and his best horsemen. Everything relies on urgency! The timing of this mission is crucial, and if you don't arrive by the fourth night, the longboats will not wait. Good luck."

In the tradition of the Imperial Roman Senate for a safe journey, the tribune and ambassador grip each other's sword arm in a firm embrace, and with their other arm, they close their fist and bring it to their chest in a respectful gesture. Tribune Verlairius then turns to General Pontus and says, "I'll await you on the shores of Gaul."

As the wagons are hastily loaded for the peace mission's departure, they are prioritized over all other preparations to ensure the camp's departure with one hundred cohorts. They will travel with the peace party up to a precinct still under Roman command and then turn back; the ambassador and his party are afforded no protection beyond this point. Legionnaires mount their horses while others ride through the camp, burning the vacant tents with torches.

The day of the meeting with the Roman ambassador and the tribune has long passed. The waiting time is over for many who sit around the banquet table inside the huge ceremonial tent, where the final signing of the peace treaty was supposed to take place. The agreement was that all would sign and affix their family seals to the document, but the patience has run out for many. Their council leaders try desperately to maintain order as they engage in heated debates. One nobleman shouted above the rest, "We wait here, and all of us are vulnerable, Jameous! An attack at this time would result in the deaths or capture of all our warriors. I dare not spend another night here! We should never have waited and put ourselves in this camp! We are defenseless from a Roman attack! We have no fortifications here; I suggest we retreat to our fortresses before it is too late! When will it come? At night, when we sleep? Our warriors are lazy and full of wine! I will not spend another night waiting for the Romans!"

Cheers erupt throughout the tent as another nobleman stands up in the crowded room and shouts, "Jameous! I agree we must retreat north to our fortresses to protect our villages and lands! I feel it in my bones, Jameous, that the Romans are planning to attack!"

Jameous shouts out to quell the crowd, "Lads, if it is peace or war again, Jameous of Shawnwood, will stand this ground till the winds of winter! For I cannot leave ... I must know and free my mind if there is treachery by the absence of the Romans on this day that we agreed upon!"

Turning to his cavalry captain, who is one of the strongest men of the Shawnwood warriors. Jameous says, "Captain, you will find the Romans for me, but now, let us indulge in the bounty before us... By your example."

The mood has changed as the abundance of large trays of cooked deer meat and red wine heightens the festivities. The laughter and jubilant conversations can be heard beyond the large tent walls while other lower-rank warriors eat meat cooked in open fire pits and consume strong-spirited drinks outside the tents. Sitting amongst the most senior leaders is one of the noblemen by the name of Lukas, who seems to be transfixed in deep thought and does not take part in any of the celebrations.

As a female servant approaches and offers him food, her

hospitality is quickly dismissed as Lukas abruptly gets up and leaves the table. He paces back and forth and shouts, "Where are these, Romans?"

He hastily walks towards the entrance and pushes open a large door made of animal skin. Turning towards Shawnwood, he says, "I grow impatient with these Romans!"

Exiting the tent, he stares at the horizon toward Hadrian's Wall. A large warrior with a red beard and long red hair sits in the center of many tables set in a semicircle. As Jameous Shawnwood lectures on the peace treaty's benefits and conditions with the Romans, an occasional outburst from several other warriors interrupts him.

As he pauses to speak, they erupt into an argument, stressing their dislike of certain parts of the peace agreement. Some are angrily shouting about the delay in the peace treaty and claiming that the Romans should not be trusted, despite having signed it.

Another warrior calls out, "By not signing this agreement, you will only prolong the fighting that has caused death and destruction since the Romans arrived on our shores!"

Standing by the tent entrance, Lukas turns away, walks towards the large feast table, and says, "The argument of 'DRUNKEN FOOLS 'plays well to the Romans' plans!"

Jameous is about to take a bite of his meal, but allows it to drop from his hands. As it hits his metal plate, the entire room becomes silent. He shouts out to the impatient Lukas, "You would do better to find the Romans at this gathering than to find the Romans by yourself, my friend! Come and supper with us, and don't be so impatient."

Lukas at once turns and stares at Shawnwood. "Ah... YES!

Jameous Shawnwood! By vote, you are our leader. You will tell me what to do today because I am in this tent with you!"

Laughter erupts and fills the tent, and Lukas raises his voice above the crowd as he sits at the table directly across from Jameous Shawnwood. "And what about my warriors, Jameous? Would you be so gracious as to order them about as you do me?"

Shawnwood smiles attentively as he puts down his goblet of wine and says, "Indeed, I speak for many, Lukas, but I offer you this meal in friendship. But never should you forget, I command great men and many warriors loyal to me as I am to them."

Cheers can be heard as goblets are raised in pride at Shawnwoods' words, and Lukas stares at him again and calls out, "Servant, bring me my cup!" As his cup is placed on the table in front of him, he brings the cup up to his lips and merely sips some wine. He then returns his cup to the table and stands. "I salute you, Jameous, and your brave warriors! I will go to my tent now and grow weary of this day!"

As he exits the sizeable ceremonial tent, laughter and celebration continue. Sitting beside Jameous is a close friend of a nobleman; as he leans over, he discreetly whispers, "Jameous, shall I release the scouts now to find the Romans?"

Shawnwood nods. "Thank you, my friend."

The following day, six riders of the Shawnwood elite cavalry and trusted companions prepare their mounts for their assignment. All six scouts are dressed in green plaid, and their horses are covered with a light blanket of the same-colored material. This will enhance their cover, ensuring the Romans do not see them as they ride through the tall grasses of the savanna towards Hadrian's Wall. Three riders will leave the camp, and the other three cavalrymen will wait as a precaution before leaving. They will keep the first three scouts at a safe distance ahead of them so they can relay their observations to Jameous if they succumb to a Roman attack.

The long morning ride across the savanna has given way to the midday sun. The first scout party that left the camp rested their horses. The lead scout raises his arm to block out the bright sunlight and looks south across the tall grasses. He can make out a great outline of what appears to be a long grey serpent over hills, valleys, and forests, cutting across his beloved land as it stands before him, Hadrian's Wall.

The three scouts continue their ride south to the wall, hoping to confront the Romans. They shout out to the Roman centurions, who are generally at their garrison posts, as they ride up to a watchtower. Despite their insults, they receive no reaction. Jameous's scouts then turn their horses, ride west along the wall to the next watchtower, and find it vacant of centurion guards.

As they continue to ride the length of the wall, they come upon two peasant merchants in a covered wagon. The lead scout calls out, and they immediately try to ride off. He quickly rides alongside the wagon and grabs the reins. "Why did you flee from my call, beggar?"

The merchant looks up to the mounted scout and replies, "I thought you were a Roman, my Lord?"

Looking down at the beggar, the lead scout asks, "Do I look like a Roman, you vagabond? And what of this knave?"

As he turns his attention towards the other merchant sitting beside him, the lead scout asks, "Do you have a tongue? Why do you remain silent?"

As he points his green flag-draped lance at the silent merchant, he asks, "What reason can you tell me before you feel this lance!"

The merchant pleads with the mounted warrior, "My Lord, I have only to bear witness to my disrespect to you. I fear for my life; may you grant mercy, my Lord?"

The scout leader then lowers his lance. "Now speak to me, knave... Tell me a good tale; you see me before you by the request of Nobleman Jameous of Shawnwood."

The frightened merchant replies, "My Lord, in my travels by word of mouth, I hear many things. From the shoreline, south to Hadrian's Wall, the Romans fled. With my eyes, I have seen many Roman legions. They leave the lands south of the wall and board their war boats. I told you this before, my Lord, their camp on Forest Road is no more. All this I told was before the heavy rain came."

The scout captain turns to his cohorts and says, "While we gathered in trust of a Roman man of peace, we waited in our tents, and what he speaks of, I cannot imagine it to be true! But where are the Romans? How could this happen? Why would the Romans leave the land that they so savor and pay for with their blood?"

He then asks the quiet one, "Do you have a name?"

"Yes, my Lord, they call me Aron; I live in the poor Village of Monks Road. Before the heavy rain came from my village, we could see the flames of the Roman camp at the edge of the forest."

The scout captain then tells him, "Aron, you live in the lands of Jameous of Shawnwood; he is your master, not I. You must carry your tale to him! And now, I will see what you carry in your wagon."

The scout captain dismounts from his horse, looks through the merchant's wagon, and then asks, "How did you come by a centurion war helmet, Roman swords, Roman pickaxes, and what's this?"

Pushing aside a burlap cover, he finds a horse feedbag with the mark of the emperor. "Aron, how did you come by these?"

Aron nervously answers, "My Lord, they were found in the forest by the trail of the Old Monks Road; in a gully below the sliding cliff wall was a broken chariot. The war helmet, swords, and feedbag were lost beyond the broken chariot. Nothing could be seen of Romans or any other man."

The scout captain looks at the merchant with mistrust. "Aron, take me to the Old Monks Road, that I may know your tale to be true."

The party of five travels to the area Aron spoke of, and suddenly they are confronted by debris and mud-drenched garments lying along the trail. The scout captain picks up a purple robe, representing the color of high honor, and asks, "Aron, why have you not told us what we see before us in your tale?"

"My Lord, we could not travel further into the forest on this old trail with falling trees and soft ground. So, we turned back."

The scout captain then turns to the other merchant and asks, "By what name are you known?"

Looking up, he replies, "Hector, my Lord."

"Hector? Are you a loyal friend of Aron's?"

"Yes, I am Sire!"

Looking at the other merchant, the scout captain asks, "Aron, does he speak the truth?"

"Yes, my Lord!"

"Very well, then you bear witness."

After questioning Hector, the scout captain turns his attention to the area before him, thinking that he might find other violations of the sacred sanctity of the Shawnwood realm. "This is not to be Hector!"

The scout captain pulls back on his horse's leather bridle reins and says, "Follow me, Hector."

He proceeds with his scouts and travels further into the forest along Old Monks Road until he comes to a clearing where he sees a friar outside a small monastery tending to some flowers. The friar abruptly stops as he is surprised by the warrior horseman. The scout leader shouts out to him, "Don't be alarmed! I am not here to do you any harm! I ride with the orders of Nobleman Shawnwood, which states that your sacred house is shared with his land."

The friar shows signs of relief from the fear that he experienced a moment ago. The scout leader says, "The devil has done his work here today!" The friar points to a small cemetery alongside the monastery and says,

"The peace ambassador could not be saved... He died in my arms."

The scout leader states and states, "Then the Holy Law has been done on this day in the lands of Shawnwood. I have but one question, were there others with him?"

The old friar replies, "Yes, some received wounds, but they were all able to escape."

The scout captain reaches into his pouch, removes a silver coin, and places it into the friar's hand.

"For your trouble, may you never see the devil's work again. Now we ride to Jameous of Shawnwood! We will take the ridge of the highland road back to camp."

The three scouts who were delayed on their departure have never lost sight of their lead scout captain as they turn their horses and follow him back to the camp. Before nightfall, they ride through the compound's guard post, and the two merchants are immediately taken to Nobleman Shawnwoods' private tent, where they are allowed to rest and partake in a light meal. Jameous sits across from them at his large oak table, listening to their story.

When the two merchants discuss what they have seen, Jameous and the elders listen attentively to them without interruption.

The stories they tell agree with each other and end with their arrival at the camp's gates. Jameous turns to his scout captain and tells him, "Give them a tent to rest in. Come morning, let these two merchants go in Peace, give them provisions, and let them go back to their trade."

As Jameous pushes the Roman weapons off the table, the room becomes silent momentarily. He reaches for the leather bag and empties its contents on the table. His attention is turned to a scroll tied together with a velvet cord. He opens it, and he begins to read its contents. He then looks at the scout captain and says, "We now have our peace treaty with the Romans! Take this scroll to the council tent; the long night for the council has just begun!"

While the night gives way to the early sunrise, it sends its warmth and light over the camp as the noblemen assemble in front of Jameous's tent and sign the peace document.

Like a strong wind or storm waves crashing against the shore, the bagpipes could be heard throughout the camp and the rugged mountains of the highlands. With the mix of the thunder from mounted horsemen, the two sides charge as they would to defeat an enemy. Before reaching the middle ground, they pull back on their mounts to a slow gallop while crossing their lines, side by side, with raised swords and cheers of victory.

    They are now truly united in this land of peace and prosperity, this fortress known as the Highlands.

Chapter 2:
Andromeda 2217

With the last phase of construction completed and every steel eyebeam in place, the vast project to build a settlement on Mars is similar to the old port ship-launching factories on Earth.

These extensive facilities, commonly known as Navy yards, would play a crucial role in space exploration and serve as the foundation of *Project Carousel*, the *Human Life on Mars Program*, which will support the establishment of the first human colony on the red planet. The Aerospace Alpha Company constructed these sections on Earth as part of the United Nations Space Exploration Program. Reviews of technical systems and their binary codes confirm the presence of a robotic EVA (Extra Vehicular Activity).

After construction is complete, all systems and remote coordinates will be relayed to the Mars site *Project Carousel*. The Star Unit identification codes are exchanged simultaneously with Computer Base Control, starting with Star Unit 1 Alpha-1 and ending with Star Unit 1 Alpha-20.

Delivery of the first drone ships, assembled on the space station and launched on their journey to the red planet, occurred several months ago, before the launch of the *Star Transport Andromeda*. It carried foundation containers consisting of building supplies, a wide variety of food, and other essentials to sustain life on the planet Mars. They were robotically assembled into a circular camp built by Central Command.

The exterior and interior cameras are placed in every unit and constantly relay visual images to all telescreens on Earth. They will remain permanently under the control of the EVA base headquarters on the moon. The space program's activities can be viewed 24/7 by a worldwide audience.

The personnel quarters and multi-level workstations are designed for a comfortable and healthy lifestyle on Mars. Each second unit offers a health spa and a shared lounge with an upper-floor observation deck. In the future, the automatic bore gear dig-out machines will place additional drone shipments of living quarters onto the Mars base to accommodate new personnel. Their tubular lock system is followed by a double-hull extension, which extends the initial automated lock sequence. The inner core of the double seal is filled with a magnetic particle proton field to protect the base personnel from the Sun's harmful rays as they travel throughout the multiunit stations.

Twenty-one hundred hours is the launch sequence for the two shuttlecraft that will enter orbit around the moon. These were constructed and assembled at the space station and will be part of the *Andromeda* on its launch date. The shuttles' projected launch time is on schedule, as the gantry control begins to pull away from the support sections of *Star Transport Andromeda's* MDSP (Mars Drone Settlement Program).

The gantry becomes engulfed in flames from the shuttle's triple photon-atomic engines as red lights and sirens sound. As they slowly leave the gantry port rails of the space station, they enter orbit under robotic control and wait to be united with the *Star Transport Andromeda* on its voyage to Mars.

The shuttlecraft's crews will remain in orbit and wait for the launch date of the *Andromeda*. This series of shuttlecraft was first introduced in the twentieth century when the original space station was constructed.

Once the twenty-star units are activated on Mars and their

computers are online, and all information is then relayed from Moon Base Control. The countdown for *Andromeda's* launch date is already in progress. The vast building complex of domed structures at MOON BASE CENTRAL COMMAND casts shadows across the lunar terrain's dusty fields at the edge of the massive crater in the *Sea of Tranquility*. This moon complex comprises a communal area of structural and support technologies responsible for constructing the luxury *Star Transport Andromeda*.

In complex Unit A, personnel have undergone rigorous training programs and field exercises that simulate Mars's orbital changes. Unit B contains the medical unit and survival center, where medical specialists can perform emergency surgical procedures immediately. Unit-C is the Officer Command College located in the building complex, where new officers are trained for their first command mission. All of these specialized personnel will serve on the *Andromeda,* which was completed three months before the last launch of MDSP Alpha-20.

When the *Andromeda* leaves the moon's surface on its maiden voyage, it will be the last time it touches a planet's surface. Andromeda's flight plan to Mars will become the service ship orbiting the red planet. Its two shuttlecraft will travel to the Mars base and then back to the *Andromeda*, carrying supplies and exchanging personnel with the complex on the red planet.

The *Andromeda's* construction specifications are nine hundred and eighty-nine feet long and two hundred and seventy-five feet wide. It comprises four decks and a company of 358 officers, technicians, and volunteers. Its weight is 5,486 metric tons, and its steel construction is composed of a double hull layer, which is compression-resistant to cosmic and gamma radiation.

It is powered by six triple photon-cold fusion atomic engines, with two emergency backup power units for transfers and lifting of saucer platforms. The solar lift platforms are two dome-shaped discs that generate an interior gravity, accommodating up to 120 passengers for comfortable, safe transport to the planet's surface. These dome-shaped discs feature four engines that generate an antimatter field, enabling them to land and take off from the planet's surface and carry a multitude of supplies and passengers. Voyage time on the completed ship's quality control units is on standby for the launch sequence.

The three-month departure schedule has passed with the completion of the Mars *Carousel* project. The ship's clearance mode and activation centers are awaiting the final countdown. As Captain John Jameous Shawnwood and his staff accept each section's personnel specialist's boarding, he acknowledges their salute and greets them aboard. He then takes their personnel folder, which contains their qualifications and length of service. These crew members will represent various services, including the Air Force, Aerospace, Navy navigational experts, NASA, Army topographical image evaluation specialists, and medical field personnel from multiple services, ranging from surgical to pre-diagnostic specialists.

After the duty officers are all welcomed aboard, the captain and his forty-four bridge Star Rank Officers will be responsible for the mission and the well-being of their crew and passengers, who will rendezvous with the Mars base *Carousel*.

The captain will not greet the passengers as they come aboard the *Andromeda* on their journey to the Mars base. He is preparing the ship for its launch time countdown while his first officer cordially greets and escorts the Mars base personnel to a ready prelaunch safety zone. There, they will suit up in comfortable, lightweight pilot uniforms made of a special material that simulates Earth's gravity, while aboard the *Star Transport Andromeda*.

After all the personnel have been outfitted, they are instructed to secure themselves in module command chairs equipped with a view screen to observe the liftoff of the star transport. The first duty officer signals the captain when all the passengers are secured. After the captain receives the first duty officer's message, the take-off alarms can be heard throughout the ship.

Moments later, the roar of the antigravity thrust engines can be heard beneath the *Andromeda* as six thrust engines lift the ship off the Moon's surface into a prelaunch personnel position. Its six columns of atomic blast fusion combine to yield 1.9 million pounds of thrust, sending the *Andromeda* up to thirty thousand feet. After breaking away from the moon's gravity, the blast-lift engines cut their power to half-thrust.

A stillness of several moments allows the ship to enter a stabilized orbit as its triple aft, photon-cold fusion atomic engines ignite. This sends the giant ship into orbit to rendezvous with the two shuttlecraft and continue its journey to Mars.

Aboard the *Andromeda*, the crew will travel over forty-eight million miles. In eight months, the ship will arrive in a Mars orbit at variable speeds, allowing it to slow down and enter a Martian orbit.

The flight time will be spent when the passengers and crew become acquainted with the captain and their respective duty assignments on the Mars base. The interior of the *Andromeda* reflects a modern, comfortable, and convenient look one would expect on an extended interstellar mission. They will meet the captain for the first time in the large banquet room, where he will introduce his star-rank officers and staff.

Tour guides escort passengers to a briefing room, where they are given instructions and provided with personal inter-ship communication devices. These devices are interference-free, allowing passengers to have conversations with one another. They also enable direct intercommunication with the ship's courtesy personnel department.

While the passengers receive instructions from their tour guides, an announcement comes over the ship's intercom: "Dinner will be served at seventeen hundred hours."

The personnel tour guides announce to their groups that they will have an hour to freshen up before dinner. The announcement also includes instructions on how to take the voice-activated elevator system to the dining hall on deck one.

As they leave the elevators and enter the dining area. The large banquet hall is decorated with murals that tell the story of man's achievements in space, from the first flight at Kitty Hawk to others representing periods from the 1930s through the twenty-first century. All stand for the advancement of in-flight technology and conclude with the conquest of the Luna Module Eagle landing on the Moon, accompanied by the inscription: *"**That's one small step for a man, one giant leap for mankind.**"*

At the center of the large room is the banquet table, which will accommodate all the dinner guests as the chefs prepare the first meal for the Mars personnel.

This will be the first of many dinners they will enjoy on their eight-month journey to Mars. They take their places at informal seating arrangements without specific assignments. As their conversations continue, they are greeted by dining room attendants who take their orders from a wide variety of entrées. A room service number is available 24/7 for those who prefer to dine in their cabin.

The Mars personnel will spend time attending to their transmissions to family members and friends back on Earth while getting acquainted with some crew members. They will share general conversations while answering many questions about their experiences on the Mars mission. The majority of the questions will be answered with strict attention to avoid disclosing classified information.

Fourteen days into the voyage, the Mars passengers and some of *Andromeda's* high-ranking officers are invited to celebrate the captain and his wife's fourth wedding anniversary. Most of *Andromeda's* crew are familiar with Lieutenant Deandra Shawnwood and her rank as a Star Officer in charge of all the ship's communications. She was the top-rated student in her class at the Officers' Command Central Moon Base Academy. She is now celebrating their fourth wedding anniversary with Captain Shawnwood and the birthday of their son Johnathan, who is now three years old. The crew and all the Mars base personnel will work a five-day week, following a routine of technical meetings and study sessions. As part of the program for their journey to Mars, they will also have access to a comprehensive fitness center.

The final touches are added to the cakes for the significant anniversary and birthday. The dining hall is decorated with fresh flowers, fine table linens, and crystal candleholder settings, complementing the traditional dinnerware. The chefs are busy preparing meals for the guests, who will be served their dinner in the large dining room. The ship's on-duty personnel will take their meals at their workstations and complete their regular shifts in accordance with the rules outlined in their duty roster. They can participate in the festivities while viewing interdepartmental communication view-screens and speaking to the dining room's dinner guests via relay telescreens.

The dinner guests begin to arrive at seventeen hundred hours and take their reserved seats. Lieutenant Deandra and several of her department crewmembers come together and start to remark about the decorations of the dining room, especially the decorative gift boxes piled on the captain's chair. She smiles and says,

"The captain is going to be in for a big surprise!"
Some guests who had already taken their seats at the table answered

her with a bit of laughter.

"Well, Lieutenant, we thought we'd make the captain happy; I'm sure he will be surprised!"

She responds with a bit of laughter, "Well, if anyone hasn't noticed, my chair is empty!"

Her Second Lieutenant, who entered the room with her, says, "I'm sure he will be surprised... Most of the gifts are for you and baby Johnathan, Deandra!"

Laughter amongst the guests adds to the festive mood as the captain enters the room and asks, "Is there a party going on here?"

A chorus of "Happy Anniversary, Captain!" fills the room as Captain Shawnwood raises his hands. "Thank you very much, ladies and gentlemen, and thank you, my beautiful wife, Deandra!"

As he kisses her on the cheek, the kitchen staff members begin filling the crystal glasses with champagne, while others take orders from the guests regarding their dinner preferences. One of the kitchen orderlies sets up a portable folding table and removes the gift boxes from the captain's chair as the rest of the guests take their places at the banquet table. As the last box is removed, the orderly salutes the captain. "Happy Anniversary, Captain!" The captain smiles and replies, "Thank you, Mister Martin."

Before taking his chair, the captain reaches into his jacket and removes two small, gift-wrapped boxes, as his wife, Deandra, does not notice while conversing with a crewmember seated to the right side of her. The crew member stops talking, smiles, and taps Deandra on the hand. "Deandra, I think someone wants your attention."

Deandra stops talking and immediately turns to face her

husband, who smiles. "Thank you, Lieutenant." Captain Shawnwood then picks up a spoon and taps on his glass to bring attention to something he wants to say. In a few moments, all conversations come to an end.

Leaving his chair, he takes his glass of champagne and holds it up towards his wife. "Every toast deserves a speech, and I promise to make it a short one."

Bringing smiles to the reception guests and Deandra, he says, "To my lovely wife... I love you and baby Johnathan very much!"

Turning towards the guests, he raises his glass again. "Ladies and gentlemen, to our mission, *Carousel*."

The entire crew of officers and staff immediately rises, holds up their glasses, and repeats the captain's toast, "To *Carousel*!"

As the kitchen staff finishes serving the main entrée and most guests sit back down, another crew member, a friend of Lieutenant Deandra, shares her warm gestures. "Okay, Captain, that was great! Now is a good time to open the presents!"

Laughter follows as Deandra reaches over to grab his hand. "That was a short speech, John, and a lovely one, too. I love you very much!"

Another crew member shouts, "Come on, Mommy Lieutenant, open your presents!"

Lieutenant Deandra proudly smiles. "I don't know where to begin. Let me see... Hmmm... I'll start with baby Johnathan's presents first."

She opens the large present and reads the name tag aloud. "It's from the crew!"

As she opens the box, she takes out a blanket with the

embroidered inscription *"Baby Shawnwood"* on it. "Thank you very much, and my little captain thanks you also!"

She then removes an array of soft-squeezed baby toys and remarks as she holds them up. "Oh, how sweet!" The following items include several pairs of pajamas, one of which is styled like a crewmember's uniform with an ID name tag stating, "Captain Johnathan Shawnwood."

Deandra holds up the uniform and says, "Now look at this! This is nice! I thank you, and little Johnathan thanks you, too. Now I have a question. How did you hide all these gifts from my inspection tour?"

Several of her crewmembers respond cheerfully, "It wasn't easy... But we did get a little help!"

Deandra turns towards her husband. "John, you were in on this?"

The captain answers, "I decline to answer until I have proper counsel!"

Laughter fills the room again as the captain points to the gifts he placed on the table. Deandra picks up the one with her name tag on it. "This one is from my dear husband, who pleads innocent of all charges!"

The crew members laugh again while she opens the gift and removes a gold bracelet. She then reads the inscription on the inside: ***Happy Anniversary to the love of my life... John.*** She then presses a clip, and the top opens, revealing a holographic photo of their wedding day. "OH! This is very sweet, John. Thank you!"

Smiling, the captain hands her the other gift. "This is for Johnathan."

Deandra opens baby Johnathan's birthday present, holds it up, and tells the guests, "This is baby Johnathan's birthday gift from his dad!"

The guests applaud, and she then reads the inscription inside the small gold bracelet: **Johnathan Shawnwood – Scotland Earth.** She pauses and says, "John, this is lovely!"

She picks up her glass of champagne, holds it towards her husband, and replies, "Happy Anniversary, John, and Happy Birthday, my little Captain Johnathan!"

Arrival time: Two days from a fixed Mars orbit, crewmembers and Mars base personnel prepare for the *Andromeda* to enter orbit and discharge passengers to its surface. This marks the beginning of the Human Life on Mars Program, as it adapts to a planet vastly different from Earth, posing a significant challenge to its existence. This will mark the beginning of the Mars base operation *Carousel*, where full-time personnel will live and work in an environment similar to their training at *Crater City* on the moon, allowing them to adapt to life on the Mars base.

Communications from *Andromeda's* central computer to the base on Mars have already activated all functional sections of life support, such as anti-radiation shields and pure oxygen control, to normal life-support levels.

The *Andromeda's* shuttlecraft transports are prepared to take the one hundred eighty full-time-based personnel to the surface. Its landing target will be in the center of the sixteen units that are now fully functional on the surface of Mars. Communication signals and teleview transmissions are being sent from the *Andromeda* to view screens worldwide and *Crater City* on the moon, where millions watch this outstanding achievement.

Last-minute packing of personal gear and equipment status is fed into *Andromeda's* central computer systems. The *Reliance Program* will provide a benefits check on all essential base equipment that is ready for deployment at the *Carousel* landing site. Ninety-seven permanent Mars personnel are already at the command module unit one. They will be the first passengers to the Mars base inside the large antigravity transport dome.

    The programmed electronic sector equipment will guide this large transport disc to the surface of Mars, checking out operational antimagnetic fields. The photoelectron spectrometers transform information for future transport disc landings, which will be stored in Andromeda's computer banks.

    Before docking into Mars's fixed orbit, each department must report its status preparation to the central computer bank. This will control the *Andromeda's* atomic engine symmetry and slow the ship's speed. Each atomic engine will shut down individually, and the vessel will be put into a glide mode projection, enabling it to enter a low-orbit trajectory gradually.
.

    The topographic computers will take over command of the ship and search for the land formations to establish base *Carousel*. When the *Andromeda* is directly over the base, reverse engines will perform a fixed maneuver and lock the craft into a permanent docking orbit. Robot control will take over the antigravity transport disc's trajectory release, and the transports will land on their preprogrammed landing targets in the center of the base *Carousel*.

    As the transport passengers hurry to their assigned command sections within the transport disc, they activate their computer screens to relay information to the ship's captain's control center. Alarms and emergency entrance signals indicate that the landing sequence and countdown have become operational. Boarding of personnel becomes the priority, and once the antimagnetic field is engaged, shutting down the ship's main computer is impossible. It will release the transport vehicle from the *Andromeda* and land on the surface of Mars.

Once onboard, the Dome Disc *A-1 Mars Transport* commander will be the last to report to the ship's captain as the shuttle disc transport is released. The flight commander, in charge of descent operations, speaks over the intercom system and can be heard throughout the *Andromeda*. "Forward motion... Banking, banking, forward motion. Lock release A-Alpha, lock release B-Beta, lock release C-Control, lock release free-flight motion in progress. Geometric analog control in motion, the Disc *A-1 Mars Transport* is on its way to the surface of Mars." As the *Andromeda's* vacant transport compartment automatically closes, it becomes air-pressurized with natural oxygen. "Data Control... Mars target progressing. Right on program source correction—seventeen degrees north by the precision target on-site."
In the background, a bell sound continues to echo behind the flight commanders' correction control console of Disc A-1 in its progress toward landing on the planet. This continues until the ascent corrections are made to ensure a safe landing of the *A-1 Mars Transport* dome unit.

On the way down, Mars's north polar ice cap, a titanium-white reflection, reflects off the underside of *Star Transport Andromeda,* sending bright fusion light through the portals into the interior of the ascent vehicle.

Moments later, the passengers are given a panoramic view of Mars's enormous, ridged landscapes, with backdrops of huge mountains, some reaching heights of 170,000 feet. Below the inundated ridges of crimson red, the passengers see fields of tossed landscapes, the burnt orange desert sands of Mars.

The passengers' final view through the landing craft's portals reveals the circular base platform-gantry lock mechanisms that have been activated automatically. The base's magnetic force field conflicts with the surrounding colors of burnt orange, creating a blue-magnetic haze as the transport vehicle lands at the center of *Project Carousel.*

In a few moments, the computer communication exchange receives confirmation of the successful landing of Disc A-1.

The lockdown of the large exit access gantries is precise, with the domed exit airlock vacuum doors sealing. This allows passengers to walk along the interior corridors of the access gantries' tunnels and carry their luggage to their designated quarters at base camp. After settling in, all *Carousel* team members will make their way to their assigned quarters and workstations as they have rehearsed many times at the training academy on the Moon.

One by one, each department will communicate with the Command Center back on the *Andromeda*. After receiving a "Well Done!" message from Captain Shawnwood, Lieutenant Deandra routinely sends other messages back and forth to the communications officer. Multiple display screens activate, congratulating the first humans to set foot on Mars.

Cheers can be heard in the background from crewmembers back on the ship while lengthy conversations of excitement and congratulations continue from Mars base *Carousel* to the *Andromeda*. Captain Shawnwood and his staff officers have scheduled a program meeting with command clearance, approved by majority vote, to allow crew members to visit the Mars base. The vote of affirmation is unanimous among crew members and staff. The personnel groups and their section command officers will proceed to the base together in teams via the second transport. This program will continue to leave a diminished crew of personnel aboard the *Andromeda* to operate the aeronautics division and communication controls, which will remain in constant contact with *Carousel*.

As the passenger transport program continues, the *Andromeda* will remain locked into a fixed orbit, operating at eighty percent of its engine capacity in a neutral field following the shutdown of its atomic fusion reactor. Most crew members are allowed to go down to the Mars base in groups of equal size, which will require several trips on the emergency transport Disc System A-2. This is due to its limited personnel capacity and smaller compartment circumference compared to the *A-1 Mars Transport.*

    The compartment doors open to allow a second party to be sent to the planet. These crew members, along with the captain and his wife, Lieutenant Deandra, will be the last of *Andromeda's* staff personnel to visit the base for a short time.

    Before entering the transport, Lieutenant Deandra stops by the medical stat unit and the nursery to check on little Johnathan. In a low voice, she speaks to the attending nurse, Susan, "I won't be long. As soon as we get back, I'll take little Johnathan off your hands. I just want to leave little Johnathan's bracelet; I don't want to lose it while I'm down on the planet." She puts the gold bracelet into the astronaut uniform's pajama pocket of baby Johnathan's uniform, closes the zipper, and straightens the wrinkles on his name tag, which reads, "Captain Johnathan." "Now there, you're all set, big guy!"

    Turning to the nurse, she says, "Thank you, Susan. Johnathan is asleep. We'll probably be back before he wakes up." The nurse smiles and says, "Please, Lieutenant, take your time. It's my pleasure. Enjoy your shore leave."

    Lieutenant Deandra rejoins her husband aboard the Transport Unit as Captain Shawnwood takes his place at the launch screen computer console and activates the launch unit.

    The second transport is released and begins its descent towards the Mars base facility.

    The *Andromeda* locks its second circular transport unit hatch, filling the exit transport dome with oxygen. The time sequence of departure is zero to eight hundred hours, and the empty station quarters are silent throughout *Andromeda*, with the exceptions of the quartermaster division, aeronautics operations, and the medical staff unit. All personnel on liberty will enjoy the Mars base facility along with the captain, his wife, and his bridge rank officers.

The walkthrough of the interlocking tubular connectors that separate the visitors' groups has now taken on a life of its own. Communication officers are at their posts, making contact with the Moon base at regular intervals. At the same time, other staff members assign Mars personnel to their section work posts on the *Carousel* Mars base and then give guided tours to *Andromeda's* visiting staff officers. These comfortable units will accommodate all future arrivals and scientific programs for the colonization of Mars.

Several hours later, while most of *Andromeda's* crew enjoy their shore leave on the planet, the department navigator in computer analysis in geo-astro astronomy picks up a strange space occurrence. Its heading is in waves of energy that cannot be immediately identified. Coming in from the universe's outer reaches from the explosion of a dwarf star, it enters the Martian planetary system with a destructive force from one point seven light-years away.

Waves of energy from its gravitationally charged nuclei send charged particles that will engulf all of the outer planets in our solar system. This magnetic energy storm and its destructive effects will be absorbed mainly by the two giant planets, Saturn and Jupiter. This astronomical anomaly will reach Mars with the same deadly force of its magnetic energy waves, resulting in a massive dust storm on the planet. The winds and ripples of this dimensional space-time storm are releasing their fury on the giant ship *Andromeda*.

Emergency computer beacons are activated as communications with the *Andromeda* and Mars's base become disrupted with broken, barely distinguishable messages.

Finally, the captain sends an emergency message through the

interference-free laser communication system: "GA section, do you copy? This is the captain, over, *Andromeda*!"

Static waves of radiation persist in high-force winds that lift debris from the Martian surface, once again blocking communications with a force of antimagnetic particles.

Some of Captain Shawnwoods' transmissions reach the *Andromeda* as the high winds dissipate. The giant ship attempts to maintain control of its orbital velocity while finally receiving the captain's communication. "GA Section, do you copy? This is the captain!" This time, his message is received loud and clear. "This is GA, Captain! Affirmative, we hear you!"

"Flight Colonel Athens, you must leave orbit now! We're monitoring another heavy solar magnetic disturbance coming in destructive waves. It can bring the ship down! According to our interstellar computer readings, it has already caused extreme damage to the surfaces of our system's outer planets. Again, I say DO NOT attempt to stay in orbit! As your captain, this is a DIRECT ORDER!"

Athens replies, "Affirmative, Captain! We're leaving orbit."

"Colonel Athens, keep our communications in code seven constant! I want to know your exact location and conditions aboard the *Andromeda*. Despite the Astro-Magnetic interference, we will monitor you down here as best we can. Athens, do not accept any communication that does not come from operations. I don't want the people down here to know what's happening, no exceptions! You will communicate only with me while I'm in operation. In the event of my absence, you will communicate with Colonel Richards."

Communications with the *Andromeda* at zero-twenty-four hundred hours discontinue, as laser-guided transmissions cannot break through the second wave of the storm and reach the *Andromeda*.

Mayday calls from the giant ship are lost in this atmospheric storm. None of their messages reach the planet Mars as the *Star Transport Andromeda* is swept away in a massive current of pulsating magnetic gamma rays at the edge of the colossal anomaly.

    As the storm retreats and gives solace to the surface of Mars, three Earth days have passed, and still, no messages have been received from the *Andromeda*. No outgoing coordinates of binary codes have been registered on any of the Mars base computers. Dispatches from the moon base and Earth Central Command begin to fill the airwaves with urgency and dismay. Captain Shawnwood becomes the center of the inquiry, and he must yield to the support he receives from all levels of space operations command when he is ordered to the search-and-rescue assignment by taking command of the scout ship *Solar-Star*. The completion and launch date from the gantry base are set for two months from now. A scaled-down shuttle crew will take the *Solar-Star* to Mars' orbit, where Captain Shawnwood, Lieutenant Deandra, and the team will exchange with the transfer personnel.

    Somewhere lost in the solar winds, the *Andromeda* is engulfed in a time-sequence distortion as the ship's atomic clocks accelerate. They match the speed of the gravitational waves that carry *Andromeda* beyond the outer reaches of our solar system. The life forms on the ship evolve transparently in multiple shifts of atomic light. The twenty-nine life forms aboard the *Andromeda* have now tripled and become eighty-seven entities.

    At the control center, radar specialist Lieutenant Stevenson turns to the com-officer and receives a course change order from the three com-officer entities. Three babies are crying in their cradles in the nursery while three attending nurses attend to their needs. The ship's interior is displayed in a three-dimensional hologram as the elevator opens, revealing passengers from a lower level. They deliver essential food supplies to feed the crew.

As the three crew members step off the elevator platform into the affected deck area, they instantly become three holographic images of themselves. The affected crew members deliver the multi-crates of food supplies to the galley. The transformation has the same effect on all crew members throughout control deck operations and all inanimate objects.

The radar scan officer turns to his senior operations and provides the heading and course-altimeter adjustments to his star bridge commanders. As he speaks, his voice distorts in intervals as he looks at his holographic duplicates. He shows no sign of alarm, as if a binary-coded equation created him.

The three identical Star Bridge officers received the message of a course change. As one turns, they all turn and give verbal orders to the three navigators, who will then change the course on their navigational screen consoles. In the preceding moments, emergency alarm beacons are tripped, signaling throughout the ship that a failsafe condition is in effect. The master operations control computer attempts to break through all audio emergency alert indicators as it attempts to make contact with the Mars base. It has no identification that the computers can lock onto due to the storm's interference, as the vessel constantly moves at light speed across the dark voids of the endless universe.

The last message finally breaks through to operation control on the Mars base audio emergency alert indicators to Chief Henderson just before the *Andromeda* left our star system. Turning to Captain Shawnwood, he hesitates for a moment and says,

"Captain, we have a big problem… The *Andromeda,* Sir, it's gone! It's off our screens!"

"Henderson, what are we talking about? A moment ago, you received a message from the ship's master computer!" Rechecking his controls, Chief Henderson states, "Yes, Captain! That's correct! That last message came from Pluto's orbit. Its electronic signature has left a trace indicator that the *Andromeda* has left our star system! It came by way of the coded subatomic signature!" In a low, solemn voice, Captain Shawnwood responds, "So… It's GONE! My crew and my son, Johnathan!" Chief Henderson replies sadly, "I am sorry, Captain…"

    Moments of silence have Captain Shawnwood transfixed on several command screens, which are now sending visual and photographic imagery of the planets Jupiter, Saturn, and Pluto. These planets were in the destructive path of this solar storm. Subatomic photographic imaging is transferred into high definition on all the computer screens at the Mars base. "Captain, we now have surface visuals, and they're changing by the minute."

    "Don't lose them, Henderson! Right now, this is all we have if we're going to find my ship!"

    The screens remain activated, and the command technicians move away from their keyboards, daring not to disrupt a single incoming transfer that has somehow taken on a life of its own. As each picture holds still for a moment, it then shifts to a different field of observation. This visual information can be replayed to enhance analysis of the various fields of surface information, graphic isolation, and collateral damage to the planet's surface.

    The computers have changed the subatomic information of space and time within our solar system to their ship's photographic picture screens. On a second module, another visual display tracks the massive storm as it travels across our solar system. Looking at a conventional digital computer time readout, the captain turns to his command officer. "I'll need some time to speak to Deandra. Henderson, notify all Base Personnel to meet me at the central auditorium at fourteen hundred hours."

    The doors close automatically, and the lift takes Captain

Shawnwood down to his unit's personnel quarters, where he will wait for Deandra. His emotional state has reached the point of despair. The quiet quarters are broken by Deandra's entrance. "John, I went to operations looking for you, and no one would tell me anything except Chief Henderson! All he would say is that you were waiting for me in our quarters. John, what's happening? What's going on?"

As he puts his arms around her, he says, "Right now, as far as we can tell, all we have is the deep space Stella Communications that lets us track the speed and location of the *Andromeda* before it left our star system. The teller-transfer photos of the planets Jupiter and Saturn give us data on the *Andromeda,* as its high-velocity engines have left a heat signature as they tried to outrun the storm. As of now, we just don't have clear information about the storm that carried the ship away." He pauses. "As soon as Space Central releases the rescue ship *Solar-Star*, we will be in command. It features high-speed thermo-velocity engines, enabling it to travel at higher speeds than the Andromeda, and there are plans to track its thermonuclear signature. When the *Solar Star* arrives here with its transfer crew, you'll be with me on board, Deandra, on a direct route to find the *Andromeda*, its crew, and our son, Johnathan! You'll do your job as always, Communications Officer. As far as we know, the *Andromeda* remains undamaged. No debris is detected within the heat signature past the planet Pluto as it left our star system."

As tears roll down Deandra's face, she says, "John—" The captain then interrupts her, "I know Deandra, but we have a job to do. We'll find Johnathan and the crew, and I'm sure they'll be just fine. There's plenty of food and supplies on that ship for a four-year mission at full crew capacity. Let's go up to operations and see Chief Henderson so he can bring us up to the latest information."

As the captain wipes away her tears, she says, "John, you're going to have to be strong for both of us because right now, I feel very weak!"

Smiling at her, he says, "Nonsense, Deandra… You're an officer in charge of one of the greatest operations in the history of humankind! Your achievements speak for themselves, and you have the strength and the ability to keep pushing forward until we find the ship and our son. And that's an order, my love!" She smiles and, in a low voice, responds, "Aye, Captain."

High solar winds continue this anomaly's journey, creating massive meteor showers while clearing the atmosphere of the planets in its path. The solar storm diminishes in the vast darkness of Star Quadrant Omega, 1.8 light-years past the faint star Proxima Centauri. The Omega Star Quadrant's asteroid belt will be the final voyage of the enormous *Star Transport Andromeda*, bearing the wounds of discarded history on its maiden voyage.

Chapter 3:
The Android Doctor

    At the advent of dawn, in the star constellation of CANTIOUS CENTAURUS, all seems unchanged for endless moments. The giant asteroid that ended the voyage of the ill-fated *Star Transport Andromeda* remains dormant again. Due to the *Andromeda's* impact, the plume of dust and rock has now dissipated into the dark shadows of the tall monolithic ridges that make up this section of the asteroid's rocky terrain.

    The stillness has returned, and so has the silence of the universe that has taken away the lives of the *Andromeda's* crew. The moments pass in ten-quarter sequences of atomic-cesium space-time that seem to last forever. Then, the star of life appears on the horizon; the sun of Star Quadrant Omega's system now casts its light and warmth upon the planets it created endless ages ago. It will also bestow its benevolent warmth on the ill-fated Andromeda; now that all the debris has settled, the giant ship will lie there and bask in the sunlight.

    Inside the ship, the first rays of morning light make their way to the secured section and chamber exits leading to the Medical STAT Unit Nursery. Oxygen levels remained normal in this section throughout the horrific ordeal. The ship's reserve facilities and backup energy quartz continue to give life force support to the two survivors in the STAT quarters. Nurse Susan slowly regains consciousness and tries to move, finally gaining the strength to focus on her surroundings. Fighting to stay conscious, she reaches out to any object that would help her regain an upright position.

    At first, the climb up to the console module chair is so difficult that she wants to give up the challenge. Her determination rewards her with the last moments of her inner strength as she falls back into the module chair and gives out a sigh of relief. With the comfort of achievement, her strength begins to return, and her military training reinforces her determination. Reaching out to the failsafe console panel, she activates the ship's emergency intergalactic distress mayday beacon. The call for help will continue indefinitely via an electric sonic-patch sequence to all existing universal monitoring receivers. Nurse Susan now reaches over and turns on the teller-support sequencing cameras outside the ship. Topographic images begin to flood several of the large module screens, pausing momentarily to show different views of the outside landscape.

Now fully aware of her surroundings, Nurse Susan struggles with the vagueness of the last moments she recalls and what her duties entailed. Disregarding the missing time, she can't quite remember why the present circumstances are the way they are. She will not waste time thinking about it right now. She must perform for what she was trained to be in life; pushing aside any further thoughts, she leaves the console and calls out, "THE BABY!"

Gaining extra strength while disregarding her discomfort and dizziness, she immediately attends to baby Johnathan in his climate-controlled toddler bed. Finding him asleep, she notices his breathing is not as normal as it should be.

She immediately picks him up, carries him over, and places him inside a sonic life support unit. The room becomes a challenge again as she loses her ability to maintain her consciousness. As she makes her way back to the large console chair, she waits for a response to her emergency rescue signal. Control Command at Star Central receives constant, evasive, and indistinguishable transmissions with no match to the Androidian binary code.

The Android command officer in charge of Penal Colony Nine-Nine-Four Division Alpha types into his superior officer's secret transmission code computer, informing him that an incident has taken place in the VESTELLA ASTEROID FIELD mining area. Code Sequence Con Nine-Nine-Four Division Alpha is immediately signaled. He instantly receives confirmation, followed by an audiovisual topography of the control commander with orders to relay urgent transmissions to a mining craft in the section of Nine-Nine-Four Division Alpha.

With orders of immediate confirmation response from command headquarters, a small mining unit boards a utility life-support flightcraft and proceeds to follow the orders given by the transmitting superior.

The small group leader takes the control seat and activates all unit relay indicators and the craft's life-support systems. Removing her spherical helmet, she gives out a sigh of relief while dropping her dirty helmet to the floor below the control console.

She then removes five packets from the console storage compartment and automatically tosses four of them back to her crew members. "It's clean-up time, guys."

Tearing open her package, she removes a moist cloth and begins to wipe her face while waiting for the flightcraft engines to warm up in the cold environment of the asteroid belt. Looking in a visor mirror, she is satisfied that she is as clean as she ever will be in these conditions as a forced laborer inside an asteroid mine.

Using the cleaning cloth again, she wipes off her helmet and turns to her four Humanacerean crew. "Ready for takeoff, guys?"

Jokingly, one of the four miners shouts, "Captain Reanna, is this going to be a long trip? I forgot to pack my bags!"

Smiling for a moment, she says, "Not funny, Prisoner Miner Sixteen!"

The miner sarcastically responds, "Captain, I have a name, you know!"

Annoyed, Reanna replies, "Yes, you do, and it's called Prisoner Sixteen! By law, only the leader of a prison detail is allowed to be called by their first name. Isn't that right, Miner Eighteen?"

He immediately replies, "Yes, Ma'am, Captain Reanna!"

The crew settles in as the ship leaves the asteroid mining district for the search and rescue of the crashed *Andromeda*, and seven quarter-time sequences pass before they arrive at the large asteroid containing the crash site. The crew had long been asleep in a well-deserved rest while Squad-Leader Reanna was constant and efficient in her assigned duties. Switching on the interior overhead console lights, followed by a continuous landing alert bell-tone indicator, the four crew members are awakened. "It's time to get up, guys!"

Looking at the rearview reflector screen, she replies, "Suit up, everybody! Test your life support systems and prepare for search-and-rescue operations. The readout diagnostics on my screen identify that there are two life forms on that wreck!" Reanna ties back her long blonde hair and reattaches her helmet to her life support suit.

As the craft lands one-quarter-sequence mile from the crash site, the crew hastily packs all necessary equipment before disembarking on their mission.

Upon exiting the flightcraft, they encounter a hostile environment. Dealing with the winds and the dust from the asteroid debris obstructs a clear view of the ship for most of its journey. The asteroid's rugged terrain takes its toll on the rescue party as they make their way to the ship.

Inside the *Andromeda*, Nurse Susan's last memory is fixed on the console screen as she sees figures approaching, giving her a sense of hope. She will close her eyes, wait patiently for the rescue crew to arrive, and then fall into a deep sleep.

The approach to the crash site has taken a little longer than anticipated. The constant solar winds and the asteroid's uneven terrain have made their short journey difficult. Finally, Captain Reanna and Miner Eighteen approach the *Andromeda*, while the others are delayed carrying the heavy rescue equipment in silence, and for the first time, she can see the mammoth ship with clear vision. Miner Eighteen steps up beside her, and as he cleans off his helmet's view-visor, he says, "Where the hell did this come from? Look at the size of it!"

In a low voice, as if talking to herself, she says, "I wish I could tell you; I have never seen anything like this!"

She then takes out a metallic micro-helix key and separates it. Handing half of it to him, she continues staring at the massive ship while telling him, "Go back and get our weapons! I'll wait here."

As he leaves, he retraces his path through the rugged terrain and arrives at the rest site of the other crew members, who are carrying the large supply container. He gestures for them to open it as he hands the micro-helix key to Miner Sixteen. He opens the container and immediately leans over to see what he might like to pick through, to satisfy his curious mind and his long history as a thief.

Suddenly, he is pushed aside aggressively and now has a laser rifle pointed at him by Miner Eighteen. After removing another laser weapon, he tells Miner Sixteen, "Close the supply container, lock it, and follow me!"

As he locks the supply container, the micro-helix key lights up in a brilliant flash of blue light, and Miner Sixteen asks, "What are the weapons for?"

He gets no response and is told, "Just follow me!"

The other two miners pick up the supply container and continue carrying it towards the ill-fated ship. Miner Sixteen then says, "You know, there are other planets out there, and you know damn well it'll take eons for them to find us! My guess is, they won't even try! Why don't we take this ship and get off this desolate place?" Prisoner Twelve lets out a little laugh that can be heard over the intercom. "Yeah, we'll just walk off this damn asteroid, and everything will be just fine! The flightcraft, how do you get it to fly out of here when you only have half of the micro-helix key?"

Miner Twelve then pats Miner Sixteen on the back with a slight smile on his face and says, "You're not so smart; none of us are going anywhere! The ship won't fly with only half of the key! Reanna has the other part! I suggest you do your job and return it to Reanna and give her one of your lame stories. This one should really impress her! I'm sure she heard what you said over the intercom!" As he laughs again, the other two members of the mining crew respond simultaneously, "Just give her back the key and say nothing!"

Still, with somewhat of a burst of reserved laughter, Miner Twelve says, "Just play dumb; it worked before, and she let you get away with it!"

The other two crew members agree to stop the bickering, and the four finally get on with the mission. As they continue, the beleaguered crew finally arrives, where Captain Reanna remains, still looking up at the crash site. She turns around and asks, "What took you so long?" The crew remains silent, not knowing what to expect next from Captain Reanna. A little out of breath, Miner Fourteen responds, "Speaking for myself... Can we stop here and rest awhile before we climb up into that thing?"

Reanna looks at the four and exclaims, "Let's go, guys!"

Having a laser weapon pointed at him again from Miner Eighteen, he is told, "Give Reanna back the key!" As Reanna takes it, she attaches it to the transport helix ignition code key and then begins to climb into the wrecked ship.

The ascent becomes not an easy task; loose sand and rocks make it almost impossible to reach the substantial gaping fisher on the ship's port side. Finally, Reanna completes the job despite the loose sand and gravel that have been continuously slipping beneath her in a downward motion with every step she takes on her climb. Her petite body and lightweight life-support flight suit contribute to her successful task.

Once inside the ship, she inspects the interior, much of which is shrouded in debris and torn metal sections. She then turns on her helmet visor lights, giving her a better perspective of the overall damage. Reanna looks back at her crew struggling up the loose, rocky, and broken terrain. Her attention now turns to the ripped electrical cables hanging above the command sectional console. Pulling on each one of several torn cables, she's able to find one with the length she needs to immediately tie one end to a jagged steel beam and throw the other end down to the struggling climbers, allowing them to climb up into the ship.

As they make their way into the dark void of the *Andromeda*, they automatically activate their helmet visor lights, thereby revealing the large command operation center of the ship. The five-miner rescue group will continue to wear their emergency oxygen container units as they inspect the debris of the several command module sections of the enormous ship.

Casting full light on the interior command sections, they discover *Andromeda's* fatal command crew on duty and at their posts with the striking appearance of when the ship was in complete operational order. Captain Reanna walks over to the command console and takes a close look at one of the uniformed figures. As she puts her hand inches away from the crewman's face, she moves it in a semicircular fashion as if to see a chance of eye movement. She then says, "There's not even a scratch on him! His eyes are open, but he's not alive!"

Looking at her Dial-Date life support readout for the crewmen's heartbeat, brain function, and circulatory conditions, Reanna sees that the respiratory indicators on all life support statistics are negative. Turning to her crew, Reanna again looks down at her Dial-Date, which functions as a diagnostic medical computer. It performs to the capacity of its high-tech scientific design and function.

Words appear on her Dial-Date screen: ...THEIR LIFE-FORCE WAS TAKEN AWAY INSTANTLY... THE SUBJECTS SUFFERED NO PAIN AND REMAINED IN A FROZEN STATE... THE SUBJECTS' DNA REMAINS IN A CODED PRESERVATION STATE...

The tiny wrist computer has no more information to offer and automatically shuts down. Reanna activates her arm-cuff computer touch relay to code essential field operations. Immediately appearing on the screen is the structural composition of the enormous ship *Andromeda*. Photon-Electro Scan adopts the methods and skills of the original architectural design. Reanna immediately announces to her crew, "We have life support, guys! Cabin pressure and temperature conditions are acceptable midship!" Looking at the relays on her arm computer again and waiting for a change in information, she receives interior amplification position directions and life-support readouts of the midship section. "Follow me, guys!"

As Reanna hits the exit exchange lever on the ship's operations control exit door, the small party follows her.

The vast corridors echo the remote party's conversations while amplifying their words across other sections of the ship. As they journey along the main walkway to the midship, the readouts on her computer display estimations and calculations of atmospheric conditions and continue to display information on life-support essentials.

Suddenly, Reanna stops the walkthrough when an alert on her arm computer indicates that two life entities are in the midship section.

Reanna then speaks into her computer, "Computer... Identify life-forms?" Readouts appear across the screen: **...LIFE- FORMS... HUMANACEREAN...**

"Computer, life-support conditions on life-forms?"

The computer continues to give Reanna the information she requested: **...CONDITION ON ENTITIES NEAR FATAL... EMERGENCY ASSISTANCE REQUIRED...**

Moments of silence, and then Reanna shouts out to her crew, "Computer, M-Code Medical Section! Midship! Let's get in there, guys!"

Hitting the exit exchange door locks, which give access to the various sections of the M-Code Medical Division Units, she enters the nursery. Reanna's attention is drawn towards a figure of a woman sitting in a command console chair as if asleep. In front of the console command, the view screen continues its functional program, scanning the giant ship's exterior field and pulsating emergency distress signals.

Reanna quietly walks up to the command console, hoping the female figure is, in fact, just asleep. Referring to her arm-cuff computer again, she directs its diagnostic scan to life support conditions. The readout immediately flashes: **... CONDITION VITAL... POOR TO HIGH RISK... IMMEDIATE MEDICAL ATTENTION REQUIRED....**

Turning to Miner Fourteen, who has just entered the nursery, she orders, "Just don't stand there! Open the Med-Vac kit and give me one of the O.N.C. cartridges!"

After he hands it to her, Reanna removes the emergency O.N.C. mask and quickly straps it onto Nurse Susan in an attempt to revive her. Miner Fourteen then says, "Hey! There's a baby in this box!"

Turning towards Miner Fourteen, who is about to lift the clear cover on the life support unit, Reanna shouts out to him, "DON'T LIFT

THAT COVER!" He pulls his hand away and steps back as Reanna hastily walks up to the incubator unit and pushes him out of the way.

"You never open these things! Not without first taking a medical STAT readout! Now, give me a hand over here; we're going to place the nurse into the atmospheric life support unit; just follow what I tell you!"

After securing the nurse in a hibernation state cylinder, she turns her attention back to the full-life support unit. She looks closely at the display module readout, which provides continuous information on the child's condition. "There's good oxygen and clear exchange field capacity with no malfunctions. We won't need our EVA support helmets, guys, as long as we stay in midship."

Looking at the console screen, she says, "This ship has a cryogenics unit just below our deck."

Turning again to her four rescue crew members, she tells them to take all of *Andromeda's* deceased crew and place them below deck into the cryogenics chamber. Following her orders, they leave the nursery compound and go about the task of collecting all the deceased crewmembers.

Reanna would not waste a moment of their departure time to learn as much as she could about this ship and where it came from. Deeply intrigued by the information from the ship's computer readouts and language acquisition, it becomes easy to read in her language while the computer changes the characters in a millionth of a second. Then, a signal is received that another rescue ship is en route to the crash site. After removing her utility vest that contained her laser weapon, she placed it over one of the console chairs.

Upon completing their tasks as she ordered, Reanna's crew returns to the nursery and tells her that all the crew members have been placed in the hibernation center. As Reanna is still focused on *Andromeda's* knowledgeable computer bank technical resources, she pays little attention to the four men. Miner Sixteen immediately removes the micro-helix key and Reanna's weapon from her utility vest.

Finally becoming aware of their presence, she refocuses her attention on her supervisory responsibilities to the prisoner. "You can lose the EVA helmets now, guys!" Miner Sixteen then says, "I don't think so! We're going to need them!"

Turning again from the computer screen with a somewhat puzzled look on her face, she responds, "What do you mean, you're going to need them?" With a smile, Miner Sixteen replies, "Well, it's like this: we're leaving you, captain, so we are going to need the helmets! We're taking the flightcraft, and we're getting the hell off this asteroid, and there's nobody that can stop us! We're not going back to the mines!"

Reanna takes her attention away from the four men and discreetly focuses on her utility vest on the console chair. Her attention is quickly acknowledged by Miner Sixteen, who is holding up the micro-double helix key to the transport flightcraft and her laser weapon. While he laughs, reacting to what he thinks is an amusing outcome of her negligence, he says, "Are you looking for this, Captain?"

Reanna remains frozen for a couple of moments, still entirely focused on her utility vest. She says, "You think it's going to be that easy?"

Staring at her, he says, "I know what you're thinking, Reanna, but you can't stop us!" With a perplexed look on her face, Reanna turns her attention towards the planetary orbital scanner that relays the screen's information data.

Turning back to her four crewmembers, she remarks, "You have seven-quarter sequence's of time left before the android security ship arrives on this crater! If you're going to take the flightcraft, you'd better do it now!" While turning away from them, Reanna's focus returns to her duties of caring for the child.

As the four crew members exit the nursery and follow the path back to the operation center, they leave the *Andromeda* and return to the transport flightcraft.

After attending to the child and checking the medical readouts, she sits at the console and watches her transport flightcraft blast off from the asteroid with her four crew members. The moments when she lost control begin to occupy her every thought. Fighting for a possible conclusion, she finds it difficult to separate herself from the responsibility of claiming to be innocent in allowing them to escape.

Sitting back in the console chair, she allows herself a tranquil moment to escape the disturbing thoughts of finding the correct explanation for the events that took place.

Suddenly, the audio alert beacon appears on the screen in front of her, and she is startled momentarily as the beacon is accompanied by the *Andromeda*'s artificial, metallic voice: "**...A FLIGHT-SHIP HAS JUST LANDED ON THE PORT SIDE OF THE *ANDROMEDA*... VARIANCE TIME ZONE BINARY SEQUENCING TRACKING ALERT...**"

Reanna operates the console keyboard as five large screens become activated, displaying angle observations of a governmental flight-ship approaching the *Andromeda* and landing.

As the flight-ship reduces its forward thrust to make a soft docking maneuver with the *Andromeda*, a large port bay hatch opens, allowing Doctor Lasara and two sentry robots to walk along the exit platform ramp and enter the destroyed interior of the *Andromeda*. Following her Life

Force Vital Computer, she receives information on two entities and their locations.

Upon entering the midship, she removes her life support helmet following the indicator alert on her arm-cuff computer, informing her that she is in an oxygenated life support environment.

Doctor Lasara and her two sentry robots continue until they reach the nursery section. She then begins to remove an emergency medical pack from her carry-on med kit. As the panel doors open instantly, Doctor Lasara and her robots enter the nursery. Placing her life support helmet down, she releases the shoulder harness on her carry-on medical kit and lets it fall to the floor, relieving her of its weight.

Reanna remains silent while carefully observing the famous Android Doctor's every move. Doctor Lasara removes her EVA gloves and then uses them to brush off the asteroid dust from her medical kit. As she observes the child inside the life support unit, she remarks,

"These asteroids are Horrendous!" Checking her Dial-Date computer and commenting to Reanna as if they had been acquaintances for a long time, she asks, "How did you ever survive on these damn asteroids? I can't imagine living and working on an asteroid mine."

With a slight smile on her face, Reanna responds to the doctor's question, "It's not easy... But you get used to it."

The Android Doctor is satisfied that she has cleaned off enough of the asteroid dust from her EVA suit. She then focuses her attention on Reanna. "Well, Reanna, you lost your crew, and obviously, they left with the flightcraft, which is a government issue, and adding that violation onto your sentence, it looks like you are going to be spending the rest of your life on an Asteroid!"

Looking around the nursery and observing the life support units, one of which contained a young child, Doctor Lasara turned her attention back to Reanna. "We can't let that happen, Reanna! You're too valuable, and you're not going back to the asteroid mines!" A look of relief on Reanna's face is replaced with one of confusion. Doctor Lasara then asks,

"Do you know who I am, Reanna?"

Reanna slowly shakes her head, and her response can hardly be heard coming from her confused state of mind. "No, I don't."

Lasara smiles. "Well, Reanna, my name is Doctor Lasara, and I am a member of the Supreme Council of the Government that sentenced you to the asteroid mines. Now, as far as the others are concerned, your crewmembers, they're not going to be in my report."

After checking her Dial-Date computer and linking it to *Andromeda's* computer console screen, prisoner Reanna's image appears, displaying her sentence violations, to which she pleaded no contest and was found guilty. She was assigned to a supervisory position on an asteroid mine, where she oversaw law violators for an unspecified period.

Turning back to Reanna, Doctor Lasara gives her a shocking response, "They don't sentence anyone to the asteroid division anymore, Reanna! According to the information I have, you and your crew were the last ones to be sentenced to an asteroid. Now, they just lock you up in Central Detention! It seems that the prison authority just clearly forgot about having a mining detail out here! This incident might have saved your life as well as the others."

Working on her arm-cuff computer and rendering the results to the large console screen, Doctor Lasara tells Reanna, "Stop looking at me and look at the screen!" Below, Reanna's photo description of prisoner information format appears in large bold letters
**...CLASSIFICATION PRISONER NAME REANNA...
RESOLVED OF ALL FAULTS AND MAY ENTER BACK INTO**

**THE GENERAL POPULATION... SENTENCE COMMUTED...
BY ORDER OF THE HIGH COUNCIL...**

Reanna turns again and looks at Doctor Lasara. With a slight smile on her face, Lasara says,

"Now you can look at me, young lady. You're free!"

Reanna is hesitant at first, trying to find the right words to express her gratitude. She remains silent for a moment, and in a slight whisper, she says, "How did you know what happened here?" Lasara smiles as she tells her, "We monitored everything that took place. My flightcraft's computer received everything before our arrival. Unfortunately, our flight course was too far out from the Asteroid Belt to intervene."

Looking at several large screens revealing the interior sections of the *Andromeda*, she says, "Now, let's see if we can find out where this wreck came from." Typing coded information into the ship's computer banks, Doctor Lasara is transfixed upon the screen as she collects further information at an accelerated rate, both in picture and language form. Turning and looking at the nurse and the baby, Doctor Lasara again remarks, "These life forms are not from our star system, and they may not even be from our time! Reanna, we must not tell anyone about this. Do you understand? I have my reasons, and I will explain them later. Now, where are the other crewmembers?"

Reanna remains in a state of disbelief, which began with losing control of her crew and then being left stranded on this wrecked ship. Now, she doesn't know what her fate would be, nor what the future would hold with the arrival of the Android Superior. Reanna hesitates for a moment as if in a state of daydreaming, then answers the request by Doctor Lasara, "Oh! I had put them into the cryogenics center..."

Lasara turns to the screen and types in the ship's graphic design, revealing the cryogenics center and its operational form capacity. Pictures show the twenty-seven-chambered occupants in a state of sleep preservation. As Doctor Lasara turns off the computer, she states, "Reanna, let's get the child off this ship where we can get him the medical attention he might need!"

While briefly checking the baby's diagnostic readouts, which indicate that everything is normal, she observes his name tag embroidered on his pajamas as he sleeps. She now turns her attention to Nurse Susan and immediately activates her Portable Life-Support-Energy Monitor, and the news is not what she had hoped for. Nurse Susan has passed. Doctor Lasara then instructs one of the sentry robots to remove Nurse Susan and follow her programmed command to the cryogenics unit, where the nurse is placed.

Observing the telescreen, she tells Reanna, "Let's remove everything we will need, and nothing pertaining to the child, and let me find out what his name is on his little uniform tag."

Typing in the symbols on his name tag into the computer's language acquisition reference data banks, Doctor Lasara finds that the results are of no possible match. The computer responds: "**... J... J... JOHNATHAN... REFERENCE MEANING... NONEXISTENT... ORIGIN UNKNOWN....**" Doctor Lasara smiles and says to Reanna, "We have a little boy by the name of Johnathan!"

Upon the return of her sentry robots, she orders them to load all of baby Johnathan's essential belongings onto her flightcraft. After Reanna gathers up some of baby Johnathan's clothing, she follows Lasara down the long corridor with the two sentry robots carrying the child's life support unit past the cabin quarters of the ill-fated Star Craft *Andromeda*.

Once onboard and all the passengers are secured, the tractor beam trans walkway retracts into Doctor Lasara's flightcraft. The craft's longitude gyrotronic launch sequence engages, and moments later, the ship is airborne, making its way across the asteroid belt. In evasive aeronautic anti-collision maneuvers while avoiding the massive debris that makes up the vast asteroid field, the ship will continue on its journey in the direction of Lasara's country estate.

After leaving the asteroid belt, the ship will head home across the dark side of the planet, avoiding the sun's harmful rays and the extreme heat. Dr. Lasara occasionally checks on baby Johnathan, who is now in her care, while Reanna gazes out at the endless horizon filled with the fading morning stars. The sentry robot turns and speaks to Dr. Lasara, breaking the silence from the journey's preprogrammed escape velocity from the asteroid belt.

"...DOCTOR LASARA... WE ARE FAST APPROACHING QUADRANT A-1-A AND ARE RECEIVING A REQUEST CODE THAT MUST BE PROGRAMMED INTO THE SHIP'S COMPUTER COMPLEX... STAR PORT CENTRAL COMMAND MUST KNOW YOUR FLIGHT PLAN IF YOU INTEND TO ENTER STAR PORT CITY'S MAIN COMPLEX FACILITY..."

Doctor Lasara responds to the sentry robot, "No, we're going to bypass Star Port City heading due north, past the winter zone. Our travel sequence course 00.92 will be under the heat shields."

The sentry robot responds, "...MISSION MESSAGE RECEIVED... COURSE ADJUSTMENT OF 00.9 IS INITIATED... EVASIVE FLIGHT COURSE AND HEAT SHIELD PROTECTION ARE NOW ACTIVATED...TRANSFERRING ALL NAVIGATIONAL COMPUTER READOUT COMMAND ANALYSIS TO BYPASS TRANSPORT FACILITY AUTHORITY... ON COURSE CHANGE TO PRIVATE FREE ZONE SECTIONS BEYOND CRATER FIELDS – NORTHERN HEMISPHERE... ALSO BYPASSING FIELD OPERATIONS AND ALPHA HOME REGIONS..."

The sentry robot turns towards her again and responds, "... MISSION GRANTED, DOCTOR... WE MAY PROCEED TO THE SAFE ZONE..."

The sentry robot initiates an accelerated thrust blast sequence, propelling the ship at high speed as it passes from the dark side of the planet and begins its journey into the light of a new day in the safe zone.

The ship lands in front of her luxurious compound, which facilitates a private residence, a medical research lab, and an observatory. Doctor Lasara is privileged to control her security, and, due to her high rank in the government, no one in the Supreme Council can initiate or conduct inquiries into her personal life.

When the ship locks down on the tarmac, Doctor Lasara awakens Reanna and then contacts Chef Eleanor, "We're back, Eleanor!"

The teleview becomes activated. "Yes, I know, Doctor... I can see you on my kitchen screen. What is all that stuff you're carrying?" Lasara smiles. "I'll tell you later. We have two extra guests for dinner tonight." The port bay exit ramp opens and is completely illuminated, allowing the passengers to exit the ship.

As they make their way into Doctor Lasara's private compound, the sentry robots are given instructions to place the young child into Lasara's Astrophysical-Nuclear science lab and turn the entire facility back on the service line.

The once indistinguishable massive complex becomes fully illuminated, from the private living quarters to the lab facilities, including the opening of her observatory dome, which contains a large telescope. Radio-transmitted pictures of the night sky are displayed on view screens throughout the complex, revealing the multitude of stars, as well as the two outer planets, Eetrainer and Cataform. Doctor Lasara's instructions to her robots are to report to the science lab to have a memory scale down to check for accuracy before putting them into a dormant sleep. Once this process is complete, Doctor Lasara removes any memory of baby Johnathan from them.

After completion, they will retain only parts of the mission, without any reference to the child. Young Johnathan has been placed in her lab on an MRI-3D processor that conveys crucial medical information on an imaging screen. Different color-coded three-dimensional images of the brain patterns and electronic impulses appear on a monitor. A series of parallel pathways of the child's brain shows no malfunctions to necessitate relay functional sequences of the VAT-NAC synaptic pathways due to the possible lack of oxygen in the nursery.

After inputting and cataloging general information on baby Johnathan, Doctor Lasara realizes that the child is remarkably similar to the species on her planet. Doctor Lasara observes the diagnostic readouts, which indicate that the child is approximately four and a half to five years old. The planet's origin is unknown. Securing the patient for further medical analysis, she turns her attention to Reanna. "Tell me about yourself, Reanna."

As Reanna looks at Doctor Lasara, she is reluctant at first to find the right words to answer her question. She then replies, "Are you asking me the story of my life?"

Smiling, she says, "Yes, Reanna, from the very beginning."

Thinking back for a moment, Reanna says, "Well, I was an only child, born to parents who were on in age. We lived on a small farm in the growing fields that supplied most of the produce that was sent to the Central Distribution Centers. My mother passed away first; a short time later, my father too." She pauses. "My happy life passed with them! I found myself alone and abandoned, and that's when I sold the farm and moved to the city. I squandered my transfer credits from the sale of the farm and ended up with some bad individuals, and that's how I ended up on the asteroid prison mine."

Lasara is silent for a moment. "Well, Reanna, where would you like to go from here? You can return to the growing fields, and I'm sure you must still have some friends there?"

Remaining quiet for a moment, she says, "No, I don't." Doctor Lasara asks, "Are you looking for a new life?"

Reanna remains quiet and then replies, "A new life, is that possible?"

Doctor Lasara smiles. "Reanna, anything is possible if you work to make it happen! I have an extraordinary project that may interest you. I am the director of the government program of Astro-Nuclear Science. My job is to investigate and report any unusual occurrences that occur in our star system. You were sent to the asteroid crash site by a command sequence order from monitoring satellites that protect our planet and its space. I must turn in a report about the crash site; however, my account will not include your crew or the child.

You see, Reanna, I intend to keep baby Johnathan, and being that I'm a government official, it will be impossible. There will be investigations into the child's origin, and I'm sure you're aware, Reanna, that there will be no future for him in a government program here. Think about it, Reanna. Together, the two of us can also give him a new life!

Now, let me take you into the kitchen and formally introduce you to my chef, Ellen.

Chapter 4:

The Solarist

Several days have passed, and the cold night winds surrounding Doctor Lasara's compound give the feeling of the coming winter season. Doctor Lasara's residence's rustic interior resembles the forest acres of hardwood trees and plant life of the woodlands that surround her property.

Reanna and Chef Eleanor take the food trays out into the dining room, where Aunt Lasara is spoon-feeding little Johnathan, a variety of high-protein baby food from a deluxe vitamin-enhanced assortment. "Come, Reanna, sit down." Smiling while admiring the baby, Lasara says, "Isn't he a handsome child?"

"Yes, he is, Doctor Lasara!" Looking up at Reanna, she replies, "Please, Reanna, call me Lasara! We're not in Star Port City now, where it would be required by law to address me by my title. Sit down, Reanna, and let us have dinner."

As Doctor Lasara gives baby Johnathan the last spoonful of food, she takes her place at the cocktail table, surrounded by plush sectional module furniture units designed by award-winning professionals. Before the doctor begins her dinner, she looks straight at Reanna.

"Reanna, do you mind if I discuss the rest of my plan that I would like you to be part of?"

"No, Lasara, of course not!"

Doctor Lasara continues,

"If you work for me and become little Johnathan's surrogate mother, which the law allows, no government inquiry or request for information is necessary. The government is not concerned about where children end up once they are adopted, as long as they are not in the government program. All you have to do is take Johnathan and register as his surrogate mother, and you will receive the proper certification; I will see to that! After they do a search that will register him as an abandoned child, you will officially be his mother. Of course, I will always be there to help you raise him; my home will always be your home and baby Johnathan's. Take all the time you need to think about it, Reanna."

Smiling, Reanna replies, "Lasara, I was never a mother before, but it sounds like a wonderful experience. I will do it! It will be a new life!" Lasara adds, "Yes, it will be exactly what you're looking for!"

After dinner, Doctor Lasara ignites the fireplace, and the burning embers of Alphanian wood release a sweet scent reminiscent of the Alphanian Forest as they warm the entire room. Reanna gets up and leaves the dining area without saying a word and checks on baby Johnathan, who is fast asleep. Moving some of his baby toys aside, she adjusts the cradle blanket to ensure that baby Johnathan stays warm on this changing seasonal night.

Returning to the dinner console area, Reanna retakes her place directly across from Doctor Lasara and says, "Lasara, you have given me that chance for a new life! I will be a good mother to baby Johnathan." Smiling, Lasara replies, "Reanna, I was hoping you would say that!"

The two women continue discussing their plans when Chef Eleanor enters the large living room. She informs Doctor Lasara that she has cleaned up the kitchen area and prepared a special formula breakfast for baby Johnathan. Eleanor then walks up to Reanna and embraces her. "I am so happy that Doctor Lasara has found such a sweet and intelligent friend to be part of our little family!"

With a smile on her face, Reanna replies, "Thank you, Eleanor. I appreciate that!"

Eleanor then adds, "If there is nothing else that I can get you from the kitchen, I'll have to excuse myself; I want to be up early in the morning to prepare a nice breakfast for baby Johnathan and us!"

Walking past the baby's cradle, she adjusts the bed linens and exits the living room.

As Doctor Lasara pours a vintage wine into two crystal glasses, she smiles. "Eleanor is such a character, isn't she? For the life of me, I would not know what to do without her!"

Reanna smiles as the two women share the warmth of the fireplace and discuss their agreement to raise the child who came to them from the shadows of a hidden world beyond the stars.

In the early morning hours of the next day, a dwarf star appears over the famous Crater Mountains. The fields of vegetation surrounding Lasara's compound retain the moisture of its seasonal passing rain from the night before. Wild creatures are huddled in their flight nests within the dense forest canopy.

On the ground in their burrows, newborn wildlife huddle together for warmth from the wet night rains. They all await the presence of the giant life-giving sun at the center of their solar system, which will soon cast its warmth on this region as it has been doing since the beginning of its conception. The green fields will rise to their early morning light as they receive the wealth of nourishment from the center of their creation. The skies will once again be filled with creatures of flight, and a new day will begin.

In the morning, a new routine began inside Doctor Lasara's compound. Breakfast will now become a ritual of interesting conversation and the beginning of a day with a purpose and parental care, where Reanna, Lasara, and Ellen will all share the responsibilities of raising young Johnathan. The kitchen area will become the morning meeting place where breakfast menus are prepared, as well as special formulas for young Johnathan. Reanna has now become a part of the great mystery of Johnathan's life. During breakfast, the four of them will start their day surrounded by view screens telecasting information about the planet and its cities, from the Trikinian Mountains to the low sand fields and ocean desert areas.

Several months pass in uneventful tranquility until routine periodical testing reveals that baby Johnathan has developed a hemoplatic condition resembling a blood virus with unknown origins. Doctor Lasara panics at the prognosis, with no information to rectify his situation, as she goes through every medical database on her computer. She cannot bring herself to the realization that this medical problem has never been encountered before.

Her only recourse is to find help wherever she can. She could only think of one person who could solve this problem, and her old friend came to mind. He was a professor of Astro-Nuclear Science and a medical doctor who wrote famous books on the origins of the universe. Unfortunately, he was banned and exiled to the Old City for the rest of his life.

As she searches through boxes of old university papers, she comes across a folder containing documents and a bronze medallion she had received from the professor at graduation. Holding up the cloverleaf design medallion and a card of instructions he had given to several of his students, which informed them how they could contact him, she places the medallion onto the computer screen, and a coded scale of musical notes automatically appears. This discreet musical code can only be interpreted as a simple melody when in contact with the professor.

She leaves her storage area in the basement complex. She makes her way straight to her computer platform facility, trying to contain her emotions, knowing that she could not contact any medical specialist without disclosing where baby Johnathan came from. She nervously submits his code sequence into the computer, and moments later, the words appear across her computer console screen: **...YOUR SONG REQUEST WILL APPEAR FOR YOUR ENJOYMENT AND ENTERTAINMENT...** Musical notes then appear across the screen on a musical clef chart. Some of the notes are shaded, while others are finely penciled in with the absence of color. At the end of the musical score, words appear, suggesting entering a song of your choice. Lasara then follows the Clef Program, selecting the non-shaded notes in a musical sequence to convey her message back to the professor.

Professor Zola receives Lasara's message and remains motionless, sitting back in deep thought. He thinks about all those enjoyable years as a professor at the university and about instructing so many fine young students. With his robot, Cen-Ton, standing by his side, he says, "Cen-Ton, you and I are going to pay a visit to one of my students."

"...PROFESSOR, LEAVING THE OLD CITY CAN HAVE GRAVE CONSEQUENCES FOR YOU..."

"Precisely, Cen-Ton. We thrive on consequences! What would become of us if we didn't offer our help to a friend in need?" Cen-Ton replies, "...I WILL PREPARE THE HYDRO-FLIGHTCRAFT, PROFESSOR..."

In the hidden mountain cave, a domed enclosure opens above the professor's lab. Several steps down from the central computer console area is an enclosed quarters room where he will dress for a high-speed flight in the hydro flight pod that will exit from a hidden gantry bay.

Cen-Ton helps the professor turn on his oxygen control flight suit before stepping into the flightcraft. Cen-Ton then steps back several feet into the safety area where he will not be affected by the anti-magnetic engine lift fields as the blast engines ignite, sending the hydro-flightcraft into the planet's mesosphere on a curved trajectory. This will avoid the planet's large cities and their detection of ray-waves while keeping the professor's flightcraft on a controlled, secret flight plan.

After a lengthy flight, the professor's hydro-flightcraft lands on the tarmac of Doctor Lasara's countryside estate, located in a farmland county, sixteen-quarter sequences outside Star Port City. The professor exits the craft and is greeted by one of Doctor Lasara's sentry robots.

"...WELCOME, PROFESSOR... MAY I ASSIST YOU WITH YOUR CARRY UNIT...?"

"Yes, you may. Thank you."

Complying with the professor's request, the sentry robot carries his medical unit into the house.

Once inside the mansion, the professor is struck by its ornate interior design. As he looks around, he remarks, "Very nice! Very nice!"

The sentry robot responds, "... PROFESSOR... PLEASE WAIT HERE... DOCTOR LASARA WILL ARRIVE MOMENTARILY..."

As the professor is looking at a large wall painting, he is interrupted by Doctor Lasara, who enters the room.

"Well, Professor Zola, it's been a long time! Thank you for responding to my message."

He turns to her and says,

"What is time? Isn't it just a memory that we put aside only to revisit with the joy of our experiences?"

As Lasara smiles, she says, "Your philosophy, professor, has always intrigued me! May I introduce you to my assistant? Reanna, this is Professor Zola." As he extends his hand to Reanna, he replies,

"I am charmed to meet you, my dear. "Reanna takes the professor's hand and smiles. The professor then turns his attention to Lasara. "Now, Doctor Lasara, I am sure you did not contact me without urgency?"

"Yes, professor. We have a child, and according to a routine diagnostic blood test, he has some kind of blood abnormality. Do you want me to tell you about this child, other than his medical condition?"

The professor replies, "No, that won't be necessary. We all have our little secrets in life. Without them, we could not very well choose between good friends. May I see the child now?"

"Yes, I'll show you the way to the nursery."

Doctor Lasara, Reanna, and the professor enter the nursery, where medical screens continuously display baby Johnathan's vital signs. Professor Zola focuses his attention on several screens that continually display diagnostic monitoring data. Speaking out loud, he says, "Everything seems to be normal; body temperature, respiratory system, and neuropathways seem excellent! However, his blood contains a viral discrepancy that should not be present in his bloodstream! Do you have samples of his blood type available, Doctor Lasara?"

"Yes, they are on this tray of crystal slides."

As the professor removed a small portable blood diffusion computer from his medical unit carrier, he placed it over the crystal slides. Diagnostic readouts appear on the screen ...**VARIABLE BLOOD TYPES UNACCEPTABLE... BLOOD ABNORMALITY OF PATIENT...UNKNOWN...HARMFUL...**

While the professor pays careful attention to his diagnostic readout, he says, "According to the child's blood composition, there is no match of other blood types to cure the problem, except for a chemical composite that can only be found in Trikinian blood! In my opinion, it is the only chance we have to destroy the spread of the virus that is continuously destroying the healthy hemoplatic regeneration of his blood cells."

The computer continues the readout. **...ONLY TWO CCs INFUSION IS NECESSARY TO ERADICATE AND PURIFY THE ABNORMALITY IN THE CONDITION FORMULA OF SAMPLE A-7...**

Professor Zola then says, "The mystery is solved, Doctor Lasara. Now, all we need is a small amount of Trikinian blood." With a puzzled look on her face, Reanna asks, "And where are we going to get that from, Professor?"

Doctor Lasara replies, "Reanna, we are going to get it from Trikinia!" Professor Zola adds, "We have an answer, and it requires that someone must go to Trikinia immediately! His condition cannot wait, and the only one who can help us is the Trikinian ambassador. She can grant permission as we speak."

Using his Dial-Date, the professor contacts the Trikinian ambassador.

A response is received in the professor's Dial-Date reading: **... AFFIRMATIVE ...!**

Aunt Lasara then says, "Reanna, you are the only one who can go! Neither the Professor nor I can leave without authorization! The moment we cross the border into Trikinia, our computer programming will notify the governmental authorities. You must leave for Trikinia this very moment!" Reanna asks, "Won't the government know when I cross the border?"

"No, Reanna. As of this moment, you do not exist! When we

were on the asteroid, I removed your existence from all the government files! When the time is right, I will give you a new identity!"

As the professor types into his Dial-Date arm computer, he replies, "My transport has been preprogrammed to enter Trikinia. You will land in a small mountain outpost, Reanna; they await your arrival in the frozen mountains of Trikinia. Trikinian warriors will be there to greet you; you have been granted security clearance. The hydro-flightcraft is preprogrammed to take you to Trikinia and back on auto-program when you enter the command console."

Doctor Lasara then says, "Come on, Reanna, let's get you a warm flight suit for your cold-weather journey."

Doctor Lasara helps Reanna with last-minute preparations for her flight suit as the two women walk out through the large field bay landing port doors of Lasara's compound.

As Reanna enters Professor Zola's hydro-flightcraft, beacon floodlights illuminate the hydro-craft area's takeoff sequence. Reanna then enters the space vehicle's operational interior bay, and its antigravity field immediately lifts the ship off the tarmac. As the gyro controls the craft, it reaches a safe zone altitude above the compound.

Then, blast engines carry the ship into the deep-space atmosphere above the planet on its preprogrammed trajectory to Trikinia, leaving a fiery red signature.

The hydro-flightcraft landing was not what Reanna expected, and the crude landing zone was not well-maintained on the side of one of Trikinian's highest mountains. Its elevation readout statistics on the flightcraft's computer dash screen reveal that its height is thirty-seven thousand feet above sea level in relation to the other mountain ranges in the land of Trikinia, which average twenty-nine to thirty-four thousand feet. The mountains and their surrounding areas are covered with Torknic Ice. This ice has remained frozen for millions of years, and the thick slabs resemble natural quartz crystal formations. As Reanna exits the hydro-flightcraft, she experiences high winds as she makes her way into the entrance port of the mountain.

Once inside the cave, the howling wind fades, and Reanna stands motionless, finding herself in a fluorescent blue anomaly of light. As the light disallows her to see the interior of the cave, it begins to dissipate as two large figures approach her. "Welcome to Trikinia, Reanna! Professor Zola has made all the arrangements for your visit. Please follow us to the center vale of illumination."

Following the two Trikinians, she steps across the ice sheet surface of stalactites as if one could step into a mirror and become one's reflection. She now finds herself in a world of instant change, where the cold winter exists outside the mountain, and the interior is a warm world. Removing her life support oxygen helmet, she finds herself alone and without the two escort figures. While she walks among a multitude of Trikinian people going about their daily lives, she finds herself lost for answers, as if in a dream, unable to identify anything familiar. She then hears a voice: "You know why you are here, Reanna? You must wake up and complete the task that you were assigned."

Opening her eyes, she realizes she had been asleep and that all this was just a dream. "Are you okay, Reanna?" Looking up at this kind face for a moment, the older woman bears a resemblance to her mother. Fighting to gain full consciousness, Reanna realizes that she had passed out. Her first words are "What happened to me?"

"You'll be fine, Reanna. You lacked oxygen, and you passed out. You are not used to the high altitude; you should never have removed your oxygen supply unit so soon."

Reanna realizes now that she is indoors, in a medical facility unit surrounded by Trikinian doctors and nurses. "As soon as you feel strong enough, we're going to send you home to Professor Zola with the blood supply. My name is Nurse Calaris, and I've been taking care of you since the two Trikinian warriors found you passed out in the cave entrance. You're going to be okay. All your vitals are perfect!"

"Thank you, Nurse... I feel better already that it was all just a dream..."

"Good! This will give you strength."

As Nurse Calaris places a tray of food in front of Reanna, she tells her, "You will feel a lot better once you have some nourishment. But be careful; eat slowly and enjoy."

A little while later, Reanna feels well enough to continue her mission and leave the medical facility, along with the strange experience she encountered while unconscious. Talking to Nurse Calaris, she says, "If you don't mind, I would like to go back to my ship, and now, it's important that I get the blood supply back to Doctor Lasara."

At that moment, an orderly leaves the nurse's ward, and the doors automatically open, allowing Reanna to view Professor Zola, who is talking to two doctors in front of a nurse's station out in the lobby. In disbelief, she calls out, "Professor Zola?"

The figure walks away from the nurse's station area abruptly, and Reanna second-guesses what she has just experienced. Approaching Reanna, Calaris asks, "What's wrong, Reanna?" In a low voice, Reanna replies, "I'm not sure... It was something..." She remains for a moment and then says, "I am ready to leave now, Nurse."

"Okay, Reanna, we have the blood supply right here." As Nurse Calaris hands Reanna the sealed blood supply unit. She says, "I'll have two escorts to see you safely to your flightcraft."

Out in the large ward area, Reanna will not attempt to find out what her eyes had seen a short time ago. She felt like she had endured enough without adding more of a burden; all she could think about now was getting home and feeling safe again in an environment she could understand.

As the hydro-flightcraft lands on Doctor Lasara's compound, the service doors open. Standing to greet Reanna are Doctor Lasara and Professor Zola. As Reanna exits the hydro-flightcraft, the night sky is clear, as is the air around the compound, with the fresh scent of Alphanian leaves. She pauses for a moment, looks up at the bright sea of stars, and reflects on the journey she has just endured. "Welcome home, Reanna!"

"Thank you, Lasara, it's good to be back!"

Doctor Lasara and Reanna enter the large living room, and, again, Reanna becomes puzzled for a moment, remaining motionless as she stares at Professor Zola. "Ah... Reanna, my dear Reanna, I'll take that from you." Handing the professor the sealed package, she remains speechless. The concerned Doctor Lasara feels like something is bothering Reanna and asks, "Is anything wrong, Reanna? You look exhausted."

Reanna smiles. "No, Lasara, everything is fine."

Doctor Lasara and Professor Zola immediately take the blood supply to the lab, as Lasara picks up baby Johnathan and places him into a controlled medical unit. As the professor places a tiny plastic catheter-based transfusion clamp onto the baby's arm, he attaches the cartridge of the two CCs of blood, and it is instantly absorbed into his bloodstream. Moments later, the medical control unit screen displays the results as they come across instantaneously with the positive effects of the treatment: **...THE VIRUS HAS BEEN INSTANTLY REMOVED...**

The professor sighs with relief. "It worked, Doctor Lasara; we've done it! Little Johnathan is now free of the virus! This calls for a cup of tea, Doctor Lasara, if you don't mind?" Smiling, she replies,

"Not at all, professor. Reanna, take Johnathan into the living room area and join us for tea." Lasara then remarks, "Professor Zola, how long is your stay with us?"

"Well, Doctor Lasara, you know of my unusual circumstances of not being allowed the freedom one would desire. If I may be so discreet, this is one of the very few times that I have ventured out of the Old City."

Lasara smiles. "I understand, professor. This whole episode will remain our secret, and we will never speak of it again. Reanna, while you're taking baby Johnathan into the living room with the professor, I'll attend to making the tea and gathering some snacks from the automatic bakery dispenser." She then remarks, "I can't wait until Chef Eleanor returns from Star Port City tomorrow and prepares some decent food for us! She will also be happy to hear that baby Johnathan is healthy again!" She calls out from the kitchen. "Now, where is that baby food formula?"

After entering the dining room, she says, "Professor, why don't you stay with us for a while? I would love to talk about our past lectures. By the way, whatever happened to that theorist friend of ours?"

"You're referring to Professor Portland Webster?" Lasara replies, "Why, yes, he was such a futuristic visionary with so many new theories."

Professor Zola remarks, "Theories, yes, unfortunately, that led to his dismissal. No one knows what happened to him. He was never heard from again. Many wonder if he's still alive; so much has changed since those days."

"How awful, Professor! I feel so ashamed of myself for inquiring about him."

Putting his hand up, he says, "Not at all, Doctor Lasara, you had no way of knowing! With the many decades you spent on the planet, Cata-Form, and your work in Astro-Atomic Astronomy, you had no idea of the many restrictions that took place within our government regarding scientific results of duplication and the dire effect that it would have on our society if our government did not put a stop to it. I was also accused of participating in the program and received a sentence; I was sent to Central Detention for a short period, and my case was appealed on a technicality. I was given a choice: spend the rest of my life in Central Detention or accept a self-imposed exile in the Old City, accompanied only by a robot companion. Of course, I accepted exile in the Old City. There was never a public trial regarding Professor Webster, and I was not given a trial pending a long, drawn-out appeal by my attorneys. So, here I am, with you for a short period, and then I will return to my exile."

Baby Johnathan shows all the signs of a healthy child of his age, playful and attentive to the two women he is beginning to know as Mother Reanna and Aunt Lasara. Several weeks passed, and Professor Zola overstayed his visit to the Lasara compound. His daily chores include keeping track of baby Johnathan's computer-generated medical stats. With baby Johnathan's original abnormality and no chance of it recurring, Professor Zola decides that it is time to go back to the Old City.

He enters the chef's gallery and greets Eleanor with a broad smile and a morning greeting. "Good morning, Eleanor! I want you to do me a special favor, if you don't mind?"

"Why, not at all, professor. Would you like me to make something special for you this morning?"

"No, that's not necessary; whatever breakfast foods you prepared will be just fine. My request is, I would like to take the breakfast tray out to those two wonderful young ladies if that's alright with you?" Smiling, she replies, "Why, yes, of course, professor. I'll follow you with the beverages."

Taking the tray, the professor enters the large living room and greets Doctor Lasara and Reanna. "Good morning, ladies!"

Walking past baby Johnathan's cradle, he looks down at baby Johnathan. "And you too, Johnathan, good morning!"

Lasara says, "Well, this is a surprise, professor. I was expecting you to be late for breakfast this morning when you did not show up at your usual time, and there you were in the kitchen helping Eleanor prepare breakfast."

"My dear Doctor Lasara and Reanna, I'm afraid this will be our last breakfast together. You know, I did overstay my time away from the Old City, and the safety of all of us is my prime concern. So, I must return today after I enjoy this fine breakfast prepared by your delightful Chef, Eleanor."

"We will miss you, professor; it was a pleasure, and the help that you have given us will always stay dear to me."

The professor replies, "I will always be there when you need my help."

"Professor, what do you do at the Old City, if you don't mind my asking? "A look of surprise appears on Doctor Lasara's face at Reanna's question to the professor. "I mean, there's no one there."

The professor puts down his cup of tea and responds to Reanna, "It was the lesser of two evils, Reanna, and I do have a friend, my robot, Cen-Ton."

After breakfast, the three companions engage in subjects that will apply to their future friendship and a bond of trust that will last beyond this short visit, as they care for baby Johnathan. As the professor's ship engages its antigravity force field engines, the ship lifts off the compound's landing field, allowing the chilly fall morning with its strong winds to cover the landing area with dried foliage, leaves, and broken branches. Lasara and Reanna stand inside the anti-blast enclosure and wave up to the professor's craft.

Doctor Lasara, Reanna, and Chef Eleanor settle into a family routine that includes preparations for the fall season and many holiday celebrations. Doctor Lasara will be required to entertain important government guests. She knows full well that she must have validation and government registration to have baby Johnathan in her home. She becomes concerned—she could explain Reanna's presence, but what about baby Johnathan's? The holiday season is approaching, when many dignitaries will arrive at her home without invitation, and some will have alternative motives. The government "reeks" with suspicion; the higher the person rises in the government, the less trusted they become.

Lasara will now focus her attention on Reanna and baby Johnathan to justify their presence in her home. She will focus on a comprehensive plan that will require many steps, each to be taken with extreme caution. Instinct had already played a role in one of the decisions that she had to make to keep the baby. Her choice of Reanna as the child's mother was a good one.

As a first step, she decodes her sentry robot's memory logs—this is a routine task she has done many times before. However, now Doctor Lasara will need a complete story to include in her report to the government. This report must not have any of the slightest errors linking baby Johnathan with the wreckage of the ill-fated ship. That would make it impossible to register baby Johnathan as Reanna's child. Reluctantly, she must get back to the ship, and she must do it alone. She would plan to remove or destroy any evidence of baby Johnathan's presence aboard the *Andromeda*. She will not burden Reanna with her plans should they fail. She will take Reanna into her confidence only to tell her that she will be away for a few days at her department office in the Government Center at Star Port City.

The next morning, at breakfast, after informing Chef Eleanor, Lasara tells Reanna that she will be gone for a few days. "I'll be at my office in the Government Center at Star Port City. If you need me, you can contact me with the professor's code, and please take care of baby Johnathan." Reanna smiles. "Lasara, you know I will!" As Lasara leaves, she turns towards Reanna. "I know you will take care of Johnathan... I was kidding!"

Moments later, the exit ramp opens, and the hydro-flightcraft levitates and exits the compound's underground port bay. Its journey is on a pre-flight-guided course, with stability locked in at the asteroid's destination. The determined Doctor Lasara remains uncertain about the decisions she must make. The whole picture is not clear at this moment; it will have to be one careful step at a time. She must refocus on what needs to take place first. The initial report regarding the wreckage on the asteroid is overdue and must be submitted without further delay. She must find any existing evidence of baby Johnathan in the wrecked ship and eliminate it.

Forty-eight-quarter sequences later, Lasara's craft lands on the dusty winds of the asteroid. Lasara enters the destroyed forward section of this once-great ship that holds secrets that could never be revealed in its entirety. Slowly deteriorating in the relentless winds of the asteroid belt, the ghostly interior of the ill-fated *Andromeda* now offers minimal lighting in the hall corridors due to the diminished state of the core field energy reserves.

Lasara finds her journey to the medical quarters difficult, struggling to walk two sections along pathways covered in sand and asteroid rock. She finally makes her way to the medical unit, and the doors open automatically as they have done before. She pauses for a moment before entering the dark interior of the medical quarters. She activates her helmet's EVA beacon light, illuminating the room and making it more distinguishable. Placing her hand-carried lantern light on the counter and focusing on the console computer keyboards, she begins to type in code sequences that she could access into the ship's central computer banks.

The dormant ship's computers were not damaged, and the computer banks function with clarity and high-speed accuracy as they display photo identification of the captain and his wife. She then enhances the screen's magnification, allowing her to read the rank tags on their uniforms: Captain Johnathan Shawnwood and Communications Officer Deandra Shawnwood. She continues to read the ship's last recorded mission, Orbit Mars: Shore Leave Project *Carousel*. Further information was relayed through last-minute conversations among nursery staff and personnel departures, including the captain and his wife, from the ship to the planet. It became apparent to Doctor Lasara that baby Johnathan's parents were possibly alive and not on the craft when it met its disastrous fate.

Opening a small, black compact, she removes a metallic disk and places it on the computer screen. Electronic waves begin to instantly delete the main hard drives that contain secure information on personnel and the origin of the ship. Photosensors flash across the screen, including pictures of the entire crew.

Doctor Lasara is now confident that she has deleted all the information that could reference baby Johnathan's existence and that he was ever on board the *Andromeda*. Removing the disc, she placed it back into her compact. Feeling more confident now, Doctor Lasara leaves the nursery and makes her way back to her hydro-flightcraft. Securing herself in her command seat, she feels a sense of comfort and relaxes for a moment, a pleasant smile on her face. "Computer, Star Port City, please."

The hydro-flightcraft's rearview screen allows Lasara to view the asteroid and the wreckage, which is now becoming a fast-distant memory. Twenty-four-quarter sequences pass as Lasara's hydro-flightcraft enters controlled space above Star Port City. Forcefields become activated with the backup computer's antigravity control entry shields until clearance identification is given, allowing Doctor Lasara to land in the Universal Reserved Field designated for government officials. Her identification has been cleared as her hydro-flightcraft lands.

Sitting back in her console area, she turns down a reflection mirror and, for a moment, admires her exquisite facial features while thinking to herself, "... *How could someone with such beauty be so devious? Wouldn't the government like to know? My plan is halfway completed, and where do I go from here? For now, that will have to wait...*" As she smiles in the mirror, she applies some makeup and fixes her hair.

Doctor Lasara enters the government complex, where she will undergo a series of entrance observations and identification checks to verify the official symbol on her jacket's lapel. Harmless laser beams will take identification information from her insignia badge, which contains an invisible code revealing only the title: **DOCTOR LASARA–GOVERNMENT OFFICIAL.**

Before the final checkpoint that will allow her to enter the facility's large interior hall, a harmless photo retina copy beam strikes and identifies Councilwoman Lasara. The doors open, and Lasara enters the forum, approaching the personnel at the entrance console. One of the receptionists immediately stands up, at attention, and greets her by saying her name and rank: "Doctor Lasara, Supreme Council Member, may I help you?"

"Yes, you may. I am here to see members of the consortium council."

"Thank you, Doctor. If I may, I will direct you to level one-zero-one, section seventeen, where they are meeting with emergency field officers."

As she types on her computer keyboard at a rapid rate, she

says, "You have been granted entrance into the meeting, Doctor." Glancing at the secretary's name, Lasara replies, "Thank you, Jan."

Lasara makes her way through the crowded atrium, where she encounters numerous lower-level government officials, security guards, and sentry robots on duty every day at this government center. Doctor Lasara makes her way to one of the lift platforms. "One-zero-one, section seventeen, please."

Just before entering level one-zero-one, the high-speed lift slows to a docking sequence mode, and the doors open, allowing the passengers to step off at their designated level. Doctor Lasara steps out of the lift platform, walks towards the large meeting room, and is greeted by a sentry robot. "**...WELCOME, DOCTOR LASARA... I AM PLEASED TO SEE YOU... MAY I PRESENT YOU WITH TODAY'S SCHEDULED PROGRAMS...**"

Taking the booklet, Lasara enters the large meeting room. A female attendant approaches her and asks, "Doctor, may I take your document carry case?"

"Yes, place it on my console counter while I sign in on today's meeting register code screen."

After signing in, Doctor Lasara takes her place in her assigned area and activates her computer monitor. She began entering her attendance for this meeting while several other council members were denied for filing incomplete reports. On Doctor Lasara's computer screen, the Supreme Council accepts and processes her attendance at the meeting with approval. They will send an inspection crew to the wrecked ship on the asteroid and remove the crew members located in the cryogenic section. An additional message from the Supreme Council appears across the middle of Lasara's computer telescreen. **...THANK YOU FOR YOUR REPORT, DOCTOR LASARA ...YOU MAY LEAVE THE MEETING IF YOU DESIRE...**

Doctor Lasara deactivates her computer screen and enters her package incident reports concerning the crash site. The monitor beneath her console registers several of her incident reports in the central computer archives. She leaves the council meeting room with a feeling of relief and satisfaction that she accomplished another part of her plan to keep baby Johnathan's existence a secret.

Doctor Lasara leaves the government complex and, shortly after, is at the controls of her hydro-flightcraft. She then speaks into the voice modulation console, "Airfield Security... Flightcraft section – Doctor Lasara One; request direction and permission for departure."

Instantly, an affirmative, vocal response to her request is granted. "...YOU MAY ENGAGE YOUR ANTIGRAVITY FIELD ENGINES... THE SPACE FIELD ABOVE YOUR CRAFT IS OPEN AND CLEAR FOR DEPARTURE... THANK YOU FOR VISITING STAR PORT CITY AND THE GOVERNMENT COMPLEX THAT FUNCTIONS ONLY TO SERVE IN UNITY WITH OUR CITIZENS... SAFE FLIGHT, DOCTOR LASARA..."

Airborne at a modest speed until she clears the airspace of the restricted zone, Lasara then activates full thrust to the flightcraft's antimagnetic velocity engines, and her flightcraft enters orbital space.

Sixteen-quarter sequences of travel time-lapse before Lasara's hydro-flightcraft reenters above the fields of Alphanian trees and her compound estate. Just before landing, Lasara types a message to Reanna, saying she is tired and looking forward to a late dinner with her and baby Johnathan.

Field lights around the circular tarmac glow softly in a pastel blue, glow, enhanced by pulsating, bright landing beacon lights. As the flightcraft descends slowly to land, Lasara immediately exits and is greeted by Reanna and Eleanor. Lasara smiles and says, "Ladies, everything is fine! We will talk later, and I will explain everything!"

As they enter the compound, Chef Eleanor heads towards the kitchen to prepare dinner, as Doctor Lasara inquires about baby Johnathan. "He's fine, Lasara..."

"Thank you, Reanna; I have much to tell you." Lasara then says, "Eleanor, you are not allowed to leave the room! Now sit down and enjoy dinner with us."

The three friends enjoy a casual conversation, and after dessert, Eleanor hands Lasara a shopping list of pantry items she needs. "Doctor Lasara, please check to see if anything is missing that you would like?"

"Oh, Eleanor, I think you have just about covered everything we need."

Looking at the list, Lasara falls into deep thought and remains silent; she then turns to Eleanor, who is about to leave the room. "Eleanor... Eleanor, you're not going to shop for our food supplies. I am taking Reanna; she was never there, and I want to show her around the large food courts outside the city and the transport terminal."

Lasara turns towards Reanna and asks, "Or am I mistaken? Reanna, are you familiar with that food transport area?"

"No, I was never there. I never had the resources to buy food in bulk."

"Well, you're going to have the experience now! I will show you how to negotiate with the merchants for better pricing. Most merchants are from the outer planets, and they maintain a culture of high-quality produce. They love to engage in debates about the prices. If you ask to pay less, they will go into a lengthy conversation with you and explain that the quality of the foods they grow is the best that you will find in any marketplace on the planet."

After tidying up the kitchen area, Chef Eleanor informs Doctor

Lasara and Reanna that she is retiring to her quarters. "Good night, Eleanor, and thank you for a wonderful dinner!"

"You're very welcome, Doctor."

Doctor Lasara follows Eleanor to the large exit doors of the living room. "Eleanor, I'll take care of the outside surveillance lights and have one of the sentry robots secure all exit and entry ramps. You may go right to your quarters and enjoy a good night's sleep, and I'll see you in the morning."

As the automatic living room doors close, Doctor Lasara activates the security alarms and disengages the compound's intercom communication relays.

Sitting down at the dinner module, she says to Reanna, "We can talk now; I must admit, up until a few moments ago, I did not have a plan. As much as I have searched for answers on how we would keep baby Johnathan, I could not come up with a solution. Then, all at once, it came to me! Eleanor's shopping list!"

Reanna then asks, "Shopping list? What does Eleanor's shopping list have to do with it, Lasara?"

"Reanna, you and the shopping list are the answer to our plan! It works like this: Tomorrow, you and I are going shopping, and we're taking Jonathan with us to the transport terminal's open food market, where large food bins come in from our produce farms. The open market also receives exotic food goods from the outer planets. There have been occasions when abandoned babies have been found in some of the most unusual places! These incidents do not occur frequently, but when they do, the government does not need to investigate the origin of the violation because someone is always willing to adopt the child as their own. The solution that I was looking for would never have occurred to me if it weren't for Eleanor. When she mentioned the open market, she described a place filled with busy customers making purchases. Hundreds of produce tents are set up to accommodate the multitudes of shoppers, and hardly anyone pays attention to anything beyond their purchases. Security is minimal, with only a few sentry robots patrolling the area. After we land, I will leave you and make several large purchases of crate vegetables, place them on a hover cart, and take them back to our flightcraft, where you and baby Johnathan will be waiting. We will then go back to the market area and seek out a sentry robot officer unit and make a report about finding this lovely child in one of my produce crates."

Reanna acknowledges. "It sounds like a good plan, Lasara!"

"It is, Reanna, and the difficult part comes later when the authorities will question you, and you must tell the same story, practically word for word. In the report that you will make out to the sentry robot unit, I will witness and be in full agreement. You will receive a receipt statement; trust me, Reanna, we can do this!"

The next morning, before the sun appears on the horizon over the crater mountains, Doctor Lasara's hydro-flightcraft is programmed for a direct flight to Star Port City's large food market. By the time Lasara, Reanna, and baby Johnathan arrive, the morning crowds have already become actively engaged in their routine of purchasing food supplies. Others who are commercial agents purchase large quantities of food products for commercial establishments. Before Doctor Lasara leaves on her mission, she turns around to baby Johnathan, who is actively playing with his toys. She then removes a sedative light beam from a medical kit and waves it over baby Johnathan. "This will keep him asleep until we are done here, Reanna. It will give us enough time to complete the task and then report our discovery of the child."

As Doctor Lasara makes her way from the hydro-flightcraft landing field, she immediately rents a large ride-on antigravity shopping cart customarily used to make large purchases. After purchasing several crates of produce and baskets of exotic fruits, she returns to her hydro-flightcraft.

Upon Lasara's arrival, Reanna engages the console dial that opens the large, linear side hatch and exits the ship. Reanna and Lasara immediately loaded the food supplies into the flightcraft and transferred baby Johnathan into one of the large empty baskets that contained exotic fruits. Placing the basket onto the hydro-shopping cart, they secure the flightcraft and take baby Johnathan back to the open market. Lasara stops the cart at the first security utility tower and activates its intercom system. As the cameras on top of the telescreens become instantly activated, a sentry robot's metallic voice responds courteously,

"...CAN I BE OF ASSISTANCE...?"

The sentry robot now has a full view of the individuals who have requested security assistance. "Hello, Security. This is Doctor Lasara One."

"... THANK YOU, DOCTOR... ARE YOU FILING A REPORT...?"

"Yes, I am, Security."

"... WILL YOU PLEASE GIVE ME THE TITLE OF YOUR REPORT, DOCTOR...?"

"Yes... Abandoned child."

"... THANK YOU, DOCTOR... CAN YOU PLEASE GIVE THE SPECIFICS PERTAINING TO THE ABANDONED CHILD...?"

"Yes, we found him in one of the exotic fruit baskets, asleep with no identification."

"... DO YOU WISH TO HAVE HIM TAKEN TO CHILD SUPPORT SERVICES...? OR RETAIN THE CHILD UNTIL YOU ARE NOTIFIED BY THE CHILD SUPPORT CENTER THAT WILL OFFER YOU SEVERAL OPTIONS...?"

"Yes, have the Child Support Center contact me at my residence."

"...PLEASE, DOCTOR, MAY I HAVE THE LOCATION AND DESIGNATED REFERENCE CODE...?"

"Of course, it's 0779 Storm Mountain, longitude: Alpha One Region."

"... THANK YOU, DOCTOR... YOUR REPORT IS COMPLETE... ENJOY YOUR SHOPPING EXPERIENCE..."

The journey back to the compound is routine until they reach the storm mountain area. Heavy snow has been falling for many hours on the northeast section of the vast forest region, but it has little effect on the flight plan of Doctor Lasara's craft.

The safe, uneventful landing at the compound is the culmination of a successful guided flight. The snow is already knee-high on the tarmac, and the strong winds push back on the passenger hatch as Reanna tries to disembark from the craft. Raising her voice above the howling winds, she says, "Give me baby Johnathan! I'll take him in and then come back and help you with the supplies."

"No, Reanna, the supplies can wait. I'll follow you in and have the sentry robots unload our food supplies. Eleanor has already opened the utility dome hangar."

Doctor Lasara and Reanna make their way across the tarmac, which is covered with a heavy accumulation of deep, drifting snow.

Once inside, they brush the snow off their garments, and Reanna looks at Lasara, and the two friends begin to laugh. "Do you believe this storm? It was so nice when we left."

Lasara smiles. "I know, Reanna, that's how the weather is up here. The morning could be full of sunshine, and by nightfall, we can have a storm. You'll get used to it."

Doctor Lasara, Reanna, and baby Johnathan settle in for the evening and enjoy one of Eleanor's fine dinners in the living room console area in front of the fireplace. Their conversation was mostly about their day's activities and how they had accomplished everything they set out to do.

The following morning, Doctor Lasara is awakened by a signal message alert from her government security code computer message bank. She quickly leaves her bedroom suite and enters her restricted computer study. Standing in front of the large computer console, she waits for the full transfer messages to be documented into her main computer for reserve access before entering her code. As the last statement is transmitted, she immediately types in her government access code, which contains twenty-nine-character symbols.

Seconds later, the computer begins printing the documents that appear on the screen simultaneously. Most of the documentation includes legal rules associated with adoption-related material. She places her hands on her hips and waits impatiently for all the rules, regulations, and government penalties to end.

Finally, the documentation containing the official approval, listing Reanna as the mother of Johnathan, is complete. To Doctor Lasara's surprise, her impatient wait is rewarded. She received the last of the documents, which state that a six-month probation period is not required since the client, Reanna, is documented as a special assistant to Councilwoman Doctor Lasara.

The snow has stopped, and the sun shines through the large, paneled windows. The floor plants around the large breakfast table absorb the energy of their creation. Halfway through breakfast, Doctor Lasara stands holding up two documents. "I have an announcement, ladies, and you too, baby Johnathan... to your new Mommy!"

Handing the certificate to Reanna, she smiles. "This is yours! You are now officially Johnathan's mother! Now, this document here is the waiver of the six months' probation." A big smile appears on her face as Eleanor gets up from the table and hugs Reanna. She then picks up baby Johnathan and says to him, "You're a lucky, healthy baby!" Doctor Lasara and Reanna raise their glasses for a toast. "To baby Johnathan!"

Chapter 5:
The Academic Experience

When he's six, Reanna registers Johnathan in a home academic program required by the Governmental Educational Program Authority, which he attends until he reaches the age of fourteen. The in-house tele-program features continuous electronic tutoring on various subjects by pre-planned, government-supervised instructors who monitor and convey students' progress, including scoring and evaluation.

The government's academic programming will separate students from family life after the homeschooling period ends. A private study room is established next to the observatory dome on top of Doctor Lasara's large mansion. Educational technicians set up the classroom, where young Jonathan will attend daily periods according to a standardized school schedule within a governmentally planned curriculum. Professors of literature, mathematics, social sciences, and various fields of science, including paleontology, paleoceanography, astrophysics, and specialized courses in the development of modern societies and astronomy, present all subject matter.

After each study program ends, Jonathan completes a value test, and his performance is consistently rated above average. Johnathan's free time becomes an obsession with the observatory, and it becomes a routine where his mother, Reanna, has to remind him to come down for dinner and insist that he should not spend all his free time stargazing. On a typical night before dinner, she calls up to him, "Johnathan, come down for dinner!" She gets no response and decides to go up to the observatory. She finds Johnathan in his usual place, staring at the star-clustered telescreen.

As the observatory is in its rotating mode, she stops it and tells him, "Johnathan, it's not good to be alone all the time! Aunt Lasara is waiting for you to come down for dinner."

She pauses, then says,

"The stars will be there forever! Now come down and have dinner!"

"I'm sorry, Mother, I find the universe very interesting."

"I know you do, dear, but you must come down now."

As Reanna and Johnathan sit at the dinner table, he apologizes to his aunt, "I am sorry, Aunt Lasara, for being late to dinner again."

"That's quite all right, Johnathan; I am glad you find your studies interesting. There are two types of food in life, Johnathan; there's food to keep the body healthy and the food of knowledge that feeds the mind. Now, let's enjoy this dinner."

As family life becomes routine, the moments of change can hardly be noticed, except that Johnathan is now becoming a young man. Many months ago, he received a gift of companionship that became the primary focus of his somewhat sheltered life, shielding him from the prying eyes of strangers.

During that winter holiday, he received a three-month-old Canis lupus, which he named Pup. Then, without notice, in this contented world where everything had a logical reason created by Doctor Lasara, time has passed, and things have changed. Jonathan's homeschooling is nearing completion, and some routines have remained the same. As Reanna is about to call up to Jonathan, Aunt Lasara says, "Don't bother, Reanna, he's outside with Pup!"

Lasara and Reanna engage in a general conversation about the cold weather and the enormous amount of snow this early in the new winter season.

As Chef Eleanor is busy setting the table for dinner, she

eventually joins in on their conversation. The three women engage in a lengthy discussion about general topics, and then Eleanor remarks about the heavy snowstorm and the need for more wood in the fireplace. Reanna replies, "Yes, I agree. There is a chill in here! And talking about the heavy snow, where is Johnathan? He's been out there too long!"

Reanna and Lasara urgently leave the dining area and immediately open the large glass doors to the back atrium. Confronted by deep snow, the figures of Johnathan and his ice wolf, Pup, are tumbling around playfully.

Reanna calls out to Johnathan, "It's ten below out there! You'd better get in here, Johnathan, and take Pup with you!"

Johnathan stops playing, and Lasara calls out to him, "Get in here, my little Trikan!" Johnathan gives in to their pleas and immediately enters the atrium with Pup.

As Reanna closes the large glass enclosure, she says, "Look at both of you all covered with ice and snow!" She removes Johnathan's insulated winter cap and uses it to knock the chunks of snow and ice off of him and Pup.

Later that evening, before leaving the dining area and retiring to his room, Johnathan places his pet in a restricted area that is also used as an exercise gym. Part of the gym has been set up as a makeshift kennel, allowing the large pet Ice Wolf to be with Johnathan, who often uses the gym's facilities. Reanna and Lasara will enjoy the evening hours as they usually do, sipping herbal tea and indulging in conversations of interest to them.

After the evening ends, Doctor Lasara becomes much more interested in young Johnathan's daily routine and begins adding to the journal she started when she first took him from the *Andromeda*. In this secret journal, she has recorded every step of her plan from the time Reanna was granted the adoption certificate.

After that, she did not regularly record her observations. She has kept it a secret from Reanna from the beginning and will continue to do so. She is now entering a new phase of changes in his behavior as he transitions into adulthood. She observed that when Johnathan would not immediately come in when Reanna called out to him, he would continue to play with Pup in the extreme subzero temperatures. She records that his behavior pattern has become more resistant to taking orders and decides to begin another observation; this time, she will pay closer attention to him.

As she notes in her diary, ***Johnathan has a very healthy appetite and an abundance of energy; he excels in his studies and has a remarkable memory.***

On occasion, Doctor Lasara deliberately interrupts his study period with nonessential questions, addressing trivia, folklore, legends, and made-up stories by fiction writers. To her amazement, he gives the correct answers to every question she asks, including the author's name and the story's title, and then returns to his studies. After observing Johnathan many times, she unintentionally titles her notes "My Little Trikan," and then her journal entries stop once he is preparing to enter the military academy.

Johnathan's next five birthdays pass with the wonders of family life, living on the estate of his Aunt Lasara, and the joys of growing and learning in the care of his mother, Reanna.

The fields around the compound are filled with wildlife and the joys of seasonal change; he develops a love for the tiny creatures that emerge in spring and summer.

In the wintertime, young Johnathan learns how to ski on the great mountains of the storm region peaks. On routine trips to Star Port City with his mother and Aunt Lasara, he enjoys meeting other young students in his age group now that he is attending the military academy. He also memorizes the science journals available to him in Doctor Lasara's document library. Two passions have become a way of life for him: excelling academically at the academy and reading her journals.

Back at home, he will now have to face reality when he is told that he must let Pup run free. Johnathan reluctantly agrees, knowing that Pup has become an adult, now fully grown and belonging with the other wild wolves that run free in the ice mountains of Trikinia.

That evening, Johnathan leaves the compound with Pup, which will become the moment he must come to terms with the decision to leave the past behind.

The cold night air lets him be accompanied by his beloved companion one last time. The night is clear, and the large moon is like a beacon of reflections of days past. It is constant, and its reflection casts shadows of a young man and his faithful friend, now a majestic creature of the wild; he, too, has changed, and now they both must be set free. Johnathan unhooks the collar around his pet ice wolf and lets it drop into the deep snow. With the feelings of uncertainty, Johnathan holds onto him one last time and says, "You have to go now... You have to go home!"

As Jonathan lets go of the past, Pup looks up at him, the moonlight reflecting in his eyes; he hesitates to say a final goodbye, then runs across the large snowdrifts into the forest.

Moments later, the silence is broken by the typical wolf howl calling up to the moonlit night. It will run its course; the mental anguish and the feeling of loneliness will continue for Johnathan. Time will not replace the empty feelings that Jonathan feels inside for his pet Pup and the winter nights that they shared out in the cold woodlands around Aunt Lasara's mansion.

As winter passes, the new spring season brings life and the sounds of all the creatures that nature has created. The broken limbs of the large Alphanian evergreens lie dormant and generate an abundance of firewood that will be used in the fireplace in Doctor Lasara's dining area. This arduous task is part of the sentry robots' routine: gathering firewood and heavy tree limbs, then loading them onto a tractor for transport to the wood mill section complex for processing.

While preparing breakfast, Chef Eleanor glances out the kitchen atrium to see the sunrise and enjoy the early-morning sounds of spring. "Oh my GOSH!" Eleanor drops what she is doing and rushes out to inform Doctor Lasara and Reanna, who are waiting for breakfast. "Do you know where Johnathan is?"

A look of no surprise is on Reanna's face as she slightly nods, acknowledging Eleanor's question. "Yes, Eleanor, he is out with those damn sentry robots again! We hardly ever see him at breakfast anymore. He runs out every morning and does routine chores with those robots!"

"Yes, I know, but you must see what he's doing this morning! He is lifting heavy tree limbs and loading them onto the garden tractor!"

Lasara and Reanna get up, leave the table, and rush into the kitchen. The three women stare out of the atrium enclosure in astonishment as the words escape from Doctor Lasara. "I don't believe what I am seeing. That is incredible! Where does he get that kind of strength?"

Eleanor folds her arms, saying, "Well, don't look at me! It has nothing to do with my food!" Doctor Lasara, somewhat puzzled, answers Eleanor in a lower voice, "I wish it were that simple! There's something else going on here..." Lasara turns to Reanna. "I want you to talk to him when he comes in, and in no uncertain terms, he must never skip breakfast again."

"I will; Lasara and other things must be brought to his attention, too!"

In a low voice, Doctor Lasara adds, "I will have to reprogram those robots; they retain too much information that can be down-tracked and censored by the authorities, and this is becoming a normal routine when Johnathan gets involved with them! Reanna, please call him in here before he injures himself."

Reanna hesitates for a moment before going to the door and then calls out to Johnathan several times. After no response, she decides to go outside. He stops loading the tractor as Reanna approaches him.

"Johnathan, what are you doing?"

"I'm just gathering some firewood."

"I know, Johnathan, but Aunt Lasara doesn't want you picking up those heavy logs; it's the robots' job! You know what Aunt Lasara said: never let anyone see how strong you are! Now, she has to reprogram all the sentry robots. I do not know anyone who can lift those heavy logs like you. Now, come in and eat breakfast, please."

Smiling, he says, "Okay, Mom."

Johnathan and Reanna walk back towards the house. Upon entering the atrium, Doctor Lasara stands there and says, "Johnathan, we must have an understanding. In the future, you will not leave this house before breakfast."

Aunt Lasara then points to the dining area and continues, "You will be at that table every morning and enjoy breakfast with us, together, and never again will we have to come looking for you! Is that understood, young man? Your military academy training will continue in this house from now on!"

Reanna adds, "Your Aunt Lasara is right, Jonathan!"

Jonathan responds, "Am I in trouble, Aunt Lasara?"

Smiling, she replied, "No, not at all, Johnathan, but I have something very important to talk to you about later."

After breakfast, Aunt Lasara hands Jonathan a progress report on his academics; she then compliments him and says,

"This report also shows that you have unusual strength for someone your age, and you excel in your field, track competitions, and win most of the events! This, Johnathan, has to stop! You must keep your extraordinary strength and abilities a secret from everyone! The academy officials are part of a very suspicious government program, and I do not want you to end up as one of their experiments! Their job is to educate students attending the academy and monitor each student's progress and behavior. When a student shows extraordinary differences from the rest of society, they will investigate the student's background and family. Your mother and I cannot be put into a government inquiry.

If that happens, we will lose everything! Do you understand me, Johnathan? I cannot tell you everything now."

"Yes, Aunt Lasara."

"As you get older, Jonathan, you will understand what I am saying. Remember, DO NOT let anyone know about your unusual strength from now on!"

Doctor Lasara then embraces Johnathan.

"This will be your first challenge in life. Be strong and aware of your surroundings. Make friends, but remember, your privacy is the most important gift you can give yourself in life! Understand and listen very carefully to your instructors; there will be times when you and other students will be asked questions unrelated to your studies. Again, I must say, listen very carefully. These questions will be about your loyalty to the government and your family. Your answers must always be of a positive sense that you are a loyal citizen."

"Aunt Lasara, can I ask you a question?"

"Of course, Johnathan, what is it?"

"When will my father be back?"

Doctor Lasara hesitates momentarily and then replies, "I don't know, Johnathan. He is on an important mission, and please, don't ask anyone other than your mother or me about him! He must be safe, and no one must know anything about him; when he returns, he will be happy to see you again, and that's a promise, Johnathan! Now, let's enjoy the rest of the day, because we'll have to leave early in the morning for Star Port City. When we get there, I will drop you off at the academy on my way to my council meeting."

Early the next morning, Doctor Lasara calls out to Johnathan, "Johnathan, are you ready to leave?"

"Yes, Aunt Lasara!"

"Okay. Then meet me out by the hydro-flightcraft!"

Turning to Reanna, she says, "Reanna, I'll keep in touch. I don't know how long my committee meetings at the council will be."

"No problem, Lasara. Have a safe flight!" Turning to Johnathan, she says, "Be safe, Johnathan!" Smiling, he replies, "I will, Mom!"

Reanna steps away from the flightcraft as it begins to leave the landing field. Once back inside the mansion, she speaks with Eleanor for a while before deciding to keep herself busy. She starts by removing discarded boxes of Johnathan's new uniform that were hastily left behind.

On her way to the lift platform, she passes Doctor Lasara's study and notices that her private office door has been left open. Aware that Doctor Lasara does not want anyone in her private office unless invited, her curiosity overcomes her better judgment when she notices a cabinet door has also been left open. She violates Doctor Lasara's rules and enters the office, unable to resist the attraction of the available cabinet. She finds several folders and recognizes a personal diary; she removes it, hesitates for a moment, then is overcome by curiosity and begins to read its contents.

As she skips through earlier entries that contain no meaningful reference dates, she abruptly stops at an entry titled *"Crash Site Andromeda."*

While she reads the diary, it becomes a personal experience that will forever be a part of her memory. As she continues, she is reminded that Doctor Lasara does nothing on impulse. Everything she experienced from the first time they met was part of Lasara's plan. As she continues to read, she turns to another page, and it is titled:

"THE ALIEN CHILD"

Upon entering the nursery section of the crashed ship, my first observation was of a young male child asleep in an auto-feed medical unit that gave intelligent information and life support readouts in continuous reference order. Immediately, I realized that this crashed ship was not from the two outer planets in our system. This unit's technology was similar to our type of nursery unit equipment, but its design and capabilities were definitively different. I realized then that this ship was from another world and star system. The deceased crew members were in uniform, and there was no evidence of any Androidian existence registered on my sensors. While conducting a further inspection of the ship with my two sentry robots, I decided to keep the alien child and the girl, Reanna, who was the first to arrive, on the order of emergency services. I did not hold her responsible for the other prisoners under her charge who escaped. My trust in Reanna's good nature has given me confidence from the moment we met that she is caring, honest, and willing to help. Giving her the responsibility for my position, she did not hesitate or question my plan to keep what we experienced a secret...

At that point, the entry stops, and Reanna realizes everything Doctor Lasara has done is to protect Johnathan from the governmental authorities and raise the child as her own. She then thinks to herself... *And where would I be? Back on the asteroid, serving out the rest of my sentence. Doctor Lasara cares about her little family, and I will never do anything to jeopardize her trust in me...*

Reanna decides not to read further entries as she closes the diary and returns it to the cabinet. She quietly leaves Lasara's study and closes the door behind her. Holding onto the door handle, she pauses for a moment and leans back against the door with a feeling of comfort. Her eyes take in the high ceilings and the expensive surroundings of Doctor Lasara's mansion as she begins to think again... *How did this all happen to me? Was it a dream...? No, this was far better than a dream; this is reality!* Her thoughts are suddenly interrupted by Chef Eleanor calling her on the intercom. "Reanna... Reanna... Would you like a cup of tea?" Smiling, she answers, "Yes, Eleanor, I would love one!"

Johnathan will now enter a new world environment that is very different from the one he was used to. Star Port City's wonders offer an excitement he has never experienced before.

For the first time in his lifetime, he is enjoying the fast-paced city life. These experiences will remain with him and become an integral part of the structural components of his mind. He would continue to excel in his academic studies and make many friends. In every class he attended, his instructors considered him a pleasure. Two of his favorite subjects were anti-gravity propulsion and quantum dynamics, in which he excelled, developing an unproven theory of the planet's trajectory around the sun and other celestial bodies.

As Aunt Lasara and Reanna visit Johnathan for the last time at the Air Flight Military Academy, Aunt Lasara continuously tells him how proud she is. Reanna agrees and says, "You only have three months before you graduate; I can't believe how fast it went by!" Smiling, he says, "I know, Mother, look at me now, a Flight Commander!"

The three of them laugh as he helps his aunt and mother step up onto the flight transport. He then says, "Safe trip home!"

As the flightcraft lifts off, he steps away and waves goodbye. Across the field, an extensive military transport lands, and recruits quickly disembark, forming a straight line outside the transport. Johnathan stands watching for several moments as an academy officer walks the line in a first inspection for the recruits, and he thinks to himself... *That was me not too long ago. Where did all that time go?...* He turns and enters the Great Hall of the Air-Flight Academy and relives for several moments the time he first arrived at the academy. Johnathan has now reentered a familiar place in time, unbeknownst to him, that will forever change his life.

Chapter 6:
Trikan

At the council meeting, Aunt Lasara arrives early and is greeted by some associate council members who pretend to be her friends; she is not well-liked because of her power and prestige, and the fact that she is in charge of a large government department, with loyal subordinates who refuse to share information with other council members.

Upon Johnathan's return to the base, several weeks pass, and the routine is less than usual as the academy graduates prepare for the final ceremony. The military staff meets daily to coordinate the preparations for a well-planned graduation experience for the cadets and their families. Staff officers are assigned to hand-deliver promotional rank certificates to every graduating candidate, from Flight Coordinator – Third Class, Flight Lieutenant – Second Class, to Star Flight Captain – First Class. In a short time, Johnathan Shawnwood will officially receive his rank as Captain.

As the day of celebration draws near, the graduates will step from their past into a future world where their choices will become the foundation for the rest of their lives. Their certificates will remain in a glass frame, while their spirits will travel beyond the horizons of their imagination.

After a workout at the gym, Jonathan stops and talks to the gym coach, while a mail-order courier delivers packages and mail to his barracks. Calling out the postmarked units by name, he reaches Johnathan Shawnwood but receives no answer. The mail orderly walks over to Johnathan's locker, opens it, puts the small package on the top shelf, but fails to completely close the door on his uniformed field locker, which is packed with his gear and laser weapon.

Before his return, three uniformed security Androids enter the locker room as the lead officer calls out, "Scout Commander Johnathan Shawnwood, step forward!" As he looks around, he gets no response, and then one of the unit's troopers says, "He's not here, Sir!"

As the Android security commander notices that Jonathan's locker is unlocked and the door is slightly ajar, he says, "Look at this, and they made him a flight captain!" He walks over, opens the door, and carelessly inspects the contents of Johnathan's locker. He then calls out, "Does anyone know where Shawnwood is?"

At that moment, a small trans-mail package falls to the bottom, and the security commander picks it up, saying, "What's this?"

He tears open the seal and opens the box, which contains a small gold bracelet and a note. He then reads the message from Aunt Lasara out loud: "Dear Johnathan... My Little Captain Trikan!"—the name she jokingly called him so many times as he was growing up—"Congratulations on all your accomplishments! This is your gold bracelet; keep it with you at all times. Good Luck, Captain. Love, Aunt Lasara." Looking up, he says, "Who is this, Aunt Lasara?"

One of his subordinates replies, "Sir, if I'm not mistaken, I believe it's Councilwoman Lasara." He then says, "How interesting." He takes trans-photos of the note's contents and gold bracelet with his arm-cuff computer, then says, "General Brogas will find this very interesting!" In a low voice, he repeats part of the inscription, "We shall see about this, my little Trikan!"

The Android commander puts the bracelet and note back into the small box, throws it to the bottom of the locker, and then attaches a citation to the locker door.

As they leave, the ranking officer remarks to his second-in-command that there is a Trikinian spy in the academy, and he cannot believe the spy was promoted to flight captain. He states, "I have to get this report to General Brogas immediately!"

A short time later, Johnathan returns from his gym workout. As he enters the locker room, several troopers try to tell him what happened. Johnathan raises his hand and says, "Okay, one at a time!"

One of the troopers then tells Johnathan what happened. "Commander, you had a visitor a short time ago! An Android lieutenant and two of his security officers were here. The lieutenant security officer went through your locker. They were laughing when the lieutenant read the contents of a package that was sent to you, and Johnathan told his support officer that he thinks we have a spy in our air base!"

Johnathan picks up the trans-mail package from the bottom of his locker, courtesy of his aunt, and reads it. He then placed the gold bracelet inside a small pocket in his military vest. He slams the locker door shut, rips the citation off the door, turns to his fellow cadets, and says, "From now on, I don't answer to the name of Johnathan... My name is Trikan!"

Trikan tosses his towel over his shoulder and walks towards the locker room's exit as one of the troopers says, "Captain, there was nothing we could do!"

Trikan stops and says, "That's okay; I'll take care of it!"

As he returns to the gym, voices reverberate from many echoes in different sections of the workout areas. Participants engage in conversations while the sounds of vigorous lifting and heavy iron being dropped onto the floor mats fill the air. In this gym, several heavy-weight units with computer screens are electronically connected via a large cable, which is only authorized for Android use. This cable is attached to a hollow steel lifting bar with a charged atomic weight, forming a protonic mass that becomes heavier and increases in weight after several lifts. Trikan waits patiently for one of the protonic weight-units to be available.

After a short period, the uniformed Androids complete their workouts and leave the gym. Trikan then activates one of the units and lifts the protonic bar. As he placed it back on the floor rack, he reached over and triggered maximum isotope infusion into the atomic weight bar. He then lifts the bar repeatedly over his head. Still thinking about what happened in the locker room, he engages the automatic process of the atomic weight elements to increase further.

As the weight increases, several gym participants stop their workouts and are transfixed by Trikans' ability as they watch the number of protonic weights multiply on the screen. They call out to others who are engaged in their workout activities. "Hey, look at this guy!"

Trikans' extraordinary lifting power has impressed all the workout teams, who have now become his audience in the gym. As the mass weight on the screen reaches 3,000 pounds, he continues to lift heavier weights, and his unbelievable strength becomes the focal point of everyone in the gym. Seconds later, he breaks the Androidian lift record, as it appears on the screen at 4,000 protonic pounds.

At this point, the unit machine has long exceeded its molecular overload and begins to melt its metal components into a fusion meltdown. Before these molecules can reach the bar section, which he holds through the trunk line, he throws the fusion bar forward into the unit screen and lets out an upset sound of anger. As it hits, the entire unit implodes within its molecular core, destroying the record-breaking point of 4,000, which had never been achieved before. The explosion of black smoke billows to the ceiling's height, followed by a loud ovation from the other gym members, as if a victory event had just taken place. Emergency alarms are immediately activated throughout the entire sports complex.

As two security guards enter the gym, they are confronted by the applause that continues to overshadow the ear-piercing alarms. As one of the security officers approaches Trikan, he asks, "Are you responsible for this?"

Trikan looks at the security android. "Are you talking to me?"

The other security officer steps closer to Trikan and says more forcefully, "You know he is talking to you! Just answer the question!"

Trikan picks up his towel, throws it over his shoulder, and pushes past the two security guards; he stops momentarily, turns to the second guard, and says, "Did you say something? I wasn't listening."

The two security guards remain silent as Trikan walks towards the exit door, surrounded by applause. He has passed the Androids' four-thousand lift mark and has changed how Humanacereans would think about themselves in the future, in a society ruled by Androids.

As Trikan returns to his barracks section, unit command troopers pack for their home leave. He walks to his locker without saying a word and begins packing some of his belongings to take home on break before graduation. Some of his command troopers tell him they wish they could have done something before the security officer went through his locker. Trikan turns around and tells them, "Hey, don't worry about it! You guys are okay. We're heading home on leave and looking forward to enjoying ourselves! What happens here stays here!"

Arriving home in a hydro-taxi, Johnathan turns on the two-way communication screen and types in his home code, which activates all the telescreens in Aunt Lasara's mansion. "Hello... Hello... Anybody there? Where is everyone?"

Chef Eleanor breaks a moment of silence as she carefully places a dinner tray she prepared back onto the counter. Turning around and facing the telescreen at the far end of the kitchen, she says, "Johnathan! Hello, dear, where are you?"

"I'm on my way home. What is that behind you? It looks good!"

"Well, it just happens to be one of your favorites!"

"I can hardly wait! Please tell my mom and Aunt Lasara that I will be home shortly. This transport robot is lost again! He's in a diatomic condition and should have been replaced a long time ago!"

Chef Eleanor laughs. "Tell him to wake up!"

"Hey, Robot! Wake up, or I'll take the controls from you!"

The outdated Taxi-Transport robot responds, "... **SORRY, SIR... BUT IT'S AGAINST THE LAW FOR A PASSENGER TO FLY A HYDRO TAXI TRANSPORT... IF YOU TELL ME THE DIRECTION CODE AGAIN... I WILL BE HAPPY TO GET YOU TO YOUR DESIRED DESTINATION...**"

Chef Eleanor lets Aunt Lasara and Reanna know that she just spoke to Johnathan through the in-house telescreen as they return home from their early morning walk.

The three women rush excitedly to the landing field tarmac and wait as the taxi transport touches down. The cabin door opens, and a large duffel bag is thrown out as Johnathan exits the transport. Before leaving the transport's takeoff area, he asks the robot, "Do you remember how to get back to Star Port City?"

The transport robot replies,"**...AFFIRMATIVE, CAPTAIN...**"

Johnathan immediately clears the takeoff area as his mom and Aunt Lasara embrace him. "Why did you take one of those antiquated taxi transports, Johnathan? You should have called. I would have been more than happy to pick you up!"

"Aunt Lasara, it was a last-minute announcement from Command Headquarters to let us return home earlier than scheduled before our first deployment."

The child that she has rescued is now beyond Doctor Lasara's control. She responds to him with a selective tone, "After dinner, I would like to speak with you in my study. Reanna, do you mind?"

Reanna could see Lasara's frustration and replied, "No, Lasara, not at all."

Breaking the tension, Chef Eleanor intercedes. "Well, is everyone ready to sit down for dinner?" Johnathan agrees, "Yes, I am as hungry as a wolf!"

Aunt Lasara adds, "I think they're called Ice Wolves, Johnathan!"

"Yes, Aunt Lasara, and I still think about him." Reanna takes his hand. "We all loved Pup very much, Johnathan. Now, let's sit down and have dinner."

After dinner, Lasara walks over to Johnathan. "Whenever you're ready. I'll be in my study."

"Yes, Aunt Lasara, I'll be there shortly."

After Lasara leaves the dining room, Reanna cannot hold back her feelings about something she does not understand. "Johnathan... will you please tell me what's going on?"

"It's not important, Mother; it must be something that has to do with Air Command."

"Like what, Johnathan?"

He places his hand on her shoulder and says, "Not to worry, Mom! I'll talk to Aunt Lasara." Reanna then adds, "I am so proud of you! Now go and straighten out whatever it is with your Aunt Lasara."

Johnathan knocked on the door, left slightly open, to Doctor Lasara's study. "Come in, Johnathan, and please, sit down. I have been working very hard on the government report documents regarding an incident involving you at the academy. To be quite honest with you, I'm not sure how to begin this conversation. Can you please tell me what happened at the academy?

You have the entire administration there, looking for answers to questions that they cannot find. I thought we had an agreement?"

"Yes, Aunt Lasara, we do have an agreement. They pushed, and I pushed back!"

Aunt Lasara remains silent momentarily, then says, "Okay... I'll return these forms to the Air Academy. They're mere formalities. They don't mean anything except for this one!" She hands him a resignation form. He takes it and says, "I'm not resigning; I'm going with the mission!"

As he hands it back to her, she smiles. "I knew you would say that!"

As she submits it to the Government Air Command website, she gets up, walks around her desk, and embraces Johnathan. "Now, let's go down and enjoy a hot cup of tea, Captain!"

At zero-eight hundred hours, an adjunct officer enters General Brogas's office at Air Command Control. "Good morning, General! I have the folder that you asked for on Captain Shawnwood." The general is about to thank the adjunct officer when his phone rings. He picks it up and listens for several moments, then says, "I understand. Yes, the council." He remains silent for several moments and then says, "Striker...I understand!"

He then hangs up and tells the adjunct, "Take the folder and place it back in the file; we won't need it."

The long wait on the Martian horizon has finally arrived. The spring colors beckon to the new population of Mars. The original base, *Project Carousel*, has evolved into a town that has elected its first mayor, with most of its population residing in developments situated on government land. They commute short distances to their work assignments within the town on original Mars Rovers. Thanks to the creative engineering department, they were upgraded to a dune buggy-type vehicle.

The primary developmental project was a ten-year program completed two years ahead of schedule. It opened up areas for population expansion, extending from the original *Carousel* Base 150 miles to encompass Victoria's Great Crater. This two-lane highway system has fulfilled its initial purpose, enabling essential personnel to travel to the outlying areas and conduct archeological research, which is crucial for the new world's inhabitants. Some of these professionals have chosen to build private residences near their work rather than travel back to the town of *Carousel*.

The selection of structural types is very similar to the original two-story, prefabricated, dome-shaped units installed at the beginning of *Project Carousel*. Each dome-shaped unit features spacious indoor living areas on the main floor, with a section of the upper dome level offering a telescopic view of the Martian sky.

After completing the highway project, Captain Shawnwood and his wife, Deandra, were among the first to purchase these private residences. Their choice was a unit seventy miles out from the town of *Carousel*, which requires Captain Shawnwood to commute each Martian day, with extended work hours that allow him to spend more time at home on personal leave. His wife, Lieutenant Deandra, who is now semi-retired, performs her limited work assignments at home.

A flare of Martian soil is pushed aside from the central lane by a vehicle traveling at 120 miles per hour, with radar-stabilized cruise control, in the direction of the great crater. This self-driving vehicle will stay on the highway path using performance indicators, signaling the vehicle every quarter of a mile along the trip. These performance indicators extend the entire length of the two-hundred-and-fifty-mile highway.

Captain Shawnwood arrives home at the usual time, closing the pressurized garage dome section, and enters the spacious living quarters. Removing his required anti-radiation flight suit, he enters the kitchen area and notices that the dinner arrangement settings haven't been put in place. Deandra's workstation area is still on, indicating that a report has not been completed, while the computer relays are about to shut down. He turns the computer off and calls up towards the observatory. "Deandra... are you okay?"

"Yes, John... I'm up here!"

Captain Shawnwood steps into the two-passenger elevated lift system, which takes him to the observatory floor. Deandra replies, "You always know where to find me, John!"

"Yes, I know, Deandra..."

She stares at the heavens and replies, "I had to come up here especially tonight! Tomorrow is Johnathan's birthday."

"Yes, Deandra, I know."

"John, do you think he remembers us? I mean..."

He puts his arms around her, looks out the observatory portal at the stars, and says, "I'm sure wherever he is, he must be thinking of us, and I feel he is just fine. So, what do we have? We have hope!" As she looks at him, her eyes fill up with tears. "Yes, John, and I'll never give up hope!"

The following day, Johnathan awakens early after a restless night of sleep, and the feelings of discomfort will stay with him through the morning. While stepping off the lift, he is greeted by Chef Eleanor, who is busy setting the breakfast table. "Well, good morning, young man!" Johnathan replies, "Good morning, Eleanor."

"It looks like another chilly fall day out there, Johnathan!"

"Yes, it's that time of year again."

"Are you okay, Johnathan? You don't seem like your lively self."

"I'm just fine, Eleanor, thank you."

Voices from the kitchen interrupt further conversations between Johnathan and Eleanor. Without further thought, Johnathan helps

Eleanor with the place settings at the table. The kitchen doors automatically open, and Aunt Lasara and Reanna enter the large dining area, carrying out the breakfast trays. Aunt Lasara says, "Well, Eleanor, I see you have a nice young man in your employment! Good morning, Johnathan!" As he speaks, he bows his head in a motion of respect. "Good morning, Aunt Lasara."

Smiling, she says, "Well, I was right! He is a nice young man and a very polite officer!"

"Good morning, Mom."

"Good morning, Johnathan!"

Halfway through breakfast, it becomes apparent that Johnathan has not engaged much in the conversation, and Reanna asks, "Johnathan, why are you so quiet this morning?"

"It's nothing important, Mom." Reanna puts down her cup of tea and curiously looks at Johnathan. "What's troubling you then?"

"I'm not troubled at all..."

"Well, something is bothering you, Johnathan; what is it?"

"I just had a restless night's sleep." He remains silent for a couple of moments and then continues, "I dreamt that I walked into a nursery and looked into a child support unit where a baby was asleep, and he was wearing a gold bracelet! At that moment, someone called out; I turned away to see where the call was coming from, and when I looked back, the child was gone!"

Reanna looks at Lasara and can hardly take her eyes off her. Lasara stares back at Reanna, saying, "I'm sorry for your restless night of sleep, Johnathan. I'm sure it was nothing. Dreams are dreams, and the more we know about them, the better we will understand them. Now, would anyone like another cup of tea?" A smiling Reanna replies, "Yes, please!" Suddenly, an urgent message appears on the telescreen. Doctor Lasara receives a communication from an old friend, Professor Hollander, with whom she worked before becoming a councilwoman.

She activates the messaging platform. "Hello, Doctor Lasara, it's been a long time!"

"Hello, Professor Hollander... Yes, it has. How nice it is to see you!"

"May I speak freely, doctor?"

"Why, of course, Professor, the messaging sequence was redirected to a noncompliance signal the moment you appeared on my screens. You can speak freely. Should I be concerned about something?"

"Yes, doctor... I wish I could tell you everything right now, but I can't. All I can say to you now is that you have been placed on an informational watch list. Your sentry robots cannot be trusted! They have been reprogrammed, and as of sixteen hundred hours, everything you say will be coded and transferred to a special unit in Central Intelligence. It all has to do with a young officer; that's all I can tell you now, and I hope to see you soon!"

The telescreen goes blank as Doctor Lasara again takes her place at the table, and Reanna asks, "Is everything alright? Lasara, what was that all about?"

Doctor Lasara does not reply at once, and when she does, she says, "We'll talk about it later, Reanna."

Johnathan then says to his mother, "It's about me, Mom, don't worry about it!"

Aunt Lasara affirms, "They pushed, Reanna!" Looking at Johnathan, she smiles. "And Johnathan pushed back!"

At that moment, Johnathan receives an incoming holographic call on the indicator screen on his Dial-Date. Reanna instantly reacts, "Now what?" Johnathan says, "It's okay! It's just a call." He then responds to the holographic image, "Go ahead, Lieutenant Davis, I hear you!"

"Captain, we got our departure time orders. We all report to Hydrocopter Command seventy-two hours from now at zero-eight hundred!"

Johnathan smiles. "I'll see you guys there!"

Breaking her silence, Lasara smiles and says, "It's good to have friends, Captain!"

"Yes, it is!"

Reanna would also share her concerns with Lasara if she felt out of sorts about something she couldn't discuss with others. Why would she have to wait until later for Lasara to tell her the truth about things? Johnathan says, "Well, ladies, I'd better get my gear together. I'll be leaving early tomorrow. I have to get back to the base!"

As Johnathan leaves to pack his gear, Lasara turns towards Reanna. "We have a big problem, Reanna! It will take a lot of careful moves, and we may not be able to rectify the situation. I will share this with you and use Johnathan's term. The sentry robots are bugged! Anything you say goes into a secret government information file. When I deactivate them, their message code relay monitors may remain activated! From now on, you must be mindful of what you say. I have no control over them!" Reanna replies, "I'm sorry, Lasara. Those damn machines!"

"It's not your fault, Reanna; it's nothing that you have done! No one can go through life without making a mistake! We all have moments of misjudgment! It's not always what we think about ourselves; it is mostly what others think about us at any given time!"

Chapter 7:

The Rain Forest

A full complement of six hydrocopters makes their way to the tropical skies of the primordial forest region of the giant planet Omega.

Time has never evolved to bring about the total extinction of all creatures on this planet, from its ancient past. Large lizard types survived and posed a peril to all who dared to enter this tropical forest. The loud noise of the hydrocopter engines makes the conversation between Mission Command Officer Striker and the troop personnel almost impossible.

Aboard Striker's hydrocopter is a squad of troopers whose mission is to capture escaped criminals and bring them back, where they will face a court hearing under the command of Captain Shawnwood. Shawnwoods' crew does not take this mission seriously; they treat it jokingly as if it were just another training mission. Some try to communicate without using their helmet modulation devices over the noise of the engines. Captain Shawnwood makes hand gestures for them to use their modulation communication extension systems, which are attached to their helmets.

The devices use a micro voice speaker designed electronically to eliminate engine noise and high optical wave frequencies. The scout troops finally comply with Captain Shawnwoods' orders and use their electronic communication devices while making light of the situation.

The Mission Command Officer Striker is one of the most disliked service officers in the Androidian Flight Core, with a record of issuing the highest number of suspensions to air flight personnel. He approaches Trikan and complains to him about the readiness of his squad.

"Captain Shawnwood, must I remind you, as I have done several times before on training missions, that you are too lax with your unit personnel!"

Trikan responds, "Let me think about it... Refresh my memory!"

"Captain, your sarcastic humor does NOT entertain me! You are not at the military training base anymore; this is the REAL THING, Mister Shawnwood! If you can't demand discipline from your men, I'll see to it and relieve you of your rank as Captain! I suggest that you fix this problem immediately before you leave this ship! I warn you, the Rainforest is no laughing matter!"

Trikan stares at him and asks, "Are you coming down with us, Commander?"

"You know damn well I'm not!"

"Well, then let me handle it, Commander."

"Captain, perhaps you will take this mission more seriously when half of your squad does not return!"

"Respectfully, Commander, that sounds like a threat to me!"

"I don't care what it sounds like to you! You and your men have orders to follow, whether you like it or NOT! Anyone who steps out of line, including YOU, CAPTAIN, will be dealt with appropriately. There are plenty of empty cells in Central Detention! Do I make myself clear?"

"I hear you, Commander Striker. Stay in your ship, and I'll handle it!"

Trikan turns away, and Striker says, "You have your orders, Captain!"

As Commander Striker leaves the gantry area, he shouts out to his flight crew over the noise of the engines. "Ready time! Approaching target!"

The ship's alarm alert system is activated moments later, with blinking beacons of bright caution lights permeating the hydrocopter's aft section. The huge sectional hatch opens, extending a ground platform outward. Trikan shouts out,

"Okay! You heard the Commander! Get ready to disembark! Weapons up front. Inspection!

Sergeant Cress, get up here! Ready arms! Inspection! It's all yours, Sergeant! See to it that their rocket packs are all locked and fully charged!"

Sergeant Cress yells out,

"Come on, Guys! Form a steady line and get ready to drop! Point man! Weapon inspection! Ready! Neutral! Clear to make ready for rocket flight descent! Arm weapons!"

The sergeant quickly checks the weapon screen. "Neutral. Make ready to drop! Come on! Come on! Double time! Larsen, weapon neutral! Clear to disembark! Laurel! Weapon Inspector Scout Laurel!"

The sergeant continues shouting orders to the troops as they prepare for their mission over the noise of the craft's open ramp. As the First Scout enters the final phase before takeoff, the ramp sergeant changes from mission instructions to shouting, "STAND CLEAR OF BLAST THRUST!"

One by one, all twenty-four crewmembers of the squad leave the platform with a blast of neutronium engine rocket fuel. The ship also begins to drop separate supply provisions to the surface. Their hydro jetpacks allow them to descend and travel above the rainforest canopy several hundred miles from the departure zone. Each man has been previously given an emergency provision kit containing food and a freshwater container with his gear pack. These provisions are also necessary for a short-term mission in the high temperatures of this tropical region.

As a sentry robot hands out the emergency kits to the squad, the last kit he is about to give to Trikan is taken from him by a flight deck technician. Commander Striker yells his orders to the robot over the noise of the engines, "That kit is missing its water supply! Go to my office; there's a new emergency kit there, and make sure you give it to the captain before he leaves the ship!"

The robot responds, "...YES, SIR...!"

Commander Striker shouts, "Captain Shawnwood, don't leave without your supply pack!"

The sentry robot hands it to Captain Trikan just before the last trooper leaves the ship. Trikan clips the supply pack onto his flight gear and is preparing to jump. Striker yells to him over the noise of the engines, "Safe Mission, Captain Shawnwood!"

The Rainforest's silence is broken by what first seems like a strange animal's cry, echoing through the heat of the midday sun as the hydrocopter pauses in midair and drops its cargo. Clearing the ship in a free fall, the flight troops ignite their retro-rocket packs to full blast, adding a blistering sound across the rainforest terrain as they travel and seek their prey. The hydrocopter leaves its drop point, and the silence returns to the jungle again. All the creatures within their natural habitats remain still; they dare not leave their safety confinement. Many will wait until nightfall, when they are given their release, and then venture out into the cool night air once again.

Trikan lands in a small clearing upon touchdown, several yards away from the heavy, thick foliage. He then removes his rocket pack harness and lets the unit drop to the ground. He adjusts his laser rifle to a non-lethal takedown setting. Placing a viewfinder scope screen on the laser rifle's breach section, he immediately receives close-up imaging of the forest terrain. He sees a shadowy figure taking a few cat-like steps in the deep foliage of the Rainforest. He positions himself and fires a cold beam of light made up of positively charged neutron particles above the shadowing target area.

The power beam strikes a wide area of Alphanian trees and explodes, sending foliage debris to the thick forest underbrush. Waiting for several moments, Trikan fires again, and another bolt of energy explodes over the forest with the sound of thunder that brought the rain the day before, and then silence returns.

Leaving the bright sunlight, Trikan enters the dark, hidden world of danger and secrets. His viewfinder on his weapon is useless, and there is no light below the Alphanian trees to cast shadows that can be identified. He scans this hidden realm of secrets and folktales with his arm-cuff computer. He receives a faint directional indicator light, which points him toward the shadowy figure he had seen moments ago.

The standstill of time is evident as tiny beads of sweat run down his face. Trikan approaches his target and says, "I know where you are! You can't get away. Come out so I can see you!"

Pushing aside large leaves, vines, and fallen debris, a female of his species crawls out from beneath the foliage, and Trikan says, "You are my prisoner! Identify yourself. Do you have a name?"

She says, "Of course, I have a name! Don't you have a name?"

Trikan remains silent for a moment and replies, "Yes, my name is Trikan."

She immediately begins to laugh, "Trikan?" Looking at him, she says, "You're NOT Trikinian!"

As he stares at her, why does he hesitate before calling in his position? Is it the sheer beauty of this female? Or is it the sudden feeling of some guilt that has taken over his emotions? He knows that he is under strict military orders not to talk to escaped criminals or render medical aid to them. He violates these two rules and is unaware that he will break many more in the future.

Captain Trikan opens his first aid kit, removes a gauze-like patch containing an astringent skin lotion, and hands it to her.

Looking up at her adversary, she attempts to grab Trikans' sidearm laser weapon, but he immediately throws the weapon aside. He holds her arms and pins her down to the ground. As she struggles within his grip, she yells,

"LET ME GO... LET ME GO, OR I'LL DESTROY YOU,

CAPTAIN!"

"Hey! Hey! Take it easy! Calm down before somebody gets hurt!"

"You're the ONE that's going to get hurt, Captain! I'm going to destroy you!"

"Hey, you're not going to destroy anybody! Maybe if you stop struggling, we can find out what both of us are doing here!"

She increases her resistance and shouts, "Let Go Of Me! You're Hurting Me!"

Trikan relinquishes his hold on her and says, "Do you have a name?"

"Yes, my name is Elisa! Now LET ME GO!"

"Okay, Elisa, tell me what you are doing here?"

"What do you think I'm doing here? I had to get away because of creatures like you!"

Elisa looks at the medallion on his uniform. "So, you're a captain, and you're not Trikinian! They don't make Trikinian's Captain in your military! So, what are you? An Amonadite?"

He laughs as he asks, "What's an Amonadite?"

"You don't know what an Amonadite is? I'll tell you, it's a creature that shapeshifts to accommodate its surroundings! It becomes adaptable to other creatures it encounters, just like that lizard over there." She points at a harmless six-legged reptilian creature foraging in a nearby field. "All you have to do is look at it, and you will become exactly like it! Now, look at it and crawl away with it! Go on and get your hands off me!"

Trikan continues his brief conversation with his beautiful captive, just long enough to place the electronic wrist cuffs on her, which will allow her freedom from his grip. "Elisa, do you know what these things can do?"

"Yes, Amonadite! I had the pleasure of wearing them before in the halfway house!"

These electronic devices will not allow her to run beyond a ten-foot radius of Trikan. If she attempts to do so, an electrical charge will travel down the tether line, instantly immobilizing her with a painful but nonlethal beam of light. The loud noise of another hydrocopter abruptly ends Trikans' encounter with Elisa.

This unit patrol copter contains only sentry robot passengers. Captain Trikan receives a report from the unit stating that three sentry robots will land and assist him in his mission. Trikan contacts the automated sentry robot craft. "Squad Captain to Unit Seven, Alpha One reporting... Affirmative on your drop off, will continue sector zone patrols, over and out!"

Moments later, three sentry robots land in the vicinity of Captain Trikan and his prisoner, along with the turbulent noise of their rocket packs. As the sentry robot command leader approaches Trikan, the robot communicates in a monotone voice, "**...WE ARE HERE TO SUPPORT YOU IN THIS SECTOR... DO YOU NEED ASSISTANCE WITH YOUR CAPTIVE...?**"

Trikan replies, "No, everything is under control. There are no other life forms in this sector. I don't need your assistance here. I suggest you assist the other scouts!"

Trikan looks at the sentry robots with distrust—this sentiment developed during his training and educational experiences at the military academy. Trikan then says,

"Stay in your assigned sector zones, which I am transferring to your program control units. Report back to me in quarter sequence variables that I have logged into your programming. Do you understand my instructions? They will be returned to Star Port City alive and well after you capture the runaway criminals!"

The highest-ranked of the three robots responds to the captain in a mechanized voice: "**... BY YOUR COMMAND, CAPTAIN...**" The other two robots mimic their leader and repeat the exact words in a monotone voice, "... **BY YOUR COMMAND, CAPTAIN...**"

As they depart, Elisa becomes agitated. "I guess you don't like robots, Trikan."

Trikan wipes the sweat off his forehead and takes his weapon off the safety lock position. He steps back into the shadowy canopy of a large wild Agaloid Vine, where he had placed Elisa away from the extreme heat of the afternoon sun. He turns and faces her and says, "What's to like about them?" Sitting beside her in the shade, he says, "Listen, I'm letting you go. This whole thing never happened, okay?"

She looks at him in disbelief as he releases the electronic tether line from her. She says, "You aren't serious, are you?"

He remains silent, and then she says, "Is that what you do when you capture someone? You let them go?"

He gives her a silent look. "You're my first, and it's not going to happen again!" Walking out into the sunlight, he says, "Come here! Look along the tree line; what do you see?"

Elisa focuses her attention on the direction of the tree line, pauses for a moment, and then says, "The Sentry Robots!"

Trikan interjects: "And... Can you tell me something about them?"

"Yes, it looks like they are coming back...Why are they coming back?"

"Elisa... they have been programmed to do exactly what they're doing! They can't be trusted!"

Putting his backpack on the ground, Captain Trikan removes a large red cylinder from his equipment pouch and loads it into his laser rifle. Elisa notices the label on the cartridge. "What are you doing? Trikan, what's that for?"

He first ignores her and continues loading the highly volatile protonic cartridge.

"It's just a precaution, Elisa. It takes a uranium blast to take down sentry robots! I didn't ask for those robots; what were they sent down here for? I haven't figured it out yet, and as you can see, they are heading back towards us! They are walking along the tree line, avoiding the open field, and hoping not to be noticed!"

Trikan raises his laser rifle and takes careful aim through the view scope. Registering a full ninety-degree angle beneath the massive canopy of forest trees, he fires the maximum radius scope capacity. As a bright burning ball of flame hits the three sentry robots, they are instantly disintegrated, leaving only burning embers on the ground. He turns to Elisa and says,

"We can't stay here any longer! If I release you, where will you go?"

"To a place where you can't follow me, Captain!"

"And what if I do follow you?"

Laughing out loud, Elisa raises her arms, emphasizing her wrist restrainers, and replies, "You will be wearing these things instead of me!"

As Trikan looks at her in slight disbelief, he asks, "Does this place where you're going have a name?"

"Yes, Captain, it's called Trikinia, my home!"

As she continues to speak, Trikan recalls the sad memory of the night he had to set his best friend, Pup, free to go home to Trikinia. He reaches down to Elisa, and with a preprogrammed reverse code calculation that he has pre-set into his arm-cuff computer, her wrist restraints unlock and fall to the ground. "You're no longer my prisoner, Elisa. You're free to go home. Tell me, how are you going to make your way back to Trikinia from here?"

Rubbing her wrists while trying to ignore the pain, she looks directly into Trikans' eyes. "To be perfectly honest with you, Trikan, I was relying on the others in our group. We were supposed to make our way to the old abandoned Great Forge town, where they used to make

Banishean steel. It's at the edge of Sub-Vector Fourteen. They have a ship hidden in one of the large warehouses. If we could make our way there, we could all escape to Trikinia. You'll have to understand this is a new experience for me. I was never a runaway criminal before!"

"Criminal? You don't look like a criminal to me, Elisa."

"Looks don't have anything to do with it, Captain! You go on with your life in Star Port City and try to make the best of it. You step out of line or say something against the Android-controlled government, and then they accuse you of being a spy in contradiction of their most precious authority! They make the rules, and the rest of us must walk that fine line between obedience! You should know more about it than I, Captain; you're one of them!"

Shaking his head again, he states, "How many times do I have to tell you you're free to go? I'm not charging you with anything. No report, nothing!"

She replies, "I realized that, and I shouldn't have said you were part of them! The moment you destroyed those robots proved that differently. Now, where do YOU go from here, Captain? You're NOT a Trikinian, but you might as well follow me to Trikinia. At least you'll be safe there!"

As she looks around at the considerable foliage that makes up the Rainforest, she says, "There are a lot of places to hide in this forest. But you know what, Captain, the Androids will find you. Right now, they're probably blowing their circuit banks trying to figure out what happened to their robots?"

A smile comes to his face as he agrees, "You're right, Elisa. Let's follow your original plan and go to the Great Forge town in Sub-Vector Fourteen. Is that alright with you?"

She smiles. "Why not? Let's go,"—she pauses and calls him—"Captain Trikan!"

As they make their way through the thick underbrush of the Rainforest, the midday sequence hours pass, and nightfall begins to cast its cloak of darkness over the forest. The two of them, now sharing the adventure of escape, are faced with the peril of defending themselves from the beasts of prey that lurk in the forest's dark shadows where moonlight cannot enter. They will endure the struggle of body and mind with determination to survive. The sounds of wild animals in lethal combat permeate the bleak darkness of the night. The reality of their journey becomes unreal compared to their ordinary experiences. It is as if Trikan and Elisa have stepped across a time portal into the Star Quadrant World, as it were, at the beginning of time, where creation did not play by the ordinary rules of existence. Their survival could no longer be interpreted as a time frame of the present; they will have to endure these horrors in the long night until the break of dawn, when they will be given benevolent relief. Only then will they know that they have survived the evils of the Rainforest.

As the morning approaches, Trikan and Elisa are presented with a clear view of the river that cuts through diminished fields of forest growth. The reflection of sunlight sends rays of silver over rocks along the shoreline in the fast-moving currents of this river as it cascades down from the mountainous terrain. Elisa wipes off her wrist Dial-Date Rangefinder to locate the navigational guidance coordinates. "Trikan, we have to follow the river south until we come to the riverbed crossings, and it will take us to the Great Forge Town at Vector Fourteen."

By mid-noon, at the height of the sun's heat, Trikan and Elisa refrain from the conversation for much of their journey as they focus on their mission to reach Sub-Vector Fourteen. Elisa has reached the point where she can no longer keep up with Trikan and is now lagging behind. Trikan turns to her, and in an exhausted breath, she quickly responds as she falls to the ground.

"I can't go any further! I need to stop!"

Trikan takes Elisa's water supply canister and helps her drink slowly without spilling its precious contents.

"Did that help? Do you feel better? We'll rest here until you regain your strength."

"No, Trikan, it's too damn hot to sit here; I'd rather keep moving!"

Helping Elisa to her feet, he agrees, "You're right, let's keep moving!" She asks, "Where are those damn heat shields?"

Trikan looks upward towards the distant skyline. "They don't cover this section of the Rainforest. No life forms, no heat shields!"

Elisa stares at Trikan and says, "Is that a JOKE?"

"It's not, Elisa. The heat shields predominantly protect the cities; very few are in orbit to protect the rain forest."

A short time later, they finally reach the riverbed crossing and are in full view of the Great Forge facility. Wiping the sweat from his forehead, Trikan sets his Dial-Date to a time-shift hologram and views the facility in a three-dimensional hologram. He remarks to Elisa, "It looks suspiciously quiet. I don't see any activity!"

Elisa looks off in the same direction as Trikan. "Check out building seven in Hangar J-11. See if you can detect any movement. The escape ship is supposed to be in the hangar, and there's a tunnel breakout exit at the end of the J-11 structure."

Trikan follows her advice and then says, "Sorry, Elisa. There is no activity and no flight-ship below ground level." Elisa takes the hologram viewfinder from him, and her disappointment becomes immediate.

"How can that be? They are supposed to be here! This was planned way in advance. Where are they? They were utility personnel and were only supposed to supply the escape ship and wait for us to arrive! Something must have gone wrong."

She stares at Trikan, and he says, "Hey, don't look at me; I had nothing to do with it! I didn't even know you existed when I got stuck on my first real assignment out of the academy, chasing runaways all over the tropical Rainforest!"

She reaches over and pats him on his arm. "Not to worry, I believe you! Now, what are we going to do?"

Wiping the sweat off his forehead again, he opens his freshwater container and drinks from it for the first time since he left the ship.

"Well, we have no choice, Elisa. I suggest we head to Hangar J-11 and escape the heat! We could be in Trikinia before nightfall if we could arrange for a pickup. Or we can wait to see if some of your late arrivals show up, that's if they haven't all been taken by the scout patrol force."

They follow along the path of the river that takes them to Great Forge and the old landing facility of Hangar J-11. Uncomfortable, strong seasonal winds continue to whip up sand as they enter the hangar. Once inside the cool confines of the building, Trikan looks around and says, "Elisa, as I said, there's nothing in here!" Looking around the empty hangar, she notices some discarded large storage bins and replies, "I just don't know what happened."

At that moment, Trikan begins to experience blurred vision and difficulty maintaining his balance. Dropping his gear to the ground, he begins to complain that he doesn't feel well. "Trikan! What is wrong with you?"

As Elisa reaches out to him, he turns to face her, missteps, and falls to the ground. Elisa immediately reaches down to him and tries to pull him up, but she can't. She now finds herself in a state of panic as she kneels alongside him. Holding Trikan, she says, "Trikan! "Can you hear me? What's wrong?"

Incoherently, he tries to respond to her pleas to no avail. She shouts to him, "DO YOU NEED WATER?" As she reaches for the water container he previously drank from, she removes the cap and tries to make him drink. Unable to speak, Trikan manages the strength to push the container away. She smells the open container and says, "Trikan, this water is bad!"

Releasing the strap on her supply case, she opens it and quickly discards several of its contents until she finds the packet she's looking for. She breaks the seal on the package containing herbs and places them into her water container while repeatedly coaching him to drink. "Come on, Trikan, Drink! Drink it all! Maybe it will save your life! It's for snake bites, but it may still work. It tastes sweet, Trikan. It's made from the leaves of the Alphanian trees! It's good for you. I think someone tried to poison you!"

Swallowing most of its contents by her command, he continues to awaken and regains some of his physical ability to drink at an average pace. He gently pushes her hand away, and she says, "Just drink a little more. The more you drink, the more you will dilute the poison."

He acknowledges her with a slight nod as he closes his eyes and falls asleep. Elisa spends the rest of the day sitting beside him, listening to his restful sleep. Captain Trikans' normal breathing returned as the snakebite antidote diluted the poison's effect.

At the first light of morning, Trikan awakens to find Elisa asleep beside him. He puts his hand on her shoulder, smiles, and says, "Are you going to sleep all day?" She opens her eyes and smiles back. "We almost lost you! Someone tried to poison you!" He replies, "And someone saved my life!" As Trikan thinks about the events that have just passed, he says, "Striker! It had to be HIM!" Elisa then asks, "Are you going to be alright?"

"Yes, I'm fine. Now, let's get out of here, check the other hangars, and see if we can find your people and the ship!"

Trikan and Elisa are back out in the open, and their search continues. With the absence of sandstorm interference, he checks his Dial-Date and says to Elisa. "I'm not picking up any life forms." Elisa suggests, "Perhaps they made their escape before we got here?" Trikan replies, "I hope so, Elisa. Now let's try the next hangar."

As Trikan pushes against one of the large hangar doors, it opens, allowing them space to enter. The morning light shines in from outside, giving them an interior view across the midway section of the hangar.

Once inside, he tells Elisa, "I'm getting a bad feeling about this place. If your friends were here, they must have left in a hurry. Look, one of them did not stop to pick up his viewfinder, and there are some broken parts of a Dial-Date on the ground. Maybe one of your friends was trying to leave us a message?"

Suddenly, in a darkened area on the far side of the hangar, a sentry robot's metallic voice calls out to him, "... **CAPTAIN TRIKAN... SURRENDER IF YOU VALUE YOUR COMPANION'S LIFE... YOU WILL OBEY MY ORDERS...**"

He then instructs his sub-warrior robot to take its weapons. Before the sub-warrior robot can complete his Commander's order, the command sentry robot shouts a second order to Trikan: "**...CAPTAIN TRIKAN... NOW SLOWLY REMOVE YOUR SUPPLY PACK AND PLACE IT ON THE GROUND IN FRONT OF YOU...!**"

Trikan follows the sentry robot's orders and places his field pack on the ground while releasing the shoulder strap attached to his laser rifle. As he lowers it, he deliberately points the rifle's viewfinder directly at the sentry robot and his assistant. Trikan purposely never took the precaution of putting the firing cartridge in a neutral position after he destroyed the three sentry robots. The weapon is still on open fire, and the slightest movement will release the firing lever to full blast. Once pushed forward, it will fire continuously until the subnuclear cartridge becomes deactivated. The discharge from the weapon contains solar radiation and subatomic particles that can melt any form of Banishean steel.

Trikan suddenly kicks the firing lever forward, and the weapon fires, sending destructive radiation waves across the vast hangar in a hundred-and-eighty-degree radius, instantly vaporizing the two sentry robots to ashes. As the laser rifle continues to fire, Trikan grabs Elisa's hand, and they both exit the hangar. Trikan and Elisa never look back as their escape continues far into the night.

The next morning, the two beleaguered companions wake up tired from their ordeal yet with a feeling of gratification. They escaped with their lives on a journey that ultimately failed; while feeling bad about being separated from her group, she remains determined to find them. Taking his eyes off the crimson colors of the new dawn, he sits up and turns to her.

"Shouldn't we get something to eat before we continue?"

"Are you kidding? I'm famished! Do you have food in there, Trikan?"

Smiling, he says, "Yes, I'll cook if you wash the dishes!"

As he pulls two packets out of his military field bag, he throws one to her. She looks at it and asks, "Is this breakfast or lunch?" Jokingly, he replies, "If you eat it for breakfast, you won't want it for lunch." She agrees. "Okay, I get it!"

Trikan and Elisa are energized by the high-protein food they just ate. They begin replenishing their water supply from the pristine river, whose strong currents flow toward their new destination. "We'll have to move on, Elisa; it won't be long before Hydro Command figures out what took place back at the hangar."

He checks his computer Dial-Date and tells her, "I'm picking up the small town where they mine neutron copper ore. If we follow the river, it will take us to the place where they have a land transport facility that carries the workers back and forth to Star Port City.

Before Trikan could explain the rest of his plan, the sound of the river rapids cascading over rocks and splashing into pools at lower elevations in the river was drowned out by the sound of several large military hydrocopters overhead. As they look up, they see the holographic irregularity of a flying platform for a few seconds, and then the vast command hydrocopter becomes visible. Trikan realizes they can't escape. "Elisa, you're not going to like this, but you will have to become my prisoner!"

She looks at Trikan, surprised. She is about to speak when Trikan cuts her off. "Elisa, you are going to have to trust me!"

She replies, "What are you doing?"

He shouts, "Just listen to me! You're my prisoner, okay? They got us, Elisa! We can't escape! Just Listen and Trust Me!"

Trikan activates his voice communication device with the hydrocopter. "This is Captain Trikan to Unit Seven Alpha One, reporting. One zone violator has been immobilized and may need medical assistance."

Elisa interjects, "Trikan... Medical assistance?"

"Yes, I told you to trust me. Now, play along with me. Pretend that you have an injury!"

The hydrocopter's lieutenant commander checks the ground view screens on his console and receives an ID report on the two subjects: **...CLASSIFICATION: CAPTAIN... KNOWN AS JOHNATHAN SHAWNWOOD... FUGITIVE: TRIKINIAN... FEMALE KNOWN AS ELISA...**

The lieutenant commander then opens communications with base control and requests a report on Captain Trikans' status. His message is intercepted by Commander Striker, who forwards it to the Copter Command Officer: "**... Message delivered to rescue copter commander. Captain Trikan has disobeyed orders from the high command and committed acts of insubordination. He is to be left on location while military court committee council members make other decisions...**"

As Trikan secures Elisa in the lift harness, he asks her, "Elisa, what's wrong? You're too quiet! If there's anything I can do, just let me know. Tell me what you're thinking."

Staring at him, she replies, "You owe me, Trikan. I saved your life!"

"Yes, you did, and I'm going to save yours!" He tells her again, "Elisa, when they question you, you don't remember anything that has happened to you. When you can talk, you tell them that I knocked you unconscious when you were trying to escape. You were nearly killed when I blasted the Alphanian trees behind you, and you were hit with falling debris. That's all you remember!"

She smiles. "I believe you, Trikan."

Placing a strong magnetic locking strip around her wrists to restrain her, Trikans hand signals up to the ship to lift his prisoner on board.

After Elisa is taken aboard, the hydro commander instructs a female medical assistant to administer a sedative to the patient. When the medical assistant is alone with Elisa, she asks, "Do you really want to take this?"

Elisa responds, "No!"

The medical assistant smiles. "I agree with you. Just pretend that you took it. It's supposed to put you into a twilight sleep and render you harmless, but it will make you say what they want, and you will be condemning yourself." She wipes Elisa's face with a soft cloth and says, "We need to get you some dry clothes. I'll give you one of my uniforms."

Elisa replies, "Thank you."

Trikan calls back to the ship as he is soaked by a mid-morning tropical rainstorm that intensifies. "Hello... Alpha One, surface calling! Rank Captain, waiting to get picked up!" He receives a communication call back from a sentry robot: "**...WILL YOU IDENTIFY PLEASE...?**"

Once again, Trikan holds back his anger and responds. "Captain Shawnwood... Assignment, rural quadrant, Rainforest! Mission accomplished! The prisoner has been safely transferred to the ship. Do you need more ID information?"

The lieutenant commander communicates back to Trikan. "That will not be necessary, Captain. I am only following orders from Base Command. I am the lieutenant commander of this ship. My orders are not to rescue or assist you in any way. Fact one, you will not be terminated. Fact two, you have permission to find your way out of the rain forest." Then the lieutenant commander shouts orders to his pilot crew, "Get this ship out of here!"

Before the Commander could say another word, the aft bridge gate opened, and a large survival unit was ejected from the flight-ship's cantilever platform, containing food supplies and a computerized flotation module. Inside the ship, flashing emergency beacons engulf the entire flightcraft in a red glow. The lieutenant commander shouts orders over the ship's intercom, demanding an answer from someone responsible for ejecting the survival pod unit and simultaneously ordering the bridge gate and all emergency hatches closed.

Moments later, the lieutenant commander enters the ship's gantry section and demands an answer from the air flight crew on who is responsible for launching the survival pod. Most of the gantry crew remain silent, except for the technical specialist who quickly responds to the Commander, "Blow Out in the C-12 circuit unit sections, Sir! I was lucky to shut down the complete circuit relay and prevent the launch of the other five support life units, Sir!"

The lieutenant commander says, "You're telling me, Sergeant, that you could not have prevented that launch from happening?"

"Yes, Sir, that's correct!"

"And the other units are secure, Sergeant?"

"Yes, Sir, that's correct!"

I will have to go along with your explanation in my report. Good job, Flight Sergeant, carry on!"

Before the lieutenant commander exits the aft-release gantry flight chamber, he turns to the crew, "How many of you trained at the academy with Captain Shawnwood?" The sergeant replies, "We all did, Sir!"

"How interesting... I'll put that in my report!"

As the life support rescue craft free-falls seven thousand air flight kilometers from the ship at its launch point, an automatic heat-sensing device picks up a life form on the surface. An electromagnetic, infrared tracking system will ignite fusion rockets to travel the topographic distances and engage the target area of its subject. A soft landing takes place several quarter sequence yards from Captain Trikan.

    Trikan approaches the survival unit and aligns his Delta Star military arm insignia with a locked plate on the craft's side. He takes a few steps back as the unit's sides open, revealing the flotation craft's interior. He enters the interior and activates the control computer, and words appear across the screen: "Good Luck from Your Scout Troops, Captain!"

Chapter 8:
Escape Across the Desert

Back on the hydrocopter, the large bay ramp hatch is closed and sealed, allowing the quarter ship's crew to release themselves from their cumbersome life support flight suits. They can now breathe fresh oxygen-rich air and engage in a conversation without using their helmet intercoms. After securing the gantry locks, the flight technician turns to the unit scout flight sergeant and asks, "Do you think Trikan will make it? There's a lot of rugged terrain down there, Sergeant."

The sergeant pauses momentarily and then replies, "If he makes it to the town of Oric, it's a small mining town that has a tram terminal that carries people back and forth across the desert to Star Port City."

The flight technician asks, "And how about the flight lieutenant? Do you think he's going to file a report on the malfunction story?"

The unit scout flight sergeant smiles. I'll bet five-thousand-unit transfer credits that he will not! Unless he wants to join Trikan down there, this is storm season, and it's unlikely anyone can survive!"

Inside the flotation survival unit, Trikan activates a teleportal screen and watches the hydro-craft airship fade over the horizon with Elisa on board. Immediately switching his attention to central command headquarters, his anger is heightened again by the reality that he has been left behind, yet he will pursue this dead end.

Trikan makes contact with the central command, and the voice on the other end is preoccupied with other functional order codes that come in daily. The readout comes back on the module's computer screen: "... **PLEASE HOLD... WE ARE ATTENDING TO OTHER SERVICE COMMUNICATIONS AT THIS TIME...WE WILL GET BACK TO YOU IN AN ORDERLY FASHION...**"

Trikan pushes the voice microphone aside and changes the screen modulation to a weather analysis report. The topographic picture reveals mudslides due to the heavy rains and lightning strikes in the general area of his flotation survival unit. For the time being, his landing site will give him protection from the storm.

Seconds later, a call back breaks the transmission from climate control to person-to-person communication. A programmed robot's voice makes contact with Trikan, "... **PLEASE IDENTIFY... IS THIS AN EMERGENCY CONTACT TRANSMISSION...?**"

Trikan responds, "Yes, I will identify... I'm Captain Shawnwood. I need to be picked up! The hydrocopter command abandoned me after completing my mission!"

A hollow, almost tin-like voice echoes over the modulator, "**...CAPTAIN... I WILL CHECK WITH MY SUPERIOR...**"

Moments pass as the heavy rain continues to fall, and swirls of pale grey clouds and blue light explode across the sky, marking the passage of the thunderstorms. The sounds echo throughout the vast canyon area that separates the mountains from the forest's tree line. Trikan patiently listens to the returning message, and the chilling metallic entity shatters his thoughts as it speaks, "... **COMMANDER...WHERE IS YOUR PRISONER? WHAT TYPE OF SPECIES... MALE OR FEMALE...?**"

Trikan shouts, "How long does it take? This is a routine mission. I want out of this place! You know the orders! Right now, I should be back at Star Port City's Base Command!"

As the storm interference clears on the screen, the robot's figure comes into view. The robot can now also receive a clear picture of Captain Trikan. The state of mind, which reflects emotions such as anger, fear, joy, and laughter, cannot be processed in the creation of robots; they are only programmed to understand the orders they were designed to follow. Hostility would be met with a repetitive, preprogrammed response, lacking thoughtful consideration. Their message to Captain Shawnwood would be repeated over and over again, "**...YOUR HOSTILITY MUST NOT GO UNPUNISHED, CAPTAIN! ...REPORT TO YOUR BASE AND SURRENDER YOUR WEAPONS...!**"

Trikan shakes his head. "Yeah, right. I'll do just that!"

Turning the screen off, he switches to the survival craft's onboard computer console as the storm increases its velocity. Suddenly, the navigational anchor system fails, and the survival craft is carried farther into the untamed forest region by the strong winds, where wild animals forage for food. Trikan struggles to stabilize the tiny craft and finally reactivates its onboard computer. A prerecorded audio voice is activated: "**... WELCOME ABOARD SURVIVAL UNIT DELTA ONE... I AM COMPLETELY AUTOMATED TO YOUR VOICE MODULATION DIRECTION CONTROL... YOUR REQUESTS WILL BE FOLLOWED WITH CONFORMITY TO THE SURVIVAL MANUAL... YOU CANNOT FALTER ANY DIRECTIONAL PROCESS OR CHANGE THE PROGRAMMED DESCRIPTION PERTAINING TO YOUR SAFETY... MAY I PLEASE HAVE YOUR IDENTIFICATION CODE...?**"

Trikan removes his arm-cuff computer and allows his military identification implant to be recorded onto the screen console. The onboard survival craft's voice modulation is activated again: "**... FOR YOUR PROTECTION AND SURVIVAL, RELEASE THE LANDING LOCK STABILIZER... ALLOW THE FLIGHTCRAFT TO ELEVATE TO A REQUIRED DISTANCE**

OF SIX HUNDRED FEET ABOVE THE SURFACE... THIS IS NECESSARY FOR YOUR SAFETY... LAND CREATURES IN THIS SECTOR HAVE BEEN KNOWN TO PREY ON THEIR VICTIMS WITH NO CHANCE OF SURVIVAL..."

As the storm subsides, nightfall approaches. Trikans' only friend and salvation will be the onboard computer, and he must rely on its preprogrammed artificial brain without exception. As he secures the tether line forcefield, the survival craft remains anchored six hundred feet above the forest. He activates the exterior camera screens to observe any activity outside his survival screens; feeling safe again, he falls into a deep, restless sleep.

Trikan suddenly finds himself at the edge of another world; what was just a moment ago is no longer so; he is now in a lake full of stars and a path leading into another universe. The emptiness of the dimension engulfs his every thought, pulling him into a vacuum of distorted sounds of prehistoric serpent-type creatures. Moments later, he wakes up in a cold sweat just before becoming one of the creatures. The agitated, hypnotic state breaks as Trikan regains his usual strength and breaks the mind-distorting spell, becoming fully awake.

Now, removing his helmet, he looks at himself in the reflection of the computer's view screen and feels safe again. The distortion of his dream has become an experience of the past, and a thought comes into his mind: ... *Where are you, Captain? You told me to trust you!...* As he closes his eyes again, he continues to think of Elisa, and he knows what he must do, and it will not be easy. He will find Elisa and free her, along with his guilt for allowing her to be taken.

In this strange quadrant of the universe called *Cantious Omegas*, all is unchanged for what seems like endless moments. Then, the massive sun that gave life to this seven-planet star system from its inception appears on the horizon. Once again, this giant's intense heat permeates the desert lands, unchecked by the lack of enormous orbital heat shields that protect wildlife, forest resources, and other populated areas of the planet. The intense heat from this sun will not affect life on the two outer planets, *Norium* and *Leavion*, because of their elliptical orbits that will take them further out from the sun, and, upon their seasonal return, they will exist in a normal temperature range, as the shadow of the giant planet Omega blocks them.

Trikan must remain in the survival craft until the sun crosses over the planet's equator and disappears into the southern tropical hemisphere, marking the end of another night. He was saved by his squad troops and the survival unit craft, which had everything he would need for the next morning's journey to reach the small work complex with transportation to Star Port City. Food, water, and a heat-resistant flight suit with a helmet that converts hot desert air into a pure-oxygen mixture are all included to help him cross the desert.

His destination is the small mining town with minimal restrictions and no security, where *Oxyon Ore* is mined. *Oxyon* is the steel that trams are made of, and it is highly resistant to the heat of the sun and its deadly rays.

The *Ore* is manufactured for levitated surface trams, allowing the underside of the trams to travel over the planet's magnetic fields at high speeds.

Once Trikan reaches his destination, his plan cannot fail due to the lack of security and the frequent personnel changes; he will have no trouble boarding a tram to Star Port City.

The next morning, a vast *Bio Lab* ship appears a short distance from his survival craft, and he is awakened by the onboard computer, which informs him that a large ship is approaching: "**...CAPTAIN...**" **DO NOT ATTEMPT TO LEAVE THE SURVIVAL CRAFT WITHOUT YOUR PROPER HEAT-RESISTANT FLIGHT SUIT... WE HAVE AN INTRUDER WITHIN A SHORT**

DISTANCE OF YOUR SURVIVAL UNIT... YOU ARE IN DANGER... A LARGE SALVAGE CRAFT HAS ENTERED THIS QUADRANT..."

Immediately, Trikan activates the tether line retrieval mechanism, allowing the survival craft to be lowered to the planet's surface, where he can escape into the forest region. However, it malfunctions, and Trikan looks at the computer display screen as it reads: ...GAMMA RAY DAMAGE TO ALL EXTERIOR MOTORIZED MECHANISMS... THE SURVIVAL UNIT IS IN A STATE OF COMPLETE MALFUNCTION...

Trikan shouts out, "Computer, respond again!"

The screen remains frozen, displaying the same information as initially indicated. He then activates the auxiliary exterior cameras and observes a large *Bio-Lab* craft retrieving the dead carcasses of nocturnal creatures that fought to dominate the forest's nighttime territory. Their massive bodies are pulled up by crane devices and placed inside the large *Bio Lab* ship.

Trikan observes the *Bio Lab* as it approaches overhead and comes to a dead stop. Aboard the craft, several figures can be observed by the emergency pod's cameras as they look down at Trikans' flotation survival unit. Trikan remains transfixed at the receiving end of the photographic screen as the camera's angles change their view of the large craft overhead.

Opening his command door, the Android *Bio Lab* Captain shouts out in his usual angry tone to the five members of his crew,

"What are you lazy anthropomorphics doing?"

He grunts several times, "Goofing off, as usual! What are you looking at, YOU FOOLS? Get back to work, or you will find yourselves on the planet tonight, where the beasts will have you for dinner!" The Android captain grunts again, and this time, he laughs out loud.

The frightened crew chief of this small band of poorly treated personnel shouts back to the captain, "The survival craft, Captain! It's a life support survival craft down there!"

The Android captain walks up to the crew chief and pushes him aside while not relinquishing his grip on the chief's worn-out, dirty flight jacket. Looking over the side, he says, "Well, what do we have here? An emergency survival pod!" He then mutters to himself in a low voice, "A nice tidy sum!" Relinquishing his grip on the crew chief, he tells him, "I'll be in my cabin: let me know when you have my prize on board."

The crew chief then tells his men, "Make ready the big crane!" The large offboard crane is lowered to the flotation survival craft, and the magnetic grappling hooks are fastened to its sides. The lifting process begins immediately as the *Bio Lab* ship rocks port to starboard, causing the survival craft to rock back and forth on the tether line. Trikan adjusts the exterior viewfinder again and observes the large industrial airship's protruding steel crane, which hangs over its side with the survival craft in its steel jaws. Trikan activates the tether line retrieval mechanism again, but it remains in a malfunctioning mode.

The crushing sounds of the survival ship's structural integrity, along with the pulling motion of the tether line, jolt Trikan back and forth in a spiral-like motion again. The *Bio Lab's* Android captain is thrown around inside his cabin as some unsecured items fall onto the cabin floor. He becomes enraged, flings open his cabin door, and yells to the crew chief, "What are you doing to my ship, you incompetent fool?"

The crew chief yells back to the captain, this time not in a timid voice, "Captain, something is wrong! We cannot lift the pod." The Android captain pushes the crew chief out of the way and looks over the side of the ship. "You FOOLS! A tether line is holding it! Must I do all the work? Get the laser cannon and mount it over the side!" The Android captain fires a fusion antimatter projectile from the laser cannon, destroying the tether line.

Following the onboard computer's instructions, Trikan secured his helmet to his flight suit as the large steel crane hit the survival pod's exterior. Suddenly, he hears a loud blast outside the survival craft, and he is pulled upward in a whip-like motion by the steel crane, without the restraints of the tether line.

The *Bio Lab's* laser cannon blasts the survival craft free as the crew chief yells out to the Android captain. "We did it, Captain! We have the survival pod!"

The Android captain shakes his head and yells back, "You finally did something right! I'm beginning to think that there is some hope for you! Crew chief, tell your men to lower the pod to the deck! Do you know what that's worth? More than the slop we picked up in the hull of this ship. Have your men remove all of its valuable contents; as it stands right now, we are to gain special privileges and six-quarter sequences of leave time off this rotten craft, and I won't have to look at you fools until our next assignment! After you remove the valuables, put the empty hull into the crusher!"

As he enters his cabin, he remarks in a low voice, "We'll get a lot of transfer credits for this one."

Inside the survival pod, Trikan can hear his captors' conversation through the intercom channels. Desperately trying to exit the survival craft, Trikan fails to open the side passenger hatch. As luck would have it, the damage to the craft by the steel claw is on the exit hatch side, and it is sealed shut. The crew chief orders his men,

"Release the rear cargo hatch cover. I'm anxious to see what its contents are worth."

The crewmen are unable to release the rear hatch cover of the pod, so the crew chief picks up a large angle wrench and breaks open a center valve lock, which releases the rear hatch cover where supplies are stored.

In the survival craft, Trikan feels relief for a couple of moments as he once again can relax in the helm chair and breathe fresh air from outside the craft. The crew chief looks into the survival craft and can see only a small portion of its interior because it is packed with boxes of supplies. He takes several steps back from the opening of the compartment.

He remains speechless as he observes a prominent, uniformed figure wearing a helmet with its visor-luminous down covering his face, pushing aside the storage crates so that he may exit the compartment.

The other members of the work detail stop their routine duties and look on apprehensively for a moment. Not hearing a sound from any of his work details, the Android captain shouts out to his crew,

"WHAT'S GOING ON OUT THERE? I WANT SOME ANSWERS!"

Receiving no answer, he grabs his leather whip and makes his way to his beleaguered workforce to discipline them as he has done so many times before. As he approaches them, he shouts,

"WHAT ARE YOU GOOD-FOR-NOTHINGS DOING? WHERE ARE THE GOODS? I don't see any work being done; did you forget my orders? Make ready to unload all the goods from the survival craft! Must I tell you again?"

The workers respond to the angry Android captain and begin to remove the supply crates. The agitated Android shouts, "If you had followed my orders, that craft would already be empty and in the crusher!"

Pushing aside the crew chief, he turns towards the open hatch and is startled by a uniformed figure standing there. Trikan says, "What's the rush?"

The Android captain drops the whip and is momentarily lost for words, and then says, "What do we have here? Who are you?"

Trikan responds, "This survival craft is military equipment, and I'm its passenger!"

"What? What did you say? Giving me orders on my ship?"

As the Android captain removes a laser-type weapon from his utility belt, he points it directly at Trikan. "Now, whoever you are, you will comply with my request. Remove your helmet, and if you refuse my order, I will fire this weapon!"

Trikan complies and removes his helmet as the Android captain says, "Now you will tell me your name and rank!"

Trikan replies, "No problem...!" He then abruptly punches the Android captain, knocking him to the deck of the craft while disabling him from using his weapon. The stunned, overweight Android captain cannot get up on his own and yells at his crewmembers in his disoriented state for help, and his request is ignored. The Android captain yells out again to his crew, "SEIZE HIM! Where is my weapon?"

Crawling along the ground, the Android captain searches for his laser weapon but fails to find it. He is unaware that his crew chief has picked it up and concealed it away.

The Android captain now finds himself in a desperate situation as he is finally helped up by several of his crew members. He yells out while pointing at Trikan: "PUT HIM IN CHAINS! PUT HIM IN CHAINS NOW!"

As he removes a broken tooth, he remains silent as he examines it, then says, "Place him in the cage, where we put wild animals!"

Captain Trikan puts up a brief struggle against three crew members with little effort and allows himself to be taken prisoner, knowing full well that this transport is his only means of returning to civilization. Again, the Android captain yells out to his crew members,

Activate the ship's solar reflector shields!" We have lost all communication due to a severe ultraviolet sun storm. Without the sun shields, I'm unable to contact Star Port City's security command and obtain any information on this creature that is now my prisoner!"

He grunts once again and laughs as he looks at Trikan.

"I'll eventually find out who you are, and I'll deal with you accordingly."

The elevated structure of the salvage transport rolls down its heat reflectors to cover the deck's top, creating an awning-like effect that protects the ship and its personnel. After this process is completed, the Android captain approaches Trikans' cage again.

"Whoever you are, I promise you, YOU WILL PAY DEARLY FOR THIS! If I find out that there is no reward for you, I will be happy when I put you in the CRUSHER!" He then orders his crew to remove all the items of value from the survival craft, adding, "And be careful not to think any of these items belong to your greedy hands! I will be back when I get information on our prisoner!"

Still feeling somewhat disoriented from his encounter with Trikan, he neglects to think about his lost weapon.

No one could have known at the time that Trikans' resistance was nothing but a ploy, allowing him the opportunity to end the conflict and avoid further inquiries into his identity and the purpose of his plan. He was aware of the *Bio Lab's* destination. Once onboard, he knew immediately that this would be his transportation out of the desert to the mining town, where the tram transport service was available. The events that took place were decisions he had to make, as the encounter with the crew and the Android captain occurred spontaneously, including the storm that blocked all communications, thereby denying the *Bio Lab's* captain the ability to notify the authorities. It was a stroke of good luck that the storm rendered the ship completely blacked out for communications.

Trikan sits in the cage and is content for the moment as the *Bio Lab* ship resumes its course, while its crew members carry out the captain's last order. Trikan intends to spend the rest of the voyage as a prisoner until the massive *Bio Craft* docks at the outpost flight terminal, where all the *Bio Lab* flightcrafts offload their cargo. He will have no resistance at the terminal because the entire complex is robotically operated, with no personnel present. The crew chief approaches Trikans' cage and, without saying a word, respectfully salutes him.

"Captain, can I get you something? We have a small galley and a variety of food preserves; most are organic and meet military diet requirements.

"No, but I can use some fresh water!"

The crew chief tells one of his men, "Get the captain some fresh water!" Hesitantly at first, the crew chief respectfully asks permission.

"Can I ask you, by what name do you go by, Captain?" Trikan smiles as he says, "Just call me captain."

The crew chief smiles back at him. "Yes, I understand."

The crew worker arrives with the water and hands it to Trikan while saluting. Trikan drinks the water and then hands the cup to the crew chief. "Thank you."

The crew chief replies, "My name is Kalpen, Sir!" The other crew members give in to their curiosity and approach the cage, saluting Captain Trikan in line order.

Trikan then says, "Okay, Kalpen, it looks like your commander is outnumbered."

The remark brings smiles to their faces as the crew chief is reassured that he can speak freely.

"Captain, don't underestimate the commander. He's evil and corrupt! He cheats us out of our pay rations and our food supply and puts us on report for the slightest errors!"

Trikan then asks, "When you and your men have leave time, why do you come back and work for him?"

The crew chief replies, "We are under contract and have four more seasons before we can leave and earn the credits for transportation back to the outer planets."

Trikan pauses for a moment. "What if I told you that there's a possibility that your passage could be paid for without you having to work for four more seasons?"

The crew chief asks, "How is that possible?"

Trikan answers, "Before we reach the docking station, find a way to get me out of this cage, and I will find your transportation to the outer planets!"

Early the next morning, the Android captain remains angry and frustrated as he attempts to gather information on his prisoner. He slams his hands on the console several times and says, "When will this storm pass?" The metallic voice of his computer becomes activated: "**... SOLAR STORM CONDITIONS WILL LAST UNTIL LATE THIS EVENING... IF THIS IS AN EMERGENCY, FIND SHELTER BELOW GROUND...**"

Slamming his hand on the computer console again and looking at his lost tooth in a glass jar, he speaks out loud.

"I must control my thoughts...how foolish of me!"

For a moment, he thinks to himself... *His Dial-Date... it has all the information I need!* Looking towards the cage from the cabin window, he says, "Well, my fine Captain! There are winners and losers, and this day you will beg me for mercy!"

As he approaches the cage, he shouts out to the crew, "Are all the goods out of the survival pod?"

The crew chief calls back, "Yes! All the goods have been removed; there is nothing left of value."

The Android captain smiles. "Good! Have your men make ready the crane lift!"

Turning back to the cage and Trikan, he says, "Captain, I'll make a deal with you... I will provide you with safe transportation to the transfer station, and the price is your Dial-Date. I can get one hundred and ninety transfer credits for such an item!"

Trikan does not answer him and remains silent.

The Android captain then says, "I understand, Captain, your silence is a refusal! Very well, then. I'll make you more comfortable. You're going back into your emergency rescue pod! But don't worry, Captain, you won't be leaving the *Bio Craft*! You'll find the life support unit more comfortable when we put you in the crusher!"

As he laughs out loud, the Android captain does not expect what comes next. Trikan steps back a few feet from the cage and, with brute force, he kicks the cage door off its attachments, and it strikes the *Bio Craft* captain, knocking him down to the deck.

Suddenly, he's hit with a blast of fusion light that melts the iron bars of the caged door and also destroys the *Bio Craft's* captain.

Standing there, holding the laser weapon, the crew chief remains silent as he slowly lets the weapon drop from his hand. He says out loud, "What have I done?"

Turning to the crew chief, Trikan replies, "You just paid for transportation to the outer planets for you and your crew!"

Captain Trikan then instructs him, "Get your guys together, and when we arrive at the bio transfer terminal tonight, we will offload your cargo as if nothing had happened." The crew chief responds as he salutes, "Yes, Sir, Captain!"

Upon their arrival, there were no security personnel in any of the docking areas. The only work being done is the automated offloading of bio cargo, performed by drone robot laborers. Several of the other *Bio Ships'* flight transports are in the process of being unloaded, and Trikan and the crew members will have no problem disembarking without being noticed. After a short wait, Trikan and the *Bio Crew* leave the ship once automatic docking is complete and assimilate into the general work population upon exiting the terminal.

For a short period, they take jobs in the mines, loading *Core-Mite* minerals, while earning credits to travel to the desert outpost like most workers. This is a government requirement to use only work credits for transportation and other services applicable to workers at the mines. These rules do not apply to tourists or other registered employees at the terminal complex. Each worker is paid at the end of each shift and may use these credits to purchase a tram ticket. Work crews would constantly change shifts, and many of them would be replaced by new workers to prevent long-term exposure to the toxic ore.

At the end of several work periods, Trikan goes directly to the terminal, buys his transportation ticket to return to Star Port City, and then pays for the flightcraft transportation to the outer planets for Chief Kalpen and his crew.

The town is full of mine workers, as small railcars that usually carry *Core-Mite* minerals are now occupied by those coming in from the mines. The first stop is the Residential Station, a complex where many miners and their families live. Other miners stay on the railcars that will carry them to the last stop at the tram station terminal, where they will board trams to Star Port City or flight transports to the outer planets. This facility offers a variety of gift shops, restaurants, and a large health spa, where miners can clean up before their trip to Star Port City.

The atmosphere at this terminal is commercially efficient, offering a high level of service to both miners and tourists alike. The spa features a natural waterfall shower, a unique design element typically found in tropical rainforests. Falling from a high elevation resembling a natural cliff, the water cascades into a pool where customers can wash and relax in a comfortable water temperature.

For passengers with little time to spare before boarding the tram, the spa features a dry, neutralizing cycle facility that removes bacteria from soiled garments by cleaning them with micro-reflecting neutronium white light. It also cleans the subject using a 360-degree base-turning cycle within a tubular glass enclosure, without removing the customer's garments. Travelers may spend the night in one of the many luxury suite complexes located near the terminal.

The entire structural complex of the terminal slowly turns, allowing restaurants and hotel apartments a full view of the sun as it travels across the *Lanzorieon Mountain* skies.

As the morning sun's rays cut across the mountains, the neutronium color channels of light change the grey mountain peaks with blasts of sunlight. Cutting across the valleys and leaving rainbows of many colors that linger in the lower elevations, this section of the desert is known as the *Crater Crown Desert*. This is one of the many popular tourist attractions that also attracts visitors from the two minor planets in this star system. Captain Trikan planned to delay his entry into the transportation terminal until the *Bio Crew* was safely on their way home.

The busy terminal, along with the heavy volume of passengers, gave him the time he needed to begin his carefully planned exit from the mining facility. From outside the terminal on a conveyor walkway that encircles the vast facility, Trikan has a view of the large, crowded main floor. The slow-moving walkway carries passengers around this massive tubular structure, which contains forty-eight upper levels serviced by robotic personnel on trams. Trikan will remain on the lower conveyor walkway and observe the main floor from the large glass archways of this enormous facility.

The architectural design features open arches spanning 300 meters across, with the height of the enclosed glass panels reaching 1,000 meters, allowing natural light to enter the terminal.

Carefully making a mental note of the security presence among the multitude of passengers, Trikan observed one sentry robot at the main entrance of the health spa and two sentry robots checking carry-on luggage after passengers had purchased their boarding tickets.

He observes what the mine workers do before entering the spa as they drop off their soiled anti-radiation deflector suits into a large collection bin.

Trikans' plan for delayed entry into the transport terminal is working better than he could have imagined. He could now see the bio crew following the same procedures as the other mine workers. The crew chief goes before the others and drops off his soiled reflective suit. Before entering the spa, he looks up at the crowded pedestrian crosswalks and smiles, a gesture that Captain Trikan well receives. Trikan remains on the slow-moving walkway until it takes him down to the main floor of the terminal. He will follow a pattern very common among travelers and will waste time looking at the large, three-dimensional information board screens that display scheduled departures from the terminal.

On a large screen, photos of interesting national environmental areas periodically change to spark the visitor's curiosity. He will continually pass the time, making his way to other information screens that show a variety of departure time readouts. Patiently waiting for them to exit the spa, Trikan tells Kalpen, "Here are your tickets, paid for in full."

As Kalpen looks at the tickets, Trikan tells him what they say, "Kalpen: Land Surveyor and Work Associates." As Kalpen smiles, he says, "Thank you, Captain!" Trikan replies, "The name is Trikan, and don't thank me yet—not until you're on board." Good luck!"

Their departure was uneventful, and for a moment, Trikan thinks to himself, *they are on their way to freedom*. He will now make his way to the anti-radioactive deflector bins, where he will follow the same procedure that he observed from the mine workers and discard his *Bio-Suit* into one of the disposable collection bins. Trikans' plan was to follow the rules of his military training and avoid spending too much time in one place, which meant avoiding a deadly encounter with sentry robots.

Captain Trikans' thoughts would not be distracted by the crowds in the tram port, for his feelings were deep and haunting. The fact that he survived the rainforest was indeed a unique experience. He looks at his dirty uniform, and he knows that he must have a clean one to board the tram for Star Port City. He enters the spa entrance and, without saying a word, pulls up his sleeve covering his arm computer and holds up his military microchip insignia to the screen. The sentry robot salutes him and responds, "... **THAT WOULD NOT BE NECESSARY, CAPTAIN... WILL YOU REQUIRE A SECURITY LOCKER...?**"

Knowing full well what to expect, Trikan responds, "No, I will not require one. I'm due back at my base, in Star Port City." Looking down at his Dial-Date, he adds. "In fact, I'll have to be aboard the next sky tram."

"**...GO RIGHT IN, CAPTAIN... THERE IS NO NEED FOR ID CONFIRMATION... HOWEVER, YOU MUST BE EXPEDIENT IF YOU INTEND TO BOARD THE NEXT TRAM FOR STAR PORT CITY... MAY I PURCHASE AN ADVANCED TICKET FOR YOU...?**"

"No, thank you, I already have my ticket."

Avoiding the water showers, he now enters one of the circular, clear-glass hydro units that complete the dry neutralizing cleaning cycle.

Trikan steps out of the unit and stands in front of a mirror to conduct a final inspection as he reloads his photonic cartridge into his laser weapon and returns it to his sidearm holster. When the locker room door opens, he is approached by a service robot.

The robot attendant hands him clean linens to dry himself off, which is a routine courtesy in the locker room section. The robot attendant focuses on the rank and insignia on the captain's uniform, and as the captain is about to exit the locker room, the robot attendant responds, "...IT WAS MY HONOR TO SERVE YOU, CAPTAIN..."

Trikan then looks at his Dial-Date to check his preprogrammed departure schedule. He has a one-quarter sequence of time to make his way through the crowded terminal and enter the departure ramp for the next departing tram. Exiting the spa's main entrance, he stops by the sentry robots' console, which all military personnel must do.

A sentry robot responds, "...CAPTAIN, CAN I ASSIST YOU...?"

"I'm checking out as required by military law."

"...WHY, YES...OF COURSE, CAPTAIN...ONE MOMENT PLEASE..."

As Trikan encounters a slight delay, he feels a sense of apprehension.

"...CAPTAIN... IN THE PROCESS OF PURCHASING YOUR ADVANCED TRAM PASSAGE... I AM REQUIRED TO GIVE INFORMATION TO REPORT ON THE PURPOSE OF MILITARY TRAVELERS' DUTY STAYS AND RESPONSIBILITIES AT THE MINE FACILITY... CAN YOU PROVIDE ME WITH YOUR TOUR OF DUTY SO THAT I MAY

UPDATE THE FIELD INQUIRY PROGRAM...?"

Trikan responds, "Why, yes, of course. How neglectful of me. My assignment was to conduct a military inspection of the large silo air vents that expel mining exhaust fumes and draw in fresh, clean outside air for the mining operations. A rather dirty job, wouldn't you say?" The robot responds,

"...THANK YOU, CAPTAIN... IT WILL BE FILED AND TRANSFERRED TO THE PORT AUTHORITY..."

Trikan turns and is about to leave as he observes the sentry robot inserting his explanation into the console computer regarding his military assignment there.

"...JUST A MOMENT, CAPTAIN... THERE IS SOMETHING THAT I MUST CHECK BEFORE YOU LEAVE..."

Trikan cautiously looks at the sentry robot and places his hand over his sidearm weapon as the robot opens a sliding console, removes a packet, and hands it to Trikan.

"...CAPTAIN...YOU ARE FORGETTING YOUR TOUR GUIDE PACKET FOR THE SPORTS GAMES AND FAMOUS ATTRACTIONS TO VISIT AT STAR PORT CITY..."

Taking the packet from the robot and moving it up and down in his hand, as if testing its weight, he looks at the waste disposal collector unit where he would like to drop it in and says, "Thank you..." I'm sure I'll enjoy Star Port City."

Trikan hastily makes his way to board the next departing sky tram, while his destination at this point becomes what seems like an impossible task. The crowded terminal is filled with its usual undisciplined movement of travelers. Boarding gates present a challenge for passengers who mistakenly attempt to board a tram with a purchased ticket that does not permit passage to a tram that is not yet ready to leave the terminal. Trikan makes his way as quickly as possible, and some travelers give him the courtesy of pushing open a path in response to the presence of his military uniform. Trikan slips through the boarding gate as it is about to close, taking on its last passenger. The blaring announcements over the terminal's loudspeakers demand that all passengers stand clear of the disembarking Antigravity Maglev transports.

Again, the announcement is repeated. "...DANGER... SOME TOPICAL RADIATION CAN CAUSE SEVERE BURNS... STAND BACK FROM THE TRAM GATES... DEPARTURE IS IMMEDIATE... LAST CALL....!"

The message is brief: the tram is already in antigravity, traveling on the skyway trans highway around the planet's magnetic field, its rear compartment's atomic engines pushing it forward. Captain Trikan checks his loading pass for his section console accommodations, and after finding the level ramp lift, he feels energized by his new mission to find Elisa. Before entering the elevator platform, Trikan asks one of the deck hostesses if his module section is still available. She smiles and replies, "I'll check it for you, Captain. One moment, please." As she checks her wristband computer, she says, "No, sorry, it's occupied, but I do have another section unit available at my assignment level, Captain, Section Seventeen." She smiles as Trikan responds, "I'm sure that will be just fine."

As he enters the elevator lift, the giant sky tram begins to levitate above the terminal and onto the planet's magnetic field. The cool, refreshing low-humidity temperature of the tram starts to have a calming effect on its passengers. Trikan finds his reserved module compartment and immediately turns on his screen, which displays the departing tram leaving the terminal as it engages the planet's magnetic gravitational field skyway.

The turbo-thrust engines propel this express tram over the high *Crater Mountains* in a nonstop direction to Star Port City. Many passengers will go up to the elevated, glass-domed lounge and enjoy panoramic views of the mountain range and the famous lake regions of the planet before reaching Star Port City. Trikan touches the view screen, and a segment of temperature and weather forecast readings of various locations around the planet appears, including the orbital heat shields that protect the planet from the sun's harmful solar flares, while ending the weather report segment. Then words appear across the bottom of the screen: ... **LAW VIOLATORS... NETWORK NEWS REPORTER INTERVIEWS A GOVERNMENT COUNCILMAN...**

A news reporter appears on the viewscreen. "Councilman, can you tell me about the individuals who were being held in the safehouse?"

The government official responds, "They were all charged with minor violations, and they all refused to exercise their rights to appear in court with defense representation. As you know, all laws must be obeyed, and no one is above the law."

The reporter then asks, "Has anyone been able to interview them while they were in the halfway house?"

This time, the official says, "As far as I know, they have refused contact with everyone, and there's new evidence that this group was conspiring to overthrow the government by their actions that I am not at liberty to discuss with you at this moment! It's still an ongoing investigation. However, I can assure you that the matter is very serious. We have one missing captain who was part of a mission in the rainforest to apprehend them, and unfortunately, he may be part of their group. If this is true, he must also be brought to justice! Trikan then turns off the telescreen as he hesitates for a moment, evaluating the report. Now, as a wanted man, he cannot afford to take the chance to stay on this tram when it arrives at the terminal in Star Port City.

The sensors at the disembarking ramp will detect his military insignia identification before he takes a step off the platform. He now realizes that he must take action to get off the tram before it reaches Star Port City. He then activates the screen to a three-dimensional view of all the interior areas of the giant tram. He familiarizes himself with one particular section for a possible escape before the tram enters the large Star Port City Terminal.

The thrust of the tram port engines adds life to the bleak desert stillness as the tram recedes into a lower electronic rail track GPS at 15,000 feet above the desert sands. This flight plan will allow passengers to view the passing desert scenery and the changing colors of the drifting sands as the tram's engines blast through the air. The global transportation system encompasses public transport, including air travel, eliminating the need for surface travel for long-distance destinations. It's a comfortable travel experience that lets passengers ride in luxury and enjoy exotic dishes prepared by certified chefs from around the world. Trikan falls into a restless sleep as the flight attendant returns to check on her passengers' comfort and notices the captain's discomfort. She awakens him with a slight touch on his shoulder, and he instinctively grabs her arm. Immediately, she says, "Sorry, Captain, I didn't mean to startle you." He interrupts her, "Please, excuse my reaction." Smiling, she says, "My scan monitor indicated that you were having restless sleep. Would you like a sedative?"

"No, thank you."

She then smiles again. "Captain, would you care for some refreshments?"

"No, thank you; I'm fine." As she was about to leave, he

reconsidered and replied, "On second thought, I do need something; perhaps you can help me? I left an important part of a transcript in my luggage, and I must read it before we arrive at our destination. It was foolish of me to leave it there; can you direct me to the lower bay luggage compartments?"

"I'm sorry, Captain, but that area is restricted to authorized personnel only."

Admiring the handsome captain, she leans over and whispers the flight security code to him, then smiles and walks away.

As she exits the corridor, he turns on the telescreen again for a moment to the government's news channel, and a governmental report appears across the screen: "All suspects in the halfway house incident have been apprehended and transferred to Central Detention." The court hearings will proceed without their presence, and the search for the missing captain remains the military's top priority.

Turning off the telescreen, he casually leaves the console area and heads towards the escalator units that will take him down to a lower level of accommodation.

In a large lobby, other passengers buy food from an array of food dispensers, and automatic kitchen doors open and close constantly as waiters and waitresses take food trays up to the main passenger level. Trikan waits patiently online until he can make a food purchase at one of the large food dispensary machines. He hesitates for a moment as he follows the flight attendant's advice and walks past the escalator. He looks specifically at the crowd to identify any sentry robots before entering the luggage compartment, which leads him to the emergency escape flight pods. Suddenly, there is an announcement from the accommodation officer to the passengers:

We are about to approach the *Great Crater*, which is located on the outskirts of Star Port City, before we land. You may view this natural formation on your viewing screens."

      As Trikan arrives in the lower luggage complex, he quickly checks the sequence indicators on the chamber doors until he finds the correct one. He types in the code that the hostess whispered to him, and the doors open. Trikan enters the large luggage bay storage area, which also contains emergency escape flightcrafts. These passenger crafts are positioned for an immediate launch sequence. As Trikan types in his military code into the central flight console, the launch bay door opens. The flightcraft begins to move into its blast mode sequence. Before exiting the giant tram, alarms blare in accordance with emergency procedures across the main security computer screens, alerting security personnel to ensure that the emergency exit doors have not been breached. Two sentry security robots enter the large emergency storage area with weapons drawn and attempt to fire at the captain. Trikans' reflexes are too quick for them, and he fires first, destroying both robots in an instant.

      He then enters his military override attack code into the escape flightcraft's computer, activating the craft's laser weapon. As he blasts off through the vast gantry opening of the tram's escape hatch, he pre-programs the flight course that will take him to Star Port City before the tram arrives. The giant tram's computers report a malfunction, and all computer screens continuously display: **...WE HAVE AN UNLAWFUL EMERGENCY FLIGHT EXIT..." ALERT ALL COMMUNICATION PROGRAMS FROM TRANSPORT TRAM'S TERMINAL...**

      Over and over again, the same message continues on all of the computer screens. Finally, the gantry bay doors open again, allowing two security flightcrafts, piloted by robots, to blast free of the tram at full velocity as they pursue their mission orders to destroy the security violator. Trikans' indicator alerts on his Dial-Date, informing him of pursuing armed security crafts, as the navigational control guidance systems on Trikans' flightcraft announce, "...EVASIVE ACTION... INCOMING BLAST FIELD..."

Trikan immediately accelerates his flightcraft into satellite orbit, and the craft becomes part of one of the many satellites that orbit the planet for a short time. Captain Trikan then turns off the engines to allow them to cool down and avoid detection by his craft's heat signature, as he monitors the two security robots in their flight patterns below.

The silence of orbital space allows Trikan to view the planet before reentry begins and to evaluate his next move, when suddenly the reentry alarms activate as he turns on his forcefield engines. A beacon indicator display appears on Trikans Flightcraft's computer screens and announces: "... SENTRY ROBOTS ARE IN A STANDARD PURSUIT PATTERN, CAPTAIN..."

Across the screen, another message is presented: "...EVASIVE ACTION IS IMMINENT...THEY ARE NOW IN YOUR FIRE ZONE... THE SECURITY CRAFT ARE CLOSING IN ON YOUR TARGET AREA BELOW..."

Immediately, Trikan ignites the blast engines, sending his flightcraft into a lower projection to avoid the heat zone of the sun's powerful rays. This makes Trikans' craft invisible, and he fires a laser missile, destroying the two security crafts as they cross one another, creating a single target. Trikan then ignites his flightcraft's engines to full forward thrust, adjusting the instrument computer finder to Star Port City. A short time later, a beacon alert indicator appears on the computer screen and broadcasts: "...ENERGY RODS ARE CRITICAL... EXPLOSION IMMINENT... THE SHIP'S HEAT SHIELDS ARE MALFUNCTIONING... NEGATIVE RESPONSE... NAVIGATE FLIGHTCRAFT TO THE DARK SIDE OF THE PLANET AND EJECT SEQUENCE... OUTSIDE TEMPERATURE FIELD CRITICAL..."

Trikan ignores the computer and pushes on to Star Port City, as the interior of his flight-ship now begins to smoke due to the overheating engines. He then puts on an emergency breathing device and activates its full engine capacity, aiming to enter Star Port City before the tram arrives.

The overheated flightcraft now enters above one of the old, deserted archway-designed air dome terminals that were deactivated and left without security or operational personnel in the far eastern quadrant, outside of Star Port City. The faulty retro rockets burn out before the entire landing sequence can occur, causing the flightcraft to cross the abandoned, old landing field and crash into a receiving terminal. Immediately, Trikan ejects into a low-altitude escape, avoiding the sizeable structural overhang of the abandoned receiving terminal. The tiny jets in his command chair module activate, allowing Trikan to land softly. At the same time, the flightcraft continues on its journey into the concrete hangar, leaving behind a twisted mass of metal debris in an explosion.

Moments of silence return as shadows of universal light dance across the desert quadrant where the old airfield is located, outside Star Port City. The cool night's silence and the absence of desert heat give Trikan a sense of comfort as he observes the last crackling embers of the destroyed flightcraft. The crash site of the flightcraft has left Trikan a distance of 965 kilometers from the mammoth walls of Star Port City.

The Tram will now arrive before Trikan, and after its passengers are offboarded, security will not find him aboard. The results will be the same; despite a different set of circumstances, he will still benefit from his original plan: not to be on board the tram when it arrives at Star Port City. The emergency service robotic rescue division is notified of the incident at the crash site in the vicinity of the old landing field. The online computer message continues to register on all screens as an emergency airbus dispenses with rescue procedures.

As Trikan looks up at the endless universe, he finds within himself a new existence. He is surrounded by old technology and ancient control towers that beckon to a sense of power long past. Nevertheless, Trikan will follow his mission, regardless of the risks.

A signal from his Dial-Date arm computer alerts him to a readout of a large drone craft approaching the old hangar facility. As the extensive medical-assisted service drone lands, two emergency medical robots immediately exit without delay. Trikan removes his micro-code chip from his arm computer and places it inside his war boot. While the two rescue robots approach the captain, they carry a medic-vac trauma stretcher, and Trikan will now play the part of a crashed and injured casualty. One of the rescue robot's questions, Trikan, as he inquires about his name and service identification, **"...CAPTAIN...WERE YOU ON A MISSION...?"**

Pretending to be disoriented, Trikan does not answer the robot. Again, the robot asks, "**...CAPTAIN... PLEASE STATE YOUR MISSION...!**"

Trikan hesitates for a moment as he looks at his Dial-Date arm computer while still declining to answer. He then lies back and pretends to be unconscious. The other Emergency Service Robot says, **"...HIS DIAL-DATE IS OFFLINE... IT'S MISSING ITS MICROCHIP..."**

As the (ES)-Robots place the captain onto the medic-vac trauma stretcher, the first ES-Robot remarks, **"...REPORT... CENTRAL CODE ONE TO EMERGENCY SERVICE STATION... UNIDENTIFIED CAPTAIN WITH LOSS OF MEMORY... POSSIBLE HEAD TRAUMA..."**

The other robot responds, "**... LET'S GET THE CAPTAIN INTO THE AIR FLIGHT TRAUMA UNIT...**"

A short time later, they are airborne on the emergency air track that will transport their casualty to the large medic-vac emergency treatment center in Star Port City.

Trikan is placed in the crash casualty section of the extensive medical facility and is evaluated by several robotic medical specialists. He is then placed in a private room with automatic technical readouts of a unique enhanced micron radial imagery brain scan. A female robot medical assistant will check in on a scheduled program period and evaluate the patient's MRI data about why there is no response from the patient, who has suffered no brain trauma or bodily injuries.

She will talk to him and continually try to engage him in a conversation about his injuries. His response to her questioning remains the same: "I don't remember."

She asks him again, "Do you know your name? Can you tell me your name?"

Trikan makes a feeble attempt at fulfilling her request as he responds, "I don't know..." and then falls back into what appears to be a deep sleep.

She remains by his side, recording the data, and after receiving no response from him, she notices the missing microchip in his arm computer and says, "Oh, great!" Now I have to go and find a technician!"

After the robot nurse leaves the trauma unit room, Trikan removes the microchip from his war boot and places it back into his arm computer, which provides him with the interior dimensions of all the rooms on his floor. He locates the utility garment room where medical uniforms are stored. He then makes his way discreetly down the corridor and enters the storage room. He puts on a medical doctor's uniform and casually leaves, walking across the front lobby and out the medical center's doors.

Outside of the front lobby, he is approached by a courteous transportation hostess. "Doctor, do you require transportation?"

"Why, yes, I do. Thank you!"

"And where is your desired location, doctor?"

"Star Port Cities Trans Terminal."

The hostess types in Trikans' request on her dashboard and hands him his code-key ticket. A robotic hydro taxi transport arrives, and Trikan gets in, thanking the hostess as he inserts his ticket into the console. The robot driver receives the ticket information and speaks, "... **DIRECTIONAL FINDER... CALCULATING...SPC-TIME... STAR PORT CITY'S TRANS TERMINAL... IS THAT CORRECT, SIR...?"**

As Trikan looks out the window at the busy front lobby, the thought of being trapped echoes throughout his mind. As the cab pulls away, he replies, "Correct... Trans Terminal."

Upon arrival, he does not expect that the terminal will be as easy as walking out of the Medical Center lobby. Once detected inside the rail-tram tube system, he would not be able to escape due to the numerous security checkpoints. Sentry robots and their cybernetic supervisors may already have been notified of his general location.

Inside the large terminal, the multitude of passengers transferring from sky trams to the lower-level tube system gives him a sense of relief, as he believes he will not be detected at the moment. He makes his way through the crowd, gets online, and waits to purchase his transport ticket. As he approaches the ticket counter, he is greeted by an attractive Android hostess, and she asks,

"Can I help you, doctor?"

"Yes, I need a transport ticket to the Flight Base Barracks Quarters."

The Android hostess is very receptive and cooperative. "Very good, doctor. Will you also require a return purchase ticket?" Looking at her name tag, he says, "Yes, Cindy, that would be more convenient, thank you!"

She types in the double-ride request and pauses for a moment. "Oh, I'm sorry, doctor, there are no single occupancies available. Are you traveling alone? I'm afraid you'll have to take a double-occupancy compartment. It will cost you extra, but you will have more room!"

Trikan smiles. "That's fine. It would be nice to have someone to share it with. It's a long ride back to the Flight Base." The hostess smiles back as she leans towards Trikan while handing him his compartment ticket. "Doctor, you're my last customer. My shift is over. Let me keep you company at the departure gate. Perhaps on your return trip, we may have more time to spend together?"

As she turns over her post to another ticket hostess, they make their way towards the departure gate. They continue their friendly conversation when suddenly she stops and pulls back on Trikans' jacket. While trying to be discreet, she responds, "Doctor, something is wrong! We are being observed by platform security personnel at your departure gate! I may be imagining this, but they seem to be focusing on you!"

Trikan looks across the crowded main lobby and says, "Not only are you very charming, but you are also very perceptive." I just noticed it myself. I'm afraid that we're going to have to end this conversation. He then says to her, "Don't follow me!" She replies, "Too late! I have no choice!" They make their way through the crowd toward one of the many escalators that take passengers to the terminal's upper level. Just before reaching the upper level, Trikan turns around and sees one of the security guards about to fire his weapon, and he grabs Cindy's hand. "Cindy, come on!"

As he pushes his way through the crowd on the upper level of the escalator, he feels a sharp pain in his arm from the blast of the agent's silent laser weapon. As they reach the top platform, she says to Trikan, "Something is wrong. I can't go on. Leave me!"

He holds her in his arms when a security agent in plain clothes suddenly confronts him.

"Captain, you're wasting your time... You can't help her!"

Trikan gently places Cindy down and kneels alongside her. She opens her eyes and says, "You're bleeding... Go! Save yourself! It's all part of the..." She stops speaking for a moment, then, on her last breath, she says, "Plan... Amulet... Take It...!"

Trikan releases the gold chain and takes the star amulet from around her neck. He remains silent for a moment as the security agent tells him, "Captain, if you have a weapon, turn it over immediately!" Trikan looks up at the security agent's laser weapon pointed directly at him, and he pauses for a moment before answering, "My weapon... It's in my carry-all bag." The security agent tells him, "Now get up and slowly unfasten your shoulder harness and hand me the bag!"

Trikan complies with the order and unfastens his shoulder strap harness. Suddenly, he forcibly strikes the security agent with his carry-all bag, knocking him over the railing three station levels down to the main floor of the transit lobby. The crowds respond to the continuation of violence in a state of panic, due to what they just experienced moments ago. Trikan then fires his weapon in a continuous blast sequence, destroying several security guards on the main floor as they attempt to fire at him. Trikan is about to fire at the central electronic-computer relay bank that supplies energy to this massive transport terminal when a voice from behind yells out, "Captain, follow me..." NOW!"

In his anger, Trikan takes a few steps back, turns, grabs the female, and for an instant, places his laser weapon against her. Then, realizing she is wearing a military scout uniform, he slightly releases his grip on her and asks, "Who sent you here?" Who are you?"

She resists. "LET GO OF ME! We don't have much time!"

"Time for what?" She grabs Trikans' hand, which is holding her. "DAMN YOU! She answered you. Escape! Now follow me!"

Before releasing her, he turns and fires his laser weapon at the principal electronic energy resource computer bank that supplies the energy to the terminal's lighting and electronic rail functions. This causes the terminal to experience an energy blackout, halting all transport systems except for emergency exit lighting. Without further thought, Trikan follows the young female scout trooper down an exit stairwell several floors until they reach the basement of the enormous transport facility. They then exit through an emergency exterior hydro-supply ramp, which takes them up to the street outside the terminal, where they join the crowd on the main thoroughfare of travelers waiting for surface transportation. Staying together, they board one of the commercial outland buses that will leave the city for several small communities in the rural desert quadrant.

After leaving the city, the coach transport enters the Sky-Way bridge complex, as most passengers give in to the comfortable ride. Looking out through the portals at the black silhouettes of trees, with the moonlight reflecting off them, has a relaxing effect on most passengers, allowing them to drift off into a restful sleep. Trikan and the female scout trooper also surrender to the scenic effects of the outside environment. Before falling asleep with a feeling of guilt for what happened back at the terminal, Trikan says to the young female who helped him escape, "You know, you can never go back!"

She smiles, "I'll be okay, Captain, but someone has to look out for you!" As she closes her eyes and leans her head against his shoulder, they both fall into a long and restful sleep.

Chapter 9:

The Old City

The transport makes several stops at its preprogrammed destinations during its scheduled tour program. At each of these locations, passengers disembark discreetly, being careful not to disturb others who are asleep. The last scheduled commercial stop drops off passengers except for two travelers in the upper level of the large transport, who are still sleeping in one of the secluded cabin areas. The transport will travel several more kilometers to the end of its route destination, where layover time will charge its solar power units for the new transport day schedule. The metallic voice of the robotic transport operator awakens Trikan and his companion with the announcement: "...THIS TRANSPORT SERVICE HAS ENDED... PLEASE GATHER ALL YOUR BELONGINGS WHEN YOU EXIT THE TRANSPORT VEHICLE... SERVICE WILL RESUME AT DAWN WHEN THE SOLAR PANELS ARE RECHARGED..."

Upon exiting the transport, Trikan discards his doctor's uniform and momentarily looks towards the vehicle operator. The female scout trooper says, "He's asleep on recharge, Captain. He doesn't even know we're here." Looking around, Trikan says, "This place is a huge junkyard!"

"Yes, it is, Captain. It's more than just a junkyard; it's also part of the Old City, which was destroyed in the Androidian War a very long time ago. Now, we're all friends, helping one another. A moment of silence passes, and she asks,

"Captain, may I ask you something?" Where are you from?"

"What kind of a question is that?"

"Some very important people are trying to save your life, Captain."

As she opens the lower section of the transport, he says. "And you, how did you get involved? By the way, do you have a name?"

Stopping suddenly, she turns. "Are you kidding me? Of course, I have a name!" Smiling back at the captain, she extended her hand. Reciprocating, he replies, "We were never formally introduced."

"Well, my name is Kriena. How do you do, Mister Captain?"

She hesitates momentarily and then adds, "Mister Captain Trikan..." She then continues to remove the antigravity hover-based platforms when he suddenly asks, "Why are you helping me?" As she begins to assemble one of the antigravity platforms, she responds, "Secrets, Captain! We all have Secrets!"

She stops and looks at Trikan as he removes his visor-luminous helmet and war vest from his carry bag. She then continues, "Trust me, Captain, you will find what you're looking for in the Old City."

Trikan takes one of the antigravity hover-based unit platforms while Kriena assembles the control handlebars and activates the power units that will allow them to travel along the ground without walking. "Did you ever use one of these, Captain?"

"No, but I know what they are. Very easy to operate, but I prefer walking."

"The distance is too far to the Old City, Captain, and we don't have time. These antigravity lifts will get us to the new construction site. When we arrive, you'll need to board a construction crane to lift you onto the other side of the crater wall. After that, you're going to use your arm computer to assist you with all the e-quad navigational sequences. You will receive a faint signal on your computer screen; follow it! It cannot be traced or picked up by security satellites."

The antigravity lift platforms move forward at variable speeds, controlled by the two passengers. A short time later, they arrive at a construction site where automatic lift machines continue on their preprogrammed functions, lifting large granite megaton building blocks while reconstructing the Old City on the other side of the vast crater. Raising her voice above the construction noise, Kriena shouts out to Trikan, "This is as far as I can go! Security sensors are everywhere. When you enter the Old City, the government will be aware, so you must continue moving until you reach the safe zone. The government cannot go there. There's a treaty of some kind with the Trikinians! Get moving, captain... your hover platform can get you onto one of the granite blocks before the crane picks it up! Most of the Old City is in ruins! Do you enjoy walking, Captain? You got your wish! The large caverns you must reach are located at the far eastern end of the crater, outside the Old City. He shouts back to her over the construction noise, "Hey, wait! How do I know when I'm in the safe zone?"

When you arrive, you will enter the large caverns that lead to the safe zone, where you will find the old professor. Rumor has it that he's some kind of skywatcher! He was exiled many years ago for defying the scientific community. Some say that at the time, he had lost his mind. That's just a rumor, Captain, don't believe it! He helped me, as well as many others, and he will help you, too! He's also a great medical doctor, and he'll take care of your arm wound."

Using the antigravity platform, Trikan elevates himself to the top of one of the large building blocks, just moments before the automatic crane begins to lift the heavy object in slow motion. Kriena calls out, "Captain, please, may I have the amulet?"

As the granite block is being raised, he searches through his uniform pockets and finds the amulet. As he removes it, it opens, revealing a symbol of the helix, the code of life.

Before throwing it down to her, he calls out, "What is it for?"

Kriena calls out to him, "You may see her again... someday, perhaps. No time to explain now!" She is my sister!"

Trikan throws the amulet to her. She catches it and then places it around her neck, and it precisely matches the one she's wearing. She raises her hand to her eyebrow and salutes him. He then touches his brow and respectfully salutes her, and they both smile at each other. She shouts up, "Good luck, Captain!" and she disappears into the night without ever explaining why she helped him escape from the Star Port Terminal.

The question would have to wait. Why did the two beautiful females risk their very existence for him? His thoughts would have to focus on the perilous journey of evading capture by government agencies that would never relent in their pursuit of him. The giant magnetic crane has now carried Trikan to an area of newly constructed wall foundations inside the Old City. The mammoth block is being lowered several yards above the ground before being put into place. Trikan jumps off into an area that appears to be one of the interior sections of the Old City.

Walking through sections on the interior side of the wall construction, Captain Trikan observes several abandoned military anti-magnetic hydrofoils. The captain looks down at his arm computer and attempts to activate one of the abandoned units by typing in a code sequence that will generally operate most hydrofoils. He opens the first one that he comes to and removes an energy lock cylinder while disengaging its power source. The power cartridge remains on discharge; with his arm computer, he makes a sweeping motion across the area where the other foils have been abandoned. He then receives a signal from one of them at a short distance, and he can activate its energy field by entering the correct variable sequence code on his arm computer.

    Trikan reflects upon the departure of Kriena, saying, "Good luck, Captain!" while he hastily climbs onto the hydrofoil platform and takes the controls. It lifts off the dusty, old terrain and becomes magnetically charged as it rises above the broken ground of the Old City. The hydrofoil is on a predestined course, programmed eons ago to transport passengers across the giant crater from the Old City to an entrance of caverns under the eastern end of the crater.

    These passengers were scientists who worked on a secret government program located deep within the caverns, and the work they did was never made public or shared with the general population. When their work was completed, the caverns were abandoned, and the project's secrets were never fully disclosed or documented in scientific journals. Rumors began to circulate that it was related to telepathy. No conclusions to the stories were ever revealed.

    As the hydrofoil nears the caverns, it begins to malfunction. Low energy readings appear on the computer screen before the screen blacks out. The antigravity lift slows and begins a pre-landing descent. The dim landing lights become automatically activated and then fade out as the craft begins its slow descent outside the cavern entrance. Trikan preferred it this way; Kriena had wished him good luck, and that luck was still with him.

    He did not care to enter the large cavern on the hydrofoil, not knowing what to expect. He would take his time and use the moonless night to his advantage; he activated the topographic hologram device on his Dial-Date computer and saw that the faint blue signal was still there.

He then puts down his ocular night visor eye frames, so he can now see with sharp, night-telescopic, spectacle-distant vision. He also types into his arm computer, activating interior scanning of the cavern with real-time feedback, and receives information on various types of cold-blooded life forms, commonly known as serpents. Each picture scan appears on his arm computer, covering a one-square-mile radius in the cavern, as he receives confirmation of an all-clear area.

After entering the caverns, Trikan thinks he can hear what sounds like a huge aircraft landing in the crater a distance away. Looking back towards the far end of the crater and scanning the airspace with his Dial-Date, he receives a negative readout. The eerie silence in the great crater gives Trikan a sense of uneasiness. Was something there? Did he imagine the sound that he heard? Trikan checks his sidearm laser weapon and sets it to full blast before entering further into the caverns.

Once inside, he realizes that the caverns are not all natural formations; they contain many fabricated chambers of varying sizes that branch off in different directions. He looks at his holographic device, and it reveals a type of life form deep within the caverns, located under the eastern part of the crater, past a volcanic fault that remains active, releasing harmful gaseous fumes from beneath an elevated ledge that can be used as a walkway. Automatically, his Dial-Date directional lens lights up, indicating some movement outside the main entrance of the crater. He now finds himself at a tunnel entrance that leads to a large, constructed dome, held up by steel columns that support an air-flight hangar. He crosses the middle of this constructed dome and realizes that this facility was once a transport center. Several exit ramps that would have facilitated air flight vehicles to depart from this location are in disrepair and have been abandoned a long time ago.

Upon entering a dimly lit area of the large hangar, Trikan checks his Dial-Date directional finder then receives a positive reading of a life form. He proceeds down the dimly lit corridor and draws his laser weapon from his side belt holster as he approaches a sizable concave door made of Banishean steel. He pushes the heavy obstruction inward and enters an old abandoned medical lab with dimly lit dome lights. He enters another room with a medical symbol above its doorway.

    Once inside, Trikan notices a picture frame containing an old ceremonial photograph of dignitaries and scientists who once ran this center. He picks up a photo plate and inserts it into an antiquated but still functional slide photo camera unit. On a screen across the large conference room, holograms appear, celebrating the doctors and scientists assigned to this installation when it was fully operational. Trikan is about to insert another photo plate into the photo projector when a voice from a dark area of the conference room speaks out, "Does this place interest you, young man?"

    Captain Trikan is startled; he abruptly turns and points his laser weapon at the figure of an older man as he steps out of the darkened area of the room.

    "Will we never learn? Must all we do is kill one another?"

    Trikan lowers his weapon and says, "I was told I could find the hermit sky watcher here." Professor Zola is slightly amused. "Skywatcher, yes! Hermit? Not likely... I have a companion, and he's standing directly behind you.

    Trikan turns to look back and sees a robot with a laser weapon pointed directly at him. He then puts his weapon into his side harness as the professor informs him, "Had you not lowered your weapon when you did, Captain, we would not be having this friendly conversation. Now, may I help you?"

    Trikan picks up another photo plate from the table. "Who are these people?"

"They are long gone, Captain. Before I satisfy your curiosity, let me tend to your arm wound, and then I'll explain this place and what it was like a long time ago.

Trikan sits down on a medical gurney, and he removes his forearm utility computer weapon unit, exposing his burnt flesh. The professor immediately applies a liquid pain-enhanced healing solution to the wound and reveals to the captain a summary of his life. "You know, Captain, I started as a medical doctor before becoming a scientist. I have seen many wounds of this type; they are very painful! You seem to have a tolerance to pain." Trikan nods as he replies, "I'm just trying not to think about it!"

"Yes, I do agree with you. When we get into favoring the difficulties that we are confronted with, the pain seems to worsen and delays the healing!"

The professor picks up the first-aid applicator and continues treating Trikans' laser wound while continuing the conversation about medical procedures.

Putting back the first aid applicator onto the counter, he accidentally knocks over a small flask of highly corrosive acid that burns his wrist and part of his hand, which causes some blistering. With no reaction, he ignores the effect of the acid and immediately rinses his hand in freshwater. He then continues to attend to Trikans' injury, remaining silent for the moment. "Professor, you seem to have a tolerance for pain as well! That flask is labeled highly corrosive acid!"

The professor ignores the captain's remarks as he places a sizeable antibacterial dressing pad on Trikans' arm wound. "This should do, for now, Captain. The healing process will take some time. This pad will prevent any infection from occurring. There, you're all done!" As Trikan runs his hand over his injured arm, he replies, "It feels a lot better, professor, thank you!" The professor smiles. "Now that you know about this place and who I am, Captain, how can I assist you?"

"I was told to come here."

"That's interesting. Tell me more about this, Captain."

Trikan explains, "Her name is Kriena!"

Putting down his medical tray and turning back towards Trikan, the professor replies, "Yes, Kriena was a student of mine, as well as her younger sister, Cindy, a long time ago. She was very intelligent, as most of my students were." I am not surprised that they are aware of my presence here, but you, my friend, are in danger! I am sure they are aware that she helped you escape. When she assisted you, she was fully aware of the consequences of her actions.

The professor then activates a view screen. There is something I'd like you to see. What I am about to show you is not publicly available.

He adjusts the monitor to the secret government archives and then enters a code into the teleview until he reaches the word "defector." A picture appears, and the teleview continues to read the description out loud: "Johnathan Shawnwood... Alias Trikan."

The professor then asks, "Does this look like you, Captain?"

Trikan stares at the screen as the professor continues to read the information: "A military officer who was in good standing until he broke the oath of loyalty to his scout command unit." A government reward is offered to anyone with information that will help lead to his capture. Judgment and incarceration will follow. Participants' help will remain confidential."

Trikan turns the screen off in front of the professor and adds, "That's a bad picture of me, Professor!"

As the professor takes his glasses off, he explains, "The reason I wanted you to see that posting is that I'm not sure if you're aware that military leaders will keep this from the general population." You seem to be an exception to something that was never done before. You have already destroyed several sentry robots that were sent to capture you, and you have also destroyed the Great River Installation. He laughs at himself as he shakes his head. What you have done has never been done before! Your actions have caused them grave embarrassment. They want you badly! That's why I showed you that 'wanted' bulletin; this is a first!"

Trikan remains quiet and then remarks, "I don't like drinking poison, Professor!"

The professor asks, "Poison?"

"Yes, professor... It left a bad taste in my mouth!"

Trikan walks towards the cavern entry control screen and looks at it. "You had me on your monitor the moment I entered the cavern? Nice work, Professor!" He pauses for several moments, his attention still fixed on the screen, which displays the main cavern entrance. "Professor... I experienced something when I first entered the cavern. I heard a sound like the ground being pushed aside as a large craft landed somewhere in the crater. I turned and looked through my helmet's visor-luminous across the entire area, and there was nothing there! Then I heard another faint sound that I couldn't identify; it lasted only briefly. But the more I think about it, the more uneasy I feel!"

The professor spends a few moments of silence and then replies, "Hmm... a sound that you could not identify?" He turns to his robot, "Cen-Ton, can you add something of value to what the captain has just said?"

Cen-Ton responds to the captain, "...CAPTAIN... YOU WILL HAVE TO PROVIDE ME WITH MORE INFORMATION...THE

ORIGIN OF THE SOUND...WAS IT EMANATING FROM THE INTERIOR OF THE CAVE... OR IN THE OPEN SPACE OF THE CRATER...?"

"That's part of the puzzle, Cen-Ton, I can't say for sure in what direction the sound came from." The professor adds, "Well, captain, you seem to have heightened my curiosity as well! Let us check my exterior computer screens and find out where the sound came from. I am more interested in the first one that you heard. This sound of air being pushed along the surface of the crater - could it have been a weather anomaly?

Cen-Ton replies, "...WEATHER ANOMALIES ARE NOT PRESENT INSIDE THE CRATER, PROFESSOR...REASON EVALUATION BEING...THE HIGH RIDGES OF THE CRATER KEEP ATMOSPHERIC WEATHER ANOMALIES AND STORM FIELDS FROM CHANGING PATTERNS IN THE HIGHER ELEVATIONS OF THE PLANET'S ATMOSPHERE... IN FACT... THERE IS NO PRERECORDED DATA OF THE CRATER EVER EXPERIENCING THE PHENOMENON OF LIQUID RAIN..."

The professor smiles. "Thank you, Cen-Ton." He begins submitting scanned pictures of all the caverns, along with recordings of natural phenomena such as desert birds and other creatures wandering into the crater. The feedback distinctions have very little to do with the sound that Trikan heard. The professor suggests, "Captain, let's try the still photo frames on my computer."

The professor rearranges the computer frames to create close-up views of the entire crater. "There you are, Captain! Getting off the antigravity hydrofoil at the exact moment that you arrived, when you heard the sound that you could not identify!"

Looking at the captain, he continues, "Look at this photo plate, directly behind you, in the center of the crater, there are two impressions that should not be there!"

Watching closely at the photo plate, they observe a slight distortion in the cubic formula of the undisturbed ground area of the crater. "Cen-Ton, what do you make of this?"

"...PROFESSOR...I CALCULATE SOME TYPE OF HEAT SIGNATURE FROM HEAVY ARMOR FLIGHT WAR TANKS... THERE IS A DISTORTION OF ALGORITHMIC WAVES THAT BLENDS THE STRUCTURE FROM THE DISTANT BACKGROUND OF THE CRATER WALLS, MAKING THE WARCRAFT INVISIBLE..."

Suddenly, an explosion destroys Trikans' hydrofoil and most of the front entrance of the cavern while sending smoke and debris down into the main tunnel area and the professor's lab. Before the dust and debris clear, the professor shouts, "Captain, we'd better take refuge in the storage area of the lab! We will be safe there!"

Once inside, behind the heavy steel door of the storage room, the sounds of the falling interior of the cave walls can barely be heard as the invisible war tanks fire several more times into the cavern. Then a long period of silence remains. "Captain... We must make sure you survive! Their mission is obvious: you will never return to Star Port City. They will most likely not give up until they find you!"

The professor activates the exterior topographic cameras, and several moments go by. All that can be observed is what Cen-Ton described before: a heat signature of stealth, magnetic-photon weapon rail tanks. Trikan then asks, "Is it possible that they have achieved such remarkable science, Professor? To make a craft that large, invisible? The computer must be in error!"

"When was the last time a computer made a mistake, Captain?"

As Trikan moves away from the view screen scope, he remarks, "You're right, Professor!"

The professor then adds, "Their patience will eventually run out, and there is no telling what they will do next. We must leave immediately and travel north through the natural tunnel system." Cen-Ton then interjects, "... PROFESSOR... I AM AFRAID THAT IT IS TOO LATE... I DETECT TWO GROUND-LEVEL SENTRY ROBOTS THAT HAVE JUST LEFT THEIR INVISIBLE WAR TANK AND ARE ON THEIR WAY TO THE ENTRANCE OF THE CAVERNS..."

Trikan responds at once, "We Need Weapons, Professor!"

The professor answered back, "What we need is to retreat into the lower chambers of the caverns; we'll be safer down there. You and Cen-Ton will have your weapons. Just let me check something first."

The professor moves towards the large computer screen and activates its keyboard. He then types in the requested information ... Z199-WT... The computer then displays: **... CLASSIFICATION ... WAR TROOPS... GENERAL USE HEALIOCON ASSIGNMENT... WEIGHT VARIES APPROXIMATELY SIX HUNDRED TO EIGHT HUNDRED POUNDS... SPECIALIZED CLASS TYPE KNOWN AS SENTRY ROBOTS EQUIPPED WITH DEATH RAY WEAPONS... SPECIAL ASSIGNMENTS... TAKE NO PRISONERS...**

Turning off the computer, the professor opens a large cabinet and removes two high-energy, charged proton laser rifles, each armed with a missile. He hands one to Trikan and the other to Cen-Ton. "Remove your blast cartridges from your weapons; I don't want those robots destroyed; I need the devices that they are wearing; they can be a great asset to us! The fusion fire from your weapons will be adequate to disable them."

Trikan then says, "Wish us luck, Professor!"

The professor replies, "Be careful, Captain!"

Trikan and Cen-Ton leave the professor's lab and are on their way to what is left of the main tunnel complex that the war tanks indiscriminately destroyed. They find most of the main tunnels blocked by debris when Trikan checks his Dial-Date and gets no reading. "Cen-Ton, my Dial-Date is all clear; are you picking up anything?"

Cen-Ton replies, "...NO, CAPTAIN...I AM NOT PICKING UP ANY ABNORMAL READINGS..."

In a low voice, Trikan says, "That's not good."

As he rechecks his Dial-Date for area surveillance, he receives a negative indication of any movement of the flight war tanks. He then says, "Cen-Ton, that's it! No movement, no sound! They're not going to be able to walk through all that debris in the tunnel without giving their position away. That's when we fire full-blast radius degrees and immobilize the sentry robots. Cen-Ton, I'm going to need your help. When they attempt to enter the main cavern, you will already have your weapon adjusted to fire in an octagon-field radius, a five-hundred-yard sequence distance downfield, and use your full-charge firing blast. When they are in position, whether they are invisible or not, we'll fire and immobilize them!"

Turning towards the captain, Cen-Ton reports, "... CAPTAIN... MY SENSORS HAVE GIVEN ME THE INFORMATION THAT WAS NOT AVAILABLE BEFORE... THAT THE IMAGE WE RECEIVED IS, IN FACT, AN INVISIBILITY DEVICE... A DISPLAY SCREEN THAT FORMS IN FRONT OF THE SUBJECT MATTER CONTAINS ATOMIC PARTICLES OF HIGH ENERGY... FORMING A HOLOGRAPHIC IMAGERY OF THE BACKGROUND STRUCTURE OF THE CRATER WALLS AND MOVING WITH THE SUBJECT'S ENERGY WAVES... THEREBY CONCEALING THE WAR TANKS AS WELL AS THE MOVEMENT OF THE SENTRY ASSAULT TROOPS..." Trikan adds, "I hear them! Full radius, Cen-Ton, and FIRE!"

The blast from their proton laser rifles travels down the tunnels in a whirlwind of antimagnetic energy, immobilizing the sentry robots. Looking into the dark tunnel, Trikan shouts, "Fire Again, Cen-Ton!" The high-intensity blast ignites the interior of the cavern walls as the energy field breaks forth in a destructive force out of the mountain.

The explosive energy strikes the sentry robots again, depriving them of their electromagnetic power and placing them in a frozen vortex energy field. In an instant, the energy of the invisibility shield dissipates for a moment, and it allows Trikan and Cen-Ton to see the war tanks for the first time without their invisibility shielding.

As Trikan and Cen-Ton walk up to the cave entrance, they see the sentry robots in an animated state. Trikan removes their Dial-Date arm computers, and he notices a circular magnetic disc attached to the arm computer's subatomic nano processors. He then says, "Take their weapons, Cen-Ton; they won't need them anymore."

On the way back to the lab, Trikans' thoughts remain as confident as they can be in his mission to free Elisa with the help he is receiving.

As the captain and Cen-Ton return to the professor's lab with the invisibility devices, the professor is overcome by the captain's accomplishments. His plan had worked perfectly, and the return of Trikan and Cen-Ton was living proof of the success against the sentry robots.

The professor says to Trikan, "Excellent, Captain! Now we must prepare to leave the safe zone!" He then instructs his robot, "Cen-Ton, to pack up as many supplies as he can and prepare for our journey to help the captain escape to Trikinia. For now, that is the only safe place for him." Trikan then says, "Hey, professor, look at this!"

As he removes the circular magnetic disc he took from the sentry robot's arm computer, he places it onto his computer Dial-Date.

He then asks, "Professor, what do you think of this thing?" The professor, who was talking to Cen-Ton, turns around to acknowledge the captain and does not see him. "Captain, where are you?"

"I'm standing right in front of you, professor."

"I can hear you, captain, but I can't see you."

For some reason, Trikan does not remove the disc; he slightly rotates it and then reappears. The professor is lost for words. "So, that is how it works! For a long time, it was just a rumor: an invisibility device that could render someone unseen without the need for heavy armor plate shielding. A long time ago, I was part of the governmental team developing such a device, which is to say, before my services were no longer needed."

The professor then instructs Cen-Ton to help him, and the captain puts on the heat-resistant, ambient-protection suit. Again, he tells the captain, "Without these suits, we will not be able to pass the volcanic magma that's active in a large section of the caverns that we must travel through. By no means should any part of our body be exposed, and we must breathe pure silicate oxygen through our helmets' masks, and as you know, captain, an active volcano—" Trikan finishes his statement, "... produces poisonous gases. Yes, professor, I know!" The professor smiles. "I see that you have knowledge of volcanology!"

Upon leaving the lab, Trikan looks back for a moment in the direction of the destroyed sentry robots. The distance is too far from the lab for the captain to see anything unusual that may have manifested itself in the incident of the sentry robot's destruction. The moment of distraction is just a human reflex that warriors experience and is passed down from their forefathers' ancient past. A bloodline that remains strong with a family of warriors that Trikan will always carry within him.

Trikan, Professor Zola, and Cen-Ton travel down a walkway that leads to a world of natural subterranean creations. Their journey will take them through slippery, wet natural corridors formed by the impact of a celestial body eons ago. The mysteries of nature have created a world beneath the surface of this giant planet where life forms live in an eternal midnight of time. Their only life source is their pools of corrosive magma, as these serpent-type creatures have never experienced the light of the outside world. Giant stalagmites create barriers of creature-type shadows as they continue on their journey; spectrums of light appear from the burning magma and fade within the chambers of the world around them. In a low voice, the captain asks, "How are you holding up, professor?"

"Just fine, Captain. I seem to have developed an abhorrence for the shrieking sounds that these cave creatures make before diving into the lava pools. I have never gotten used to them!"

"I agree with you, professor. What would happen if we were bitten by one of them?"

The professor stops walking for a moment. "Captain, I neglected to tell you that these serpent creatures are highly poisonous! If we lose our source of light, we will be dead in a matter of seconds. They usually attack in groups!"

Trikans' handheld laser lanterns' powerful light source deflects upon the hypersensitive serpent creatures, and they immediately submerge themselves in the lower depths of the corrosive lava pools. "Thank you for telling me now, Professor!"

The professor replies, "It wasn't necessary to tell you back there, Captain. There was no other way to reach the abandoned Trikinian airbase."

As they continue their journey, they encounter an underground world of ghostly shadows and illuminated reflections of colorful, winged cave insects that feed on vines that nurture their existence. The maze of tunnels leads them into a world of ice-covered stalagmites and into part of an old, abandoned underground city. Looking at his arm computer, the professor reveals to Trikan, "Captain, several sentry war troops from a second patrol group have entered and destroyed my lab quarters. Something that they enjoy doing when they fail at what should have been a simple mission: to take you captive! Am I correct, Cen-Ton?"

Cen-Ton responds, "...THE PROFESSOR IS CORRECT, CAPTAIN... MY TOPOGRAPHIC SENSORS CONFIRM THE LAB QUARTERS ARE IN A STATE OF DESTRUCTION..."

The captain turns back towards the professor for a moment and asks, "Are we still undetected?"

The professor replies, "Yes, for the time being. Let us keep moving along." Just before nightfall, they exit the hot caverns of the volcano, and the cool air is a refreshing relief from the high temperatures that Trikan and the professor experienced in the caverns.

The sky above the crater has now given way to the radiant moon and the infinite concert of endless stars. Trikan looks up at the stars as the moonlight reflects off the dark cavern walls, setting forth a surge of light across the fields before them. As they continue their journey to the northern mountain region, Trikan turns to the professor, who has been lagging since they left the caverns. "Professor, are you alright?"

"Captain, I can't go any further... I must STOP!"

"Very well, professor, then we will stop here and set up camp." Dropping his bag, the professor falls to the ground alongside it and gives an exhausted sigh of relief. The captain relinquishes his backpack and also drops next to the exhausted professor. "Well, professor, we made it!" The professor replies, "Indeed, we did, Captain!"

"I guess this is where we are going to make camp, Professor?"

"You're a reasonable man, Captain, and your perception is excellent! You don't have to be told that I am exhausted. Cen-Ton, would you please set up the tent?"

"...YES, PROFESSOR... I WILL SET UP THE TENT IMMEDIATELY..."

Looking at the professor, Trikan opens his supply pack. "Here, professor, eat some of this." Trikan hands the professor a sealed package of military-issued, genetically designed field rations. Tearing open the package, the hungry professor quickly consumes the contents. "This stuff is very tasty, Captain. What is it?"

Smiling, the captain replies as he continues to eat the genetically altered food. "I don't know, professor, it's something I picked up back at the rainforest from the survival flightcraft. But you're right, it is tasty!" The professor stops chewing and stares at Trikan. "The RAINFOREST?" Trikan then smiles as he looks over and notices the professor's eyes are closed. "Professor, are you falling asleep?"

"Yes, Captain, I am very tired. If you don't mind, keep talking, and I will engage you in a conversation to the best of my ability when I wake up."

Trikan looks up at the tranquility of the night sky and observes the stars of the winter night solstice. "Hey, professor, what type of life forms do you think live out there, past the two outer planets?"

The professor's eyes open. "I don't know, captain... Perhaps very different than ours." Silent for a moment, Trikan asks again, "Is that the opinion of a scientist? Or just your personal feelings?" As the professor sits up, he says, "The origin of creation and the natural state of existence are the wonders of creative life. It's out there, captain, somewhere amongst those stars, hidden away for some adventurer who's willing to travel the great adventure to discover it."

Trikan smiles as the professor closes his eyes. "Good night, professor; good night, Cen Ton."

Cen-Ton stands guard all through the night until the first event of sunrise. His sensory eye receptors transfer the early morning sunlight into thought waves through the process of reverse tri-conical lens color patterns. Due to his target-tracking brain sensors, the light-color shapes are transferred into artificial synaptic circuits. Cen-Ton awakens from a program of standing guard all night to a day-functioning robot and the morning sounds of scavenger ravens that echo across the mountain range. As Cen-Ton receives the sounds of the morning call from these predatory wild creatures, he turns his head and pauses for a moment. Another sound catches his attention: the sound of hydrocopters.

Turning towards his two sleeping companions, he calls out to awaken them, "... CAPTAIN TRIKAN...PROFESSOR ZOLA...!" In urgency, he calls out again, "...CAPTAIN...!"

His second call to Trikan awakens him, and in an instant, he reacts, shouting, "Cen-Ton, what is it?"

The alarmed exchange awakens the professor as Cen-Ton responds, "...HYDRO-FLIGHTCRAFTS, CAPTAIN...! MY SENSORY RADAR RECEPTORS CALCULATE THAT THEY ARE EIGHTEEN KILOMETERS AWAY IN-FLIGHT FORMATION...!"

"Good job, Cen-Ton! Well, professor, we have a choice. The nearest cave entrance is about fifty yards away. Shall we take it, professor, or do you have a preference for another location?"

"Just a minute, captain. That is precisely why I chose to make camp here! We are right outside the entrance to our journey. Once inside, we will find an old, abandoned Trikinian air dome. We will wait there until we are rescued."

Inside the cave, the interconnecting structures are inundated with huge stalactites hanging from heights within the northern mountain range. Their journey takes them deeper into the caverns, where they encounter rivers of cold, fresh streams of water. Suddenly, Cen-Ton alerts them, "... PROFESSOR... MY SENSES HAVE INDICATED THAT THE LEAD HYDROCRAFT HAS JUST LANDED..."

"Thank you, Cen-Ton."

Suddenly, the professor loses his footing on the ice and is about to fall off the permafrost ledge when Trikan quickly pulls him back onto level ground.

"Careful, Professor! We don't want to lose you!"

"Thank you, Captain."

Checking his Dial-Date, the captain observes the seismograph reading. "Cen-Ton's right, professor, they haven't given up!"

All of a sudden, the tranquility of their journey is interrupted by a massive explosion outside the northern caverns. The ground shakes with the echoing rumble of the huge stalactites crashing down throughout the elevated sections of the tunnels.

Trikan then states, "Well, that's no surprise, Professor!"

"They want to let you know that they are here, Captain, and they intend to capture you!"

The captain looks at the professor and remarks, "We're not going to let that happen, right, Professor?"

Smiling, the professor replies, "Not at all, Captain; however, we can't stay here; it's not going to take very long for those assault robots to catch up to us. We must keep moving, Captain."

Trikan then says, "Professor, you and Cen-Ton go ahead; I'll catch up with you after I take care of these sentry robots! They are too close, professor; they must be destroyed!"

After the professor and Cen-Ton leave, Trikan waits until the assault robots are halfway from his location. As they approach the middle ground, he fires at the ceiling structure, which is composed of a thousand years of permafrost ice, timber, and stone debris as it closes the entire length of the tunnel under the mountain, destroying the sentry robots. After a short period of silence, the hydro crafts can be heard at a distance as the sentry robot enforcement team leaves.

Trikan makes contact with the professor, "Take a break, professor, let me catch up with you and Cen-Ton."

"Captain, it's so nice to hear from you! What about our company?"

"They're all gone, professor. Now, let me catch up to you!"

When Captain Trikan arrives, he sees the professor looking at a large stone statue of a warrior clad in battle armor. Trikan walks up to the professor and asks, "What do you make of this, professor? Is this a statue of a Trikinian Warrior?"

"It's not Trikinian, Captain! The war armor and the helmet are far too advanced for their culture!"

Trikan wipes away the accumulation of snow and ice from the base of the statue, revealing ancient inscriptions carved in stone.

For several moments, Trikan remains silent and then says, "Professor, I'm going to need some help here."

The professor takes a closer look at the statue's base. "This is an ancient language, Captain!"

With his Dial-Date, the professor scans the symbols into his relay decoder screen, and suddenly an indicator alert appears on his Dial-Date as Trikan asks, "If he's a warrior, professor, where are his weapons?"

The professor remains silent for a moment, looking up at the statue. "That's very observant of you, Captain. There are no weapons."

Suddenly, the statue begins to move forward, revealing a large entrance archway behind it. Trikan steps back as sheets of ice and ancient sections of permafrost break away from the archway opening, revealing the open chamber. He then hesitates for a moment as he remarks, "Professor, look at this place."

As he continues, dim ancient fluorescent lighting becomes activated as he walks into a large circular structure with a vaulted ceiling. Trikan is unable to identify his surroundings at first due to the structure's massive size. He shines his handheld spectra-light-scope up into the dark, domed chamber, and the light fails to reach the height of the construction.

As the professor follows Trikan into what was thought to be a simple chamber, he finds walled compartments filled with books and ancient scrolls. As he shines his handheld spectra light along the interior, he remarks to Trikan, "Magnificent! Absolutely Magnificent! A place of learning and ancient wisdom! Cen-Ton, can you tell me the age of this cavern?"

"...YES, PROFESSOR... ONE MOMENT PLEASE... I AM SORRY, PROFESSOR... I AM UNABLE TO GIVE YOU A SPECIFIC DATE SINCE THERE ARE NO EXISTING RECORDS..."

There is a pause before Cen-Ton continues, "...PROFESSOR... MY CALCULATIONS HAVE CHANGED... BY MY BEST ESTIMATE... THE AGE OF THIS STRUCTURE IS REGISTERED IN ORBITAL SPACE-TIME SEQUENCES SEVERAL THOUSAND

YEARS BY THE AGE OF OUR PLANET..."

Upon examining several manuscripts, the professor becomes focused on an ancient language that has never been spoken in his lifetime. His Dial-Date computer could instantly translate the ancient language. The particular scroll that attracted the professor's interest was labeled in bold letters: **ACROMENTI**. As he opens the scrolls, he reads some of the titles silently, and then in a low voice, he reads one particular title that strikes his attention: **"DEEP SPACE OPTICAL TRANSFER WAVES OF LIFE- CONTAINING PLANETS."**

He begins to read a specific part of the document to Trikan: *"Life-bearing systems of magnetic fields of Life-Force energy... Reference Point Acromenti."* Trikan asks, "What did you say, professor?"

The professor looks up from the scroll. "Yes, Acromenti, Captain!"

Trikan curiously asks again, "What's Acromenti?"

The professor explains, "It means life forms in other star systems, Captain; we're not alone! The rest pertains to the operations of a starship that traveled through a four-dimensional space-time continuum and carried passengers to the four mentioned star systems and then landed somewhere in the Trikinian mountains."

Their conversation is interrupted by Cen-Ton. "... CAPTAIN... PROFESSOR... I AM PICKING UP A LIFE FORCE IN THIS QUADRANT OF THE CAVERNS... IT EMANATES FROM OUR DESTINATION IN THE OLD HANGAR AREA..."

Placing the scrolls into his provisional travel bag, the professor states, "We'd best leave now! Captain, do you remember the code on the statue?"

Trikan acknowledges. "Yes! I do, professor."

"Very good, Captain!"

Upon exiting the chamber, Cen-Ton takes the lead with the professor following him down a long corridor that will take them to the underground flight hangar base. Captain Trikan stays behind for several moments and types in the entire ancient code into his Dial-Date. He will need more time to think about this secret place as he watches the giant statue move back, sealing the entrance and closing the portal atop the dome of this ancient structure, which has become a mystery of the past and an adventure into his future.

Trikan catches up with Cen-Ton and the professor, and they continue their journey until they arrive at the hidden air hangar within the mountain. The massive hangar complex contains an old air-flight personnel barracks and field office buildings that once served as the nerve center of operations for the enormous Trikinian Mountain Ranges. Now, it is used only during the stormy winter season by Trikinian personnel as an emergency flight rescue facility.

Trikan and Cen-Ton enter the vast hangar and find an eerie emptiness in the large quarters. "Cen-Ton, do you still have a clear reading on the intruder?"

Cen-Ton replies in his robotic voice, "...YES, CAPTAIN... I AM PICKING UP A LIFE FORCE ENTITY..."

The captain looks over at Cen-Ton. "Trikinian?"

"... NO, CAPTAIN... THE IDENTIFICATION READOUT OF BODY MASS DOES NOT COMPLY WITH TRIKINIAN... MY READINGS INDICATE THE INTRUDER CARRIES A SIDEARM LASER WEAPON..."

Smiling slightly, Trikan replies, "Thank you, Cen-Ton. Now, let's get into the unit quarters and find out who this intruder is."

Trikan and the robot enter a large barracks facility and quietly walk through the sleeping quarters. Row after row of empty bunks, unused since the facility's closure, tell a story from long ago, when many pilots could be heard discussing their flight assignments.

Down the long corridor of the barracks, Trikan and Cen-Ton can see lights and hear running water in the clean-up shower area. They follow the sound of the running water as Trikan sets his laser weapon on a low fire setting, not to kill but to render the intruder unconscious. An intense light blast from this setting will momentarily immobilize the intruder in a field of bright, glowing energy, enabling Trikan and the robot to subdue him quickly.

As Trikan enters the shower facility unit, he observes a typical area with mirrored cabinets above each wash-up fixture. This allows the intruder, who has just finished shaving, to become aware of a spectrum in the kaleidoscope of mirrors that is not his reflection. He tries to hide the tensions that run through his mind as he slowly turns to give the impression that he is not yet aware of Captain Trikans' presence.

The intruder continues to dry off and places the towel on the counter near a chair with his scout field military jacket hanging over it, along with his weapon. Captain Trikan looks at several of the glass panels that reflect across the large shower facility and becomes convinced that this trooper knows of his presence.

Trikan waits for the trooper to make the final adjustments to his makeshift sling, which holds his left arm in a fixed position.

The trooper then makes a feeble attempt to reach for his laser weapon, which is holstered on his jacket. Captain Trikan breaks the silence, "Touch it, and you're dead!"

His commanding voice is more than enough to convince the trooper not to attempt his foolish action. Looking at the captain's reflection in the mirror, the trooper says, "Don't you remember me?

Captain Trikan, it's me-Larsen!"

Trikan hesitates for a moment. "Where do I know you from?"

The trooper replies, "I was part of the crew in the Rain Forest Operation... I was one of the guys in the backup helicopter!"

Trikan is still holding his laser weapon directly at the trooper. "Oh yeah... So, you were one of four hundred guys in a squadron assigned to the second hydrocopter operation. So, how am I supposed to know you? Do you think I remember everybody in the morning roll call before flight operations began? What are you doing here?"

The trooper remains silent as the professor enters the room and says, "Well, captain, who do we have here?"

Trikan directs his question to the trooper again, "I'll ask you one more time, what are you doing here?" The professor interjects, "It's his right not to answer you, Captain; he's wearing a military uniform."

"Yes, I know, professor, and it's his right to answer me as well!"

Before the professor can speak again, the trooper answers Trikan, "I'll tell you whatever you want to know, Captain."

"Okay, trooper... Your name and rank? Then, give me your best shot! I'll listen ONE TIME ONLY, and it better be good!"

"Okay, captain... I agree! I am Sergeant Larsen, in charge of computer communications. We were a support unit on the same flight operations in the rainforest when we were hit by a heavy downpour of rain and the lightning strikes as we entered the operational zone. You and your crew arrived early that morning at the control area ahead of us, and you were lucky enough to avoid the heavy downpour! After we were hit by lightning, we lost control and were ordered to put on our rocket pack flight suits."

Trikan continues, "Okay, then what happened?"

"The airship was damaged, and we couldn't keep up with you! Upon landing, we were rescued by your command hydrocopter, and you were not aboard!"

Trikan lowers his weapon. "That was a while ago. How did you wind up here?"

"After we got back to the airbase, I already knew that something was not right. Two of the injured air scouts were taken to the Air-Vac Rescue Facility. I was given medical attention for my arm injury back at the barracks. The rest of the crew was put into lockdown quarantine. They said it was for their protection."

Trikan asks, "Whom are we talking about?"

"The commanding officer, Captain."

"You mean to tell me that the company commander ordered you to be officially put into quarantine?"

"Yes, captain, something big was going on, and it had something to do with the mission." Trikan then asks, "What gave you that idea, Sergeant?"

"Well, Captain, it all started after we were rescued and were on our way back to the base. Your lieutenant colonel was angry that your guys sent down a life support unit! He spoke about it briefly and then dropped the subject! Your Flight Communications Officer, Jakens, wasn't feeling well and asked your Fleet Control Officer if he could be relieved. I was then ordered to take his place in operations, and on the way back to air fleet command, a transmission came to your ship's lieutenant major. The transmission didn't sound right to me. It was absent from military protocol and contained part of a conversation that had already taken place; it had nothing to do with flight command! This person identified himself as Superior Officer Lennox!"

"So, what was the message, Sergeant?"

Larsen hesitates momentarily before answering. "Word for word, captain. No specific orders were given, the message was brief, and it came over the com: 'Did you take care of it?' The lieutenant major's response was, 'It has been taken care of!' Then, a short time later, the communications officer was feeling better and returned to flight control, relieving me."

Trikan responds, "Okay, but that still doesn't answer my question. What was the message about?"

Larsen continues. "At the time, Captain, I had no idea what the transmission meant."

Turning to the professor, Trikan asks, "Professor, who is this Superior Officer Lennox?"

The professor replies, "He's more than a name, Captain! He's a code and a rank; he belongs to a secret social order called the Pteranodons. It's made up of governing council members, and no one knows how many belong. They have the power to eliminate anyone when given orders by military or political authority. The Pteranodon Society is a secretive organization that worships its own moral code. Other members of the government dare not speak a word of them, and in my opinion, the president of our government refuses to believe that they exist!"

"Was anything else said, Sergeant?"

"Yes, the lieutenant colonel said that you would not be coming back, Captain!"

"Did he say anything else?"

"Yes, Captain, he said to the lieutenant colonel, that he was very pleased with his performance on the assignment, and when he gets back to the base, he has another important assignment for him. Then the transmission ended. A few moments later, your communications officer felt better and returned to relieve me. I went back to the drop-off section of the ship and listened to some of your guys talking about what happened to you. About the fact that you would not have survived without the drop-off of the survival pod! When we arrived back at the base, everything seemed normal, and we were all in our barracks. After that, this quarantine order hit me. Then, everything that happened — communication with this guy, Lennox, and you being left down in the rainforest—it all made sense! There was something more going on than the mission!" Turning to the professor, Trikan asks, "Well, professor, what do you think?"

"I'm not surprised, Captain, that they want you out of the way!"

Agreeing, Trikan states, "I would say, more than out of the way, Professor! Did I mention to you that I was poisoned?"

Smiling, the professor responds, "Yes, and if I remember correctly, it left a bad taste in your mouth!" Trikan remains silent as he puts his laser weapon back into his side holster. "It did, professor, and it's still there! Well, lieutenant, what happened after the quarantine?"

The lieutenant continues, "The next morning, the first sergeant came in and told us that quarantine was over and to clean up and get over to the Mess Hall. They were celebrating a successful mission that marked the capture of all the escaped prisoners. I lagged behind, looking through my locker for a clean field jacket, and if it weren't for that delay, I would not be here. I would be in Central Detention with the rest of the guys! When I went over to the Mess Hall, they were all being led away to Central Detention by sentry robots. I was lucky to escape that night with the help of some friends from the Central Air Command base. I have been hiding in this old hangar ever since."

Turning to the professor, Trikan asks, "Then perhaps we would be safe here for a time, professor?"

The professor insists, "No, Captain! You must go to Trikinia with Cen-Ton! On the way there, you will drop off the sergeant with me in the safe zone; I have friends who will help us avoid being captured. However, I must warn you: when speaking to the Trikinians, choose your words carefully, as they tend to be suspicious of strangers. Their leader is called Alden, and he will help you! Give him this anagram message from me." The professor hands the captain a small, cryptic bronze computer disc.

Agreeing, Trikan replies, "Okay, professor... now let's see if we can get one of these old hydro-flightcrafts airborne if we are going to get to Trikinia before nightfall."

Turning to the sergeant, Trikan says, "You were a big help, sergeant... I owe you!"

The sergeant nods his head, "You're welcome, captain, as far as a flightcraft that is available, there's only one without damaged energy rods that, unfortunately, can only accommodate three passengers!" The professor interjects, "Then what will become of you, sergeant?"

"Don't worry about me, professor; I will stay here. I doubt that they will be looking for me in this old Trikinian air facility!"

The professor replies, "Yes, sergeant, perhaps you're right. Stay safe!"

The professor and Cen-Ton climb aboard the flightcraft as Trikan shouts above the turbo-lift engine noise to Larsen, "Thanks again for your help, Sergeant!"

Sergeant Larsen salutes and shouts back, "Anytime, Captain!"

As Larsen begins to close the hangar doors, he watches the flightcraft disappear into the star-lit night.

At the **Central Command Hospital Research Center**, a doctor walks into a patient's room and says, "Hello, Sergeant, I'm Doctor Anderson. How do you feel this morning?" Slowly opening his eyes, Larsen replies, "Do I know you?"

"Yes, you do, Sergeant. We have been friends for a long time; my name is Doctor Anderson." Remaining silent for a short period, Larsen opens his eyes and asks, "Where am I?"

Doctor Anderson doesn't answer him and asks, "Do you have any difficulty remembering me?" Larsen's eyes shift from left to right several times, and he then hesitates before answering, "No... where am I? Do I know you?"

Doctor Anderson moves closer to Larsen's examination table. "Yes, you do; I would like to ask you a question, Sergeant Larsen... can you tell me where our friend Captain Trikan is?"

He hesitates momentarily, then responds, "Mission..." Doctor Anderson replies, "That's very good, Larsen. Can you tell me about the mission?"

Larsen remains silent as the doctor continues to talk to him. "Your mission, Sergeant! Can you tell me where Captain Trikan is?"

Larsen hesitates again before he responds, "I can't remember. Is that called lost time, Doctor?" Larsen's eyes close and open again; while looking directly at Doctor Anderson, he asks, "Do I know you?"

Doctor Anderson replies, "No... that's not necessary."

Looking at the nurse, the doctor says, "Nurse, the sergeant is ready; take him into surgery; he is ready for the infusion memory implant transfer."

Chapter 10:

The Northern Fortress

The large Gantry Bay Doors begin to close onto the old military hangar as the flightcraft leaves the tarmac. In the blistering snowstorm that has been raging, the gantry bay doors are barely visible to the adventurous travelers who have escaped the danger of the Androidian military powers. As the gantry doors close, the young Sergeant Larsen steps back from the high winds and heavy snow accumulation, sealing the mountain cave.

Standing there for several moments, he wiped off the snow and ice that had quickly accumulated on his uniform and covered the surrounding gantry tarmac. As he had experienced the fury of a Trikinian winter for a short time, his thoughts of a successful mission for Trikan, Professor Zola, and the robot Cen-Ton will rest heavily on his mind.

Captain Trikan pilots the flightcraft three thousand miles through the stormy night to the clear skies of the next morning. Just before the flightcraft lands, a ground transport is waiting for Professor Zola. "There they are, Captain. They're waiting for me and right on time!"

Trikan looks at the surface surveillance dashboard and focuses on a large ground vehicle transport. Shouting over the engine noise, Trikan tells the professor, "It looks like a big reception party for you!"

"Yes, yes, captain, it was all prearranged."

The professor, now shouting over the landing engine noise beneath the craft, says, "Now remember, captain, be very careful with the Trikinians! They are very suspicious of anyone in uniform who's not Trikinian."

"Will do, Professor!"

"I will see you soon, Captain. Good luck!"

As the craft lands, the professor disembarks, steps away from the landing area, and waves back to Trikan. Trikan then says to Cen-Ton, "Next stop, Cen-Ton, the Trikinian Security Quadrant!"

The flightcraft continues heading north, and several hours pass before it enters Trikinian territory, where it is suddenly struck by a blast of fusion from an undisclosed location. The blast jolts the airship momentarily off course, and Cen-Ton informs the captain that they were hit by a military mobile flight drone that detected their flight signature.

Cen-Ton is about to notify the captain further when he is interrupted. "I know, Cen-Ton! They have us in their target range! We can expect to be hit again at any moment! I'm taking the flightcraft down to ground level, and we'll get some protection from the mountain range that we just flew over!"

With the landing of the flightcraft, Trikan orders Cen-Ton to eject the upper section, which disengages from the craft as the lower portion converts into a standard mobile tractor foil. Leaving the disengaged upper section, they travel a short distance with the tractor foil before several drones hit the flightcraft's domed shell again, destroying it. The technicians who operate the drones do not receive high-quality photo transmission. The absence of sun shields in this area prevents clear telescreen pictures from the operators at the **Android Drone Control War Base Headquarters**. The photos they contain identify destroyed sections of a flightcraft with blurred ground-level distortions. The debris field around the large area of the flightcraft gives the impression to the drone control commander that they have accomplished their mission and destroyed Captain Trikan.

After the destruction, the snowfields remain silent except for the constant turning of the snow cleats on their vertical axis, giving the tractor foil power to cross them on the rest of its journey into Trikinian territory. Trikan removes a vortex scope from a compartment inside the tractor foil and adjusts it to a distance of one thousand meters. He focuses on the windswept ridges that periodically cast powdered snow mounds across the ice-laden fields they will travel. "Cen-Ton, after dark, is this area safe to travel?"

Cen-Ton immediately replies, "... CAPTAIN... OUR PROJECTED COURSE WILL TAKE US TO THE GATES OF THE TRIKINIAN OUTPOST IN THE MOUNTAINS... OUR ARRIVAL IS APPROXIMATELY ONE HUNDRED NINETY-TWO SEQUENCE HOURS... THERE IS NO NEED TO WORRY ABOUT THE PREDATORY ICE MAMMOTHS... DO YOU SEE SOMETHING THAT CONCERNS YOU, CAPTAIN...?"

"Yes! There's a lot of them up there, on that ridge."

Trikan begins to count and says, "Forget it; there are too many of them to count! What did you say about predatory?"

"... CAPTAIN... I NEGLECTED TO INFORM YOU... IF I MAY CLARIFY... WHEN YOU FIRST ASKED ABOUT THEM... THEY ONLY FEED ON LARGE EGGS OF MIGRATING BIRDS THAT MAKE THEIR NESTS ON THE HIGH RIDGES... THERE IS NO NEED TO WORRY, CAPTAIN... HOWEVER... THEY ARE VERY TERRITORIAL..."

Trikan puts down the vortex scope, and as he zips up his heavy hooded snow jacket, he remarks in a low breath, "Large predatory mammoths feeding on bird eggs!"

"...CAPTAIN...DID YOU SAY SOMETHING..?"

"Yes, I have never been this cold in my entire life, Cen-Ton, and now, it's beginning to snow again!"

By nightfall, the Captain and Cen-Ton will have to travel past the Northern Fortress, as a report comes in at Android Drone Command, informing members of the Government Council that the flightcraft and its passengers have been destroyed. The cold columns of Banishean steel reach upward into the dark shadows that conceal **Scout Battle Arm Security Complex Control**.

    This pantheon-designed fortress in the Northern Defense Base near the Trikinian Territory accommodates a strike force that needs no explanation for a mission of destruction. Equipped with a unit of heavily armed warriors trained to attack immediately and annihilate their enemy. This fortification controls the Northern Frontier, and beyond its elevated heights, in the cold spectrum of mysteries lie the Trikinian Mountains with their hidden secrets. This war command fortress is an enigma, manned by disobedient scout troops that have violated their code of conduct, ranging from serious breaches to minor infractions of military protocol. Rather than accept prison time, they were allowed to spend most of their lives, depending on their sentences, in this cold fortress of constant winter storms.

    The fortress troops change posts without much as a spoken word as they routinely go about their duties, while the cold winds of Trikinia echo throughout the complex. Rumor has it that the giant granite blocks that support the enormous Banishean columns allow shadows of the past to enter, as if life has been given back to lost warriors who fell in battle against adversaries that still exist in the cosmos of space. Now, their spirits are lost, and they must return to this fortress and endure the many winters of their past.

    The cold winds of the constant snowstorms unite their allegiance in many ways, not to their government but to their very existence. They depend upon one another to survive in this cold, forsaken fortress and complete their mission of eternal damnation.

Cen-Ton picks up a signal. "... CAPTAIN... I HAVE JUST BEEN STRUCK BY A FINDER WAVE... FROM AN ELECTRONIC PROBE... IT IS A DEVICE THAT SENDS OUT A DEMOGRAPHIC DESIGN OF CHANGING DIMENSIONAL TRANSPORTERS..."

Trikan immediately asks, "Cen-Ton, have we been identified?"

"... YOU HAVEN'T BEEN, CAPTAIN... YOU DO NOT HAVE THE ELECTRONIC CIRCUITRY... AS YOU ARE AWARE... I POSSESS THE MULTITUDE OF TRANS-ELECTRONIC CIRCUITS... IF THEIR PROBE DIRECTION FINDER IS FUNCTIONING PROPERLY... THEY WILL SEE THE TRACTOR FOIL AS AN ELECTRONIC BLUEPRINT SIGNATURE WITH A ROBOT AT THE CONTROLS..."

"So, what you're saying, Cen-Ton, is that they know a robot is operating this tractor foil?"

"...YES, CAPTAIN..." Trikan then asks, "Cen-Ton, have you ever referred to yourself as a robot before?"

Cen-Ton looks away from the dashboard screen towards the captain. "... NO... SHOULD I HAVE CAPTAIN...?"

Trikan smiles as Cen-Ton says, "I ADMIRE YOUR SENSE OF HUMOR, CAPTAIN... EVEN THOUGH I DON'T QUITE UNDERSTAND IT..?"

After a short pause, Cen-Ton continues, "...CAPTAIN...THE SIGNAL IS GETTING STRONGER... IT WILL NOT BE LONG BEFORE THEY SEND OUT A SENTRY SCOUT SQUAD WITH BATTLE FORCE ARMS..."

"Cen-Ton, I'm stopping the tractor foil! Turn all components off and let them come and find us!" Trikan gets off the tractor foil and takes some of the provisions he will need, including removing the vortex scope from the storage compartment. "Cen-Ton, can you receive their signal probe and tell me if they have left the fortress?"

"... I WAS JUST ABOUT TO INFORM YOU, CAPTAIN... MY READOUTS HAVE IDENTIFIED A LARGE HOVERCRAFT THAT HAS JUST DEPARTED THE FORTRESS...IT'S HEADING FOR THEIR SIGNAL RELAY PROBE..."

"That's us, Cen-Ton! Activate your invisibility disc unit."

"...AFFIRMATIVE...!"

The Captain and Cen-Ton become invisible as Cen-Ton asks, "...WHAT IS YOUR PLAN, CAPTAIN...?

"We're going to walk toward the finder beam, Cen-Ton."

"...CAPTAIN... I DID NOT HEAR YOU CORRECTLY...?"

Trikan raises his voice over the high-velocity winds of the snowstorm. "Do you hear me now? We're going to take that hovercraft from those scout troops! When they disembark, they'll be following military caution protocol! They will stay several hundred yards from their target, and if we're lucky, they won't leave anyone behind, making it much easier for us to take the craft without using force. Do you like my plan, Cen-Ton?"

"...YES, CAPTAIN... IF ALL GOES WELL...WE WILL THEN CONTINUE ON OUR PLANNED JOURNEY TO TRIKINIA..."

Trikan agrees, "Very good, Cen-Ton; we'll keep to a wide area, allowing the troops to pass between us as we approach the warcraft. The scout troops will not be able to see us and will walk right past us!" Trikan and Cen-Ton's foot-tracks in the deep snow disappear instantly, as well as the trail of the warcraft that has departed from the sentry fortress due to the high snowstorm winds.

Large steel hatch covers are forcefully opened, allowing the disembarking war troops to enter the fierce, frozen world of the Trikinian mountain region. They immediately push forward in their assigned mission, wearing heavy-laden winter gear and carrying photon laser weapons.

The storm's effects are immediate, as some troops fall into deep snowdrifts and struggle to regain their footing while continuing their mission. When the squad finally reaches the abandoned tractor-foil, they receive a readout and classification of what they observed—an old, outdated military war vehicle that was constructed and discontinued long ago.

The war-unit commander removes his winter protective mask from his helmet visor, and his second-in-command shouts, "It's Trikinian! How did this get here? It was not here when we last made our patrols of this quadrant zone!"

The war-unit commander shouts over the storm, "The high mountains! It must have been up there a long time. This is an antique tractor foil! It has happened before in the deep snow of the glaciers on those mountains; snowstorms have been known to take down flightcraft and freeze life forms that have been abandoned and buried in those high ridges. This quadrant has experienced numerous incidents of avalanches, and this tractor foil was likely brought down by one of those storms. The high winds carried it across the open fields of the frozen lakes. My opinion is that we leave it where it is and get back to the fort before these high winds carry us away with this tractor foil! We'll come back when the storm ends!"

"What about the robot we identified on the tractor, Commander?"

"Don't worry about it; he's probably buried under a ton of snow by now! Before the storm is over, it will probably be carried into the next quadrant by then. Let the Trikinians figure out how it got there! Let's get back to the fortress!"

Trikan takes control of the scout troop's war tank and engages the low-octane fusion engines, which shift into an elevation mode. As the craft lifts, its engines automatically convert into a military attack hovercraft. Its aft engines ignite as it turns one hundred and eighty degrees, sending the craft on a projected course north to the Trikinian military territory at a flight speed of six hundred miles per hour. Its heading will constantly lift the tank five hundred feet above the topographic snowfields.

With the coming of the sunrise in the morning, Trikan rubs his eyes as he approaches the control command station with Cen-Ton at the helm. For a moment, the bright morning sunlight prevents Trikan from reading the dashboard instruments, which show how far they still have to travel before entering the Trikinian field base. "How far out are we from our projected arrival time, Cen-Ton?"

"...ONE AND ONE-QUARTER SEQUENCE, CAPTAIN...UNTIL OUR PROJECTED ARRIVAL TIME..."

"Good... Then I have time for some breakfast."

Turning to a military provision computer, Trikan types in a basic breakfast order and receives a cup of berry juice and a high-protein breakfast biscuit. As Trikan looks out at the snowfields and the bright sunny morning, he remarks to Cen-Ton, "Big difference from the night before, Cen-Ton."

"... IF YOU ARE REFERRING TO THE SNOWSTORM, CAPTAIN... I AGREE..."

Trikan looks over at Cen-Ton with a smile. "I wasn't referring to the snowstorm, Cen-Ton, I was referring to the fortress!"

A short time later, the warcraft enters the Trikinian restricted zone and loses all power and its technical systems, including its navigational ability. Concerned, Trikan says, "NOW WHAT?" He immediately tries to switch to the craft's auxiliary power grid, but there is no response. A magnetic course finder beam locks onto the warcraft, and after shutting down all of its navigational electronics, it takes the craft down to a soft landing. After reaching the control screen, Trikan types various command prompts with no success. Trikan and Cen-Ton remain silent for several moments. Then a communication response comes over the control view screen: "**...YOUR CRAFT IS IN A LOCKDOWN MODE FOR VIOLATION OF ENTRANCE INTO A TRIKINIAN RESTRICTED ZONE...**"

The transmission repeats several times before the screen goes offline. Cen-Ton responds, "...WHAT IS YOUR PLAN, CAPTAIN...?"

"I guess we'll have to put on our snow boots and start walking!"

Trikan and Cen-Ton have to lift the large, heavy side exit hatch, which is not easy because the ship's hydraulic system is malfunctioning. None of the backup systems can operate without the information transfer directed by the ship's computer. Trikan takes an emergency fire mallet and strikes the large steel pins several times, knocking them out and releasing the cylinders. This allows Cen-Ton and the Captain to lift the heavy steel exit hatch open, as Trikan pauses for several moments to take in the view of the bright, sunny morning.

A multitude of giant pine trees hid the magnificent snow-covered fields and sheltered gorges from deep within the valleys to the heights of the Trikinian mountain summits. Captain Trikan takes in the clean, fresh air for a moment, and his thoughts turn to a time in his life when he would go out onto the snowfields on a clear, sunny morning with his pet, Pup, and his hydro sled. He would pretend it was not just a snow sled but a flightcraft that would take him to other worlds. "...CAPTAIN..." Not answering immediately, Trikan asks, "What did you say, Cen-Ton?"

"...CAPTAIN...WE SHOULD CONTINUE ON OUR JOURNEY IF WE ARE TO REACH THE TRIKINIAN OUTPOST BEFORE NIGHTFALL..."

Still somewhat distracted, Trikan replies, "Yes, Cen-Ton, of course, you're right!"

The Captain and Cen-Ton remove their gear from the craft and begin their long journey toward the Trikinian mountain outpost across the snowfields. Suddenly, they are besieged by the sounds of wild animals and come to a sudden halt. In a low voice, Cen-Ton tells the captain, "...THIS AREA CONTAINS MANY WILD ICE MARTINMUS PREDATORS... BUT JUDGING BY THEIR SOUNDS, THEY ARE A GOOD DISTANCE AWAY..."

Looking through his binocular vortex scope, he says, "Yes, they are on the outer ridge, and I could make out the Trikinian outpost!"

By late afternoon, they reach the outer ridge of Trikinian Base Squadron Command. Looking around, Trikan says, "Well, Cen-Ton, this looks like the best place to climb up past the ridge. Do you think the Trikinians are expecting us?"

"...YES, CAPTAIN... ACCORDING TO THE PROFESSOR'S INSTRUCTIONS..."

At that moment, a giant predatory beast appears on one of the ice-laden ridges, and the hairy creature leaps off the ledge toward Captain Trikan and Cen-Ton. Instantly, the beast is struck down by a crude phosphorus arrow-like weapon that explodes in midair. If it were not for the flash of the explosive light rays, the creature would hardly be noticeable because of its white fur, which perfectly blends into its snowy mountain background.

A huge marksman motioned to several of his companions to throw down rescue lines for the two climbers. As the Captain and Cen-

Ton grabbed hold of the lines, their ascent became less of a task as they climbed upward to the top of the snowy ledge.

Upon completing their climb to the top, Trikan turns to give Cen-Ton a hand and is suddenly grabbed from behind and thrown into a snowbank by two Trikinian warriors. Trikan struggles to be released and is informed by their commander that they are a prisoner under the terms of the Trikinian Treaty. The female commander tells him again, "You have violated sacred territory, and as an uninvited guest, you will remain our prisoner!"

Twenty Trikinian nomad warriors now surround Trikan. The larger group holds up a set of shiny silver arm-cuff restrainers and dangles them while smiling directly at him. Trikan looks at the group and realizes there is no point in continuing the fight; he is outnumbered! He holds his arms out to the smiling Trikinian nomad warrior and says, "Alright, let's get this over with!"

One of the other Trikinian nomads attempts to put another set of arm-cuff restrainers onto the robot until Doria, the female tri-leader of the group, shouts out to him, "Not the Robot! He's no threat!"

A faint, distant rumble echoes across the vast valley. Before Captain Trikan can fully identify the sound, a large commercial passenger ship flies overhead, heading directly for Trikinia. The nomad warrior who put the arm restraints on Trikan now leads him down the side of the ice-laden, snow-covered ridge. Trikan is being taken to a Trikinian military mobile snow tractor. This large tractor will take the prisoners and the Trikinian snow troops back to the outpost.

On his way down the ridge, Trikan observes the ICE MARTINMUS that leaped off the ledge and remarks to the nomad warrior who is taking him to the craft, "Is the animal dead?"

The nomad warrior responds, "No! He's just lifeless from the blast! It will wake up and run off in a little while. If you don't cooperate, you will be at the bottom of the ridge with that MARTINMUS!"

Doria shouts to the big Trikinian, "Don't you talk to him like that! He is a captain in the Androidian Star Command! You know, we have a treaty with them! All prisoners have to be treated with RESPECT!"

Trikan looks at the rank leader and replies, "That's okay... No offense taken."

Tri-leader Doria tells Trikan, "We treat our enemies with respect!" Trikan then says, "Hey, wait! I'm not your enemy! I'm here to visit the outpost!"

She stops and stares at him. "Okay, then show me your visitor identification pass, and why weren't you on that commercial transport that just passed moments ago?"

Trikan stares back at her. "I don't have one!"

Smiling, she replies, "Then, you're my prisoner!" Trikan looks up at the sky, closes his eyes, and says, "Okay...I give up! Whatever you want me to be. Let's just get on with this!"

Doria orders her troops, "Take the captain and his robot to the outpost camp and see that he doesn't escape!" She then looks at Trikan and continues to smile at him.

At the helm of the large commercial transport, a young Trikinian lieutenant flight commander is conversing with the highly honored Trikinian General Brenton. "Lieutenant, I enjoy sitting up here at the helm with you! It brings me back to my younger years as a young cadet lieutenant a long time ago. Too long, in fact! Our flightships back then did not have what you have today! I'm not saying that you have it easy. Ah, yes, it is much the same as it has always been. We had our responsibility, just like you have yours today!"

The lieutenant responds, "I agree with you, General Benton, and may I add that your long career and what you have achieved inspire all of us!"

As the general glances out the high-tempered port shield glass, he replies, "Say, did I just see an Androidian War Tank down there?"

"Yes, general, I did not intend to interrupt you while you were talking. I did enter the incident of an officer and his robot walking away from their battlecraft into my main surveillance computer."

The lieutenant turns the mobile screen unit toward General Brenton and continues, "As you can see, the computer readout has acknowledged and confirmed that they have already dispatched a security patrol."

"Good work, Lieutenant!"

As General Brenton sits back in the copilot command com, he remarks, "What is an Androidian War Tank doing in our Trikinian quadrant?"

A moment later, a communication officer from the command patrol transmits a priority code to the outpost and the commercial transport via audio: "The Hydro-Foil Tank Is No Threat, and Our Patrol Is Presently Questioning Its Occupants."

After the large passenger ship lands within the confines of the Trikinian fortress facility, the passengers disembark and are greeted by the commander and his honor guard. These outpost troops are dressed in their battle arms regalia as they stand at attention in the windswept hydro-craft port landing field. The newly arrived passenger list includes personnel, dignitaries, and civilian subordinates who have been invited to the retirement ceremony of several Trikinian generals with distinguished careers. Most of these dignitaries have participated in this type of ceremony before and are greeted by old friends, except for one passenger. This was the first time Professor Zola would join the ceremonies and serve as a keynote speaker, as he could barely keep up with the disembarking passengers while preoccupied with a plan to make contact with Captain Trikan and his robot.

The professor enters the large lobby, and an adjunct officer walks up to the professor and asks, "May I help you, Professor Zola? May I take your bags up to your room after you register?"

"Why yes, thank you very much!"

The next day, preparations are proceeding at the Trikinian fortress facility for the ceremonial banquet in the restaurant lounge. The professor arrives early and is greeted by a security liaison officer: "Good afternoon, Professor Zola. May I escort you to your reserved table?"

"Yes, thank you."

As the professor is escorted into the dining room lounge to a comfortable seating arrangement, he begins reviewing parts of his speech for the ceremony honoring his old friend, General Brenton.

Just outside the dining lounge area in the large arched entranceway, a group of Trikinian scouts becomes the focus of an altercation. The security liaison officer tells the Trikinian scout leader that she must wait outside in the entrance hallway and allow the guest to enter the dining lounge. He will get back to her after he checks with the command security office.

Trikan then says, "Hey, wait a minute! I've been wearing these things since yesterday! Do you mind taking them off?"

Tri-leader Doria says, "How many times do I have to tell you they are NOT coming off until we know who you are!"

Looking into the dining lounge for the first time, Trikan says,

"Okay, you want to know who I am? Ask Professor Zola; look, there he is... He's sitting at that table over there!"

The security liaison officer says, "You say that you know the professor?"

Trikan replies, "YES!"

Doria interjects, "This isn't the first time he mentioned that."

The security officer then says, "If so, then why wasn't he on the passenger transport with the professor?"

Trikan insists, "Now, let me in there to speak to the professor, and this whole matter will be cleared up!"

At that moment, Professor Zola notices what is happening and contacts General Brenton on his security screen.

"General, are you aware of a commanding officer with Captain Trikan in the front lobby? From what I can see, Captain Trikan is being detained. Upon his arrival, he was supposed to be at a meeting with Alden. Can you please call the duty officer at the front lobby and let the captain come to my table?"

"Of course, professor, I will take care of it immediately!"

The duty officer instantly receives the General's message and tells tri-leader Doria, "I suggest we solve this whole thing right now! Take the captain to the professor's table, which is a direct order from General Brenton!"

Tri-leader Doria says, "Wait one moment..." She throws his flight vest over his handcuffs, and two troopers walk Trikan through the crowded restaurant to the professor's table. Professor Zola looks up at Trikan. "So, you finally arrived, Captain!"

Trikan lifts his hands, draped over his flight vest, and shows the professor the handcuffs. "They want you to identify me, professor."

The professor responds, "Oh, my goodness! Let him go! What is wrong with you? Who's in charge here?"

"I am! My name is Commander Doria."

"Oh, how nice, and where is my robot, Cen-Ton?"

Trikan quickly responds, "He's waiting for you in the lobby!" Looking directly at Commander Doria, Trikan adds,

"They didn't want that big, bad robot in here, Professor!"

The professor raises his voice, "This is insanity! Alden will hear of this!"

Trikan turns back to the scout commander and raises his arms to her, allowing her access to his handcuffs. He smiles at her and says, "I'm waiting!"

Patrons at the following table begin to notice the unusual altercation and discontinue their conversations as the scout commander lets out a sigh of exasperation. She says, "Okay, you Win, Captain!"

She releases his cuffs, and as Trikan rubs his wrists, he looks at the professor. "Thank you, professor, for this plan of yours is becoming increasingly complicated! That must mean it's a good plan; this way, no one would know your next move."

"Sit down, Trikan! Have a cup of tea and enjoy some excellent food."

He places a menu in front of him and asks Commander Doria, "Commander, would you care to join us?" As she sits down, Commander Doria thanks the professor for his courtesy. "Thank you, professor; I am sorry for the misunderstanding."

Looking at Trikan, she adds, "I had the fortunate pleasure of meeting the captain a short time ago, and I did not realize how famous he was. Half of Star Port City would like to collect the reward for him!"

The professor smiles. "Yes...but unfortunately, you'll have to wait in a very long line!"

Looking directly at Doria, Trikan remarks, "Well, you shouldn't have taken off the cuffs; next time, it's not going to be that easy putting them back on!"

Smiling, Doria replies, "Now I know why they call you Trikan!"

Trikan looks towards the professor. "Professor, what about Cen-Ton? Are you going to let them keep him?"

"Oh, right! Cen-Ton, where is he?" The professor turns his attention to the Trikinian scout leader and says, "Release Cen-Ton immediately and have him join us here!"

Commander Doria tells her subordinate Scout, "Well, just don't stand there! Go and tell the robot to come in!"

As she is about to leave, she states, "My work is done here, and again, professor and captain. I apologize for the misunderstanding."

With the scout commander's absence, the professor can now speak freely with Trikan. "Now tell me, what has happened that allowed you and Cen-Ton to be imprisoned?" Trikan interjects, "First, I want to ask you a question, Professor. How did you arrive here, at this outpost, before we did?"

"Well, Captain, civilian transportation is sometimes more efficient and is allowed by appointment to cross into the restricted Trikinian territories. I was just one of the many passengers scheduled to attend the General's retirement celebration."

Trikan asks, "So, you were aboard the transport that flew over the stalled hydrofoil tank?"

The professor nods. "Yes, Captain, I apologize for not being able to rescue you and Cen-Ton before the Trikinian troopers had taken you prisoner!"

Trikan would like to ask the professor several more questions, but realizes that the professor is paying more attention to the data readings on his computer screen.

The light emanating from the roaring heart of the Alphanian timber logs in the dining room adds a comforting, colorful design to the large stone fireplace. A waitress approaches the crowded tables, set up in a circular floor plan, and begins taking food and beverage orders. Now paying little attention to some of the data readings that were his primary interest moments ago, the professor picks up the food menu and concentrates on his choice of dinner as one of the waitresses approaches his table. "Welcome to Trikinia. May I take your order?"

Putting down his menu, the professor suggests, "Captain, you must try some of the lake trout specialties here. They go perfectly with a glass of berry wine. It would be an excellent choice!"

Trikan lowers his menu and smiles at the waitress. "Make those two lake trout specialties, and we'll have the berry wine." The waitress smiles and replies, "I'll bring the wine before dinner."

The professor and Trikan continue their cordial conversation, touching on what they have experienced since their first meeting. "Professor, I wish you would clarify some questions I have."

The professor smiles as he complies. "I will, Captain, when the time is right. I will explain everything, but not right now; our wine has just arrived."

As the waitress sets a decanter on the table, she pours the beverage into the glasses and politely apologizes for the interruption. "Excuse me, your food will be out momentarily."

As she leaves, Trikan continues a conversation with a completely different subject. "For a military outpost, I find the whole area very relaxed, professor."

"Well, Captain, it is a military outpost, which is true. However, many areas around this quadrant have various winter recreational activities. All you need is security clearance, and then you may come and stay at the many mountain lodges and enjoy the outdoor civilian activities, like two of the most popular: the Turbine sledding over the valley hills and skiing the mountain trails!"

"Excuse me, professor, captain."

As the waitresses place their dinner orders onto the decorative signature placemats, which identify the recreational activities at the civilian section of the resort, she replies, "Your lake trout specialties. Enjoy!"

One of Commander Doria's Trikinian guards interrupts the conversation. "Excuse me, professor. Your service robot has insisted that he would rather wait for you in the lobby and enjoy the large recreational activities on the telescreen. He said he would reunite with you on your way to your private quarters."

Acknowledging, the professor replies, "That will be just fine, thank you."

As the professor gives Cen-Ton a slight wave of acknowledgment, Cen-Ton responds similarly. The Trikinian guard, still present at the table, says, "Professor, I have been ordered to remind you and the captain, as well as all the other passengers that are taking the transport to Tundra—the capital city of Trikinia—that we will be leaving after breakfast, around noon, after the boarding passenger list is completed. Contact the facility superintendent if you require more information; his code identification is on your Dial-Date. Enjoy your stay in Trikinia."

The Trikinian guard leaves and continues informing the other dining room patrons. Just before their dinner is over, General Brenton arrives and makes his way through the crowded dining room to Professor Zola's table.

As he approaches the professor, he joyfully announces his name, "Professor Zola, it's good to see you! It's been a while!"

The professor discreetly responds, "It's my pleasure to be here, General, and a special honor to be one of the guest speakers!"

He then looks directly at Trikan and says, "Captain Trikan, I don't think you ever had the pleasure of meeting General Brenton?"

Trikan replies, "No, I never had the pleasure."

The general kindly smiles, "Please, don't stand up. So, you are Captain Trikan that everyone's talking about?" He laughs out loud. Well, you belong to us now! Please enjoy your dinner with Professor Zola, one of the smartest men on the planet! We go way back, Captain. The professor and I have been good friends for... oh, I can't tell you how long!"

Still in his jovial mood, General Brenton says to the professor, "Professor, I heard that you would give a little speech with the others tonight at my ceremony. Now, be kind to me, professor!"

Smiling, the professor replies, "I will mention your great service, compassion, and understanding of the freedoms we enjoy and why so many are indebted to your leadership, General Brenton." The general replies, "Thank you, professor."

Professor Zola adds, "Now, please sit down, general, and have a glass of wine with us!" Taking a seat across the table from the captain, the general asks, with a slight sense of humor, "Now, tell me, young officer, how did you manage to steal that Androidian war tank without being captured?"

Taking a sip of his berry wine, Trikan answers, "It was easy, General! The hard part was when they wanted it back."

General Brenton starts to laugh out loud again, causing some dinner guests at several tables to stop their conversations and glance over at the General's table. The general tells Trikan, "I can't tell you how many times I gave that same answer when I was a young officer. I heard about the incident: it violated our treaty!"

At that moment, an orderly approaches the table and hands the general a handheld message; as he reads it, he looks back at the orderly and says, "Thank you!" The General then turns his attention back to the professor and Trikan, "Now, if you both will excuse me. Professor, I'll see you in the ceremony hall, and captain, it has been a pleasure!"

"Same here, Sir, and congratulations!"

As the general leaves, the professor remarks, "Captain, if he didn't have to leave, he would have stayed and talked all night!" Smiling at the professor, Trikan acknowledges, "He's fond of you, professor. The two of you must have made a good team!" The professor agrees. "Yes, we did, a long time ago! Now, what did I do with that speech?"

Hastily looking through a folder, he exclaims, "He always does that to me! Listening to General Brenton, I completely forgot where I put my speech."

Trikan tells the professor, "It's right there, professor, in your vest pocket!"

"Thank you, Captain. I must leave you now before I'm late for the ceremony!"

As he is about to leave, Trikan adds, "I'll see you in the morning, professor, at the passenger terminal."

"Yes, of course, Captain."

Trikan remarks, "I'm sure Cen-Ton will remind you, professor." As he is walking away, the professor exclaims in a low voice, "He always does!"

Trikan could hear the professor's departing words and smiled to himself as the professor left the dining lounge.

Chapter 11:

Revelations

The passenger craft begins to accept boarding at the exact moment of the first sunrise sequence protocol. Abiding by no departure schedule, it will continue to receive its passengers whenever they arrive at their leisure. A scheduled format that will not depart for the capital city until the last passenger has casually entered the entrance platform, which is also used to load supplies and personal cargo containers.

The last to come aboard will be the captain's liaison officer and his staff, with a computer readout correctly cleared by terminal security before the airship departs on its non-scheduled flight. This is the typical way to travel by public transport in Trikinia when no scheduled events require a specific time to be at any given destination.

Trikan arrives at the flight terminal before Professor Zola and Cen-Ton in the morning and gets on one of the many food lines that lead to the prepared breakfast service units.

The morning food lines move slowly since the workers are still tired from the late hours of the night before, following the general's retirement party speech. Captain Trikan pays no attention to terminal information, occasionally broadcasting all departure schedules. These announcements are primarily for tourists who will depart on small craft for the mountain ski areas and for recreational activities featured in many ski lodges.

Like most passengers at the terminal, Captain Trikan is interested in purchasing a hearty breakfast before their departure. While looking up at the extensive menu display of breakfast selections, Trikan pays no attention to his surroundings. Suddenly, a familiar voice distracts him from the breakfast menu screen. "Hey, you, Captain!"

Trikan turns and looks past the line of patrons several yards in front of him and remarks, "Oh no! Not you again!"

Commander Doria responds to Trikan, "Are you following me?"

He answers her back. "If it leads me to the breakfast counter, then yes, I am!"

Several patrons in front of Trikan turn around and find his remark somewhat amusing. At the counter, Doria orders a modest breakfast assortment of juice, cereal, a wheat bun, and herbal tea for herself. For Trikan, she orders a double ski resort special, which consists of large wheat cakes, stuffed turnips, pellic-stalk eggs baked in cinnamon candy, honey shells, and a mug of hot honey rum.

As she leaves the counter, she turns and gently waves to Trikan, calling out to him, "Your breakfast is paid for, Captain! Just pick it up!"

She then makes her way to one of the circular seating sections and begins enjoying her breakfast. Unable to select his breakfast of choice and trying not to draw attention to himself again, Trikan walks up to the counter and removes the breakfast tray. He thanks the food attendant, and she replies, "Enjoy, Captain."

Captain Trikan makes his way through the now-crowded restaurant to Commander Doria's table. He places his tray down in front of the commander, sits, and remarks, "You have to be kidding? I can't eat all of this! And what is this stuff anyway?"

Doria smiles. "Eat it, captain! It's good for you. You'll have to get used to it; you're going to stay in Trikinia, and this is one of our favorite breakfasts!"

Looking at her, he asks, "Why didn't you order one for yourself?"

She looks at him and smiles again. "I'm not that hungry this morning. Now start eating before you make a scene."

Make a scene? And what was that back there when you called out, 'Are you following me?"

"Well, I needed to get your attention, Captain."

"That's a fine way of getting someone's attention!"

"Is your food good? Are you enjoying it, captain?"

"Yes, I'm enjoying it! Now tell me, what am I doing here with you? And don't tell me we are just having breakfast together."

"No, I won't, Captain, it's more than that! It's a lot more. It all started with your assignment in the rainforest. No one could change the circumstances, even for Elisa! Though she desperately tried to prevent her capture, you were persistent, and that's why you're here, Captain!"

Trikan remains silent for a moment, considering how she could know all of this. Doria continues, "It must have been something else."

He replies, "Yes, something was put into my water container before I touched down on the surface."

Acknowledging, she then questions, "Are you saying that someone tried to drug you? Or are you just using that as an excuse for running off with her?"

"Well, it almost worked... I drank it! It was poison!"

Curiously, Doria asks, "How did you survive, captain?"

"I would not have survived if it were not for Elisa. She saved my life!"

At that moment, a cheerful Professor Zola arrives for breakfast. "Well, well, good morning, Doria, and you too, captain! I can see the two of you are getting along quite well!"

Trikan smiles. "Good morning, Professor! You look well-rested."

"Ahh... Captain, I see you are enjoying the traditional Trikinian breakfast!"

"Yes, it was Commander Doria's recommendation, and it was a fine choice."

Smiling, Doria replies, "Thank you, Captain, I appreciate that!"

As the professor places his ledger carrier case on the table, he asks them, "Now, may I join you two wonderful friends?"

Doria invites the professor, "Of course, Professor! Please, sit down here by me."

"Well, this is very nice, and I must confess, a good night's sleep has left me with a list of priorities. That being said, breakfast as soon as possible, and here comes Cen-Ton with my order!" Cen-Ton places the breakfast tray on the table in front of the professor.

"... GOOD MORNING, COMMANDER DORIA... GOOD MORNING, CAPTAIN TRIKAN... PROFESSOR... CAPTAIN... DURING THE NIGHT HOURS... SEVERAL MILITARY DRONES WERE DESTROYED AS THEY ENTERED THE TRIKINIAN TERRITORY... THEY WERE THE SAME TYPE THAT DESTROYED OUR TRACTOR FOIL...." Trikan asks Doria, "Does this happen very often?"

"No, Captain, that is very unusual! They know that they can't get past our defenses, and I don't have an answer for you as to why they are doing this at this time. So, Captain, whatever happened to Elisa?" Professor Zola interjects, "Right now, we think she is in Star Port City."

Looking towards Trikan, he continues, "We have the best people working on it, but the authorities will not release any information on exactly where she is being held. I know what you're thinking, Captain, but there is nothing we can do right now."

A moment later, an announcement comes over the transport terminal's speakers: **"NOW BOARDING, ICE KINGDOM EXPRESS TRANSPORT TO CAPITAL CITY TUNDRA."**

Trikan gets up and says, "Thank you for breakfast, Commander! It was very enjoyable!"

Doria smiles as she extends her hand. "The pleasure was all mine, Captain!"

As he is about to leave, she asks, "Oh, Captain, I'm curious, how did you get the name Trikan?" Trikan smiles, "That is a long story; we'll share it some other time!"

She smiles. "Until then, be safe, Captain!"

Trikan, Professor Zola, and Cen-Ton board the transport, and as the last of the unscheduled passengers are on board, the vast ship begins to lift off its landing bay.

The transport's air-flight antigravity engines lifted this thirty-thousand-ton tourist-air-passenger ship above the tallest mountain range of the Trikinian Ice Quadrant.

Its long, sleek design will reach speeds that create a sonic distortion as it flies over the ice-laden snowy mountain regions. Inside the transport, there is no indication that the passengers are on a moving platform speeding over the planet's gravity due to the artificial aurora created by antimagnetic flight stability technology.

A Trikinian flight warrior, dressed in his traditional ancient war regalia, walks the aisles of the transport, handing out pamphlets that describe the ancient ruins of Trikinia, along with visitor accommodations in the Ice Kingdom. As he hands the brochures to the passengers, he repetitively says, "Welcome, Visitor!"

Handing one to the professor and another to Trikan, he stops and casually salutes the captain before continuing to the next passenger. Trikan looks through the visitor pamphlets describing the ancient city that was once called the Ice Kingdom and the antiquated training garrisons that protected it. The features and barracks conform to the quadrants of an earlier time when wind ships and glacier trading posts were prevalent in the glory days of the ancient empire.

A beacon indicator on all the telescreens throughout the ship signals an alert that the transport is slowing for a passenger drop-off.

The emergency drop-off signal disappears on the screens and is replaced by off-board ramp exterior cameras, which allow passengers to view the off-board parties as they leave the transport after landing. "Professor, they look like our uniformed scout troops."

Looking at the screen, the professor replies, "Why, yes, Captain, they're working with a detachment of Trikinian powerline technicians; it's a joint effort to install several towers for the new sun shields that will cover this area and parts of Star Port City. It's not often that you witness such cooperation, but the benefits of this project will help both sides by keeping the planet in the temperature range suitable for our environment."

After the last survey team leaves the ship, the transport takes off and continues on its scheduled flight. Trikan can now relax thanks to the professor's knowledge and explicit explanation of events not generally known to the public.

Trikan then asks, "Professor, why are you doing all this?"

The professor responds, "I beg your pardon, captain; what do you mean?"

"This whole rescue thing, Professor!"

"Rescue, Captain?"

"I gave the amulet to her sister when she took me to the Old City. She said that she helped me because of you!"

The professor says, "My good captain, I can't be responsible for every good deed that takes place in my name or by some nefarious mention about my name either."

"Yes, I understand, professor, but that doesn't explain why anyone would put their life in danger as you have done."

The professor remains silent as Trikan closes his eyes, sits back in his seat, and takes a comfortable position. He then turns his head slightly towards the professor and replies, "I owe you, professor."

A short time later, the transport approaches its destination. Trikan looks out the large transport's circular nautical-design port-view window and observes, for the first time, the capital city of Trikinia, with its beautiful landscape of snow-covered rolling hills and orchards of winter fruit, as well as an abundance of other types of produce.

Given the ordeal he has endured in the past, the pleasant surroundings have created a subdued, relaxed feeling in him this time. He has now set aside his anger and guilty feelings and can think clearly, as the strength of his will and the natural beauty he sees give him a breath of new life after a long task of endurance.

Thinking back to the beautiful Elisa that he reluctantly captured and allowed to be taken away by the military authorities has left him with a deep feeling of loneliness. The time they spend together remains frozen in his mind like the landscape below. He is now a fugitive, an outcast, looking down at the frozen slopes and windswept valleys that lead into the hidden trails of Trikinia's frozen landscapes.

Trikan observes the green and white rigid stems of purple, pink, and red blossoms that have broken through the orchard fields. The flowering plants become one with the spirit of the Trikinians and their memories of Elisa, allowing them to endure the harshness of nature's offerings and still survive. His thoughts return to the laughter, and the time they spent together gives him a warm sense of comfort, inspiring him to carry out his plan to free her and find a place where they can live their lives together, free from conflict and oppression.

As the transport reaches its final destination, it remains in a holding pattern, waiting for the airbase transport control landing clearance. Upon landing confirmation, the transport's massive magnetic gyrotron landing gears activate for a soft landing. Finally, the transport rests upon the vast tarmac in front of the main passenger-receiving center.

Dignitaries and a detachment of Trikinian Honor Guards await to greet the important ministers, including several Trikinian military officials who disembark with a multitude of civilian tourists. They are all greeted by a chorus of singers and the national Trikinian band playing the Trikinian anthem.

Luxury hydro coaches pull up for foreign government officials and are also available for pedestrian visitors. These transport coaches will travel and take the visitors to various resort accommodations. The officials will be taken to Trikinian government facilities, where they will be greeted by Trikinian government personnel.

Trikan and the professor are escorted into the terminal by a special security detachment, which takes them to a private office facility in the transport center. There, they will meet with a personal envoy representing Alden, who will arrange a time and place for them to

Formally meet the Trikinian leader the next day.

The envoy will also escort them to pre-arranged, private luxury accommodation at one of the major guest hotels, where they can relax and, if desired, receive a city tour with an official government security escort.

The dignitary suite comprises several large, luxurious rooms that typically accommodate very wealthy clients who prefer the high-priced accommodations and the privacy they offer. A valet escorts the professor and Trikan to their luxury suite as other attendants carry their travel luggage into the room. Immediately, they draw back the blinds while activating an array of multicolored ceiling chandeliers that contain photo cameras, which send three-dimensional holographic images to specific wall screens that receive them. The cameras capture three-dimensional scenes of the city and the outlined areas of its suburban provinces, including Trikinia, featuring hotel festivities and Trikinian holiday celebrations.

Early the next morning, Trikan and the professor prepare to meet Alden. Trikan knocks on the door to an adjacent room and calls out, "Professor, are you awake?"

"Just one moment, Captain!"

The professor slowly opens his door and says, "Good morning, Captain; please come in. I want your opinion on something. Cen-Ton and I are undecided about what I'm wearing to attend the meeting with Alden and his ambassadorial staff."

Trikan acknowledges the professor's attire to be perfect for the occasion and says, "You look perfect, Professor!" Looking at Cen-Ton, he asks, "Do you agree with me, Cen-Ton?" Cen-Ton replies to Trikan, "... THANK YOU, CAPTAIN... I HAVE BEEN TRYING TO CONVINCE PROFESSOR ZOLA THAT HE IS ADEQUATELY DRESSED FOR THE OCCASION..."

The professor then responds to Cen-Ton's remark, "Okay... You win, two against one! But I still hate this bow tie! Never liked them despite the occasion!"

Cen-Ton adds, "...I TRIED TO TELL HIM, CAPTAIN, THAT MOST OF THE DIPLOMATS WILL BE WEARING BOW TIES..."

Smiling, Trikan replies, "Well, Cen-Ton, I'm glad I'm not a diplomat! I don't care for bow ties myself!"

A short time later, they are greeted by official security emissaries of the Trikinian leader in the hotel lobby. Here, they will receive transportation that will take them across an elevated highway over the capital city to the Trikinian Mountains, commonly referred to as the *Ice Kingdom*.

The higher elevations of this snow-covered mountain range experience extreme weather conditions in the fall and winter seasons. The entire elevated highway that runs from the capital up through the mountains features heat-activated elements that prevent meteorological obstructions during the winter season's extreme climate.

After the dignitary vehicles travel on the entire expanse of the highway, they arrive at the main gates of the old historic castle in the late afternoon. Before entering the old fortress, they are greeted by Trikinian Mountain troop honor guards dressed in animal-skin garments that their forefathers traditionally wore. They stand at attention in the extreme cold and salute as the dignitaries' transports enter the castle's open gates.

As the guests leave their transports, they are greeted by ministers of the Trikinian government and escorted into the main ceremonial section of the castle. There, they will exchange personal greetings with Alden's officials, then be escorted into a large, traditionally furnished banquet hall prepared for several hundred dinner guests, including Professor Zola and Captain Trikan.

As the guests are led in, kitchen attendants prepare the dinner placements on the long, ornate table, which is fashioned from timber wood and lit by the decorative steel chandeliers that hang from the vaulted ceilings above the length of the banquet room. This large room features archways carved from Banishean stone, each containing a statue of a celebrated ancient Trikinian warrior. The guests are being led to their reserved seating, and Professor Zola steps back from the other guests as he takes a moment to speak with Trikan. "By the way, Captain, I will confidently tell you something that very few people know."

Looking at the professor, Trikan smiles. "You trust me that much, professor?"

"Why, of course, I do, captain, with my very existence! You see, Captain, we have a mission that is very important to me. My wife is Trikinian and is also a member of the Trikinian ruling council. I must keep that a secret to protect her from our government because she often travels to Star Port City to visit friends and attend official government meetings."

Upon entering the dining room, the professor tells Trikan, "Oh, there she is! I see that my wife has already arrived. Captain Trikan, may I introduce you to my lovely wife, Annora, and the Ambassador of Trikinia."

Smiling, she says, "It's a pleasure to meet you finally, Captain. My husband has told me a great deal about you! I must say, the two of you have so much in common." Trikan smiles. "I am honored, Ambassador!"

As other dignitaries enter the banquet room and take their seats, an orderly interrupts the professor. "Professor, will you please take your place at the banquet table before Alden enters the dining room?"

"Yes, thank you." As the professor turns towards his wife and

Trikan, he says, "Ambassador, captain, will you please excuse me?"

Ambassador Annora continues her conversation with Trikan, "So, captain, tell me, how do you like it here in Trikinia?"

Trikan replies, "It's very nice, Ambassador!"

"Captain Trikan, I want to thank you for the help you are giving to get my Elisa out of Central Detention!"

"It's all I think about, ambassador."

Smiling, she says, "Thank you again, captain."

The professor motions for Trikan and the ambassador to take their places at the banquet table before Alden arrives.

As Trikan takes his seat across from the professor, he picks up a glass of wine and says,

"To the mission, professor, to free Elisa!"

The professor smiles as he raises his glass of wine and repeats, "Yes, to free Elisa!"

As the last of the dinner guests take their seats at the table, a decoratively dressed footman enters the banquet room and announces, "Ladies and gentlemen, it gives me great honor to announce the presence of our brave and beloved leader, 'Alden the Great of Trikinia!'"

The guests immediately stand and begin to applaud the entrance of a prominent figure. Some of the military dinner guests begin chanting his name several times until Alden takes his place at the far end of the banquet table, which encompasses the ancient, ceremonial decorative throne. Standing before the ornate crown chair, he thanks the crowd for their warm greeting, and he then announces the presence of Professor Zola, his wife, Councilwoman Annora, and their special guest, Captain

Trikan.

He then gives motions to the professor, his wife, and the captain to stand up as he greets them by their names, so that everyone in the banquet room knows how delighted he is to have them as his dinner guests. A new period of applause continues for several moments as Alden motions to Professor Zola, Ambassador Annora, and Captain Trikan to speak to the dinner guests.

Professor Zola approaches the podium first and then insists that his wife stand beside him as he addresses the crowd. The professor begins by first thanking Alden for the support he has received from the Trikinian people.

Stepping aside, he lets Annora address the dinner guests. "I want to thank all of you! Many of you have helped me in the past, and we are a family that works together to support others in their time of need. We are people who demand justice and equal treatment for all. May peace and strength always be with you."

Alden begins the applause as Annora leaves the podium. He then introduces Captain Trikan and asks him to address his guests, "Captain Trikan, you bear the name of my people, and your reputation as a warrior has brought honor to that name. You have taken refuge here with the help of my good friend Professor Zola. Welcome to Trikinia, Captain! An ice world of snow-covered mountains and ice-laden oceans, where our adversaries dare to enter at their peril!"

The applause continues as Trikan steps up to the podium. He turns to face Alden and replies with a military salute as a subordinate would to a superior officer. He thanks Alden for his gracious hospitality. "Alden! I am a stranger to your land, and what little I know about the world of Trikinia is from the ancient texts describing legends of the Trikinian people and their love of Freedom."

The dinner guests applaud Trikans' words as he continues. "May

I also give thanks to a wise man, Professor Zola. If it were not for him, I would not be here at this incredible dinner as a guest of your most gracious host, Alden the Great!" Applause fills the room once again. "May I thank you all for making me feel part of your family in the great land of Trikinia, Valla Trikinia!" Alden's eyes widen as he stands and applauds the captain's last statement.

The festivities continue, with guests enjoying the master chef's traditional Trikinian dishes while engaging in discussions.

Some of the conversations vary from the excellence of the chef's creations to politics and fashion, as well as the curiosity of this strange visitor who goes by the name of Trikan but bears no resemblance to a Trikinian. Some of the guests wonder why this man is sitting to the right side of Alden in the place of honor.

As the dinner continues, several of Alden's officers stand up with their chalices in hand and toast their leader, "To our leader, Alden the Great! We honor you as our leader of all Trikinia!" Everyone in the room stands and applauds for several minutes, then returns to their dinner. Alden turns to Captain Trikan and engages him in a personal conversation. "So, tell me, Captain, you had freedom in the land you came from, and it was your choice to turn away from them?" Trikan hesitates momentarily before answering, "Freedom should not be dictated; it should be a matter of choice! They have no regard for those who discount their privilege and only ask for equal justice!"

Alden interrupts, "So, what is it that you seek then, captain... Revenge?"

No, not revenge... But justice! Justice for everyone and for someone special to me.

"Does this special someone have a name, captain?"

Trikan replies, "Yes, her name is Elisa. They all have names, and they are all special! One to me and many to others. If I can, I will free them all!"

Alden nods. "Ah, yes, Freedom! The sweet wine of life! How will you go about this task, Captain?"

Trikan responds, "Star Port City!"

Alden puts down his goblet of wine. "Star Port City? What chance would your Freedom have there, Captain?"

Trikan pauses momentarily. "The Healiocon Games are about to begin. The flight transports land with visitors after arriving from the two outer planets, as we speak. The Healiocon Games will draw spectators in multitudes, and I will take refuge with them to enter the city."

Alden listens attentively to the captain. "…And your plan is?"

Trikan then adds, "I will give myself up to be taken as a prisoner."

Alden laughs loudly. "This is your plan! Have you forgotten, Captain, that you are a wanted man? Once the Androids have you, they will NOT let you go!"

"Yes, they will! Trust me, and I won't need an army, just a small group to get me out of Central Detention with Elisa if she's being held there!"

Alden interjects, "It's much easier to get into Central Detention as opposed to getting out!"

Some laughter is heard amongst the dinner guests sitting at the table in the immediate area of Alden's place of honor, finding truth and humor in Alden's remarks.

He then gestured for the server to fill his goblet. "Please, more berry wine for my guests and me." Looking at Trikan, he states, "Your bravery is to be admired, Captain! You shall have the help of my warriors, but first, I would like to hear from your good benefactor, the professor." Alden turns his attention to Professor Zola. "Do you know of this young captain's mission, professor?"

"Yes, his mission...She's a Trikinian woman!"

Alden smiles and replies, "Ah, a Trikinian woman. They are very beautiful! Now I understand, she cast a spell on you, Captain! They have been known to do that to the man of their choice." Alden laughs aloud again, and some of his loyal followers who hear the conversation also laugh at his statement.

As the dinner continues, so does the conversation between Alden, Captain Trikan, and the professor at their table. Suddenly, the sounds of brass base horns interrupt their discussion, heard in the back of the theater section in this vast banquet hall. As the drapes slowly open, a maestro taps his podium, and a choir of Trikinian children begins singing traditional Trikinian folk songs.

Overhead ceiling lights in the theater area bathe the singers in pastel colors, complementing their ancient costumes of the Trikinian past.

The festivities continue throughout the night of the dinner party as groups of Alden's guests converse loudly while enjoying their food and drink. At the end of the evening, the maestro taps on his podium again; as he turns and faces the dinner guests, he announces, "Ladies and gentlemen, it gives me great pleasure to thank our noble leader and ruler of all Trikinia, Alden the Great, for selecting tonight's musical performance."

The entire banquet room erupts in applause as Alden remains standing. As the dinner guests quiet down, and before the order is restored, several in the audience begin to chant the name "Trikan." As the chanting increases amongst the guests, Alden says to Trikan, "Well, Captain, I may have to invite you to dinner again! You have certainly inspired my people!"

Some of the dinner guests find Alden's statement amusing, and laughter can be heard. Alden smiles again and motions towards the maestro. Acknowledging Alden's gesture, the maestro courteously turns to the choir and gently taps his music podium as the choir begins singing the Trikinian anthem, ending the night's festivities.

As the children sing, the maestro addresses the audience, "It has been my great pleasure to have the privilege of entertaining you during this wonderful banquet. The honor goes to our wonderful young people."

This being the conclusion of their final performance, the maestro motions to the side quarters of the amphitheater, and stage assistants come out with an array of banquet flowers, which are presented to the young performers. The maestro addresses the guests, "Ladies and gentlemen, please will you respond and show our wonderful choir how delighted you were with their performance?"

The entire banquet room erupts in applause as the young choir exits the stage; they bow and wave goodbye to their audience.

The guests start to leave the banquet hall as several dignitaries approach Professor Zolar and engage him in a conversation. After their greetings, Professor Zola introduces them to Captain Trikan, and a brief discussion ensues. Alden also engages the ministers, including the military advisors, in dialogue ahead of the next day's big meeting.

As the banquet hall begins to empty, the dinner attendants start to clear the tables while Alden, Professor Zola, and Trikan remain behind for several moments of personal conversation. As they slowly walk to the large exit foyer, Alden shares his carefully considered opinions with Trikan on what will occur at tomorrow's meetings. "You will speak to my people tomorrow, Captain. Your words they will hear; say them with wisdom! For they are wise warriors, and they will follow you by choice alone."

Trikan remains silent momentarily and then replies, "There are no words that can take the place of truth, Alden! I must do what I must do! What they believe will be their judgment of my words. So be it!"

Alden smiles. "You are indeed a brave warrior, Captain Trikan; I will also await their decision."

The next morning's ambassadorial schedule will begin with the formal dress code required by all military personnel attending. The early morning winds that have accompanied the freshly falling snow from the night before now cover the large courtyard of this ancient Trikinian castle, where Trikinian warriors are assembled. These winter troops will call out their names and ranks to their superior officers before going to their assigned posts. The echoes of their callouts can be heard throughout the hidden chambers and archways that comprise this mighty castle fortress, the legacy of their ancient forefathers. The occupants of the small mountain villages also listen to the sounds across the mountain valleys as a morning wake-up call that has been part of their lives since the day they were born.

The next day, Alden's staff and military personnel assembled in a large, circular conference room, where they engaged in conversations and discussions about their past experiences related to information prevalent in Trikinian governmental protocol. Several conversations among some will involve discussions relating to who Captain Trikan is and why this military meeting was called in the first place, when there were no indications of any problems requiring military intervention.

Alden's assistant and military staff members enter the conference room and cordially approach the groups of dignitaries. As they proceed, the staff assistant places official names and title cards in front of the dignitaries as other officials enter the conference room. As a multitude of additional military officials enter the room, Professor Zola and Captain Trikan enter with the group, then leave to wait by the steps of the elevated stage. They are then approached by a military orderly and escorted up to their special seating arrangement for guest speakers and dignitaries, which is located at the back of the speaker podium.

The conference escorts continue their duties while a high-ranking military staff officer approaches the professor and Trikan. He cordially recommends that they follow him to their assigned seating in the middle section of the stage, located directly behind the speaker platform.

Several feet back from the stage platform, the walls are adorned with heavily embroidered tapestry drapes depicting mounted warriors riding into battle. Once all guests are seated in their assigned seats, the conference escorts leave the meeting room.

Most of the dignitaries remain silent, except for a few low-ranking warriors in the background speaking as they wait for the appearance of Alden.

Several moments later, the tapestry drapes are drawn by two of Alden's men, and a large Trikinian warrior dressed in a historical parade uniform enters the conference room and walks to the front of the stage, carrying a large javelin containing different color banners of historical units of quadrant war victories in Trikinian's past.

The large Trikinian warrior raises the javelin and thrusts it down several times to the wooden platform, creating blunt sounds familiar to the ancient carpenter's wood hammer and shouting to the assembly, "THIS MEETING IS NOW IN ORDER!"

The military leaders immediately obey the command, and the entire room becomes silent. Several moments later, Alden enters from behind the large tapestry drapes, walks up to the podium, and announces the reason for calling the assembly. "My brave Trikinian warriors... I salute you as a servant of the people! We have a special guest with us who some of you met last night at our celebration dinner. Some of you might have heard of his name, while others might know of him by his actions. Now, all of you will know him by the name that was given to him by people who admired him. I present him to you—Captain Trikan!"

The entire room erupts in applause, except for several Trikinian warriors in the back. As they speak under their breath, Alden waits until the applause stops, and he then addresses these rude countrymen, "Is this how you greet a friend and a guest? I see a sense of distrust amongst some of you." He puts his right hand on his chest and then points toward Professor Zola. "I trust in my friend, the sky watcher; he knows many things, much of which he cannot reveal to you! I know him well! He speaks of the captain with great hope and a journey past many stars, a journey beyond our imagination!"

Alden looks at Captain Trikan. "You will speak to my people now, Captain Trikan. They will follow you by choice alone!"

Trikan rises slowly from his chair, and silence again engulfs the room. After approaching the speaker's podium, the captain remains silent for several moments.

He then speaks. "You know me now for what I am as I stand before you and not what I was in the past! I cannot take you back into my past, as I have no way of returning there myself. Like many of us, we would like to go back and change so many things we've done that we regret. Hear my words, for they are true! Know me now for what I am as I stand before you. I am going back to Star Port City to free someone to whom I owe my very existence! She belongs here, with her people, not in Central Detention! I am responsible for her misfortune; I failed her, and that's why I must go back and free her!"

At that moment, a multitude of warriors stood up and shouted, "FREE HER! FREE HER!" Trikan shouts back to them, "So that she may return home to her people in Trikinia!" With his last statement, not a warrior remained seated in the room.

Alden approaches the podium and stands next to Trikan as the applause and shouting continue. Alden then speaks to the assembled warriors, "Hear my words! I also speak the truth!"

Alden points to the captain. "Who will follow this warrior and spare not his own life to free one Trikinian woman and many others? Be they Trikinian or not, they shall all be free!"

The assembly stands again and begins to cheer and call out Alden's name, followed by Captain Trikans. When the room returns to order, Alden calls Professor Zola to address the assembly. The professor takes a few moments to prepare himself to speak on behalf of a mission that he cannot elaborate on in detail, as it is not meant for everyone to know. Adjusting the speaker's microphone, the professor can now look directly at the crowd as he speaks. Turning to Alden, the professor begins, "It is with great pleasure that I am here and given the privilege to address the honored guests of Trikinia! I do not have a prepared speech, nor do I feel one is needed. I will speak of something that we all need and treasure—FREEDOM! It's like a journey on a road to follow; so many others have shown us the way. Yes, we have peace and Freedom, which were left to us as a legacy by the great people who went before us and created that wonderful road that I call FREEDOM! Things change, and people change. We go into the future and be thankful that we are free in this wonderful country of Trikinia. How fortunate we are, I thank you all!"

Turning to Alden momentarily, he calls out, "Valla Trikinia!" The entire room cheers and offers the professor a standing ovation.

The following day, Captain Trikan and the professor meet with Alden, a select group of his generals and senior officers, to discuss his mission to Star Port City. Trikan follows the professor down the stone walkway that leads to the military conference room. "Professor, correct me if I'm wrong, but I get the feeling that you know this place very well."

The professor smiles. "You look surprised, Captain, at my presence and ability to find my way around this old castle. Yes, I have been here many times before, and may I add, I did not have to climb the mountains to get here."

The two friends paused momentarily as Trikan replied, "You hold many surprises, professor, and don't worry, your secrets are safe with me!"

The professor and Trikan walk across the large courtyard to the stone steps of the massive, ornate timber doors, which are flanked by two large Trikinian sentry warriors. The warriors immediately salute Professor Zola and the Captain as they pull open the large security doors to let the two special guests in. As they enter the room, the captain and professor are then greeted by one of Alden's general staff members. Some of Alden's generals have already decided to provide Trikan with transportation to Star Port City, along with as many Trikinian warriors as he requires. This group of generals will be part of the mission as they are assembled into a conference room with their secretarial staff to monitor the entire meeting. The captain and professor are escorted into the conference room.

There, they will be questioned appropriately about the requests and the Trikinian military's ability to provide Trikan with the assistance he may need.

Alden's minister approaches Trikan and the professor, introducing himself by his authority. He will grant them any assistance and materials that will allow them to secretly return to Star Port City and complete their mission after they address the High Council members and receive their approval.

After the meeting, the captain and professor were fully supportive of Trikans' plan and mission objectives.

A short time later, they meet with Alden, who congratulates Captain Trikan and Professor Zola for their sincere effort to convince their generals to accept their mission objectives.

Alden tells him, "Captain, you will be contacted by my staff tomorrow."

Early the next morning, Cen-Ton answers the door to Captain Trikans' room, and the captain is still sleeping. Cen-Ton opens the door. "... MAY I HELP YOU...?"

"Yes, I wish to speak to your Captain Trikan."

Cen-Ton looks at his uniform and replies, "... PLEASE COME IN... I WILL AWAKEN THE CAPTAIN..."

Cen-Ton is then handed an official-looking document. As he walks across the living room area to the bedroom apartment, he opens the bedroom door and calls the captain in a low voice,

"CAPTAIN TRIKAN... A GOVERNMENT OFFICIAL IS HERE TO SEE YOU... YOU BETTER GET UP, CAPTAIN..."

Trikan turns over, not bothering to look at anyone. "... CAPTAIN... HE MUST BE IMPORTANT... HE IS WEARING A VERY IMPORTANT UNIFORM..."

"Okay, Cen-Ton, okay! I'm getting up!"

The colonel calls out to Trikan, "Captain, take your time. It is not urgent! It's a request from Alden, who prefers not to use any electronic communication, a preference that he desires for security purposes."

Before the colonel could say another word, Trikan entered the sitting room area of the apartment. "Good morning, Colonel!"

"Good morning, Captain, and forgive me for waking you up so early this morning. I will get right to the point. You'll find all the information you need in the packet I gave to your robot."

Cen-Ton hands the captain the envelope, and Trikan opens it, removing several documents signed by Alden. He reads the first document, which primarily concerns their meeting with the general staff.

The second document pertains to their friendship and the trust that they have built. The third and final document reads, accordingly...

> *"My good Captain and my good friend. When you sign this document, and it is returned to me, you will fully understand the grave consequences we discussed during our previous meetings. I will emphasize the gravity of the situation regarding your mission, as we previously discussed. I could not provide you with an official Trikinian transport. Secret arrangements have been made with a private vendor to meet your transportation needs, with no impact on our treaty with your government. We must proceed in this manner so that when you sign this document, you will acknowledge that you fully understand the gravity of the situation. My good captain and friend, I wish you great success in your mission."*

Trikan signs the agreement, reinserts it into the envelope, and returns it to the colonel.

"Good luck with your mission, Captain. I will take my leave now."

The colonel looks at Cen-Ton as Trikan makes a request to the robot. "Cen-Ton, will you please show the colonel out?"

"... YES, CAPTAIN... COLONEL... MAY I ..."

As Cen-Ton opens the door, the colonel exits the apartment. Trikan is sitting on the oversized living room couch, falls back into a lounge position.

Not getting a good night's rest, Trikan is about to fall back asleep when his arm computer's signal suddenly activates. Captain Trikan receives a message from Professor Zola: "Be prepared that we are expecting a severe snowstorm. I will arrive shortly, and we must travel 150 kilometers to where the ship is being stored, with air cargo freight aboard. It is located in the food warehouse complex of Trikinian antiquity."

Trikan replies with a message from his arm computer: "I await your arrival. Thank you for your advice, professor."

Suddenly, there is a loud knock on the door, and Cen-Ton replies, "...WOULD YOU LIKE ME TO GET THAT, CAPTAIN...?"

Looking at the door, Trikan replies, "Go ahead, Cen-Ton."

As Cen-Ton opens the door, a large Trikinian warrior enters while slightly ducking beneath the door frame, which cannot accommodate his height. He is followed by a distinguished-looking older man carrying bundles of rolled cloth resembling the typical dress clothing that Trikinians wear. The distinguished-looking elderly man greets the captain, "Good morning, captain. I am here to measure you."

Trikan is somewhat puzzled as he asks. "Measure, for what?"

"I'm sorry, Captain, I guess no one told you. I am here to measure you for one of our fine Trikinian uniforms. It won't take long."

Trikan asks, "Who arranged this?"

The tall Trikinian warrior, standing at attention, replies in a deep voice, "Alden." Immediately, the tailor exclaims, "Oh, I'm sorry, Captain, I should have advised you of that!"

At that moment, the beacon light above the door begins to flash as the Trikinian warrior opens it. "Well, captain, I see that you have company this morning."

Trikan smiles at the professor. "Come on in, professor, and join the group. If there's anyone else out there, have them come in, too."

The professor looks up at the Trikinian warrior and says, "Good morning!"

The Trikinian warrior stares at the professor while remaining silent. Alden's tailor takes his final measurements and is about to leave when he thanks Trikan. "Thank you, Captain. I should have your Trikinian uniform ready in a short time."

Alden's bodyguard is about to exit with the tailor when he stops momentarily and turns to the captain. "Oh, captain, I almost forgot, you must sign this document."

Slightly annoyed, Trikan replies, "Okay, okay. Where do I sign?"

As Alden's security guard begins to exit, he repeats part of the tailor's words, "Thank you, captain."

He hesitates and says, "We will be leaving you now."

Ducking under the door frame, he leaves and quietly closes the door behind him. As the professor reads their departure schedule, Trikan enters the kitchen area and discovers that the cabinets are empty. He then selects a variety of breakfast menus from the automated food dispensary. The selection menu lights up, reading, "... EMPTY... PLEASE RESTOCK..."

An early morning discomfort, resulting from excessive activity before breakfast and insufficient sleep, has left him feeling "off his game" this morning.

He calls Cen-Ton, "Cen-Ton, did the professor leave yet?"

The professor says, "No, Captain. I'm still here. Captain, don't you think you should have read the document before signing?"

"Professor, I'm in no mood to read anything this morning, okay?"

"Yes, Captain, but we have adequate time before leaving. You can get your breakfast downstairs. We have private transportation to the Village of Northrona. Besides, you have to wait for your tailored uniform anyway. We have plenty of time before we depart for Star Port City's industrial complex. It's all been arranged with regular cargo entrance security approval with its commercial clearance."

"Great, professor, can you order breakfast for me, if you don't mind. I'm going to take a shower."

The professor asks, "Captain, do you have a preference?"

Trikan does not answer as Cen-Ton interjects, "... PROFESSOR... I DO BELIEVE THAT THE CAPTAIN HAS A PREFERENCE FOR THE TRIKINIAN BREAKFAST SPECIAL... AND... THE BEVERAGE SHOULD BE A LARGE RUM HONEY-FLAVORED TEA..."

When breakfast is served, Trikan looks at it and says, "Commander Doria again?"

The professor then asks, "What did you say, captain?"

Before Trikan can answer, a message from Alden appears on the professor's Dial-Date view screen, reading:

> **"WARNING ... Record snowfall has caused a delay in your exit operational departure. Please be advised that several avalanches have blocked access to transportation exits. The storage complex is under deep snowdrifts and will require a full company of service relief personnel to dig out. Delay expected; several days ..."**

Looking at his Dial-Date screen, the professor replies, "Well, captain, it looks like you're going to have a few extra days to plan out your mission!" Trikan remains silent for a moment. "Professor, if trying to survive is a plan, then sign me up! Without your help, I wouldn't be here." The professor gives out a hearty laugh as he exclaims, "Captain... Captain! I admit that I have many friends who will oblige me when I ask a favor, but I am very much like you, Captain, taking one day at a time and hoping for the best!"

As the solar days pass, the night before the mission finally arrives, the three friends walk out to the rampart, the night before the captain and the professor depart.

This will be the last time Trikan speaks to Alden until he completes his mission. As they look down from the terrace, they see the fields of ice clinging to the mountain cliffs and deep snow-covered valleys and foothills. The moonlight illuminates the ridges across the valleys of this ancient Trikinian fortress, casting a majestic blue glow that gives the appearance of a land that will exist forever in mythical folklore.

"Do you hear them, Captain? The sounds of their wild existence!"

"Yes, Alden, I'm familiar with that sound."

The professor adds, "It's the Gen-Tor! The sounds of the wild ice wolves."

Alden interjects, "Yes, professor, the Gen-Tor, they were given that name by our ancient, legendary king. The first king of our people, King Gen-Tor, was a great leader and a great warrior who loved the ice wolves. Legend said he could walk amongst them, and they would react to his every command."

Looking at the captain, he says, "Well, captain, you are going back. By this time tomorrow, you will be on your way to Star Port City. What consequences await you? Your escape from the sentry war robots was, by chance, a victory by any standard. Very few have done what you have and lived to talk about it! You can stay in Trikinia, and if they come here to hunt you, we will destroy them together! You don't have to go back, captain. You will need more than a few of my warriors, and I sense a deep misgiving that a Trikinian garment disguise will achieve what you have in mind."

Trikan then says, "I must go, Alden. I must right the wrong and go back and change the past!" Alden looks at the captain as he puts his hand on Trikans' shoulder, a Trikinian tradition of respect for a brother warrior. "Then, good luck, my friend. I wait for the day that you return to Trikinia in victory."

As Alden leaves, he stops for a moment and says, "May the War Gods of Trikinia watch over you!"

Trikan hands the professor his small gold bracelet and asks, "Professor, take care of this for me! I don't want to lose it."

As the professor takes the bracelet, he glances at it for a moment and then casually puts it into his vest pocket as Trikan says to him, "Aunt Lasara gave it to me; she said that it belonged to me. Can I ask you something, professor? What is the *Andromeda Report*?"

The professor stays silent for a moment, reluctant to answer, and then says, "It was a crash site on an asteroid a long time ago; it's in a government report. Why do you ask, Captain?" Trikan remains silent for a moment, then says, "It's not important, professor; I was just thinking, why would a distress signal have to be turned off, professor?"

"Well, Captain, there could be only two reasons. The first is that help has arrived, and the other would be that someone did not want the ship to be found."

Trikan then says, "The night before leaving to go to school in Star Port City, Aunt Lasara asked me to go up to her office and get my school admission papers from her desk; she had spent a good part of the day moving old files around and cleaning her office.

There was a government folder on top of the pile, labeled "*ANDROMEDA REPORT.*" Next to the folders was a small black book atop her work reports. When I took my seminar application, I accidentally knocked it off the desk, and it landed with its pages open. In her words, she had written:

'I had to turn off all the electrical current in the ship to stop the distant signal transmission of the codeword EARTH, only because I had to protect them from being put through long-term incarceration and medical experiments. I did what I knew was the right thing to do at the time, and I have never regretted it! I have never been this happy in all of my life.'

Professor, this entry in her diary was written a long time ago!"

The professor remains silent as he takes the bracelet from his pocket and carefully reads the inscription. *Johnathan Shawnwood – Scotland Earth.*

He then says, "I know what you're thinking, Captain. There must be an explanation!"

Trikan replies, "It doesn't matter, professor; we can't change the past; we can only change the future!"

Still holding the bracelet, the professor says, "I will keep this safe for you, Captain." Trikan smiles. "Thank you, professor; I'll see you in the morning."

The exchange in their conversation ends as Trikan leaves the balcony. Each moment of silence seemed like an eternity; Trikan was in a state of mind that allowed him to live in the past once again.

He was back under the protection of Aunt Lasara and with his caring mother, Reanna, whom he never once doubted was who she claimed to be. It was a good life back then, and like many young adolescents, he lived in a protective environment where everything he needed was provided for him. Trikan decided he would never question

Aunt Lasara about her diary or the inscription on the inside of the gold bracelet.

If there was something that his mother or Aunt Lasara felt he should know, he knew deep down within his very existence, they would tell him at the right time.

Chapter 12:

Emissary

The morning preparations for departure are complete, and the captain, professor, and Cen Ton are ready to depart on their mission to Star Port City. Trikan reminds the professor, "We will leave before the first light of dawn and arrive at the storage complex where the cargo ship is being stored.

By then, the Trikinians should have cleared the flight tarmac of snow, and then we will take off for Star Port City. It was nice of Alden to provide us with his flight transport, Professor."

"Yes, Captain, he wanted to make sure we would have no problem entering the warehouse zone facility; it's a highly secured area."

Trikans' short conversation with the professor is interrupted by a Trikinian warrior outside the apartment. "Captain Trikan, last call!"

Cen-Ton opens the door to the shouting Trikinian warrior. "Captain, your transport is ready to leave, and here is your package with your Trikinian uniform. I will escort you down to the castle gantry section, where you will be given final instructions and clarification on how to operate the cargo lift transport. We will provide transportation to the storage warehouse, where your cargo flightcraft has been cleared for departure. Good luck with your flight destination, Captain!"

The castle gantry section contains Alden's private military airlift transport, as a Trikinian military officer then presents Trikan and six of his aides in battle arms of the Trikinian Embassy Special Forces.

They salute Trikan, and the officer hands him official documents and a code-pass insignia that will allow the captain to fly a commercial air cargo ship loaded with Alphanian timber logs through Trikinian airspace without risk of friendly fire from Trikinian ground units.

"Captain, we will escort you and remain in your charge until you take possession of your aircraft and depart. I will discuss further operational procedures when we are on board with how to navigate your air cargo flightcraft. You will have many commercial landing fields of your choice outside Star Port City; their failsafe operational systems will communicate with you electronically, and you will be given commercial clearance permission to land your cargo in the commercial zone."

The castle's observation dome illuminates the tarmac. Trikan, Cen-Ton, and a selected military officer, LamBrute, climb aboard Alden's transport, accompanied by three special embassy forces, followed by the professor. A siren alert breaks the silence of the air dome section of the castle to clear the tarmac as the flightcraft lifts off on its air flight mission over the frozen mountain peaks of Trikinia.

Now, on their journey to the cargo center, where Trikan will take possession of a transport cargo ship that will provide transportation for him and his companions, along with the professor and Cen-Ton, to Star Port City. Border computers will interlock with the high-speed reference relays in Trikans' cargo ship's computer, transmitting navigational guidance and security reference feedback data.

Embassy Officer LamBrute addresses Captain Trikan, "Captain, I'll use this time before we arrive at our destination to explain the rest of your mission concerning the cargo air flight-ship. You will be carrying raw tonnage of freshly cut Alphanian timber wood, and it's already been loaded and secured in the hull of the ship."

Trikan looks at the embassy officer, somewhat confused. "Timber wood?"

"Yes, and paid in full!"

Trikan then asks, "I paid for timber wood? That's what I signed for this morning?"

A humorous grin appears on the embassy officer's face. "It's the only way that you will be allowed to land in any of the commercial air dome facilities around Star Port City."

Trikan then replies, "Okay... I got it. Tell me everything that I should know!"

"Captain, without a weight cargo, an empty airship is considered an adversary intrusion into Androidian airspace, and the ground-to-air defense systems would destroy your ship. You see, Captain, cargo ships are rated by their tonnage. Passenger ships are exempt from this practice and are allowed to land. The rule is, you can't destroy a city with a shipload of passengers, but a cargo ship carrying a mega-ton of explosives, if allowed to land, could have a devastating outcome and destroy a large section of Star Port City."

Trikan looks at the embassy officer. "Okay... So, when do I meet the four volunteers who are going to Star Port City with me?"

The embassy officer smiles. "They're right at the back of you, Captain. They're the BEST!" Trikan turns around and says to the Trikinian warriors, "You guys are volunteering for this mission?"

The leader of the Embassy of Trikinian Warriors responds, "My name is Commander LamBrute. It's my honor to serve with you, Captain!"

As he takes hold of Trikans' right hand in a bonding gesture of trust and loyalty, he says, "These are my warriors, and now they are yours! Alden's special guards: Sergeant Cole, Ranger Rok, and Ranger Yava."

The three Battle Arms Special Force Trikinian Warriors immediately place their right hands on the top of the first Trikinian command warrior and repeat the same gesture in unison. "It's an honor to serve with you, Captain!"

A short time later, the craft arrives at its three-thousand-two-hundred-and-nineteen-kilometer destination site of the original city of the ***Golden Age of the Trikinian People.***

The ship descends into a lower orbital velocity as it passes ceremonial sites considered sacred grounds of the people of Trikinia. Captain Trikan is struck by the antiquity of the design, portraying the hidden mysteries of the creation of the Trikinian people.

Carved into Banishean stone, giant statues of warriors reveal the evolution and grandeur of their victories over grotesque creatures that once ruled the plains and mountain regions of this enormous planet. Along the landing corridor, the stories of a planet dominated by these wild and dangerous beasts are told, depicted in statues that formed the challenges this world would face during the long nights of creation.

This was the foundation of the Trikinian people in the lost time after conception, when there was just land and water, and only the voices of the solar winds that spoke the words that gave the names of King Gen-Tor and his Queen Northrona.

The transport ship lands at Air Dome Fourteen, which contains several significant cargo modes of transport that are granted treaty access into Star Port City under commercial agreements.

Trikan, the professor, and Cen-Ton, along with the four Trikinian volunteers, disembark and are met by Flight Dome Director Manis, while storm-clearing personnel pull into the air dome with their tractor equipment, still laden with their heavy snow-clearing assignment.

LamBrute compliments the flight dome director, "Well, Director Manis, how does it feel to be the chief of this facility? May I say you did a fine job of getting these doors open!"

Manis replies cordially to the embassy official. "I'll accept credit on behalf of my men, and we had to hire an extra crew to help get that ship out of here. There must be a big demand for raw lumber in Star Port City. I was told that my recent promotion would be rescinded if I had not been able to clear the air flight port exit and open those gantry doors!"

Trikan remains silent, paying little attention to the director's conversation with the embassy official, as his interest remains focused on the size of the large cargo transport ship. The embassy official agrees with the director. "I know what you mean. But this came down directly from Alden!"

Manis replies, "I had a feeling it was from higher up!"

"Well, I'll say again, Manis, you and your men did a great job! Now, let me introduce you to the captain who is going to take that cargo air flight-ship out of here."

Turning to Trikan, he says,

"Captain—" Before he could complete his introduction, Director Manis interjects as he looks at Captain Trikan. "It's a pleasure to meet you, Captain; I've heard a lot about you!"

Paying little attention to the director and not responding to his acknowledgment, Trikan says, "I see that you supplement your workforce with sentry robots?"

The director responds, "Oh, pay no attention to them, Captain. They're the older type, have been decommissioned, and are on their way to the scrapyard. We were able to get them at a bargain price and use them for the heavy lifting that my guys can't do."

Trikan is still observing the sentry robots replacing burnt deflector tubes that must be replaced before the ship departs on its next scheduled flight, and says, "We had sentry robots back at the house when I was growing up. They worked on the outside grounds."

Sensing the discord, the embassy official adds to the conversation, "Well, gentlemen, shall we check out the interior of the ship?"

Ignoring the embassy official, Trikan continues, "Sentry robots were considered very dangerous back then. Certain things had to be done to them. I have a question for you, Director. When they were decommissioned, I'm sure that you're going to tell me that their unit computer cellar-corneous brain section was removed?"

The director responds to Trikans' concern, "I see that you are quite knowledgeable about sentry robots, Captain... and that is a yes to your concerns. Those units that you referred to were removed and destroyed; I can validate that."

Trikan continues to observe the ship and the work in progress by the sentry robots, remaining transfixed as he speaks to the director. "And the trunk lines, Director, were they destroyed as part of the decommissioning regulations?"

Trikans' statement takes the director back. "Captain, my guess is it was not done!"

"Exactly, Director! That's my concern. So, what you are saying, Director Manis, is that all someone would have to do is put a cellar-corneous unit back in, and then you would have a functioning and very dangerous sentry robot under the direction and command of the Androids! Right here in a Trikinian defense unit."

The director replies, "Captain Trikan, I'm glad that you brought this to my attention. As soon as I have you and your crew aboard for a walk-around orientation inspection, I will report back to my superiors at the loading dock transport facility headquarters, and I assure you, Captain..." he addresses Embassy Official LamBrute as well, "...this will be given the highest priority. Gentlemen, I have a feeling more than a few are going to lose their commission and end up in a lower rank! Captain, I can't thank you enough for bringing this to my attention."

Trikan then says, "Let's get aboard and get on with this inspection!"

The boarding party proceeds directly to the passenger elevator, which takes them up to the Com Operations Center.

As they exit the elevator, Director Manis continues his conversation with Trikan, explaining the air freight cargo transport operations. "Captain, as I was saying, most of the operations of this craft are uniquely programmed with very little effort by the pilot commander, and there is no need for an air flight helmsman. It is all built into an integrated, pre-programmed microdot sequence system that has never failed to perform at utmost efficiency. It replaced the forerunner that was referred to as an Ultra-Tec Drive. The microdot system is a failsafe, and there are no two alike! Each one has its own coded memory and retains actual experiences, including conversations exchanged during its flight operations. It has been estimated that finding a duplicate would be astronomically improbable. To put it simply, Captain, this ship with all its safety features will not function without this operational keyplate."

Handing the captain an octagonal keyplate, Director Manis states, "This plate was electronically designed with computer codes that will only operate the navigational guidance systems of this craft. By the way, this is what you signed for, and the logs are just a decoy; they come with the ship! Once this plate is inserted and the captain is at the helm, the code is no longer visible, and the craft will operate. It's not just theory, Captain; it's an operational triumph! Upon arrival at your destination, someone will meet you at a predetermined location. Contact will be made with you after the craft lands at the port. She will take the metallic coded plate, and with it, she will return the flightcraft to Trikinia without the cargo."

Trikan replies, "Okay, what does this contact look like, and when is this supposed to happen?"

"After you leave the transport facility, Captain, you will be approached by someone whom you have met before. You will discreetly give her the code plate and refrain from engaging in conversation with her. Remember, Captain, we can't guarantee that you will not be under surveillance when this takes place."

Trikan responds, "Yes, I understand!"

Manis continues, "Let me show you the updates that were made in the computer programming of this craft."

As Director Manis explains the operational updates of the automatic computer features of the flight cargo craft, Trikan receives a message with no ID on his Dial-Date computer:

"... I'll contact you in a café a short way from the games. I will know where to find you. I'll be with some who visit and are all coming to the games, so don't look for me; I will find you..."

Trikan erases the message as Embassy Official LamBrute steps forward and extends his hand to Manis. "Thank you, director; I'll be on board with the captain. This will not be my first flight with one of these cargo transports."

The director replies, "Captain, Commander, Professor, have a safe trip! Your crew members are already onboard below deck in the crew accommodation quarters; you do not have to leave the operations cabin to speak to them. All you need to do is turn on the intercom telescreen."

As the gantry doors open, the director takes the elevator lift down and exits the transport. Alarms become activated, sending out the launch-in-progress signal as the flight cargo craft's engines begin to lift the large transport off its parking berth within the storage depot.

After reaching an off-distance elevation, it ignites its aft engines and blasts the ship forward, out through the gantry doors onto its journey to Star Port City.

Once in orbital space, Cen-Ton remains standing as Trikan and the professor can unbuckle their safety harnesses from the pilot's com chairs and walk around freely due to the ship's enhanced planetoid surface gravity. Each cargo section of the ship has its own entrance and exit walkway, leading to the crew and command officer's operation level. These entranceways to each section of the transport allow crew members to inspect cargo that is safely moored and locked in place in each area of the ship.

The design of these cargo ships provides the desired refuge for an intruder as the lead entity motions to his three companions to perform their command mission as he continues down the chambered path that will lead him to the com-ships operations. The faint sounds that they make cannot be heard over the noise of the blast engines of the flight cargo craft.

Trikan reaches forward and turns on the audio-com view screen to engage in a conversation with the four Trikinian crew members. "How do you guys like it down there?"

LamBrute, who is sitting next to the audio-com, raises his goblet to the screen and replies to the captain, "Captain, why don't you come down and join us?"

Trikan acknowledges, "I will, in a little while, as soon as we are locked down in a navigational course time sequence."

Turning to Professor Zola, Trikan then asks, "Professor, I would like to share something with you."

"By all means, captain."

"Just before takeoff, I received a message on my Dial-Date. The message was:

"I'll meet you and the five in a café a short way from the games... I will know where to find you. I'll be with some who visit and are all coming to the games, so don't look for me; I will find you."

The professor remarks, "Well, captain, I received the same coded message before coming aboard. I'm sure, Captain, I know who sent it, and it was sent with limited code frequency. However, my message ended slightly differently. It said, "If you don't see me, wait no longer; I will be with the flowers."

Cen-Ton interrupts, "...CAPTAIN... I DO NOT INTEND TO INTERRUPT YOUR CONVERSATION..."

Looking at Cen-Ton, the captain replies, "Yes, Cen-Ton... What is it?"

"...CAPTAIN... I AM PICKING UP A WEIGHT DISPLACEMENT ON MY SENSORS..."

Looking at the com readouts, Trikan replies, "Are you sure, Cen-Ton? All my com sections are reading no displacement in any section. The weight stabilization registers metric tons in equally divided weight configurations. Mathematically, all cargo chamber sections have the same proportional readings. I don't see any problem, Cen-Ton."

Trikan viewed this processed information as being correct. He was unaware that the grade level of the computer systems was not able to identify the intruders who entered the cargo sections undetected. "Professor, we're on autopilot now, so let's go down and see how those troopers are doing."

Before leaving the com, Cen-Ton alerts the captain. "... CAPTAIN... IT'S HAPPENING AGAIN... I AM DETECTING A MOVEMENT DISCREPANCY... I HAVE NEVER ENCOUNTERED ANY WEIGHT MISCONFIGURATIONS OTHER THAN PASSENGER DROP-OFFS AT SPACEPORT TERMINALS... MY QUANTUM EQUATIONS WERE PROGRAMMED BY THE PROFESSOR... THE PROFESSOR CAN ENSURE YOU THAT MY PROGRAM IS ONE OF A KIND AND PROGRAMMED NEVER TO FAIL..."

The professor adds, "Cen-Ton is right, Captain! There is a definite danger of a weight discrepancy in a ship this large! Throughout the fourteen cargo sections, the length and weight of each cargo hull must be balanced and correctly distributed."

Cen-Ton responds, "... CAPTAIN... I SUGGEST—" Trikan interrupts, "Not right now, Cen-Ton!" As he instinctively reacts, he turns on all of the cargo view screen monitors, including the emergency monitor, to alert the four Trikinian warriors in the cabin lounge below.

He quickly discovers that the Trikinian warriors are unconscious. Trikan activates the audio inter-ship com and calls out to them. One of the Trikinians reacts to Trikans' call, as he desperately tries but cannot put together a comprehensive statement. The Trikinian warrior attempts to overcome the fact that he has been drugged as he falls back into his chair in a passed-out position near his three companions, who lie unconscious on the cabin floor. Trikan immediately tells the professor, "Let's get down there and see what's wrong with those guys! Cen-Ton, secure the Com door until we get back! Weapons, off safety!"

Cen-Ton replies. "... UNDERSTOOD, CAPTAIN..."

The professor reacts to the emergency and steps onto the lift platform with Trikan while taking his medical kit with him.

A minute later, they step into the eerie silence of the crew cabin, and the professor begins to administer his medical skills to the four Trikinian troopers. After testing the food and drinks that they consumed, Professor Zola has a clear prognosis of the substance that caused them to be medically debilitated.

He adjusts a portable medical injection dispenser containing a variety of molecular antibodies that attack all poisonous chemicals in the body and render them harmless. He then proceeds to inject each of the four troopers with the injection dispenser.

Trikan is focused on the telescreen and notices a weight change in the balance of equations. "Professor, Cen-Ton is correct; there is a discrepancy in the weight displacement in the cargo bay area, and it shouldn't be happening!"

Trikans' concerned thoughts put him in a distressed state of mind, with the feelings of being surrounded by an evil force. Every moment he denies his action, his inner being yearns to break free and fight back, to destroy his enemy. His feelings of frustration cannot cloud his sound judgment. He must wait for the doctor's verdict and be assured that the four warriors will survive this ordeal, for which he feels responsible.

He asks the professor, "Are they going to be alright?"

"Indeed, they will, Captain! They are going to be fine. In a little while, they will wake up and experience a mild headache. Captain, please clear the table of the contaminated food! We are almost done here."

Trikan adds, "Good. When they're feeling better, I might need them for backup. Is that alright with you, Professor?"

"That will be just fine, Captain."

"There's something that I have to take care of... Cen-Ton can help me; I'm looking at the service history graphics of this ship. I am also seeking information and videos featuring food service supply personnel. I have a feeling that no security measures were in place when the contaminated food was transported and brought onto the ship. There is no reference in the ship's log pertaining to service dates and supply schedules. Something bothers me, Professor; why were no records kept? Before I jump to conclusions, I want Cen-Ton to run a scan and clarify my suspicions."

The heavy steel entrance hatch is pushed open as a figure silently leaves the engine section and enters the chamber cargo compartment section D-14. Moving slowly, the figure activates a three-dimensional screen module, which displays distorted reception on the portable unit. After adjusting the frequency relays, he then receives clear, sequenced readouts. The figure with the visual feedback scanner now enters a tunnel corridor with a transfer tubular section channel that will take him into a cargo hull laden with Alphanian timber logs.

This section is one of the fourteen cargo hulls filled with the heavy timber of Alphanian trees. Probing the entrance and exit cargo sections, the portable module feedback scanner provides a clear holographic view of sub-chambers leading to the operational compartment and the crew quarters.

The lead figure turns and motions to the two sentry robots behind him in a coordinated, preplanned mission. Pointing to the large cargo of Alphanian logs, fastened down with steel chains, he receives a confirmation signal that they understand their mission procedure. The lead figure then proceeds to enter the next cargo section, as he is followed by one of his intruder companions. His well-conceived plan has been successful so far; they were able to enter the ship, hide out in the engine room, drug the four Trikinians, and avoid detection.

Pointing in the direction of the next cargo hull, he receives an affirmative nod from the first intruder sentry robot as the other robot follows.

As Cen-Ton enters the operations com, Trikan turns his attention to him. "Cen-Ton, see if your configuration analysis can find any formatted information that was recently deleted from the main sectional computer banks."

It does not take Cen-Ton very long to run his analysis check on the intel-main storage computer. "... CAPTAIN... I SCANNED THE MAIN STORAGE COMPUTER BANKS... I FOUND NO DATA RECORDS PERTAINING TO THIS SHIP'S FOOD PANTRIES... THE LAST INFORMATION ENTERED WAS THE HANGAR MAINTENANCE SERVICE WORKER'S RECORDS... THEIR SERVICE WAS COMPLETED BEFORE WE ARRIVED ON BOARD THE TRANSPORT... THERE ARE NO RECENT SECTION ENTRIES DELETED..."

Suddenly, the ship's autopilot voice activation unit cuts into their conversation as Professor Zola enters the cabin of operations control. An emergency readout message is displayed on the central bank's view screen, along with an automated danger alert signal. The integrated ship's alarm screen announces the ship's trans-lift flight auto program. "... LIFT SEQUENCE CONFIGURATION IS OFF COURSE AND IN DANGER WITH FURTHER INFORMATION TO ALL PERSONNEL... TO ABORT THE CARGO TRANSPORT CRAFT BY WAY OF THE EMERGENCY FLIGHTCRAFT SYSTEM... AUTO LIFT SEQUENCE IS NOT IN PROGRESS... SECURE ALL PASSENGER SEATING... ENGINE VELOCITY MAXIMUM... ALL ENGINES IN FULL BLAST SEQUENCE IGNITION..."

Beacon indicators begin to blare out siren sounds throughout the ship. "... WARNING... THERE IS A WEIGHT DISPLACEMENT THROUGHOUT SECTIONS... SUB-CARGO D-12 AND D-14..."

The ship's gyrostabilizers are now critical and are unable to correct the weight displacement, as the large craft is now beginning to spiral off its course. The professor is knocked down to the com's cabin floor, while Cen-Ton can compromise the ship's unstable course polarity change.

While Captain Trikan struggles to stay in the com chair, he resists the G-forces created by the ship's weight displacements. The midship is out of its polarity, with most of its heavy cargo released, specifically in sections D-7, D-12, and D-14, located on the port side of the large transport, causing it to continue off course.

Trikan instantly activates the computer-audio relay. "Computer, give me the ship's complete graphics of the sections that are experiencing the weight discrepancies in a close-up visual readout... Explain the problem!"

Immediately, the computer responds, "... CONTENT... ALL SECTIONS SECURED EXCEPT PORT SIDE D-7, D-12, AND D-14 ARE CONFIRMED... WEIGHT DISPLACEMENTS ARE CRITICAL... INTERIOR STRUCTURAL DAMAGE EXTENSIVE..."

Trikan responds to the computer, "Computer... Magnify screens, close up on sections D-7 through D-14, and show all affected areas!"

The close-up of the view screen reveals that the chains were cut with a laser beam, releasing the heavy tonnage of Alphanian timber wood logs in the reported areas, which blocked the exit escape hatches on the port side of the craft. The sentry robots must now work their way back to the main orbital blast engine compartment, located in Section D-14 on the transport—the location where they first entered and remained discreetly concealed, to carry out their mission and destroy the transport after its departure. Also available in Section D-14 is an emergency escape flightcraft, where they plan to exit the ship when the damage they cause reaches a critical point, and the transport's structural outer hull will break apart due to weight discrepancies.

The sentry robots continue onto the elevated metal maintenance platform in the direction of the escape craft, where they will meet their commander. Trikan shouts out to Cen-Ton, who is still holding onto the com's operational console. "Cen-Ton, look at this! They cut through the moored chains with a laser beam!"

As Cen-Ton looks at the console view screen, Captain Trikan calls out to the ship's computer again. "Computer, give me a readout of the weight analysis on the ship's emergency passenger escape flightcraft on the entire port side section!"

The computer replies, "... AFFIRMATIVE, CAPTAIN... FLIGHTCRAFT WEIGHT... APPROXIMATELY FOURTEEN METRIC TONS EACH... SEVEN UNITS WITH FULL ESCAPE CAPACITY CAN ACCOMMODATE TEN PASSENGER OCCUPANCY EACH..."

Trikan commands, "Never mind that, computer... JETTISON THEM! Jettison all of the emergency flightcraft on the port side immediately! AND DO IT NOW, COMPUTER!"

With the release of the last emergency escape flightcraft, the large transport regains its flight course polarity as the beacon indicator lights, along with the sirens, become deactivated, and silence once again returns to the ship.

Seconds later, the transport's orbital flight course heading and speed factor lock onto the orbital magnetic sky highway above the planet's stratosphere. As Trikan sits back in his flight chair, a moment of relief comes over him, and he turns towards Professor Zola, who is now standing alongside his com-chair, observing the telescreen and the damage to the cargo sections.

"Professor, are you alright?"

"Yes, thank you, Captain... I am fine. They desperately tried to destroy this ship! Their assignment was to prevent YOU from returning to Star Port City!"

Trikan replies, "That was their first try! Those chains did not just come loose; they were cut, professor, and NOT before takeoff! They're on board, and I'm sure they'll try again!"

The professor looks at his arm computer. "Captain, my computer readout just alerted me that our unwelcome visitors are heavily armed and are working their way back toward the engine section of the craft!"

Cen-Ton interrupts, "... CAPTAIN... THE PROFESSOR IS CORRECT... MY SENSORS ARE PICKING UP MOVEMENTS ON THE ELEVATED CREW MAINTENANCE WALKWAY SECTION... THE INTRUDERS ARE WORKING THEIR WAY BACK TO THE ENGINE SECTION D-14... THEY ARE TWO SENTRY ROBOTS AND AN UNIDENTIFIED LIFE-FORM..."

Trikan pauses for a moment and says, "This might be their backup plan to destroy the engines, even though they cannot escape. They will destroy this ship with all of us on board!"

He turns towards Cen-Ton. "Come on, Cen-Ton, we have to get down there NOW!"

Trikan gets on the com unit and talks to LamBrute, "LamBrute, how are you guys doing down there? Can you take over the com and stay with the Professor?"

LamBrute replies, "Yes, Captain, and we're feeling a lot better!"

"Good, have your crew guard the forward section of operations and tell them, weapons off safety! If they pick up a reading that they can't identify, tell them not to hesitate to fire! Cen-Ton and I are going back there to put an end to all of this now! Cen-Ton, let's go. I'm not going to wait any longer to stop these sentry robots!"

Suddenly, a voice calls out to Trikan over the ship's telecom, "Captain... Captain Trikan... It's me, Sergeant Larsen. Do you copy?"

Trikan waits before he responds to the telecom, "Sergeant Larsen?"

"Yes, it's me, Captain!"

Trikan does not answer. "Captain... Please, they're after me, sentry robots! I don't know how many there are. They're trying to destroy the ship! I need your help. Please, I'll explain later!"

Trikan waits again before he responds, "Okay, Larsen, tell me what section." Larsen responds instantly, "I don't know, Captain! I think I'm lost. I'm not familiar with this ship!"

"Okay, Larsen, I'm on my way!"

Trikan shuts off the inner ship's communications, severing all incoming and outgoing messages. Professor Zola remains silent for several moments in deep thought and then says, "Captain! It is highly unlikely, Sergeant Larsen. This Sergeant Larsen is most likely a government agent!"

Trikan agrees, "You're right, Professor! The real Sergeant Larsen is most likely sitting in a cell at Central Detention! After I leave, keep all the monitor view screens activated. If you lose transmission and cannot visually identify me or hear my voice asking you to open and let me into the com, Do Not! You know better than I, professor, that the Android commanders are equipped with voice modulators."

"Yes, captain, and they use it to perfection! Before you leave, please ensure you have your visor luminous oxygen supply helmet. The oxygen content in the cargo sections is dramatically low, compared to what we need to breathe, but quite adequate for the Androids, who can adjust and function at a lower oxygen intake!"

Trikan puts on the double-layer helmet, which contains an emergency oxygen supply; he then attaches the night-vision screen and prepares to leave. "Cen-Ton, let's go... weapons off safety; Full Blast Mode!"

Captain Trikan and Cen-Ton become a life force of their own, relying on one another in an existing state. All plans and programs that previously separated them are meaningless, for they now exist united in a dimension where the universe allows them to walk on the same path, feeling united with a shared purpose.

The thoughts of Cen-Ton and the captain are now less

complicated because they are now of one mind and one mission—to survive and destroy the enemy.

"... CAPTAIN... MY MAGNITE SENSORS ARE TELEPATHIC SIGNAL RELAYS THAT ARE USED FOR DETECTION AND COMMUNICATIONS... I AM PICKING UP THE CROMION SIGNATURES THAT IDENTIFY TWO SENTRY ROBOTS... ALL CARRYING ANTIMAGNETIC WAR SHIELDS THAT CAN DEFLECT INCOMING LASER FIRE FROM OUR WEAPONS... WE DO NOT HAVE THE WEAPON CAPACITY TO DESTROY THESE SENTRY ROBOTS... CAPTAIN, MY SENSORS ARE PICKING UP THAT THE ROBOTS HAVE NOW REENTERED SECTION D-13 AND ARE HEADING IN OUR DIRECTION..."

Trikan replies, "Cen-Ton, I am familiar with the blast shield reflectors that protect the sentry robots. I agree; however, I have something else in mind! Computer, give me the entire ship's graphic relay construction prints."

The computer responds in picture form on the helmet's visor screen, without providing verbal descriptions, giving Trikan the information he requires to carry out his plan. Also appearing on his arm computer is the complete holographic readout of the transport's construction, with section-by-section capability, along with complete electronic circuit configuration and bypass form capabilities. Trikan says to the computer, "Exit processing!"

Trikan and Cen-Ton travel down a narrow corridor that takes them to a maintenance catwalk that runs the entire ship's length, allowing inspection personnel to report on all cargo sections.

Upon arriving at the transport's computer brain storage room junction maze, located in Cargo Storage Section D-5, Trikan moved boxes of durable goods stored there.

He then opens the unit control relay computer junction door to access the display units that operate the functional dielectric computer systems, which control the entire inter-base command center of the cargo ship.

The actions that he will now take cannot be undone. The slightest mistake or a simple error will jeopardize the sentry robots' success in destroying the ship, which contains the professor along with the four Trikinian warriors.

As Trikan reacts without a preconceived plan to destroy the sentry robots, his mission to find Elisa remains unchanged. He reacts without fear, setting aside any danger that might lie before him, driven by his will to overcome any force that can deny him the ability to survive now and continue with his mission.

Trikans' plan to destroy the sentry robots and deal with Sergeant Larsen was not given the time to plan every move. His reaction would be spontaneous and take the complete discipline of a brave warrior, willing to risk his life for others and Elisa.

Finding the correct computer relay, he instructs Cen-Ton to synchronize with him on his command to pull out the 31178 and 31179 computer program relay units for sections D-11 and D-12, which will bypass the mechanical operations that control and release the offload underside cargo doors in those sections of the ship.

"Do you follow me, Cen-Ton, on my command!"

"... YES, CAPTAIN... I UNDERSTAND... BY YOUR COMMAND, I WILL PULL THE COMPUTER PROGRAM, RESULTING IN THE RELEASE OF THE CARGO DOORS... THEREBY DROPPING THE ENTIRE CARGO OF TIMBER LOGS FREE OF THE TRANSPORT..."

"Correct, Cen-Ton! And then, wait for me to return to your location. Do not attempt to leave Section D-5."

"... THANK YOU, CAPTAIN... I UNDERSTAND..."

"Now to deal with those Sentry Robots!"

As Trikan makes his way to confront the sentry robots, he checks his arm computer for an open-frequency alert activator. A scan appears, revealing the interior of the cargo section that lies before him. Its heat range temperatures are 3,000 degrees outside the cargo ship as it travels on the magnetic orbital highway above the heat shields that protect the tropical regions and the vast farmlands that cover the planet.

Captain Trikan makes his way to Section D-12 and fires his laser weapon at the steel cable rods, destroying the catwalk section above the cargo area. As the rods explode, the entire section drops off its steel hangars, preventing the two sentry robots from entering section D-12 by way of the catwalk.

Unable to continue with the missing sections, the sentry robots climb down their section of the catwalk ladder and make their way slowly over the massive timber logs that now obstruct their access to Section D-11. The sentry robots are registering a life-form with a destructive weapon as they continue with their preprogrammed strategies to destroy Trikan and the large cargo transport.

Captain Trikan backs away, takes refuge in the cargo section, and continues to monitor the robots from a safe distance on his arm computer. The sentry robots' progress is slow and disabled due to the unassembled timber logs that caused the entire cargo section to become obstructed when they cut the moored chains, releasing a deluge of heavy timber.

As they continue to follow their preprogrammed command order, they are unable to anticipate a trap or a hostile plan created by their adversary, the captain.

As Trikan waits and observes their slow-moving progress, beads of sweat begin to run down his forehead. He turns off his helmet's visor luminous shield and remains motionless, standing in the dark void of the cargo section, in the absence of any light. When the sentry robots reach the midpoint of Cargo Section D-12, he sends the message of his plan to Cen-Ton. "Now, Cen-Ton, remove the section program of D-12 and manually open the cargo bay doors!"

Cen-Ton overrides the D-12 section and releases the hatch bay doors, and the entire cargo of the Alphanian timber logs, along with the sentry robots, drops from the underside of the craft. As the entire cargo lands on top of the sky platform's heatshields with the robots, they explode in energy combustion due to the excessively high temperatures of the sun's rays.

Trikan speaks to Cen-Ton again on his arm computer, "Sender to receiver... Close the cargo hatch doors, Cen-Ton. Our robot passengers are no longer with us! Now, to deal with Larsen!"

Relieved from the pressure from the deadly sentry robots, Captain Trikan is now more determined to destroy Sergeant Larsen, whom he believes is nothing more than a replica of the real sergeant. He turns on his helmet's visor luminous lens light and reenters the now-empty cargo section, where he fires his laser weapon, destroying the catwalk and luring the sentry robots to their destruction.

At the entrance, he takes off the safety harness from his arm computer, activates its warning indicator light of low fusion energy, and then hangs it on the twisted steel ladder that was part of the destroyed catwalk. Removing a small magnetic communication device, he attaches the unit to a receiving monitor above the visor luminous shield on his helmet, where he can transmit and receive communications with Cen-Ton.

Trikan now leaves the area and, from a safe distance, communicates with Sergeant Larsen through his voice modulator receiver on his Dial-Date arm computer, which is hanging from the twisted metal of the catwalk.

Not wasting any time, Trikan calls out in the darkened cargo section, "Larsen? Larsen, do you copy? You can come out now; the sentry robots are no longer onboard. It's safe for you now!" Finally, Larsen answers, "I understand, Captain! That's too bad about the robots! This is not the first time, Captain. You've done this before, in the rainforest! I'm afraid that I can't help you, Captain. You see, I was sent here to possibly negotiate an understanding with you. You must believe me, Captain; I have nothing against you. There are some things that I admire about you. But you disappointed me, Captain!"

Trikan responds, "Oh, really? Enlighten Me!"

"Well... You made a fatal mistake, Captain, and now it's going to cost you your life!"

Trikan makes his way back to the adjoining Section D-11, where he will deal with Larsen and have the added protection of the steel section wall that separates each cargo compartment. Anticipating an eighty-degree blast range radius from Larsen's laser weapon, he will remain there and let him fire first.

Suddenly, as he had expected, Larsen fired at the voice modulation coming from Trikans' arm computer, destroying the entire ladder section and sending debris throughout the cargo entrance of D-11. When the firestorm clears from the laser blast, Trikan waits and remains silent as Larsen looks at the smoldering debris and black smoke, thinking that he has killed the captain. Larsen then speaks into a recording device, "Captain Trikan has been destroyed!"

Unexpectedly, Trikan steps out from the obscured smoke-filled entrance portal and fires his laser weapon. One single blast of *Infused Proton* energy destroys the Larsen duplicate, and then Trikan communicates to Cen-Ton, "It's done, Cen-Ton! Tell the professor that the problem has been corrected! You can open all the cargo bay doors now, Cen-Ton."

From the audio-message unit inside his helmet, Captain Trikan receives a message from Professor Zola. "Captain, good news, it's in effect. I have a code frequency; it reads:

"WEATHER CONDITIONS APPROPRIATE... UNFORTUNATELY, STAR PORT CITY IS IN A STATE OF ELECTRONIC BLACKOUT... NO FLIGHT VEHICLES CAN ENTER... THEIR ENTIRE AIRSHIPS AND GROUND MOBILE UNITS ARE IN A STATE OF LOCKDOWN... CIVILIAN CARGO RECEIVING PORTS ARE NOT AFFECTED."

"That's good news for us, Captain!"

Trikan responds, "Message received. Thank you, professor. Replace the computer program relay units and close the control doors, Cen-Ton."

"... AFFIRMATIVE, CAPTAIN... THE PROGRAM UNITS ARE BACK IN PLACE... I SECURED THE COMPUTER CONTROL ROOM, CAPTAIN..."

"Good, Cen-Ton, we're done here!"

A short time later, Trikan arrives back at the operations com, and upon entering, the Trikinians suddenly confront Trikan with a celebratory greeting, with mixed emotional shoutouts and cheers in praise of their captain and friend. Professor Zola proceeds to recite personal praise of the captain. "Captain Trikan, I can't think of anyone in my whole life who has achieved such a magnificent feat! In the face of great danger and determination, I salute you, Captain Trikan!"

The Trikinians proceed to leave the control-com and go back down to the crew's mess hall, where they are preparing a celebratory dinner for the captain. After they leave the com, Trikan looks at the professor and says, "I don't think I'm hungry, professor."

The professor replies, "Oh, nonsense, Captain! All the food in the pantry has been checked and is in perfect condition. Cen-Ton will confirm that he has checked out all the food supplies and has assured me that they have not been tampered with. The food that the Trikinians consumed came from an unsecured automatic food dispenser.

Later in the evening, the captain, professor, and Cen-Ton return to the operations com without remarking to the professor, who is on the verge of falling asleep. Trikan then begins searching the computer's industrial networks of electronic listings, and the sleepy-eyed professor observes the captain and asks, "Captain, may I ask what you are looking for?"

Trikan is transfixed upon the scanner. "I'll let you know when I find it, professor. Okay, there it is!" Words of the item appear on the screen: "...Military Grade Arm-Cuff Computer...Authorization from Government Required... Department of Defense..."

"I was hoping that you could help me with this one, Professor. I had to destroy my arm-cuff computer to distract Larsen!"

The professor looks on inquisitively. "Would you care to explain further, Captain?"

"It's not important, professor."

Turning off the ship's computer, he says, "Get some rest; I'm going up to the observation dome; we'll talk about it later."

Captain Trikan climbs up the ladder to the operations console and observes the panoramic view of the zero-gravity landscape. From horizon to horizon and across this star system was the place he was familiar with. As a young child, he studied distant star charts and the asteroid belt, broken up by ominous-looking figures carved out of distant craters that had been formed at the beginning of time.

The bleak and alluring asteroid belt, now set against a new sunrise in the background, evokes memories of ancient silhouettes and shadows. Seconds later, they are lost, as the large ship is fast, leaving its past behind. Trikan climbs back down into the command console alongside the professor, who is sound asleep in the copilot's chair. For several moments at the helm of the large ship, he watches the new sunrise coming in from the side observation portal, dancing across the ship's technical and operational panels.

Trikan thinks to himself, ...*This is where I belong*... He has found that inner being, and from this day forward, that feeling will remain.

At a ship's helm where time does not exist, he belonged out here, where the restless spirit of an individual can find inner peace; this place, this excellent, endless adventure that we call the universe, where his future remains within the stars, as the transport continues on its unrestricted, pre-planned course to Star Port City.

Chapter 13:
Destination: Sports Arena

By nightfall, the transport enters orbital space above the commercial quadrant complex three hundred kilometers outside Star Port City, where these commercial zones supply food and other marketable products to its large population. Star Port City is the largest and most populated municipality on the planet. The purpose of these commercial landing supply zones is to free up the airspace and allow only passenger air travel within the city limits.

Trikan receives an online computer transmission from the commercial port landing master announcing: "Captain, we're putting your transport into a holding pattern for the time being until we clear a surge track that will place it in a cargo offloading transport removal facility. In the meantime, I will accept your code plate number."

Trikan enters the requested information into the ship's main computer, deactivates the lock code, and then the plate code numbers are immediately transferred to the port master. The commercial port landing master replies, "Thank you, captain."

Moments later, the landing sequence begins with a facility tracking beam that locks onto the large cargo transport, announcing that the landing program is now in effect.

Ship bells continue in a rhythmic sound throughout the entire transport as emergency beacon lights blink with the ship's computer announcements to secure all personnel during the reentry into the planet's atmosphere. Over and over again, the ship's computer gives status announcements:

"... GYRO-FORCES ARE IN EFFECT... HEAT SHIELDS ACTIVATED..." As the transport reenters the planet's atmosphere, the ship's computer announces again: "...TRANSPORTS REENTRY... FLIGHT COURSE STABLE... HEAT SHIELDS HOLDING... TRACKING... TRACKING... LANDING PROGRAM... ABLE ONE TRACTOR BEAM HOLDING... SPEED REDUCTION IN EFFECT..."

The ship's emergency bells cease their alarm program, and the red beacon lights remain on, bathing the entire personnel cabin and the operations cabin in an eerie red glow. Silence now replaces the emergency bell alarms throughout the ship as it continues in a free fall into the planet's atmosphere, guided only by the facility's tractor beam.

The transport reenters the planet's atmosphere from orbital space at a speed of twenty-one thousand kilometers per hour as the retro rockets ignite, slowing the transport down. The onboard computer announces the following operational procedure as the emergency alarms become activated again: "... SPEED REDUCTION... SHIP'S FRONTAL RETRO ENGINES ARE NOW ONLINE... NOW FIRING... SPEED REDUCTION... THE TRANSPORT IS NOW IN A NORMAL OPERATIONAL LANDING MODE... OPERATIONAL SEQUENCE NOW NORMAL..."

At that moment, the emergency alarms are discontinued as the computer announces: "... NOW APPROACHING LANDING BAY... COMMERCIAL ZONE SEQUENCE PREPROGRAMMED... ALL ENGINES STOPPED... ANTIGRAVITY TARMAC FIELD IN LANDING PROGRESS... CAPTAIN... YOUR SHIP HAS NOW TOUCHED DOWN IN THE LANDING BAY..."

With the landing operations completed, Trikan looks over toward the professor. "Well, professor, we made it!"

He is suddenly interrupted by a knock on the side window by a docking official robot standing on an elevated antigravity platform. He motions to Trikan to open the com's portal window as the slow-moving antigravity slide track slows down into position to be unloaded.

The docking official quickly takes a photo with a computerized camera, which quickly identifies Trikan and produces a temporary visitor's photo pass with his characteristics listed on it: Type: Trikinian ... Height: 6'4" ... Hair Color: Light Brown ... Eye Color: Blue Green ... Total Weight of Visor Helmet, Flight Uniform, Side Arm Laser Weapon: 210 lbs. He hands the completed identification pass to Trikan, which will allow him to remain in Star Port City for eight solar days. A new merchant must then report to the central port official's office and apply for a permanent commercial license to continue to transport commercial goods to the city.

Judging Trikan by his Trikinian apparel, he refrains from asking him further questions because of past experiences that Trikinians are work-oriented and not interested in official inquiries unrelated to their work mission.

As the official's elevated antigravity platform recedes downward, he says, "**...ENJOY YOUR STAY IN STAR PORT CITY, CAPTAIN...!**"

After the docking procedures are completed, the professor tells Trikan that he will contact him the next day, as previously planned, at the café. "Professor, wait! Can you tell me where you're going?"

"It's not important, captain, and I don't want to burden you! You have enough to think about!"

"Professor, tell me anyway."

"My exile has been temporarily lifted. I must report to the governing council, and I don't have the faintest idea what they want from me."

The professor then smiles and says, "Here, captain, take my arm-cuff computer and be careful not to lose it; it's government-issued and also programmed with a failsafe code sequence."

As the professor removes it, he hands it to Trikan and says, "I have other ways to keep in touch with you. I am sure that before I leave the council meeting and tell them that I lost mine, they will gladly provide me with a replacement military-grade, with something special inside to monitor my every move."

Before leaving the terminal, Professor Zola is given a farewell departure by Trikans' four special envoy escorts.

The professor enters a surface transport and calls out his destination to the robot operator.

Trikan and the four Trikinians blend into the crowd of workers outside the commercial terminal complex, where the complex workers are loading the large surface transports that carry goods into Star Port City's commercial markets.

Outside the complex, there are also commercial pedestrian transport surface buses.

Not wanting to bring attention to themselves, Captain Trikan and the four Trikinians deliberately split up and took separate land transports to Star Port City. Trikan boards one of the transports with Cen-Ton and discreetly walks to the back, taking a seat as he intentionally does not want to be surrounded by other passengers.

When the transport has received its last passenger, it pulls out onto the main Megatron Control Highway, which will take the passengers on their nonstop trip into Star Port City in extraordinarily comfortable, aerodynamic seating.

The comfort of the hydro bus provides a smooth ride to all its passengers, despite occasional surface imperfections on the highway. Captain Trikan, as well as many of the other passengers, feels the effects of a relaxed, scientifically planned mode of transportation. As he sits back and closes his eyes for a couple of moments, his meditation is suddenly interrupted by a female passenger who abruptly drops into the seat next to him and whispers into his ear, "Hey, Trikinian! Do you know who I am?"

Trikan looks at her, smiles, and replies, "Yes, and why are we whispering?"

She smiles back. "Because you are a big troublemaker! Do you know that half of Star Port City is looking for you? All the authorities are looking to collect the reward for your capture." Trikan smiles again. "Does that include you as well?"

Holding up her left hand, she replies, "If you want, you could put a gold ring on this finger and consider yourself captured by ME!"

Trikan then says, "Now I know that I'm in trouble!"

They both indulge in a couple of moments of humor as Kriena lowers her voice again, "Well, Captain, I have a message for you. When we arrive at Star Port City, we will be dropped off at the tourist-transport terminal, where you will find a hotel where you will stay. LamBrute and his troopers will also be staying at the hotel. Do not make contact with them while you're there. The next day, you and the Trikinians will visit a popular tourist café, located a short distance from the hotel. There you will wait for the Professor! If plans change and the professor does not show up soon, you must leave and go to the place of the flowers. Do you follow me, captain?"

"Yes, but I have one question. How do you fit into all of this?"

She smiles again. "I don't! I'm only the messenger, and captain, after that, my orders are to pilot the flight transport back to Trikinia!"

At one of the government's **Pro-Genesis Labs**, a medical director and research scientist conduct unlawful experiments for financial gain unbeknownst to his staff. This is where the Larsen Android was created and programmed. The director in charge of the facility receives a call from the enforcement division on a restricted circuit ban, and the caller remains anonymous. At the time of the transmission, the director did not realize that his main computer's audio system was left on:

"Director... I am calling to inform you that our prototype did not work out as planned. I'm not blaming you or your staff." There is a slight pause before he continues. *"There was a plan that had great possibilities, and we will let it go at that... I have*

just left a meeting where all present agreed that we return to our original initiative. That is why I called you. We will need the same good work you and your staff have diligently put together in your original prototype. I have full confidence that you will give us what we need."

The door to the lab was left open, and unbeknownst to Doctor Stanford, his nurse, Rose, who is more than his professional confidante, heard the entire message. She enters the lab without warning, thinking she can discourage him from dealing with this group, which she believes is an unlawful organization, unaware that it is a secret government program. She tells him, "You're not going to do this again, are you, Stan? No official documentation was sent to the proper governmental authorities. I found the file that you instructed me to prepare for the Larsen procedure, but it was never sent through the proper channels. I found it hidden away in the pile of old medical records. Can you tell me what's going on?"

Looking at her for a moment, he tells her, "Whom shall I report this to, Rose?"

She does not answer, and, judging by the look he gives her, she realizes he is angry and remains silent. "You know too much! That could be very bad for you! I think you should go home and think about what you heard, clear your mind, and refrain from discussing this matter with anyone! I want you to leave right now and be here early in the morning, where you will do your job as if you know nothing about the message that you overheard!"

She quickly responds to his instructions, "Yes, I understand, doctor. Am I in trouble?"

"Of course not! As I said, go home, and I'll see you early tomorrow morning."

She then leaves and goes home to her apartment complex, where she begins to do some chores. Suddenly, she gets a knock on her door. A voice calls out from a message delivery service, "Hello, I have a message for Nurse Rose!"

As she opens the door, she is immediately shot by a laser blast and killed.

The next morning, Doctor Stanford receives a message on his telescreen from the Hospital Security Department. He replies, "Yes, I understand! That's awful! Do the authorities have any idea of what happened?"

The caller responds, "No, doctor, the authorities are working on it. All they could come up with as of now is that she had no known enemies!"

As Doctor Stanford ends the transmission, he contacts the Trauma One Hospital staff, whom he has worked with on many occasions, and inquires about more information about what happened to Nurse Rose. Most of the staff tell him that they're sorry about what happened to his assistant, and he replies, "Yes, thank you... Please keep me informed."

The following day at the café, the professor does not show up after a lengthy period. Captain Trikan grows tired of waiting and decides to leave, following the remaining instructions he was given.

Before his departure, a large man approaches Trikans' table. He is dressed in the traditional garments that identify him as a trader of clothing and wares, a merchant from Cata-Form, one of the two outer planets. "My good friend," —he abruptly corrects himself— "Sorry, my brave Trikinian warrior, excuse me for being so intrusive! I have been looking at your outdated robot, and my business as a trader has given me a keen eye for a profitable investment that can be of great revenue. For not only my keen eye for business, but also a gratifying sum for the seller! Are you interested?"

Trikan looks at the large, robust man and replies, "Are you selling or buying?"

The overweight merchant breaks out into loud, uncontrolled laughter and recites a few words in the Trikinian language that complement and amuse most Trikinians.

"How refreshing you are, my brave warrior! A Trikinian with a sense of Humor! May I sit down, my friend?"

Trikan motions towards the empty chair as the large merchant sits down and lowers his voice.

"I do not intend to keep you waiting for a handsome, sizable profit! If I may get to the point, is your robot for sale? I do have a large collection of old robots, and I would like to include yours in my collection!"

Somewhat amused, Trikan looks at Cen-Ton and asks, "Cen-Ton, would you like to go with this man?"

Cen-Ton immediately responds, "... CAPTAIN... I AM NOT SURE THAT I WOULD BE HAPPY IN A COLLECTION..."

The merchant looks at Cen-Ton and then bursts out laughing again.

"Happy? How can a robot be happy? All of my robots are well cared for. Perhaps they are happy, too? I never thought to ask them!"

Trikan looks at the merchant and replies, "Cen-Ton is happy. You can't have him, and he's not for sale!"

The merchant stands up and laughs again while bowing down to Trikan. "My good, brave Trikinian warrior, I bid you a good day!"

Turning to Cen-Ton, he says, "And you, my happy robot... Good day to you, too!"

Trikan suspiciously watches as the merchant leaves and approaches other tables of tourists. He opens a carry bag filled with delicate trinkets and inexpensive souvenir jewelry, representing the various places of interest for tourists visiting Star Port City.

Outside the café's main entrance, two suspicious individuals are sitting at a table with no food and an empty beverage decanter. Trikan mainly focuses on the fact that they have no cold drinks on a sweltering day in Star Port City.

As he continues to observe the merchant and the two suspicious individuals, a waiter approaches them to see if they would like to order, carrying a tray with a complimentary carafe of an iced fruit drink for all the patrons in the café.

As the cold fruit carafe is placed on the table, it is refused, and the waiter is impolitely directed away. Unbeknownst to the merchant, who had not witnessed the incident at the table, he approached the same two individuals and tried to interest them in several of the souvenir items he was selling. He immediately realizes by the way the two men stare at him that they have anger in their eyes, and he abruptly excuses himself and walks away.

Trikan is convinced that they are in trouble and sends a coded message on his arm computer to the four Trikinians that he is leaving the café. The two individuals sitting outside the front entrance are not tourists, but by all indications, may be government agents.

Before transmitting, he adds, "Do what you can to find out what their intentions are. Cen-Ton and I are leaving now!"

Trikan and Cen-Ton walk through the main entrance of the café, passing the two suspicious individuals without noticing them. For a moment, Trikan stops by the merchant who is concluding a sale and tells him that he is interested in the same item that one of the tourists had just purchased.

As the merchant places Captain Trikans' souvenir item into a gift box, he continues to converse with the patrons at the table. Trikan planned for this slight delay to keep an eye on the two individuals in question.

Noticing that they are also leaving, Trikan thanks the merchant and makes a cordial departure to the tourist at the table.

The two men, dressed in almost identical outfits, begin to leave the café to follow Trikan and Cen-Ton. Before they can leave the outside area of the café, the four Trikinians pass in front of them in the crowded entrance of the café and block their exit.

One of the four Trikinians shouts out to a brother trooper that he is a "crook" and that he did not play the game fairly at the table. Upset, he punches the accused trooper, who receives a blow and falls back on one of the agents who is about to follow the captain.

The agent is knocked over onto a wooden table and then falls to the ground unconscious. The other two Trikinians join the argument as the fighting continues; with the four of them involved, it becomes a 'tug of war,' resulting in broken tables and the other agent being hit by a chair, which knocks him to the ground.

The agent then shouts out, "Will someone call Star Port Security?"

As he receives a stern look from one of the Trikinian troopers, he points and says, "You have NOT heard the last of this! I'm putting YOU in my report!"

LamBrute, the leader of the Trikinian troopers, apologizes for his friends' conduct. As he looks above the crowd, he sees that Trikan and Cen-Ton are nowhere to be found. He then announces that he will help with the situation and sincerely apologizes for his Trikinian brothers' conduct, and pays for the damages.

He walks over to a table of tourists and takes their large carafe filled with iced fruit drinks off their table. He then starts to walk away with it, and the tourist at the table looks on in disbelief at the large Trikinian wearing animal skins, but does not remark about the incident that has just taken place.

The Trikinian trooper then calls out to the waiter, "A fresh carafe of iced fruit drink at this table, please!"

Looking at the event that has just taken place, the waiter nervously says, "Yes, Sir! Right away, Sir!"

The large Trikinian then walks over to his companions, who are standing over the unconscious agent, and then pours the carafe of iced fruit drink onto his face to revive him. He then says to his companions, "Now, gentlemen, let's behave ourselves; no more fighting!"

Suddenly, spontaneous applause erupts throughout the café, as most of the patrons believe they have just witnessed a live performance by professional entertainers, a common occurrence in some large cafés and restaurants along the main thoroughfare leading to the arena where the Healiocon Games are held.

As the four Trikinians leave the café, the applause continues until they exit onto the promenade. The four of them are assigned to their mission to protect the captain, and must now separate themselves from one another and assimilate into other Trikinian groups of visitors.

They are fully aware that government security agents will be specifically looking for the Trikinians who were involved in the incident at the tourist café.

Trikan and Cen-Ton take a private taxi ride with a robot driver who is a programmed sociable entity. After Trikan and Cen-Ton are aboard, the driver remarks about the continuous news reported on his dash-com screen on the electronic power loss over Star Port City.

The repetitive reporting continues, with government officials sharing their opinions while still trying to determine the cause of the mysterious malfunction in the giant grid systems, which were considered fail-safes. Something like this had never happened before in a metropolis the size of Star Port City. Research committees have already been formed to investigate various malfunctions of the giant city that affected the terminal velocity escape ports, which also malfunctioned, preventing space transports from leaving on their regular schedules to the two outer planets. However, the occurrence did not last long, and the cause of the issue affecting the electronic grid system is under investigation.

The taxi robot driver turns towards the captain, **"… So, by the way, Captain, tell me where you and your robot are going. I'll be happy to drop you off if it's not too far off my program schedule…"**

Trikan does not answer the robot immediately while thinking to himself, "*…Did Alden have something to do with the massive electrical* *failure right after he landed in the unloading dock terminal? Or was it just a coincidence?*

Trikan then replies, "Go to the place of the flowers!"

"...Oh, you want to go to the Nature Preserve, Captain. It's not too far off my scheduled route. I know the tourists love it there. I'll be happy to drop you off. It's always packed this time of year! I've been caught in many traffic backups that last for miles on this road because of the tourists! They are familiar with only one way to the Nature Preserve, and that is on this road. However, I know a way to get you there by using some less-traveled roads that pass through small villages. It's going to take a little longer if you don't mind the delay...!"

Trikan says, "Sounds good to me; we're in no hurry."

The driver raises his voice over the noise of the rough road. "...By the way, Captain, your robot doesn't talk much...?"

Trikan looks out over the dismal condition of the highway, which is in need of repairs. Adding to the strain of the noisy engine that was not present on the main road before the turnoff, he shouts back to the driver over the vehicle's uneven drive conditions, "He doesn't talk unless you ask him a question!"

Not hearing the captain, the driver responds, "...**What did you say...?**"

Looking at Cen-Ton, Trikan remarks, "I think my robot is a little nervous."

The driver shouts back again over the rumbling of the vehicle, "...**What did you say...?**"

Trikan shakes his head and shouts, "Never mind!"

After a while, the taxi finally approaches the highway exit, which is on the main road to the Nature Preserve. The backup of commercial transports, combined with personal luxury vehicles, has overfilled the Nature Preserve parking facilities.

Visitors will now have to walk a long distance from their parked vehicles to the entrance of the Preserve, and Trikan and Cen-Ton are no exception, as they leave the taxi transport. Trikan then shouts to the driver, "Thank you very much!"

The robot driver replies, "**…Anytime, Captain. I enjoyed your company…!**"

Once inside the Preserve, the exhibits feature nature trails alongside wild animals in artificial habitats that are conducive to their species. Visitors can walk the trails or rent comfortable electric transportation modules and tour the entire 900,000 acres of this lush natural park, which also features three large vacation centers.

Captain Trikan and Cen-Ton become part of the living tapestry of holiday seekers, combined with enchanting wild birds flying throughout the parks above the giant Alphanian trees. The multitudes from the two outer planets are frequent visitors, dressed in their traditional, decorative colors that represent the popular, flamboyant garments of their cultural heritage and add to the exciting festival atmosphere of the Nature Preserve Park.

Trikan and Cen-Ton enter the Nature Preserve through the main entrance, following the majority of visitors and using the exhibit reference brochure. The captain then says, "Cen-Ton, let's go and check out the exotic flower exhibit and buy some flowers."

Cen-Ton adds, "... CAPTAIN... I BELIEVE THAT WILL COMPLETE THE MESSAGE..."

"Yes, let's approach this in a positive way, Cen-Ton, and expect to be contacted by the professor."

As they continue walking, a familiar voice calls out to him, "Johnathan, keep walking, and don't turn around. Listen carefully; there's a flower shop outside the large horticultural dome at the end of this trail. Stop and buy some flowers; we can then talk safely there. It's a safe environment where we can admire the plants and engage in a personal conversation."

Inside the center, a multitude of floral creations featuring exotic plants from various regions of the planet are on display. It features large rock formations surrounded by a variety of wildflowers and twisted, sprawling perennial bushes, which overlap and block the view of other sections as the trail continues.

This part of the large horticultural center is covered by a vast dome, leaving an equal amount of natural open-air space, which allows wild birds to enter the domed section and feed. Trikan remains silent as they continue their walk in the preserve until they reach a secluded area. Here, they can talk without their conversations being heard.

"Johnathan... What have you done?"

"Aunt Lasara... I didn't ask for this! They trained me for this, to fight back!"

As tears roll down Reanna's face, Trikan replies to her, "Hey, come on... What's this all about?" Embracing her, he says, "There's no reason to be upset, Mom. Everything is going to work out, trust me!"

Teary-eyed, Reanna says, "I'm just happy to see you, Johnathan!"

Turning back to Aunt Lasara, he smiles as she embraces him. "Johnathan, the plans have changed! You are not going to meet up with the professor; he has been taken to the government center to speak to the council members about their favorite subject these days—Captain Trikan!" Trikan asks, "Will he be alright, Aunt Lasara?"

"I'll see to it that no harm will come to him. I wish I could say the same for you, Johnathan. They took possession of my home, and everything they could think of that would give them information on where to find you. They know about you and the professor and will stop at nothing to destroy you. The professor claimed under interrogation that Cen-Ton was malfunctioning when he left the professor and joined your voice command, allowing you to utilize his technical abilities for your evil deeds.

Jonathan, I think you shouldn't travel with him into the city. I have already made arrangements that only the Trikinian LamBrute will travel with you, and Cen-Ton will travel with the other three Trikinian warriors after you leave the Preserve.

They will keep a safe distance from you, and if you should need them, they will be there to help."

Handing him a small business card with an address written on the back, Aunt Lasara tells him, "Here, take this; this is the safehouse where I'm staying north of Star Port City. Stay safe! Oh, by the way, Captain, you make a very impressive and handsome Trikinian in that uniform!"

He smiles. "It was Alden's idea!"

"Johnathan, let us not leave this area together. Security cameras are monitoring every area throughout the park. Reanna and I will leave first. Stay well, Johnathan. Until we meet again." Before leaving, Reanna talks softly to Trikan, "Be careful, Johnathan."

Trikan waits until Reanna and Doctor Lasara leave their little rendezvous, as he then plans to leave the Nature Preserve with Cen-Ton and meet the three Trikinian guards for the last time outside the main gates, where they will go their separate ways.

Upon leaving the park, the multitude of tourists has created a well-protected cover for Trikan, Cen-Ton, and the four Trikinians as they plan their next move.

Trikan tells LamBrute, "You travel with me; Cen-Ton will travel with your unit commander.

They will be looking for the professor's robot, and if they find Cen-Ton, they damn well know that they will find me!"

Cen-Ton agrees. "... I UNDERSTAND, CAPTAIN..."

Trikan says to LamBrute, "We'll leave first, and your crew, along with Cen-Ton, will follow on a separate passenger coach on their way to the safehouse; Cen-Ton has the coded directions."

As they split up and board different surface transports that carry passengers to the inner city, they go unnoticed. Doctor Lasara receives a message in the form of musical notes in a chord of a popular melody that repeats itself in a different sequence of the original scale. Their form of communication has been used successfully in the past. Now, it has become almost a daily occurrence to communicate with one another:

> *Hello, my dear Doctor Lasara and Reanna. Just to let you know, everything went well, and I am no longer in exile. It has been lifted, and I am free to go anywhere I please, including no travel restrictions to Trikinia or the two outer planets. Of course, I had to agree to their terms. The government officials have put forth several requirements; I must convince Captain Trikan to surrender if I encounter him. If such a thing were to happen, the exile would be permanently removed. One man's freedom for another man's incarceration! Until we meet again, my dear friends... Stay well.*

Transport after transport pulls up to lines of tourists waiting to enter the games and entertainment park centers outside the arena grounds. Trikan and LamBrute make their way to the far end of the transport to available seating. Trikan says. "LamBrute, you see that hostess working her way down here. Tell her no, thank you, and I don't want anything. I just want to close my eyes and get some rest."

LamBrute acknowledges. "I understand, Captain."

Minutes later, Trikan falls into a deep sleep as his last thoughts fade into a kaleidoscope of fragmented images and conversations.

Where did it all start...? In the mysteries of dreams, where the word *"wood"* becomes part of a conversation that Trikan is having with the professor, *"... A long time ago, cutting wood for the fireplace with sentry robots and picking up the large, heavy logs and placing them into a mobile sled. It was the middle of winter; back at the house, my mom was there, and Aunt Lasara told me, 'Never let anyone see how strong you are.' I did what she said for a long time, and years later, before graduation, Aunt Lasara told me, 'Trikan, I have to put you on report... You must never chop wood with sentry robots....."*

Breaking out into a cold sweat, Trikan awakens, and LamBrute asks, "Captain, are you okay? You were saying something in your sleep."

At that moment, the hostess reaches the passenger area where Trikan and LamBrute are sitting. She asks, "Can I get you two gentlemen something to drink?"

LamBrute replies, "No... I have something much better for the captain!"

Taking the cup from her hand, he opens up a small flask, pours some of its contents into the cup, and tells the captain, "Here, captain, drink this!"

"What is it, LamBrute?"

"It's blackberry rum, and it will make you feel better!"

The hostess leaves and makes her rounds, serving beverages to the other passengers on the large surface transport.

After entering the city, the first scheduled stop is at the Healiocon Stadium, and as the transport slows down, Captain Trikan turns on the view screen above his seating section. A constant traffic delay announcement travels beneath the up-to-the-minute real-time information bar across the bottom of the screen, explaining the various traffic delays. He sees the crowds in front of high-speed land-vehicle racers, live theater, and an assortment of souvenir shops, along with the War Game's main attraction.

After several minutes of observing the screen, Trikan is about to say something to LamBrute. Instead, he remains silent as he focuses his attention on the two individuals familiar to him. As he pauses, he replays the still imagery of the crowd in front of the stadium. He observes the two security agents waiting to see who gets off the transport. "Look at this, LamBrute, there they are!"

LamBrute looks at the screen and replies, "Looks like we have company again, Captain! Most likely, they are looking for you!"

Agreeing, the captain replies, "My thoughts exactly, LamBrute. Signal your unit command; tell them we have company outside the stadium!"

Becoming aware of the two café individuals that Trikan brought to his attention, LamBrute removes the safety on his laser weapon. Trikan then adds, "As soon as the transport slows down, we get off and walk the rest of the way to the stadium. We will blend in with the crowd, which will make it more difficult for them to identify us. They'll likely be looking for your command group and Cen-Ton also! You'd better warn them to get off their transport before it arrives at the stadium's front entrance!"

By the time most of the passengers have left the transport, Captain Trikan and LamBrute are in line to purchase an entrance ticket to the stadium. Trikan is still preoccupied with the two agents as they climb aboard and begin questioning some of the passengers who remain on the transport to another travel location. He suddenly observes one of the agents looking out the window and pointing at him, while the other agent is on his arm computer, talking, as the transport pulls away with the two agents on board.

At that very moment, Cen-Ton and the three Trikinian scout troops make their way through the crowd and are united with Trikan and LamBrute once again. The captain then informs the scout troops that they will not be entering the stadium with them. He is almost sure that the two agents have identified him and their Commander LamBrute. The three of them must go to the safehouse. "You must leave immediately with Cen-Ton; he has the location."

LamBrute then adds, "Follow the captain's orders. Do not leave the safehouse until I contact you."

A period lost in time, before the written words, is where it all began when the universe gave light to the shadows of the past, and life began in this quadrant of the Nebular Cloud. The ancient events that took place have been mysteriously passed down to present generations, as if transcribed into their DNA by a force from a hidden location far away in another dimension, which dictates the rules that must be followed to this present time.

Outside the main gates, multitudes of spectators are negotiating entrance tickets to various accommodations within the stadium. Better seating facilities are offered to individuals who are willing to pay a premium price for the best viewing. The expanse of the lower arena sections allows for the action events to occur close to the audience in a three-dimensional field of battle. They will experience the sounds of combat and triumph as well as the anguish of defeat.

The upper-level sections of the arena are constructed with large Banishean steel columns, holding up a roof of celestial bodies and other anomalies above the circular fighting field, including the solar storm event that takes place within the Healiocon Arena at every event. Spectators will leave their seats to view the circular fighting field, as victory is declared over the vanquished in each event.

Outside the main entrance of the Healiocon Arena, the shoving and pushing from the multitude of spectators becomes a severe problem for the crowd control sentry robots. Their commander issues a call for more security sentry robots to help contain the crowds outside the arena as dignitaries arrive in luxurious transport vehicles. Their arrival accelerates the excitement amongst the spectators who want to see the celebrities as they exit their vehicles. Computer transfer-imaging constantly relays photos of the dignitaries, which appear instantly on every screen monitor throughout the large stadium's mega-view screens. Home viewers are also offered telescreen viewing of celebrities and dignitaries walking up the main reserve ramps. They stop for a moment, engage with stadium officials, and are given special reserved seating as they are led into the Healiocon Stadium.

The population of spectators present at the Healiocon Center becomes problematic when the dangerous genetically altered prehistoric Tyrannosaurus Rex arrives in its cage. This fierce predator is used in the event called the ***Paleolithic War Games*** against a team of warriors that will end in the destruction of the Tyrannosaurus Rex before it inflicts massive casualties on them. This event is a reenactment of their ancient ancestors' struggle against these beasts for survival. The final event in the **Paleolithic War Games** is hand-to-hand combat using mounted troops on robotic Mangus-Equo Horses while avoiding being eaten by ice wolf predators.

Inside the circular combat field of the arena, participants will battle under the huge Healiocon Disk, which will discharge circular spheres of universal energy as it spins. The discharge of these energy-charged *Maglite* globes will strike the ground and explode in a deadly, colorful detonation, with a thunderous sound that reverberates throughout the enormous stadium.

At sequenced uncontrolled intervals, the Healiocon Disk will fire a fatal, destructive charge that will vaporize the combat participants who are in the line of fire.

As the competition continues, the Healiocon Disc will increase its spinning rate and discharge its deadly rays, making survival for the participants almost impossible except for the most agile and skilled warriors.

Outside the main entrance gate, regular deliveries of ice wolves arrive for the upcoming events. Director Stormis of the Healiocon Sports Complex inspects the cages that contain the ice wolves and then gives his approval upon receiving personal identification passes with order contracts relating to their transport. These cages that hold the Trikinian ice wolves have been purchased in a transcript order from the arena event minister.

After checking his computer-identification screen for clarification, the director's second-in-command instructs the delivery transport service to take the ramp to the lower sections where the ice wolves will be contained in stationary caged compartments under the arena until they are ready to participate in the games.

After the carriages containing the wolves are well within the entrance gates, Trikan and LamBrute approach the ticket-processing security control entrance unit. It seems as if the entire population of Star

Port City seeks entrance into the vast stadium complex. Long lines await to purchase entrance vouchers for the stadium, which features several levels of seating, allowing patrons to observe the games. The premium purchase vouchers will also allow visitors to access the large park's entertainment facilities, which include a live theater featuring professional entertainers, as well as an assortment of games and rides suitable for younger visitors. Complimentary dining is also available with the purchase of the premium voucher.

Beyond the sports complex is the megacity of tall structures that dominate a portion of the skyline, where private air-transport flightcraft are constantly in remote-control programs, taking passengers to their destinations.

Many of these flightcrafts are specifically programmed to land on top of the tall commercial buildings that employ a significant portion of the city's population. Surface transportation is also constant throughout the city's large thoroughfares.

Surrounding these immense structures are commercial tunnel ramps that connect to the Hydro-Express Train Transportation stations, located below the city's surface, which take passengers to local destinations and out to the extensive produce farmlands.

After completing their city station and borough stops, these high-speed, mega-electronic transports leave the city at electromagnetic speeds of 200 miles per hour.

As Captain Trikan and LamBrute approach the ticket entrance officer, he immediately touches the security information central identification screen to process the entrance tickets for the two Trikinians. Trikan momentarily turns away from the visual display, triggering an alert on the security monitor that indicates an evasive action. Instantly, their photos are transmitted to Central Command as the electronic facial indicator continuously analyzes their facial features.

An alert indicator for the two Trikinians shows no reference file on LamBrutes' screen; however, the Trikinian captain is identified as the fugitive Captain Trikan to the admitting officer. The officer does not immediately hand Trikan and LamBrute their entrance tickets and says, "Captain, I apologize; there is going to be a slight delay for you and your scout officer. I'm experiencing offline communication at the moment."

As the ticket entrance officer sends their photos to the central command, on the opposite side of the device scanner, the attendant gets the complete identification of the wanted notification on Captain Trikan. The security screen reveals a readout: **"CAPTAIN TRIKAN... FACIAL FEATURES... POSITIVE IDENTIFICATION... EXTREMELY DANGEROUS... MUST TAKE PRECAUTIONARY MEASURES."**

Upon receiving the complete identification of the wanted captain, the entrance security attendant immediately informs his superior, Director Stormis, that the fugitive Captain Trikan is standing right in front of him, buying an entrance ticket to the stadium.

The message is then transferred from Director Stormis of the sports complex to Government Councilman Lennox, who was out of his office when his secretary received the coded transmission.

Upon the councilman's return, he is immediately notified about the transmission that they have located the fugitive Captain Trikan, along with a Trikinian warrior, with the intention of entering the Healiocon Stadium. Government Councilman Lennox, who is in charge of the Department of Criminal Justice, is delighted by the news, and he remarks, "How fortunate! The illustrious Captain Trikan is not hiding out in Trikinia anymore! I wonder what made him return to Star Port City? I am not surprised that the arrogant captain would allow himself to be photographed in a public arena where there's no chance of escape! He thinks of himself as being infallible. I will show him how insignificant he is if he thinks he can avoid capture!"

He then orders his secretary to quickly send a reply message to the entrance officer, instructing them to issue the tickets and grant permission to enter the arena. Turning on his telescreen, he remains silent for a few moments, then smiles and replies, "His escape cannot be permitted! Now, send a message to notify Director Stormis of the Healiocon Stadium that I have approved the entrance passes for the criminal Captain Trikan and the Trikinian! Tell him that he must use his security to see that the captain does not leave the stadium. He is very clever, and you must have sentry robots at every exit. I am in the process now of alerting every member of our government council for their judgment on this serious ongoing situation!"

His secretary interjects, "Councilman, I have Supervisor Stormis of the Healiocon Complex on the screen."

Lennox turns to the screen and replies, "Councilman Lennox here."

Stormis responds, "Pleased to talk with you. I already ordered Sentry Robot security for all of the stadium exits. Are there any other orders that you have for me?"

"Don't do anything to him! Treat him like the other visitors unless he tries to leave the stadium. As we speak, I'm in the process of putting together a security team, and we will be at your disposal as soon as possible."

Unbeknownst to Councilman Lennox, a large tourist group of Trikinians is staying at the visiting centers in the Healiocon Complex that offer tourist accommodation facilities for extended vacation periods. Complimentary admittance is also included, and the Trikinians will attend the Healiocon Games daily. Director Stormis feels that this could become a problem when they attempt to arrest Captain Trikan; he immediately informs Councilman Lennox of his concern.

As Lennox reads the message from Stormis on his view screen, he tells his secretary, "I need to inform the members of the security council on every step we take with this problem. It will be their decision on how they want to deal with this Captain Trikan and the Trikinian!"

Lennox then sends a message to the large government chamber, and all the telescreens become activated simultaneously on every personal seating console station with a council member present at the daily meeting forum.

> *"Council members, excuse me for the interruption, but I have a pressing issue that must be taken care of immediately! We have confirmation that the fugitive Captain Trikan has just entered the Healiocon Stadium. Director Stormis has been informed of the situation and is fully cooperating with my initial request to have his security team of sentry robots at all exits in the large arena. This is the best that I can do to prevent the fugitive Captain Trikan from leaving the premises. I request a combined judgment from our council on how to proceed in this matter."*

The entire government council immediately takes up the request from Lennox regarding the decision that will be made and enforced by agreement with the majority of the members present.

After a heated debate and discussions on what action should be taken, the entire assembly that is present decides on a two-thirds majority vote to apprehend the fugitive Captain Trikan before he attempts to leave the Healiocon Complex, thereby avoiding a public display. Councilman Lennox, who is in charge of governmental security, is pleased when he is given the orders to apprehend Captain Trikan, following the council's decision, personally. He must remove the fugitive from the crowded Healiocon Complex in any way he can, using his discretion. Lennox tells his secretary, "Get my security crew and sentry robots together; have them meet me at the air flight security dome unit one complex. They will fly down with me to the Healiocon Stadium."

Just before leaving his office, his telescreen blacks out, and a complete malfunction occurs in all the office electronics.

Suddenly, an anagram message appears on the telescreen, revealing a priority-coded message for Councilman Lennox. The coded transcript informs him of what must be done. He must act according to the mandated rules to show his allegiance and the worth of the privilege granted to him to retain his position of authority. His orders are to eliminate the captain as discreetly as possible.

As the screen goes dark, the electronics in the office return, and Lennox pauses momentarily while looking at his secretary. He says, "Just don't stand there; notify them!"

She nervously replies, "Yes, Councilman!"

By the time Lennox arrives at the air flight dome, his security crew and sentry robots are already boarding the hydro-flightcraft. Taking his place up front with the pilot, he says, "When we land at the far section of the dome, we will enter the complex by a special security entrance ramp."

Immediately, the pilot engages the blast engines in a takeoff mode flight course, while shouting over the noise of the engines, Lennox tells his security crew, "We're going after the renegade Captain Trikan! He cannot escape; he's inside the Healiocon Stadium, and before we leave there, he will be our prisoner! I don't want anything to happen to him, you understand. Weapons on sequence, stop and hold!"

Chapter 14:

The War Games

During the flight down to the Healiocon Stadium, Lennox remains silent as he plans how he will deal with Trikan. He now has no intention of following the directives given to him by the council vote at the meeting.

As the hydro-craft touches down outside the flight dome of the Healiocon Stadium, Councilman Lennox and his security crew walk towards the stadium and meet up with Director Stormis. "Director Stormis, I appreciate your cooperation! This is my assistant, Commander Gorman, with whom I believe you have worked on several assignments."

Director Stormis agrees, "Yes, councilman, we have."

As he extends his hand to Commander Gorman, he replies, "Good to see you again."

Lennox then tells Stormis, "I have been given full authority to take any course of action to apprehend this fugitive, Captain Trikan. May I remind you, director, he is very dangerous! I don't want to lose him, and I hope you understand the seriousness of this matter."

Agreeing, the director states, "Yes, I do, councilman." We have taken the necessary precautions, and as we speak, we have him under surveillance! He is with a group of Trikinian tourists in Section C, located in the lower part of the stadium.

Handing Lennox a teleview computer module that locks into all the security cameras in the stadium, he scrolls through frame after frame until he finds the captain and remarks, "There he is! We got him!"

The councilman turns on the computer's telescopic view and adjusts the programming for the lower area of the arena to Section C. The camera instantly focuses on the group of Trikinians as Lennox concentrates on the telescopic computer scope, which reads voiceovers and lip-syncs and separates individual conversations to identify multiple people talking at once. Below the picture screen, the word "recording" appears as it is stored, and the conversation so far reveals nothing important about what Trikan and the others are saying. It seems that the rules of the game and the events that are about to take place are entirely the subject matter of their conversation. While Trikan listens for a couple of moments as the others engage in small talk about the upcoming events, he interjects into their conversation and tells them, "The games are about to start; we should return to our seating sections."

Councilman Lennox puts the computer camera on save and tells Director Stormis, "Let the games begin as scheduled, and then we will take care of our Captain!"

Lennox hands the telescreen computer back to the security official and replies, "I do not need this anymore!"

Lennox spends a few moments in conversation with the facility supervisor as they walk through the long corridors into the Healiocon Complex until they meet up with Stormis's official security team. This security team has carefully observed Captain Trikan with the large Trikinian group of patrons within the lower seating area of the fighting field. Councilman Lennox begins to explain, "The Supreme Council members have insisted that no harm should come to Captain Trikan when we take him into custody. If he were to have an accident, whom could they blame? You know... I have a plan that may be to the liking of our brave captain. It's called 'I'll meet you halfway!'

Smiling again, he says in a low whisper, "Yes, captain..."

Halfway!"

The director remains silent, listening attentively to what Councilman Lennox is saying. Lennox then tells Stormis to have his security ground personnel immediately arrest Captain Trikan and the tall Trikinian, who is not part of the tourist group in that section. Director Stormis turns on the identification security camera and sends a photo composite to his enforcement command unit.

A short time later, the sentry robots, led by a stadium security officer, approach the captain and the Trikinian LamBrute, placing both under arrest. The two prisoners are told to comply without creating a scene and are removed from the stadium field. Director Stormis asks Lennox, "Are you sure that's Captain Trikan?" I don't understand why he would allow himself to be taken prisoner without resisting."

Lennox looks at him with a deep stare. "Director, if you value your position, you must keep this Captain Trikan under extreme security! Do you understand?" Looking around at the stadium seating, he tells him, "Now, look for three Trikinian warriors and a robot! They were observed together and may be here to be part of Trikans' plan to disrupt the games and help him escape!"

Director Stormis remains quiet for a few moments, observing the crowds, before answering. "Councilman, with all due respect, what is it about this Captain Trikan that makes him so dangerous?"

"Director, what I'm about to tell you was once reserved for the highest-level government officials only. I can speak of it now because the necessary corrections have been implemented, and the mistakes that were made have been rectified. There is no longer any documentation of the original records. So, I can tell you about Captain Trikan and why he is so dangerous! He entered our military academy as a young adult and showed respect for his superiors' higher rank. He was an outstanding student with extraordinary academic ability. It was the sports that no one paid attention to!"

Stormis interjects, "Are you referring to the military sports programs?"

"Precisely, the competitions—they're mandatory training for the young cadets. They can participate in three competitions of their choice. Trikan wins the 110-meter sprint and also defeats his opponent in the ancient form of combat wrestling, emerging victorious once again. Must I go on? The heavyweight lifting competition, do I have to tell you who wins? He outlifted two of our heavy-lift champions, and none of the officials at the military academy took any notice of it at the time. This young man possessed such unusual strength! Some say he might very well be a cyborg spy sent here by the Trikinians to destroy us! Unfortunately, we have no way of telling! His medical records reveal no unusual characteristics, despite rumors that he might be a cyborg.

Director Stormis is silent for a few moments and replies, "Is that possible?"

"Yes, anything is possible when you can't prove it's not!"

Stormis speaks into his arm computer, and one of his security personnel appears on the screen. "Healiocon Security! This is Director Stormis. Have our two Trikinian prisoners been processed yet?"

The Healiocon security officer responds, "Yes, director, their weapons have been removed, and they have been placed in separate cells."

Stormis replies, "These two prisoners are extremely dangerous!" Have them both firmly secured to the steel Triangulum: they must not be allowed to escape. Take extra precautions, as ordered by Councilman Lennox!"

The sentry security officer of the lockup complex replies, "By your command, Director!"

Activating a support unit within the lockup complex, he orders sentry robots to prepare the two prisoners to be chained to the steel Triangulum. The security officer abruptly enters Captain Trikans' lockup cell while holding a laser weapon on him; he shouts, "STAND UP, CAPTAIN! ARMS FORWARD!"

As two other security sentry robots enter Trikans' cell, they carry in a heavy steel Triangulum plate and chain Captain Trikans' wrists to it. The weight of this long, arrow-shaped piece of heavy Banishean steel pulls the captain forward while penetrating the soft ground of the prison floor. The three sentry robots then repeat their ordered offensive procedure on Commander LamBrute in the next cage. Lennox speaks in a low voice, thinking out loud, "The steel Triangulum... This will break the captain's spirit, director, and then I am sure he will accept my plan!"

The brilliant seasonal change of the winter solstice brings darkness as the winter season begins. High winds pick up snowdrifts and cast them across Star Port City's mammoth structures until they reach the open fields of the city's spaceport. The sounds break the winter night of exploding light that lifts the massive starships, which will carry passengers and cargo to the outer planets.

The winter storms do not affect everyday transportation as they complete their scheduled passage across the Omega Star System. Several days later, Councilman Lennox arrives back with clearance orders to use his full authority to deal with Captain Trikan as he sees fit, if he feels that disciplinary action must be taken, until Captain Trikan is transferred to Central Detention.

As his transport flightcraft lands at the far end of the stadium, he enters the massive structure by the security entrance in the middle of the War Games, which have started on their regular schedule. Director Stormis once again greeted him and inquired, "How are our prisoners doing, Director?"

Stormis responds in an official manner, "Well, councilman, your captain hasn't said a word since you ordered him secured to the Triangulum. The Trikinian complains constantly! He keeps mentioning a person called Alden, and this person will take us to justice!"

The councilman exclaims, "To justice?"

The director agrees, "Yes, and there's something else; he blames you directly for his incarceration!"

At the Government Council, a lifetime member has called for an emergency meeting that all government officials are required to attend, as stipulated in the written charter of their constitution.

The distinguished Doctor Lasara arrives at the front entrance of the government complex, and several friendly supporters and a multitude of agency correspondents meet her. As she leaves her government-provided transport, she is surrounded by various media officials who ask her questions she cannot answer at once. I am currently unable to answer any questions at this time. Please understand that I cannot explain why the government called for a meeting."

Smiling, she turns around to the luxury transport that has now pulled up behind her vehicle. Still smiling, she recognizes one of the council members. "Why don't you ask Senior Councilman Barntor? I am sure he will be happy to answer all your inquiries!"

As the elderly, overweight Councilman Barntor exerts extra effort to get out of his transport, he shouts out to his chauffeur, "Well, just don't sit there, young man! Help me get out of this confounded thing!"

After being assisted out of the transport, he exclaims, "Why do they make these passenger transports so difficult to get out of?"

He says to his driver, "Thank you, my good man!"

Looking at Doctor Lasara, he smiles as he approaches her. "What a pleasant surprise! How do you manage to stay so slim and charming?"

As she straightens out his jacket's lapel, she replies, "It's a woman's secret, councilman. Now, would you please address these journalists before we're late for the meeting?"

The questions come from the crowd in every direction. He attempts to quiet down the undisciplined shouting of inquiries, which makes it impossible for the councilman to answer every question that differentiates every subject without continuity. He reaches the point of frustration and motions to the crowd to have them step away from him until their inquiries subside. "Now, I must tell you... I know as much of this meeting as you do! I will deliver satisfactory answers to every question after the meeting! Thank you very much! Now, if you'll all be so kind as to follow me to the meeting?"

Once inside the lobby of the Government Center, Councilman Barntor says to Doctor Lasara, "I should not forgive you, Doctor Lasara"—he smiles at her again— "for not warning me to stay in my transport until the crowd dispersed. But I will, only because you're so charming!"

Doctor Lasara replies, "May I say, councilman, you handled the situation like a true gentleman!"

Moments later, they are greeted by government orderlies who will assist them to their private offices, where they will prepare for the emergency meeting that is already in progress.

The events taking place back at the Healiocon Stadium cannot be described as justice for the two prisoners. Director Stormis asks, "Do you want to go down and speak to the prisoner's councilman?" Lennox hesitates to answer while he is observing one of the Hover Platform Spheroid Nebular Cloud Evolution Events coming to an end at the

Warfield. This infantry event is a reenactment of the past when warriors in combat with their enemies charged at them carrying deadly weapons. Dressed in steel plates and animal skin, they wear protective helmets as they attack one another while holding an electronically charged lance. They only have to strike their opponent with a glancing blow to activate the electronic charge that will burn through armor plating and cause fatal injuries.

The event also features a large, structurally mounted plasma disc that spins at the center of the stadium's dome-shaped ceiling. As it rotates, it releases units of plasma energy in spherical forms that strike the event field. These energy-plasma globes explode, emanating different pastel colors of deadly energy waves of electromagnetic radiation throughout the combat area. A warrior in the process of defeating his adversary, unaware of the energy spheres, is instantly vaporized if struck by one. Once this happens, it automatically gives the opposing team the advantage by having a higher number of warriors in the game.

The War Games will continue until the surrender or destruction of one side occurs. Absorbed in the carnage of the War Games, Councilman Lennox finally breaks his silence. "Director Stormis, I noticed that after the fatal blast from the protonic-spheroid disc, there is an increase in its rotation."

Director Stormis acknowledges, "Yes, it has to do that, to build up its inertial force for the radiated plasma to form into its energy blast again."

In a low voice, Lennox replies, "I see... A fatal performance of universal science!"

Looking up at the increased revolutions of the stadium's giant plasma disc, Lennox asks the director, "How is it controlled?"

"It's programmed for each event, councilman."

Lennox is still deep in thought as he shouts over the cheers of the crowds as they observe the suspenseful actions taking place in the War Games. "Did it ever malfunction, director?" Looking out at the vast, crowded stadium, Stormis replies, "Councilman, it's a failsafe program, and we do have a backup provision in the event of an unforeseen occurrence. An attendant operates a braking system that will also shut down the power source to the entire stadium. Each attendant is an expert in the conditions that could cause a malfunction. So, you see, councilman, we will never have a problem!"

Taking his eyes off the plasma disc, he looks at Director Stormis. "Well, director, let us get on with it. Let's see how receptive the captain is to my offer."

Two levels below the stadium are the lockup cells. The prison sergeant is notified to have the prisoners ready for an interview. Trikan is about to fall asleep when the prison sergeant walks over to his cell and shouts at him, "HEY YOU… CAPTAIN, GET UP! DO YOU HEAR ME? You haven't been found guilty yet! If I had my way, I would put you in a cage with an ice wolf! You're going to be spoken to by the councilman; why would he want to be bothered with you? I don't know."

As Trikan gets up, he drags the Triangulum, which he is chained to, across the dirt floor to the middle of the cell. As he stands at attention, he thinks to himself, … *Freedom of the mind...* The feeling of freedom that has always kept him in a state of well-being now weighs heavily on his thoughts. …*Could I still feel that I was free…?*

Trikans' past would return like a dark shadow from when he entered the academy. It was the same feeling now that he had back in Star Port City. Those years of regimentation have come back to haunt him. His past was as if he were existing at the edge of a high cliff, daring not to step forward in fear of where he would land.

The periods of silence without interruption have come to an end; the everyday reality of life was beginning to affect him. The past was no longer the past; it had become part of the storm of his emotions, which called for action. This storm would have victims without vengeance, and he will do what he must to gain his freedom once again.

The prison sergeant looks over to the next cell and orders LamBrute, "TRIKINIAN! Stand up at attention and look like a Real Warrior!"

After ordering LamBrute to stand at attention, the prison sergeant hears voices coming from the stairwell leading down to the prison chamber. He immediately buttons up the front of his war vest and adjusts his sidearm weapon while quickly checking the rest of his uniform for appearance's sake.

Councilman Lennox and Director Stormis enter the chamber and are greeted by the prison sergeant with a military salute. Lennox says, "At ease, Sergeant! How are our prisoners doing?" As Lennox walks past the sergeant, he stops in front of Trikan, who is standing at attention. "Well, well, now what do we have here? Chained to the Triangulum! How unfortunate it would be to be chained to it for the rest of your life! It doesn't have to be that way, Captain, but then again, it will be your decision."

Trikan stares at Lennox for several moments and says, "What do you have in mind?"

Lennox turns towards the director and remarks, "Do you hear that, Stormis? Our good captain is interested!"

Looking at Trikan, he continues, "Captain Trikan... I am here to offer you a way out!"

He stops and looks around at the interior of the entire cell block and remarks, "What a horrible place this is! I am willing to go halfway with you, Captain! If you agree, I have a plan that will grant you a full pardon. I have our government's approval to pardon your past as if it never existed if you are willing to prove to yourself, by the investment that they made in you, that you are a true warrior! You will be released from the Triangulum."—Councilman Lennox looks towards LamBrute and continues— "And so will the Trikinian. I guarantee that both of you will never be chained to the Triangulum again for the rest of your lives... A complete governmental pardon granted!"

Trikan hesitates before speaking again while turning his attention towards Director Stormis. "It's true, Captain! It came over the government's coded communication."

As Stormis hands Trikan a computer graphic reader through the openings of his cell, Trikan looks at the computer screen and then turns his attention back to Councilman Lennox. "I accept. What do I have to do to meet you halfway?"

Slightly smiling, Lennox replies, "There are just two requirements on your part, Captain. Your half of the agreement is: first, you will no longer be known as Trikan! You will use your proper name and be known as Captain Johnathan Shawnwood, the name with which you entered the military academy. You must participate in the Healiocon Games at least once. If you are victorious, you will be free from any past transgressions for the rest of your life. The Trikinian will act as your second; he will help you prepare for the event, and he will dress you in battle armor and provide you with weapons of your choice. After that, he is free and allowed to leave the stadium."

Director Stormis orders the sentry robots into the cages to assist the two prisoners in lifting and carrying the heavy Triangulum from the chambers up to the fighting field. An antechamber leads them to one of the many large, gated courtyards that cut through the stadium seating sections, where the spectators can see the warriors being equipped with their armor and weapons as they prepare for battle. This is before they enter through the Banishean steel gates that open onto the fighting field, where the War Games occur.

Trikan and LamBrute are led out into the gated courtyard, where Trikan will be dressed for battle as a previous contest is about to come to its conclusion. Lennox and Director Stormis walk up to the gates to observe the infantry event while paying no attention to the captain and LamBrute. After the sentry robots unchain Trikan and LamBrute from the steel Triangulum, they leave them standing alone, unattended, in the center of the courtyard directly across from a horse stable. As the four sentry robots reenter the arched Warfield corridor and go back down to the prison complex, Trikan picks up the heavy steel Triangulum over his head and throws it across the courtyard. The crowd observes what he has done with the Triangulum shield and the distance to where it landed, several hundred yards away; they begin to cheer for him.

The trumpets then sound again, declaring the end of the second War Game event of the afternoon. The controller of the game announces a change in the final war event of the day. It will begin when the participants have completed the entrance of new warriors, as they prepare their weapons and armor to engage in battle scenes on horseback against several of the ice wolves that will be released into the battle competitions.

An old weapon's supply attendant approaches the captain and LamBrute. With a raspy voice, he says to them, "Which one of you has to sign for the equipment? I don't care which one."

He hands the signature tablet to LamBrute, who signs his name and hands it back to the old man. As the attendant looks at the tablet, he remarks, "Name... LamBrute?" He looks up at the Trikinian and says, "I have a friend, long time ago, same name, LamBrute... Brave man. He's dead. Die in War Games here! You fight today?"

"No, the captain fights today!"

The attendant turns to Captain Trikan. "You fight in War Games?"

Trikan does not answer him. The attendant asks, "You know how to ride a horse?"

Trikan looks at him and remains silent. "You know, captain, horse is not real..." They were gone a long time ago. You ride robot horse, Captain?"

Trikan answers the old attendant, "Yes, at the military academy; it was required."

He smiles and says, "Good...then you know. Were they real horses, Captain?"

Trikan responds, "Some were, some weren't."

The old attendant looks back towards LamBrute. Take whatever you need for your friend." Looking again at Trikan, he says, "My stable boy will help you pick robot horse you like. Now, I go away. Maybe when I come back, you be dead!"

As the old man walks away, Trikan asks LamBrute, "Do you think he'll be coming back?" LamBrute replies, "I hope not, Captain!"

Like many others throughout the stadium, this courtyard is surrounded by spectators who have paid a premium price for the seating areas that offer a close-up view of the combat groups. These spectators will be privileged to observe the warriors as they are dressed in their heavy armor, accompanied by a variety of ornately designed combat regalia.

The warriors will choose their preferred lethal weapons, and LamBrute will assist Trikan in inspecting these weapons for their reliability in battle. As the trumpets sound throughout the colossal stadium, they are followed by the announcement of the final War Game, in which mounted warriors will fight.

Several renowned warriors who gained recognition in previous War Games have announced their participation in this final event. Notably, they revealed that the notorious fugitive, Captain Trikan, will also be joining the competition. This announcement took many spectators by surprise, leading to a wave of disbelief among those who heard it. As the War Games are about to begin, the audience seated above the courtyard starts to exchange questions and comments about Captain Trikans' involvement in the games.

Some in the crowd observe the two warriors being escorted by sentry robots, and suddenly, one of the young spectators recognizes the captain and shouts out loud, "Look! That's Captain Trikan!" Getting up and leaning over the embankment wall, she is followed by her friend and other spectators, who ask her, "Are you sure it's him?"

Yelling out loud, she says, "Yes! I'm sure it's him! I can't believe that he let himself be taken prisoner!"

As she points in the captain's direction, she yells out to him, "Captain Trikan!"

She says to her friend, "That's definitely Captain Trikan. I would recognize him anywhere!" Many other spectators who have heard her remarks get up and leave their seats and run over to the edge of the wall embankment and begin to call out to the captain: "CAPTAIN TRIKAN! CAPTAIN TRIKAN!" Many more in the audience leave their seats that surround the large courtyard and begin to call down to the captain and LamBrute.

Trikan responds to their curiosity and waves back to the crowd. Cheers can be heard, and they begin to chant his name again throughout the large spectator sections of the courtyard. "TRIKAN... TRIKAN... CAPTAIN TRIKAN!"

The chanting increases and begins to spread throughout other areas of the stadium. This allows more spectators to become involved in their curiosity as they leave their section seats and look down from the high walls around the courtyard. The trumpets sound again to announce the preempted start of the final War Games.

The gates remain open throughout the stadium, allowing the warriors of the last competition to leave the field and for the new battle groups to enter. With the gates open for the start of the latest games, Councilman Lennox walks out onto the open field and is followed by Director Stormis. With so many people around the courtyard calling down to Captain Trikan to get his attention, Trikan responds to the last call of the new competition. He observes that Lennox and Stormis have left the courtyard and entered the Warfield with the gates remaining open. He will keep his part of the bargain and participate in the games. He waves again as the crowd erupts in applause, and the chanting continues.

Distant sections of the arena observe the warrior and cannot identify who he is, relying instead on the chanting of his name. Lennox looks up at the packed stadium from Warfield, and level after level, he observes the crowd chanting the captain's name and becomes angry. He shouts at Director Stormis, "CAN YOU TELL ME WHAT'S GOING ON HERE?" Director Stormis responds, "I have nothing to do with it, Councilman! Perhaps YOU should not have allowed the announcement of the fugitive Captain Trikan and his participation in the games."

Councilman Lennox and Director Stormis were unaware of Trikans' popularity, causing the crowds to enter into a new period of excitement and applause as they continued to chant the captain's name.

Before leaving to prepare himself for the War Game, Trikan gives a final wave to the crowd. The pathway to the horse stables is aligned with armor and weapons of double-edged swords of different lengths that are hung up in an open-market fashion, where warriors can pick and choose whatever necessities they desire before entering the stables.

Offensive jousting poles give the impression of tall hedges as they are lined up in multitudes on both sides of the entrance to the horse stables. Trikan selects the modern version of a jousting lance, a significantly more deadly and improved version of the one used in ancient times. This electronic lance will strike its opponents with a fatal electric charge, as it can burn through armor with a direct strike or cause a burn injury by a slight glance of its high-energy photon tip.

By the law of the contest, each contestant is allowed to select a second weapon of their choice. Trikan picks up a heavy double-edged sword that was the choice of ancient Trikinian warriors. Those Trikinian nomads, at the time, were the only warriors who could wield these heavy swords effectively in combat.

Upon entering the stables, Trikan and LamBrute are greeted by the old man's stable assistant, who is working on a damaged robot horse. He is attaching new hydro electronics to the robotic animal in the shop area, which is full of used and broken parts.

Stopping his work, the stable assistant wipes his soiled hands with a cloth, and before speaking, he smiles and says, "How may I help you two great warriors?"

Trikan remains silent as LamBrute smiles and replies, "The old man told us to take what we need."

Immediately, the stable assistant says, "Yes, yes, of course. I see that you have your weapons." Picking up a work roster, he reads a late entry and then remarks, "Oh no! Captain Trikan!" Turning towards the late arrivals, he then asks, "Are you Captain Trikan? I'm sorry, but all the horses are gone!"

Trikan remains silent as LamBrute remarks, "What are you talking about?"

The stable worker replies, "Well, you see here, they added the name Captain Trikan, but there are no horses available! The weapons are available at all times, but the robot horses become damaged and are not replaced on time. As you can see, all the stables are empty. I work here alone! My boss, the old man, is no longer of any help. I tell him we need ten deliveries, and we only get one! Most of the time, he walks around talking to himself about when he was young... The same stories over and over again!"

As he picks up the supply order list from the counter, the stable assistant says, "You see here, it says, please order ten more Magnus-Equo Robotic Horses, and we got only one the other day; it's still in the box!"

Trikan takes the list from the stable assistant, looks at it, and reads a brief description of the boxed robot horse that is still in its crate. The warehouse identification tag that was attached to the delivery list reads: NEW... LATEST-MODEL IMPROVED... ORIGINAL ORDER... DELIVERY SERVICE... ONE.

Trikan then says, "Let's open the crate and see what this thing looks like." Turning to LamBrute, he states, "Latest model improved!"

As LamBrute shakes his head and replies, "It's still a Robot Horse!"

As they follow the assistant down the middle of the stable to a stall that contains the large crate, the stable assistant remarks to Captain Trikan, "If you like it, captain, and you take it without being tested, it can cost you your life!"

Ignoring the comment, Trikan replies, "Let's check it out."

The captain, LamBrute, and the stable assistant begin to disassemble the large crate. The stable assistant, still thinking out loud, remarks to himself, *"When you need it to do something, it may not work!"* As he pulls open a section of the crate, he finds a computerized tablet that provides a comprehensive readout of the robot horse's functions and abilities and hands it to the captain. Trikan steps back and lets the other two continue to disassemble the crate as he reads about the specifications of the latest improved model: "The Magnus-Equo Robotic Horse..." Weight: Nine thousand pounds... Height: Eight point seven feet... It is operated by a computerized helmet that feeds off the brainwaves of the mounted rider. The horse and helmet come together; it's part of the equipment package. All the rider has to do is think of a projected move and how fast they want the robot horse to run and jump, exceeding its standard capability of twelve feet. This will all depend on the speed he conveys, and the distance traveled by a fully charged run can average a jumping height of eighteen feet. Some of these new robot horses have reached a height range of over twenty-one feet. On occasions, the ground field conditions determine the horse's traction and enhance their jumping height ability. These new robot horses have photo-projection sensor capability to identify multiple adversaries grouped in the background, alerting their host warriors to the danger of a charged attack approaching. This will allow the mounted warrior to change his course and retreat to his side of the war grounds, where he will have the protection of his battlegroup partners."

LamBrute interjects, "What else does it say, Captain?"

Trikan continues to read the information on the tablet. "Let's see... Its eyes have a long-distance field of vision and are also equipped with night vision. What the horse sees is sent back through the helmet to the mounted rider in real-time, along with mathematical brain sequencing information about potential adversaries. A signal alert indicates whether the rider should continue their charge or retreat. Please note: The manufacturer's warranty will become void if damage occurs to any part of this product due to failure to follow the manufacturer's requirement that every robot horse must have its name programmed into it. The name will be retained in the company's databases, thereby distinguishing each product as a separate entity. This robot horse will also take voice-activated commands, and all the rider has to do is flip the switch on the computer in front of the horse's saddle."

With all the packing material removed, the stable attendant and LamBrute take away sections of the wood crate. As Trikan smiles to himself, he says, "Let's see what this ride can do!"

He places his foot in the stirrup and mounts the robot horse as he turns on the switch that activates its voice control. An audio pictogram of a female company representative who manufactures robotic horses appears on a small tablet screen in front of the saddle:

"...WELCOME TO THE WORLD OF ROBOTIC HORSE RIDING! AS YOU CAN SEE BEHIND ME, THESE ROBOT HORSES ARE TRAINED AS YOU WOULD TRAIN REAL STALLIONS IN AN OPEN RANGE. THEY WILL DO ANYTHING A REAL HORSE CAN DO WITH ONE EXCEPTION... THEY NEVER GET TIRED, AND THEY REQUIRE VERY LITTLE STABLE MAINTENANCE. PLEASE ENTER THE NAME OF YOUR HORSE TO COVER THE WARRANTY..."

Looking up at the captain, LamBrute asks, "What are you going to name him, captain?" Speaking into the computer, Trikan responds, "Victory!"

The female computerized voice representative replies to Trikan, "...AN EXCELLENT CHOICE, CAPTAIN... YOUR STALLION 'VICTORY' IS REGISTERED, AND YOUR WARRANTY IS COVERED IN FULL..."

The trumpets sound, declaring the featured War Game of the day as the large gates of the courtyards open throughout the stadium complex. They will remain open to allow the warriors to enter the Warfield and leave after the event's finale.

Captain Trikan walks Victory out through the back of the large stable by voice command, not keeping to the standard procedure when warriors traditionally take their mounts out through the front of the stable and onto the Warfield. Following this procedure and adhering to the rules, the warriors were always dressed in their armor before selecting their mounts. Not being aware of the traditional aspects of the games, including the rules of the arena, Trikan had already chosen his weapons before entering the stable.

As he walks the robot stallion out to the courtyard, the crowds become excited again, paying all their attention to Captain Trikan while ignoring a large number of mounted warriors on the Warfield in their ancient traditional armor as they wait in a disciplined line for the war flags to drop, signifying the start of the last event.

Walking alongside Trikan, LamBrute carries the war helmet the captain will wear to control the robot stallion in battle. Again, the crowd begins to chant the captain's name, "TRIKAN... TRIKAN!"

No one in their lifetime has dared to defy the rules of the game. The mounted warriors break from the line of discipline and take different positions across the large Warfield. LamBrute hands Trikan the control helmet, and a moment later, Trikan rides out to the center of the courtyard as the robot stallion is now under helmet control. The horse trots and suddenly makes the sound of aggression that a wild horse makes as it rears up on its hind legs. This robot stallion reaches up to a height of fourteen feet in its first leap as the crowd roars with excitement.

Councilman Lennox and Director Stormis turn their attention from the Warfield to see the captain's performance on top of his robot horse. As Trikan raises the ancient, heavy, double-edged Trikinian sword high above him, the crowd, especially many Trikinian visitors, begins to cheer and call out his name throughout the stadium with great enthusiasm. The captain's actions will remain in their memory for this particular day of the games. When all four powerful legs of the robot horse touch the ground again, Trikan leaves the courtyard in a whirlwind effect as his Banishean steel armor creates, for a moment, a reflection of blinding light.

As Trikan rides out through the courtyard gates onto the Warfield, the robot stallion passes dangerously close to Councilman Lennox and Director Stormis, who suffer the indignity of having the ground dirt thrown up onto them from the horse's tracks. Some people who observe this action by the captain create a new round of cheers and chants of Trikans' name. They follow the captain, and within moments, the stallion's speed increases, and the captain arrives at the battle line with his assigned group of warriors as the War Lance Event begins.

While unsuccessfully cleaning the ground dirt off his dirty garments, Councilman Lennox is overcome with anger and remarks to Stormis that the captain was fully conscious and had purposely shown disrespect to them by his actions.

Lennox reaches the point of rage and loses all rational thinking. His original plan was to see Captain Trikan lose his life on the Warfield; instead, he observes the captain striking down his opponents as they ride towards him in groups of two and three horses.

He continues to strike them all with heightened fury while avoiding the deadly high-energy plasma spheres spinning and releasing from a fatal reproduction of the Cantianious Nebular Cloud, which is located in the center of the arena's dome. Each of his actions against his opponents is followed by applause throughout the enormous stadium.

This Universal Nebular Cloud, with its circular formation, turns at variable speeds, releasing deadly energy until it peaks at a higher speed, thereby releasing an explosive cluster of destructive force. This Nebular Cloud system was designed as a weapon of destruction to be used in the War Games. As the energy plasma spheres are released, the most agile of the troops evade injury, while others fail to avoid being vaporized by the energy of the plasma-subatomic cloud. Captain Trikan avoids being hit and stops for a moment to observe the field of his opponents.

At that moment, the deadly energy plasma cloud releases a volley of deadly plasma orbs again onto the field in the captain's direction. Trikan and his war stallion, Victory, instantly leave that area before the plasma spheres strike the ground and explode with their deadly effect that would destroy the captain and his robot horse.

This replication of the Nebular Cloud exists in a distant universe, one hundred billion light-years away from the Star Quadrant Omega Star

System, where its power and energy create new planetary systems within the vast region of the Milky Way.

At the end of the first quarter of the finale event, trumpets sound, and the announcement of the first quarter rest period is made. This allows the warriors to leave the Warfield and attend to their wounded as they prepare to continue the battle event.

As the warriors remove the last of the wounded from the Warfield, the speaker's announcement informs the spectators and the home viewers of the number on each side that will continue in the War Game event. The stadium broadcast speakers announce, "Ladies and gentlemen, out of one hundred government-sponsored warriors who participated in the event's start, sixty-five will return to the battle. Of the warriors on Captain Trikans' side of the field, eighty-four will return to battle, with only sixteen not participating!"

The announcer pauses and lowers the volume on his trans-speaker microphone as he turns towards his co-anchor and says, "Could that be right? Only sixteen not returning?"

His co-anchor replies, "Let me check my field computer for the event play-by-play photo sensors; that will give me an accurate real-time count!"

A photo sequence readout displays the entire event in a relay picture, as it stops and reveals the casualty amounts. The co-anchor responds with the information on his screen, "It's correct! I can't believe it, but it's true! Trikans' side only lost sixteen of their troops!"

Surprised, the announcer responds to him, "The captain on the big horse is responsible for most of the thirty-five casualties! We'd better pay more attention to this War Game!"

The co-anchor replies, "I wonder what this finale event is going to look like?"

The broadcast announcer says, "At this rate, unless there's some change in the numbers, our government is going to be very unhappy if they lose this War Game!"

The co-anchor agrees, "It will be a first!"

The broadcast announcer declares, "Let's not even think about it! Or we will all find ourselves out of a job!"

Addressing the audience again, the announcer says, "Ladies and gentlemen, the War Games will continue, and in the next segment, you will see for the first time in any previous contest, the sponsored team will enter the fighting field in a depleted state of numbers in relation to their opponents."

Hearing that announcement, Councilman Lennox becomes consumed with anger, and he says to Director Stormis, "DID YOU HEAR THAT? DO YOU SEE WHAT'S HAPPENING?"

Replying to Lennox, Stormis says, "Yes, councilman... It's clear to me, and I can understand why you are here."

At that moment, the trumpets sound again for the continuation of the War Game. Now, in an agitated state due to Trikans' survival in the first period of the event, the councilman turns to

Stormis and orders him, "SEND IN THE ICE WOLVES!" Stormis then tells him, "The government-sponsored warriors are not in a position yet."

The event continues with massive applause from the spectators and the chanting of Trikans' name. Councilman Lennox remarks about the first period and its results, and continues to tell the director, "I was a fool to give him his freedom, Stormis! I should have eliminated him when he was chained to the Triangulum!"

The crowd cheers as Councilman Lennox realizes that his agreement with Trikan will never give him the results he had planned. As the Trikans' team of warriors forms a successful line, they hold their ground, and the spectators become captivated with excitement, beginning to chant the name of his war stallion, VICTORY, as it appears on the large outdoor arena screen.

Lennox has reached the point of despair, as his plan to eliminate the captain has failed! He tells the director, "Look at him... Look at him, Stormis! The noble captain did not pursue his wounded enemy and destroy them in the first period! That's a sign of weakness!" Muttering to himself in a low voice, he exclaims, "The noble Captain Trikan... Now, I will deal with you!" Lennox turns his attention away from the arena's large screen, back to Stormis, and says, "DIDN'T I TELL YOU TO SEND IN THE ICE WOLVES? SEND THEM ALL IN NOW!"

As ordered, Director Stormis contacts the antechamber section below the arena that leads to the caged wolves. Within minutes, the gatekeeper in charge of them gets back to the director from his control center and says, "Sorry for the delay, director; I was just about to start feeding the ice wolves." Lennox interjects, "Stormis... Did I hear that correctly, hungry ice wolves? Tell your men NOT to feed them! Let's see if our brave captain can claim a victory over these predators!"

Before Director Stormis gives the order to release the ice wolves, he says to Lennox, "Councilman, it doesn't have to be this way!"

Lennox tells Stormis, "There's still time, Director! Perhaps you would like to join the wolves on the Warfield, but before you leave, order their release immediately!"

The director makes contact with the gatekeeper again. "This is Director Stormis. Open all the gates! Release all of the ice wolves to the Warfield!

The gatekeeper responds instantly, "By your order, director, the cages are open!"

Director Stormis is not happy with what he is forced to do; he always follows the orders given by his superiors, but this time it is different. He reluctantly follows Councilman Lennox's command, which leaves him with a deep feeling of regret.

Again, he listens to Lennox but is unable to take any action that could rectify the evil he has become involved with, as the government-sponsored warriors slowly approach their battle line. With a sinister look on his face, the councilman states, "You see, Director Stormis, you are now in a much better place when you obey my orders! Would you not agree?"

Looking at Lennox, Stormis responds, "Yes, councilman, I agree!"

Lennox continues to stare out at the Warfield as he says, "Outstanding, director... I am glad that you and I can work together, and both enjoy the elimination of Captain Trikan!"

As he walks over to the closed courtyard gate and looks out onto the Warfield, he observes the large ice wolves emerging from the open transfer exits below the cutout archways of the stadium walls. As the wolves exit, they attack the sixty-eight government-sponsored troops before they reach their battle line, as other packs of wolves hunt across the Warfield towards Trikan and his men. Before they can reach Trikan and his band of warriors, a large grey wolf crosses in front of them, stopping the attack. In a reluctant manner, the vicious pack turns away and slowly retreats while occasionally looking back at the large grey wolf and Trikan.

As they leave, the attack stops across the entire Warfield as they obey their command from the alpha wolf. The large alpha wolf then turns and looks at Trikan, a glimmer of the night stars reflecting in his eyes that transcends the bond of two warriors they both shared in another life, a long time ago. Trikan smiles and says, "Good boy, Pup!"

As Trikan reaches out and pets Pup, they are once again united in an unbroken bond. The two warriors stand together, and the crowd remarks, surprisingly. Many cannot believe what they see and marvel at the large alpha wolf allowing Trikan to touch him. Most remark while others cheer and call out Trikans name several times with an added comment. "Trikan and the Ice Wolf!"

The Warfield has failed to destroy Captain Trikan, and Councilman Lennox becomes silent for a moment as he bears witness to an unsettling event. "Stormis! What's going on out there? Explain to me... Your wolves come out, attack, stop, and then retreat!" He looks out above the arena and says, "Just look at them!"

Looking up at the crowded stadium, he says, "They will not stop calling out to him, this renegade traitor! Stormis, I need to use your office computer! Let the military deal with the captain... He's their problem! They trained him!"

The director agrees, "Of course, Councilman Lennox."

As Councilman Lennox and Director Stormis leave the courtyard and are about to enter the stadium, Lennox stops in front of the director and says, "Stormis... You'd best go first; you know your way around these corridors better than I. So please, Stormis, lead the way."

As he gestures with his hand as if he were a perfect gentleman, the director complies, "Of course, councilman."

As they walk down the corridor in the complex, Lennox must make his move before they reach the crowded lobby where the elevator lifts are located. He removes his sidearm laser weapon and fires it at the director, striking him in the back. While remaining silent for a moment, he quietly steps over Stormis and enters another corridor that leads him to a tourist access stairwell that will take him up to the Healiocon Control Center.

He walks up the spiral stairwell until he reaches the top of the circular domed control center of the Nebular Cloud System. He then proceeds down the dimly lit corridor, which allows tourists to look into the circular, glass-enclosed control room that operates the Nebular Cloud.

Thick panels of clear laser blast-proof glass protect the dangerous operations of one of the many mysteries of the universe. The only access point through which one may enter or leave the Nebular Cloud control room is controlled by a code-clearance, blast-proof steel door.

The operator is the only one who possesses a security clearance profile that can open the door and let specified individuals in at his discretion. Councilman Lennox stops outside the entrance access door to the control room and waits for several moments before touching the telescreen. Immediately, it will put him in contact with the operator, and he must get it right the first time if he hopes to gain access to the control room. He has convinced himself that this could be the best way to achieve his mission, finally.

He activates the outside communication screen and speaks to the technician, identifying his authority as he does so; he then follows up with a story of his assignment, requesting a meeting with Director Stormis. He then complained that he had checked his office and other areas around the complex and could not find him anywhere. The technician observes the councilman on his view screen before responding to him, "I'm sorry, councilman, for the delay... I'm in the process of making contact with the director as we speak."

The operator has no reason to doubt what the councilman tells him, as he looks at an official identification screen that confirms the councilman is who he claims to be. The technician responds to Councilman Lennox, "I'm sorry, Councilman, I can't seem to contact the director." Looking into the communication telescreen, Lennox responds, "That's okay, young man, I have the director right here on my arm computer in a secret coded format. He's going to be delayed a while and says that I should wait here with you, and he also informed me that you are the best of the technicians who operate the Nebular Cloud."

Upon hearing the compliment, the technician says to him, "If you care to, councilman, you may come in and wait for the director in the control room."

"Yes, that would be nice, thank you."

Upon release, the security door automatically opens, and Lennox enters the control room; as he looks around, he says to the young technician, "So, this is where it all takes place, the Nebular Cloud. It looks like quite an operation?"

The technician replies, "Yes, it is, Councilman!"

The technician then begins to explain the operation of the Nebular Cloud accelerator. Lennox hardly listens to the young technician as he describes the danger of the high-speed Nebular Cloud accelerator, which cannot be canceled. Lennox is preoccupied with watching the telescreen to ensure the captain is still on the Warfield, attending to the wounded. He then says to the young technician, "So, this is how it all works!" As he fires his laser weapon, the technician is struck by a laser blast and instantly becomes another victim of the councilman's obsession to eliminate Captain Trikan.

Lennox talks into the computer, "Nebular Cloud accelerator, subject War Games!"

The computer screen immediately responds: "...ENTRANCE CODE REQUIRED..." Lennox tries again and types in "...WAR GAMES..." and the computer responds: "...NO ENTRANCE...CODE REQUIRED..."

Without a moment lost in time, Lennox begins to remove the safety track clamp from the Nebular Cloud accelerator, and again, he reacts as if in a state of uncontrolled anger to destroy the captain before he leaves the Warfield. Pushing the speed control lever to maximum acceleration, the gauges above the accelerator's operating screen jump forward, and all react to a magnetic flux while the thick glass panels of the operations room crack and break apart.

The effects of smashing atoms in the subatomic chambers of the accelerator send out waves of energy into a Nebular Cloud above the Warfield, causing it to activate a fusion override of hydro-velocity atomic particles, which destroys sections of the dome over the Warfield.

On the large computer console in the control room, words appear across the screen:
"... STOP FUSION RELAYS CANNOT BE REVERSED...A NEBULAR ENERGY CLOUD IS NOW IN ITS ENERGY FIELD OPERATION...UNIT MELTDOWN IS IN PROGRESS... SEPARATION FROM THE ACCELERATOR IS NOW COMPLETE..."

The voice-activated computer blares out: "...ENERGY FIELD IS NOW IN DUPLICATION FORM AND INCREASING IN SIZE... IT IS NOW SEPARATED FROM THE ACCELERATOR AND CAN NO LONGER MATCH THE SUBATOMIC CONTROL ACCELERATOR ... NOW MALFUNCTIONING IN HIGH MAGNETIC FORCE FIELD..."

The entire control center becomes inundated with destructive subatomic particle energy waves, and Lennox is now in a state of panic. While he is still obsessed with Captain Trikan, he makes his way from the control room down the long corridor to an exit platform.

By the time the passenger lift reaches the lower level of the stadium, the breakup of the Healiocon Dome has already taken place.

As the destructive force of sound waves of thunder strikes the entire stadium in a storm of electrically charged particles of a Nebular Cloud, it continues to destroy entire sections of the stadium. Large pieces of concrete and steel structures of the upper stadium levels have reached their state of critical capacity as sections break up and fall in the fashion of nature's mighty strength, which formed the Nebular Cloud along with its uncontrolled energy.

The Nebular Cloud is now hovering over the entire stadium as it increases in size and rises over sections of Star Port City. Any known force can no longer control the creation of the Nebular Cloud on the planet's surface. As its velocity increases, weather patterns begin to change, continuously sending heavy rains and lightning strikes to the planet's surface.

The strict authority within the Healiocon Stadium has lost its command and control over the multitude of spectators as they rush for safety and try to avoid the falling debris, as the crowds swell in the exit corridors. Sentry robots open all escape ramps to help everyone exit the stadium.

Deep within the sub-chambers of the Nebular Cloud exists the universal code of creation and destruction. The giant fusion energy force continues to increase in strength above the planet's exosphere, finally giving some relief to the surface of the planet.

As the ground destruction continues, stadium walls do not retain their integrity and ultimately collapse, leaving only a few damaged structural sections still standing. Councilman Lennox was telling the truth when he told the director that he did not know his way to the director's office.

Stepping off the lift, Lennox finds himself on the same ground-floor corridor where he left the director and is now able to exit the stadium onto the destroyed courtyard across from the horse
stables, where he sees Captain Trikan riding through the gates on top of his robotic horse. Lennox remains frozen for a few moments and then realizes that Captain Trikan did not notice him. Covered in debris, the area of the stands is inundated with falling roof fragments, creating a dusty film over most of the stadium sections and entrance archways that

lead into the courtyard.

As the entire stadium structure continues to collapse from the top of its steel arches, Lennox
shouts out, "CAPTAIN... CAPTAIN TRIKAN! Over here! Can you see me, Captain?"

As Lennox raises his laser weapon and holds it in a position like a true marksman, he watches as Trikan
gets off his robot horse, turns, and faces Lennox.

Trikan cannot identify precisely where Lennox is due to the dust clouds created by the broken concrete construction. Lennox then steps out from the dusty area of the stadium walls to let Trikan see him more clearly; he then remarks, "Can you see me now, captain? I can see you...Very clearly! Oh, too bad, Captain...! You don't have a weapon! Here, I'll let you have mine."

Still holding his weapon in a marksman position, he is about to fire when, unexpectedly, a strange twist of fate takes place; a large section of concrete slides off a roof ledge and falls on top of Lennox as the Nebular Cloud blocks out the sun, and a heavy rainstorm begins.

Trikan walks up to Lennox, picks up his laser weapon, and is met by LamBrute, who says, "You had a close call, Captain!"

Standing in the heavy rain, Trikan looks at LamBrute and agrees, "You're right, LamBrute, today is my lucky day!"

Trikan then hands Councilman Lennox's laser weapon to LamBrute and says, "Here, take his weapon, LamBrute." Trikan then picks up Lennox's arm computer. "We'll need this if we're going to find the safehouse."

LamBrute replies, "Captain, the invisibility device must still be in the prison complex."

"No, it's not, LamBrute!" As Trikan removes the invisibility chip from his war boot, he places it into the arm computer.

LamBrute then remarks, "Ah, very clever, Captain!"

Captain Trikan begins to walk across the empty courtyard towards the horse stables as LamBrute calls out to him, "Captain, there's no one there!"

Trikan continues walking as he answers, "Yes, I know, LamBrute, but I want to see if I can find some type of transportation for us."

Before entering the horse stable, Trikan stops and says to LamBrute, "I was just thinking about something... The ice wolves LamBrute; whatever happened to them?"

LamBrute replies, "They're gone, Captain. They ran off and followed their leader, the large grey one. I would say they're halfway home to Trikinia by now. You can't keep the free spirit in a cage; it has to be set free."

Trikan adds, "Everyone deserves to be free, LamBrute!"

"Yes, Captain, I agree. Captain, as you know, I stayed behind with the stable attendant. As it turned out, it was the best place to be when the destruction occurred. The stable area sustained very little damage, and when the aid workers arrived, the stable attendant left with them and assisted in removing the remaining wounded from the Warfield. I stayed behind waiting for you."

"I understand, LamBrute. Let's get out of here before we end up like the councilman!"

As enormous blocks of granite continue to fall from the retaining walls of the stadium, they crash through the lower empty seating section ramps below them on the main thoroughfare. Trikan and LamBrute make their way out to the multitudes of survivors who are waiting for emergency and commercial transportation. They continue to arrive and are given priority entrance and exit to service ramps that have not been damaged by the disaster at the stadium.

Trikan and LamBrute will eventually have to wait through the night until the next day to get transportation to the emergency supply zone within the disaster area. When they arrive with the last passengers from the sports complex, they will find medical facilities and food product tents set up by private merchants and the government emergency relief department.

The next day, aboard the transport bus, they are standing up front in the middle of the aisle, near the robot operator of the vehicle. The transport is filled as they leave the area surrounding the destroyed stadium. Trikan starts a conversation with the transport robot operator. "How many times have you done this today?"

Looking up at Trikan, he replies, "... **AS MANY TIMES AS I AM PROGRAMMED TO...**" Looking at LamBrute, Trikan rolls his eyes as LamBrute says, "Let me try this... Driver! Can you tell me where you're taking us?"

The robot operator responds, "... **YES...**" As he reaches the vehicle console screen, he activates it, and a description of transport stops appears in detail, "... **EMERGENCY FIELD MEDICAL FACILITY DROP OFF AT SECTION A... SECTION B NON-MEDICAL... SECTION C... HOSPITALITY CENTERS AND FOOD PURCHASES...**" The robot operator looks up at Trikan. "... **DO YOU REQUIRE FURTHER INFORMATION...?**"

Trikan takes a moment to look at LamBrute and then tells the robot operator, "No... The information is quite adequate."

The long ride finally comes to an end at the destination, and the passengers disembark at the medical facility. The bus enters through the gates of the relief center, and the final stop is Section C, where commercial services are available. This commercial zone is set up with tents resembling a large outdoor market where merchants can sell their products.

Trikan and LamBrute, along with the other passengers, have arrived just before nightfall and are now with the hundreds of other displaced groups that fell victim to the destruction of the Healiocon Stadium. While waiting in line to enter a large pontoon structure where fresh food is being prepared, Trikan types in the code number of the safehouse and receives a negative response. Trying it again, the results are the same, and he says to LamBrute, "I know the safehouse is somewhere north of Star Port City, but I keep getting a negative response." LamBrute adds, "I guess we're not going to be able to make contact with the safehouse until we're in their code frequency area, Captain."

Acknowledging, he says, "I agree! So, we need to find a suitable flightcraft. That's the only way we're going to find the right code to the safehouse."

Trikan and LamBrute devote most of their time walking through the markets while attempting to get information on a flight transport that could take them out of the city. Trikan is frustrated that it's useless for him and LamBrute to continue walking through the market areas that sell everything but the one thing he needs: a flight transport.

"LamBrute, we might as well go back to the main terminal and take a ground transport out of the relief area."

LamBrute then reminds him that there are numerous checkpoints throughout the city, equipped with information surveillance screens that will track his whereabouts if he leaves the market complex by ground transport. Trikan tells LamBrute that he will have to take that chance. "Sooner or later, government officials will arrive in this complex and demand identity information on everyone here."

Trikan then checks his arm computer, which provides a picture scan of the large area in this particular market section, and sees someone he knows—the salesman who had wanted to buy the professor's robot, Cen-Ton.

"LamBrute, do you remember the merchant from the café?"

Looking at the screen, LamBrute responds, "Yes... That's him, all right, Captain!"

"LamBrute, let's go over and pay him a visit."

As they make their way through the crowd and before reaching the merchant's stand, the merchant calls out, "Captain! Captain Trikan! Over here!"

LamBrute says to Trikan, "I'm glad there are no government agents around, or you'll find yourself sleeping in Central Detention tonight, Captain!"

Trikan and LamBrute walk over to the merchant's large tent, which displays a multitude of goods, including some preserved food products. The merchant smiles as he greets the captain and LamBrute. "My good Captain! It is so nice to see you again, and don't tell me you sold your robot to someone else?"

LamBrute asks, "What is that supposed to mean,

Captain?" Trikan replies, "I don't quite know. Maybe our friend, the merchant, can explain?"

They both look at the merchant. "Oh, please forgive me for picking the wrong words. I did not mean to offend! I was overcome by seeing my good friend, the captain, again!"

Picking up one of the items in the display of goods, the captain remarks, "Fifty Tri-Logs for this?"

The merchant replies, "No, No, Captain! For you, half price and a twenty percent discount besides!" Putting the item back down, the captain adds, "That's all right. I already have one!"

The merchant responds instantly, "Take it as a gift from me! Then you shall have two!" LamBrute interjects, "Captain, what are we doing here?"

"LamBrute, I am sure our good friend did not mean to offend you by not offering you a gift." The merchant then says, "Yes, yes, my brave Trikinian, to show you how much I value your friendship. Everything you see is half-price for you as well as the captain!"

Trikan smiles. "There you see, LamBrute, he is our friend, and he wants to help us find the item we're looking for!"

Pulling the merchant close to him, Trikan lowers his voice in the crowded market. "We need transportation out of here! You're going to help us, right?"

As Trikan releases the merchant from his firm grip, the relieved merchant responds, "Why, yes, of course, Captain... I have ticket vouchers for cargo vehicles in my tent that will allow you a choice of departure times to any location you so desire, and again, for you and your friend, the brave warrior, half price!"

LamBrute interjects, "At half price?" Trikan smiles as the merchant replies, "Why, yes, yes... of course, my good Trikinian friend."

Once inside the tent, Trikan can now talk freely without being overheard. "Listen... Forget about the transport vouchers and forget about the half-price off! We need a special item, and I think we have come to the right place and the person who can provide us with it."

The merchant curiously responds, "What is this specialty item that you need, captain?"

"We need a flight transport and forget half price! I'll pay full price for it!"

Shaking his head, the merchant replies, "That's not going to be easy to get, Captain! A flight transport must be registered before it is given clearance for operational control and navigation in this restricted area. Nothing is allowed to fly in or out of this area unless it's a government-licensed flightcraft. But let me think... It's not going to be an easy task, but... I will have one for you tomorrow! Unfortunately, Captain, you must pay in advance, and I guarantee it will be waiting for you under one of my large tents outside."

Stepping forward from his browsing around the merchandise, LamBrute says to Trikan, "How do we know we can trust him, Captain?"

Looking at the merchant, Trikan says, "Well, we can always return it and get our credits back, isn't that right?"

The merchant immediately responds, "Oh, yes, of course! Of course, Captain! There will be a slight charge of ten percent for any damage to a returned item!"

The captain smiles. "There, you see, LamBrute, he's an honest merchant!"

LamBrute holds up a decorative item that he picked up while browsing around the tent. "How much for this, merchant?"

As Trikan and the merchant turn their attention to LamBrute, the merchant replies, "For you, my friend, there is no charge! Now, Captain, can we conclude your purchase if you can please give me your purchase credit plate?"

Trikan hands it to him as some customers come into the tent to shop. The merchant quickly responds to them, "Sorry, we are closed! No more business today, but I'll be back tomorrow. If I don't have what you want, I'll get it for you! Half price! I bid you a good day!" Completing the purchase for the captain's flightcraft, the merchant asks, "Captain, if you don't mind, can you give me a hand taking in the merchandise outside? I am closed for the day!"

After Trikan and LamBrute help the merchant take in his goods, they remove the last of the items from outside the merchant's tent and carry them in. LamBrute comments, "Captain, look at this sign; it reads, low prices for high-quality goods! I can't wait to see what our flightcraft looks like."

"Yes, LamBrute, I can't wait to be surprised!"

Early the next morning, Trikan and LamBrute arrive at the merchant's tent and read the sign that is hanging over a large brass bell: "Ring the bell if you need service."

Trikan looks at LamBrute and says, "Should I?"

LamBrute replies, "Well, if you want to wake up everyone in this camp area, then go right ahead, Captain."

Trikan discreetly knocks on the door of the merchant's tent. After waiting several moments, a small opening in the doorway appears, and the merchant greets them, "Good morning, Captain, and my good Trikinian friend. I see that you are here to pick up your purchase! Come in, come in, my brave warriors!"

After some casual talk between Trikan and the merchant, LamBrute interrupts and tells the captain, "Captain, it's getting late. If we want to leave before the large crowds gather outside and without being observed, now would be the best time."

"You're right, LamBrute!"

The merchant then says, "Your flightcraft is ready for departure, Captain, if you will follow me into my service area storage tent. You can take possession and leave immediately."

Entering the large adjoining tent, Trikan and LamBrute observe the air flight vehicle. "Here it is, captain."

As the merchant removes the air flight clearance tag with a license code indicator that allows flight clearance throughout Star Port City, nonstop priority security allows this flight vehicle to fly beyond the border sequence limits of the entire zoned quadrant. He hands it to the captain as LamBrute looks over the flightcraft and says, "Captain, this flightcraft is a piece of junk! You paid too much for this, and it's a discontinued model!"

Turning to the merchant, LamBrute says, "Where did you get this flightcraft from? This model has been discontinued!"

The old merchant remains silent for a moment and then says, "My brave friend, this passenger flightcraft—true, it's a discontinued model—I purchased it when it was brand new, and I assure you that it is perfectly maintained and one hundred percent reliable! Please, don't judge it by its damaged outside appearance! A few bumps and scrapes, but it's perfectly reliable and safe to take you to any destination you so desire." Then he tells Trikan, "It's the best I can do on such short notice, Captain!"

Ignoring the merchant, Trikan says to LamBrute, "That's okay, LamBrute, as long as this flightcraft gets us to where we need to go."

As he holds up the merchant's unrestricted flight pass, he says, "With this, we have permission to fly over Star Port City without restrictions. You can't put a price on freedom!"

LamBrute says, "I agree, Captain!"

The quiet turbo-lift of the antimagnetic gravity field of the old flightcraft's reverse energy wave still retains the ability to defy the planet's gravity.

As the old ship takes flight in the early sunrise from the merchants' campsite, the merchant shouts at the event of their departure. "Good luck, my friends!"

Once airborne onto a flight tractor beam, the flightcraft leaves the emergency market camp. In less than several quarter-sequences, the flightcraft is now on a steady path heading north, with other flight vehicles, leaving the devastated areas of the city.

Chapter 15:

The Safehouse

As they travel north, on their journey to the safehouse, Trikan types in code sequences unsuccessfully until he activates the correct area code sequence of the GPS quadrant and receives a positive result, revealing its location. He says to LamBrute, "Now is a good time to contact your crew and tell them that we're in their code zone."

A short time later, LamBrute receives a confirmation message and tells the captain, "They are all waiting for us, Captain. Aunt Lasara just coded another message: 'What took you so long, Johnathan?'"

Trikan smiles and says, "Very good!"

Aunt Lasara receives a coded message on her telescreen computer from the Justice Department liaison office, pertaining to a schedule confirmation of a court date for a legal proceeding of a captain: "Name, Rank: Jonathan Shawnwood, Captain. Please contact this office to arrange a court date. Reference Class: Compliance Date Code 1740."

After reading her message, Aunt Lasara says, "Professor, Johnathan will be surprised when I tell him about this?"

Looking at the message on her screen, he agrees, "Yes, Lasara, and why has it taken so long?"

"You know very well, professor, the wheels of government turn very slowly!"

At that time, Reanna had already entered the room and heard their remarks while carrying a tray of tea and dessert cakes. Lasara says, "Reanna, I don't know what I would do without you. You're so good to us!"

"It's my pleasure, Lasara." Placing the tray down, Reanna asks, "Lasara, what do you think Johnathan will say when you tell him about the court date?"

"Reanna, I'm not going to tell him anything until I find out what happened after we left him at the nature preserve."

Doctor Lasara continues to look at Reanna while ignoring the teller-view alert report, which is continuously scrolling along the bottom of the screen. A flightcraft is about to land in the vicinity of the safehouse; a locked-in matching code sequence must be typed in on the computer keyboard to allow the airship to land on the safehouse Community Estate. Reanna looks at the screen for a moment and then raises her voice and announces, "Lasara, it's Johnathan! I just know it's him! The code sent down from the flightcraft matches the code on our screen!"

Aunt Lasara abruptly turns and announces, "It's Johnathan; he made it, finally!"

She nervously types the code clearance signature into the computer, allowing the craft to land without triggering the emergency detection alarms of other estate houses in their private, coded airspace.

As Trikans' air flightcraft lands on the mansion's tarmac, he is greeted by Aunt Lasara, Reanna, and Professor Zola. Trikan is the first to leave the air flightcraft, followed by LamBrute, who is restricted by the small dimensions of the exit ramp door of the old craft. Trikan hesitates and turns to LamBrute, "Do you need a hand getting out of that thing, LamBrute? I'm sure Cen-Ton will help you."

Cen-Ton says, "... CAPTAIN... I WOULD GLADLY ASSIST WARRIOR LAMBRUTE IF HE SO DESIRES..."

LamBrute shouts back, "Captain... If I were you, when you meet that merchant again, I would ask for my credits back!"

Trikan smiles as his small reception party immediately joins in on the levity of LamBrutes' comment as he struggles to get out of the copilot's section of the flightcraft. Looking at the old flight ship and judging by the statement that LamBrute made, Aunt Lasara remarks, "Johnathan, don't tell me you credited that flightcraft to my account."

He responds, "Aunt Lasara, you did say—" She immediately interjects, "That's quite all right, Johnathan... I don't care how much you spent. I was only kidding! We can always donate it to a museum!"

Located in an underground complex in Star Port City, an emergency meeting of the Pteranodon Society is called.

On stage, the host speaker calls for everyone to take their seats and remain silent as the theater lights are lowered. He then turns to a large three-dimensional view screen behind him, picks up a microphone, and walks up to the screen.

He begins by announcing to his audience that a short viewing of Captain Johnathan Shawnwood, also known as the renegade Captain Trikan, will be presented. He then says, "Please watch these short viewings of Captain Shawnwood in our competitive sporting events. In this two-hundred-meter competition, the captain wins!"

As the screen changes, the speaker continues, "In the heavyweight lifting competition, Shawnwood wins by lifting above the average weight of all the other candidates. In the event of freestyle wrestling, he defeats every opponent and wins again! The military college administrators paid no attention to this cadet's outstanding athletic abilities in his performance in these required competitions over the other candidates.

Just before graduation, in-house security cameras record him working out in the military fitness gym complex. Then, the subject somehow forcefully destroys the antigravity weight machine after breaking the Androidian record for heavy lifting.

Expert analysis determined that Captain Shawnwood must have taken deliberate action to break the heavy-lift record and conceal his defiance of the military officers' code; he had deliberately destroyed the machine.

The hologram screen now remains in a frozen state as the lights in the auditorium are turned on, and the orator walks back to the podium and addresses the audience. "Tonight, we have a special guest who has the ability to solve our problem! Yes, the problem is Captain Johnathan Shawnwood, a criminal who goes by the name Trikan. It gives me great honor to introduce to you our special guest and our newest member... Marcus, the RAS Symmetry!"

Applause begins again as Marcus walks out onto the stage towards the podium.

The host speaker steps aside as Marcus takes his place at the podium. As he waits for the applause to stop and the room to remain silent, he addresses the audience, "My mission is to eliminate this renegade called Captain Trikan! I am part of a program to track down and remove the captain, and anyone who vows loyalty to him will also be targeted for elimination. He must and will be destroyed!"

He remains silent for several moments until the applause stops and then addresses the audience again, "Why did it take so long? When we find someone who is disloyal to our authority, they must be destroyed immediately!"

Marcus's last comment is followed by applause from the entire audience membership as he receives a standing ovation. Marcus steps aside and gestures to the host speaker, who then addresses the audience. As the applause stops, the speaker says, "Thank you, Marcus, and welcome as our newest member to the Pteranodon Society!" The applause begins again as Marcus walks off the stage and exits the meeting.

Hidden away in a forest of seasonal change, the small reception party gathers around Trikan at the safehouse. Aunt Lasara tells him, "Johnathan, I am so happy that you are here. Please sit down and join us for dinner! You will not be allowed to leave here again without a full consent agreement, young man! You do agree with me, Reanna, and Professor Zola? And what is Chef Eleanor going to do with all that food she cooks? Your aunt is now officially putting you under house arrest, young man! I am sure that LamBrute will certainly agree with us."

LamBrute replies, "Councilwoman Lasara, I am honored by your hospitality, and I do agree with your decision on the captain."

"Thank you, LamBrute. Oh, LamBrute, your security detail was picked up last night at the orders of your embassy staff. Alden directed them to return to Trikinia."

Trikan begins to laugh as he puts his arm around LamBrute and says, "Come on, my friend, let's go and see what Chef Eleanor has prepared.

As Aunt Lasara redirects her attention towards LamBrute, she says, "LamBrute, it is finally nice to meet you!"

Professor Zola then turns to Trikan and says, "It's good that you're back, Captain! We have a lot of work to do!"

Aunt Lasara then adds, "Yes, we're going to have some important business in Star Port City." She then tells Jonathan that she has something important to tell him after dinner tonight. "But first, you and LamBrute go into the kitchen and say hello to Chef Eleanor."

As Trikan and LamBrute enter the kitchen, Chef Eleanor turns around, expecting to see the professor, and is surprised by her two unannounced visitors. A look of joy comes to her face as she calls out, "Captain Johnathan, what a surprise!"

Smiling, he says, "Chef Eleanor, this is my good friend LamBrute."

Smiling back, she says, "LamBrute, it is so nice to meet you! The two of you have arrived just at the right time! You both can help me prepare the dining room for tonight's dinner!"

Aunt Lasara enters the kitchen and remarks, "Johnathan, before you do anything, take that old wreck, put it on the lift platform, and take it down to the underground flight storage area; we don't want any inquiries about it from security monitor drones, and we don't want our neighbors on the other estates to see that old wreck!"

"I'll take care of it, Aunt Lasara."

A few moments later, Lasara receives a coded government message on her Dial-Date computer, informing her that a copy of the date and terms for Johnathan's court appearance is being transferred and printed out on her personal office computer. These official documents must be signed by the captain and transferred back to the government for his acceptance of his official court date, as it appears on the documents. The most serious charge of treason will be addressed in an open court hearing on the set date.

That evening, during dinner, Aunt Lasara decides to make her announcement as she holds up her wine glass and expresses her feelings of pleasure that Johnathan is back home with them. Smiling, she begins, "Captain, there were so many times when so many things were happening to you that we could not bear, nor make sense out of, the events that were taking place. Without going into details, we wanted so much to reach out to you. Without the help of our good friend, Professor Zola, I could not have ever imagined that this moment would have ever taken place again."

Trikan then adds, "Aunt Lasara, you don't have to continue... I am here now! We all make our own choices in life. Just by chance or perhaps an act of faith, the road I traveled has given me the good luck to have met so many who have helped me."

Remaining silent for a moment, he is reluctant to allow himself to go on. His thoughts of Elisa and his concern for her well-being will always be on his mind as he reflects on his past, a place he would not care to revisit without Elisa.

Aunt Lasara raises her wine glass again, this time towards the captain, and says, "I would like to propose a toast to Johnathan and LamBrute. There is no need for any more explanation. I am glad that you are both here and safe!"

As Trikan raises his glass, he replies, "I would like to make a toast to a special person who is not here at the moment, to Elisa!"

The professor immediately stands up and says, "Yes, to Elisa!"

After dinner, Aunt Lasara announces to her dinner guests, "I think this would be a good time to tell the captain the important news!"

Looking towards Johnathan, she says, "In fact, the very important news that should be taken with extreme caution. Johnathan, the government offered you a compromise: if you surrender to an inquiry under trial conditions, you would be found not guilty of lesser penalties. I was chosen to present a deal to you. To put it in simpler terms, you will have to plead forgiveness for certain incidents."

As she gets up and leaves the dinner table, she walks over to a bookshelf and removes an official government book titled **"Criminal Acts and Civil Disobedience Laws."**

Taking her place at the table again, she places the book down and puts her hand on top of it. "Johnathan, this book contains the unlawful civil disobedience acts on minor violations of private citizens, to the most serious of military personnel. All acts of reference code Section 16 cannot be reversed, regardless of whether the individual is found guilty or innocent. The major infringement of treason is the most serious charge you are facing! All the other charges are in the process of being dismissed as nonessential."

Trikan then asks Aunt Lasara, "So, when Councilman Lennox offered me his plan and told me that all the charges would be dropped—" Doctor Lasara interjects, "No, Johnathan! There was NEVER a plan to drop all the charges! Lennox knew that he had to cover up his plan, to put YOU in the War Games, hoping that you would not survive! He knew damn well that you would only have to answer to the charge of treason, and a court date was already in progress! We have to be very careful, Johnathan. He was not acting on his own initiative!"

She then adds, "I have an excellent attorney who will help you. He is one of the most intelligent counsel attorneys in government law. It's totally up to you, Johnathan."

Trikan remains silent for a couple of moments before he speaks. "I know who they are and what they're capable of... I don't trust them! But I'm open to suggestions. Aunt Lasara, if you don't mind, I'll give you the final vote."

Smiling at him, she replies, "Very well, Johnathan, whatever you want."

Looking at the professor, Trikan asks, "Professor, what do you think? Do you trust them?"

"Certainly NOT, Captain!"

Looking at his mom, Trikan is about to ask her opinion when she says in a low voice,

"Don't trust them, Jonathan!"

Trikan then says, "I don't think I have to ask you, LamBrute. I know what your answer is already!"

LamBrute abruptly responds, "My answer is the same as Professor Zola's! Don't trust them!" The professor adds,

"Well, I guess we're all in agreement?"

As Chef Eleanor begins to remove some of the dinner plates from the table, she stops by Trikan for a moment and says to him, "Don't do it, Johnathan. I like cooking for you too much!"

After Chef Eleanor gives her advice to Trikan, the room becomes silent for a couple of moments as they wait for Aunt Lasara to come forward with her guidance, and she says, "Well, I guess everyone is waiting for my opinion. I don't like this treason indictment. It's untrue and a complete fabrication! But we have to consider that all the other charges have been dropped, and we will go to court to answer to the charge of treason!"

Trikan then adds, "Aunt Lasara, you're right! Get me that very good lawyer that you mentioned. We're going to court!"

Smiling, Lasara replies, "First thing tomorrow, Jonathan. I will make all the arrangements! Jonathan, it is so good to have you home with us again!"

Several days pass, and Trikan wakes up with a feeling of new anticipation as the others in the safehouse remain asleep. He would dare not say the word, not even to himself, but the feeling he feels can be best described as one of freedom, a sense of being reborn.

This large house is not unlike the one he grew up in; the open fields and cool morning air were an early morning routine that he enjoyed outdoors before anyone else was awake. His pace down the long corridor picks up momentum, and a faint smile appears on his face. He had stayed up late last night and observed on the dining room telescreen all the work and correspondence that his aunt was able to accomplish with the most famous attorneys who had defended clients in negotiations with the government. Their success rate served as a validation of their professionalism and knowledge of government law in defending their clients. Those who were not found completely innocent were placed in a program of psychological rehabilitation.

Placing an identification card into a room sentry device, he is given clearance that allows him to proceed throughout the large safehouse complex. This enormous structure, complete with a landing flightcraft tarmac, is surrounded by probes and other security devices. Trikan thinks to himself about this complex, as it reminds him of the fortress-type residence he grew up in.

At the Government Complex Center in Star Port City, the sign on the door reads: **Dr. Evans - Director of Molecular Tryotonic Science.**

Doctor Evans' attention is diverted from a folder screen report on a scheduled interview appointment that he received from the Counterintelligence Department. As he removes the printed report from his telescreen, he receives a picture of the large hallway outside his office. His appointed visitor has arrived late, which he will note later on after the interview is over. He will also add it to the profile folder, along with his observational notes, which will help determine the off-program behavior of the appointment candidate.

Pressing the release buzzer to his office entrance, the two-panel doors separate as Doctor Evans calls out, "Come right in, Marcus."

The doctor's office is sparsely decorated with furniture, except for an abundance of bookshelves filled with texts from physiological and medical folders. Doctor Evans' desk module is clear of anything that would give a guest any indication of his professional abilities and governmental title references.

As his guest walks into the office, rather than sitting in a semicircular chair in front of Doctor Evans, he remains standing. Doctor Evans says, "So... You're the Marcus RA Symmetry-7000? I heard of a top-secret production project, but I reasoned it was only a rumor if you know what I'm referring to."

Marcus says, "Doctor, I know how government departments work. They try to outdo each other by keeping new programs secret."

Doctor Evans says, "Please, sit down, Marcus. I have been looking forward to this meeting." Doctor Evans then opens a folder report on his desk that's labeled:

TOP SECRET PROJECT

Evaluation Program

Captain Johnathan Shawnwood

Handing Marcus the folder, Doctor Evans continues, "On your document, section one pertains to you. This is your evaluation report; this section will assess your ability to complete your mission and bring an end to the renegade Captain Johnathan Shawnwood.

The remaining sections contain physical comparisons as well as assessments of your mental capability. Your physical statistics are as follows: The captain is seventy-three inches in height, as compared to your height of seventy-nine inches.

Military college status: track and field competitions; you ranked first in twenty events and won every one of them. The captain participated in the same documented events and won eighteen out of twenty! An amazing accomplishment by any means. In the long history of military-grade mandatory performance, only three other participants have achieved the feat of surpassing the average qualifying requirements by scoring above the ten mark.

Your sprint time was forty sequence seconds in the five-hundred-meter competition, breaking all records. In the same performance program, the captain's time was forty-nine!"

He turns his screen off and continues, "Everything you want to know about the captain is in your folder. Your mission is very important, Marcus. Discretion must be followed!

This Captain Shawnwood is related to someone very important in our government. Our organization cannot be compromised, and may I congratulate you on becoming our newest member? Welcome to the Pteranodon Society! May I also add, as of this moment, there's a growing opinion amongst many council members that Captain Shawnwood might very well be a Trikinian spy? Now that you know how important this assignment is, the rest is up to you."

Marcus responds, "Thank you, Doctor Evans."

The doctor replies, "Marcus, it's been good to meet you! If you need more information about the subject, my door is always open, and I will do whatever I can to assist you!"

Marcus takes the folder report and is about to leave the office when Doctor Evans tells him,

"Marcus, may I remind you, this Captain Shawnwood can be very dangerous! Every attempt that was made to eliminate him in the past failed!"

Stopping for a moment again, Marcus turns and says, "Thank you, Doctor. I can assure you that my mission will be successful; I will eliminate the captain!"

Johnathan needed some fresh morning air, so he decided to walk outside the complex for a short time. As he approaches the front exit door leading out to the landing field tarmac, he is alerted by a blinking telescreen above the exit door, with a continuous information bar running along the bottom of the screen. It informs him vocally in a robotic voice, telling him to insert his identification card, the same one Aunt Lasara gave him. He obeys the response, inserts the card, and gets rejected.

A voice comes from behind him, "I'm afraid your identification card will not allow you to leave the complex without the personal approval of your Aunt Lasara, Captain."

Turning around, he is now confronted by Professor Zola. "Good morning, Captain!" Smiling, Trikan replies,

"Good morning, Professor Zola. What are you doing up so early this morning?"

"Well, Captain, to be quite honest with you, it comes with age! The older you get, the less sleep you require!"

Trikan asks, "Does that have anything to do with breakfast?"

Professor Zola laughs. "Exactly the opposite, Captain! As you can see by my waistline, I never miss a meal!"

The two begin to enjoy a moment of levity as the professor informs the captain of their upcoming plans regarding an appointment with government officials that Aunt Lasara and her attorney have arranged.

"Tomorrow, we will leave here and be before the Supreme Council Government Officials that your Aunt Lasara arranged, along with the seven judges and that very important attorney who will represent you. You will remain absent from this first part of your trial hearing, which is standard procedure. Captain, before we go to breakfast, I have several questions for you."

"Of course, Professor, what are they?"

"What happened to the Healiocon Stadium? Do you have any idea what caused such a huge disaster?"

Trikan remains silent for a moment before answering, "They did it, Professor... They destroyed the whole Healiocon Stadium and a good part of the city, which now looks like a War zone! All I can tell you is what I witnessed at the time. I was on the Warfield, and the ground began to shake; the entire stadium was in disarray, and the concrete columns began to come apart. Level after level, the spectator sections began to collapse, and the dome above the fighting field began to lift off its construction walls, and then the Nebular Cloud dome exploded! The blast was so bright, it was like staring into the blinding sun.

For a couple of moments, you could not see anything. The blast carried the domed structure upward in a spiral motion; as it continued to fire compositional, destructive orbs, it destroyed large sections of the city. You probably know that part from the news reports, professor. Other than that, I know just as much as you do about it! The only difference is, I was there!"

"Well, captain, there is a lot more to the story of the destruction!"

Puzzled, Trikan asks, "What do you mean, professor? What are you talking about?"

"Well, Captain, someone killed Director Stormis, and it was recorded on security cameras. Someone fired a laser weapon, striking the director in the back, destroying him instantly. The time sequence on the security camera footage has been officially documented, confirming that the incident occurred before the enormous explosion destroyed the stadium. Whoever fired the weapon could not be seen from the angle of the stairwell leading up to Stormis's office. A well-executed plan from an angle that is absent from the recording cameras! The governmental authorities are concerned that it was an act committed by the Trikinians. There were a great many who attended the War Games on the day of the disaster. They have no proof, but I guarantee you that they will eventually put the blame on the Trikinians not only for the stadium but for the unprovoked attack on Director Stormis as well!"

"Professor, why would they do that? It doesn't make any sense."

"I know, Captain, I agree with you, but they have to blame someone! Had the security cameras not continuously placed you on the Warfield at the time of the destruction, they probably would have blamed you for the fatal attack on Director Stormis, also! Well, captain, let's see if we can find our way back to the dining room. I must be quite honest with you; when Doctor Lasara contacted me and gave me directions to this location, she referred to it as a safehouse. I had no idea it was going to be such an elaborate fortress!"

"Professor, when I landed, I was not surprised. Aunt Lasara always told me to provide for myself the best that I can.

As they both walk through the arched doorway that leads into the dining room, Captain Trikan stops and jokingly says to the professor, "Professor, do we know that man?"

As he looks towards LamBrute, who is sitting at the huge oval table, the professor is about to speak, but LamBrute responds first, "Good morning, Captain. Good morning, professor."

Trikan responds, "I see that you got up early as well, LamBrute."

"Yes, I did. I was awakened by the smell of breakfast being prepared in the kitchen. My room is directly over the kitchen area."

Trikan smiles as he takes his place at the table. "I thought I was the first one up this morning. There I was, wandering around trying to find an exit that would let me go outside and get some fresh morning air, and then I got captured by the professor!"

At that moment, Doctor Lasara and Reanna enter the dining room while engaged in a conversation. "Reanna, you're going to stay here with Chef Eleanor. When the professor and I leave for Star Port City, we will meet for the first hearing with the Government Council that has already been arranged by the attorney that I have chosen to represent Johnathan. Now, if I may volunteer Johnathan and LamBrute, will you help Chef Eleanor carry out breakfast?"

She smiles and then adds, "Seeing how the two of you did such a good job with dinner last evening!"

As Trikan and LamBrute are about to leave the room to help with breakfast, Doctor Lasara turns towards the professor and asks, "Professor, when the government picks a trial date for Johnathan, will you accompany me to the court hearings?"

"Yes, Lasara, I certainly will... I cannot wait to get this whole mess over with! It's been a long time since I'll be face-to-face with some of the council members who declared me a traitor and sent me to Central Detention and then into exile!"

Concerned, Doctor Lasara replies, "Professor, please do not mention anything about the past. They have released you from exile; do not think for a moment that their decision cannot be reversed. You can very well jeopardize yourself and ruin everything for Johnathan, too."

Seriously, she adds, "Temper, temper, Professor!"

Reanna states, "She's right, professor, at least until Johnathan's trial is over."

The good professor agrees and cordially apologizes for his display of ill feelings that took the best of his emotions. He could not help it; day after day, he could not get Elisa off his mind—her lonely existence in an isolation cell where most prisoners were placed after they ran away and were captured again.

Remaining silent for a couple of moments, Professor Zola thinks about the inner seclusion chambers of Central Detention, where Trikan will try to enter without some type of identification code. It would be almost a one-hundred-percent fatal attempt to avoid capture, so he must team up with Trikan and devise a plan that will increase the chances of a successful mission. Trikan would have to enter a maze protected by invisible security screens. He would be asked over and over again for a code identification classification when he entered the grounds of the Central Detention facility.

The global identification network will match his identity within their failsafe security program. Every step along the way, the long corridors are protected by deadly antimagnetic instant-firing laser beams. In a second, any false identity of anyone trying to enter the prison compound will be vaporized by the firing of the laser-charged weapons.

Before the completion of breakfast, Aunt Lasara says to Reanna, "Oh, Reanna... I apologize for not mentioning earlier that you are not required to be present at today's initial pre-trial hearing. Johnathan's attorney notified me just before coming down to breakfast. He said it would not be necessary for you to come to court with us; you stay home and keep Eleanor company."

Smiling, Reanna replies, "Yes, I'm happy to hear that! Thank you, Lasara."

Doctor Lasara turns and asks the professor, "Professor, why so quiet all of a sudden?"

Still not able to find a solution to his problem, he says, "Oh, sorry, Doctor Lasara, I was trying to put in place something essential that has to be done! Something happened a while ago, just by chance..."

"Is it important, professor?"

"I feel it's crucial, but for now, it will have to wait."

"Well, professor, we now have a woman jurist who was recently appointed to the Supreme Judgement Council, and she is an old friend of mine. I haven't spoken to her since we worked on a program together; it's been a while. We were assigned to different government agencies. She stayed in Law, and I went into Astrophysics."

As the professor puts his glasses back on, he says, "Well, that is good news, Lasara! Provided your friendship with her is still in existence."

Smiling, she says, "I'm sure it is, Professor, because Justice Calandra is an individual who lives by the letter of the law."

Looking at Trikan, the professor adds, "Captain, I'm starting to feel a little better about your government hearing; at least we know we have one supreme judge who will listen to the facts and be honest with her decision following the guidelines of the law." Trikan agrees, "Great! Now, let's all enjoy our breakfast!"

After breakfast, Trikan, Professor Zola, LamBrute, and Cen-Ton walk out to enjoy the cool morning air and experience the magnificent view of the rolling hills of pine trees and flocks of wild morning birds leaving their nests in an organized concert of flight. Doctor Lasara activates her automatic star drive, which opens the flight bay entrance doors, leading out onto a tarmac section.

As it opens, her flightcraft is elevated to the surface of the tarmac, and the professor and Trikan get on board. Aunt Lasara raises her voice over the loud sound of the hydrocopter's engines. "Reanna, after we leave, take that old flightcraft and put it on the lift platform, and then take it down to the underground flight storage area. It's been up here long enough. We don't want anyone to inquire about it."

Reanna replies, "I'll take care of it. Have a safe flight!"

As Aunt Lasara's luxury flightcraft is airborne, it is en route to the government complex in Star Port City. A message is then received on the logistical aeronautics flight computer screen, reporting a delay on the magnetic highway due to heavy ground commercial transport vehicles carrying reconstruction materials to several disaster areas within Star Port City. The magnetic highway transport reports that service air flights to areas around Star Port City are congested with personnel transport vehicles that would usually carry workers by ground highways.

Below ground, *Magna-Transport* trains are packed to capacity with the working population who are on their way to the city for their various jobs. This slow-paced entry into the city will last several days, leading to the cancellation of most government meetings. Aunt Lasara is notified on her control dash teleview that the court date has been changed, and she will be notified of the new court date. The screen reads: "... PLEASE ENTER THE CITY AS SOON AS POSSIBLE AND RETAIN RESIDENCY AT ONE OF THE MAJOR HOTELS FOR AN EARLY CONTACT DATE AT THE NEXT SCHEDULED HEARING..."

Trikan says to the professor, "Professor, I really wanted to get this court thing over with!"

The professor replies, "Perhaps this delay will work to our advantage. It will give us more time and a chance for Aunt Lasara to have a meeting with her old friend Judge Calandra."

As Doctor Lasara's flightcraft lands in the courtyard complex, she receives another transmission of a clarification notice that "The court hearing will be delayed for several days," and that her Dial-Date will notify her of the next scheduled trial hearing.

The professor then adds, "Well, this was predictable! These court hearings never go off on their scheduled dates."

Lasara then says, "I had a feeling that this was going to happen! Jonathan, Professor, I will arrange hotel accommodations for us, and I will call Reanna to ask her to join us at our hotel with Chef Eleanor here in Star Port City. We can all get some shopping done tomorrow at the mall when they arrive."

Trikan then says, "Good, I need something to take my mind off all of this! LamBrute, take us to the hotel."

The professor agrees, "That's right, captain, this delay is starting to bring back some unpleasant memories!"

As LamBrute pilots the flightcraft, he receives clearance to land at one of the luxury hotels located within the commercial district adjacent to the city's largest shopping mall.

Lasara smiles at the professor as they walk through doors that automatically open and enter the luxury hotel lobby. After signing for their rooms, they make arrangements for afternoon snacks to be delivered.

Lasara says, "There are some wonderful restaurants here, Professor. I'll make arrangements for all of us."

The professor smiles. "That's a wonderful idea, Lasara!"

Johnathan agrees, "We can all relax for a couple of days; it's been a while since we have all been together."

Lasara then adds, "LamBrute, leave very early tomorrow; this way you can have Reanna and Eleanor here before lunchtime, where we all can enjoy having lunch together."

The following day, Reanna and Eleanor become separated from Lasara and the professor while shopping in different areas of the mall. After completing her final purchase, she says to the professor, "My shopping is done, Professor. Now, let's go and find Reanna and

Eleanor."

The professor then asks, "How do you propose to find them in this crowded mall? May I remind you, Lasara, it is obvious that the government is monitoring our communication devices."

"It's quite simple, professor, just by looking in the right places where a woman would shop."

"In that case, I will go and find the captain and LamBrute, and my dear Doctor Lasara, I will leave you to your woman's adventure, and when you have completed your mission, you shall find me in the hotel's tropical lounge, relaxing!"

Smiling, Doctor Lasara remarks, "Oh, come on, professor, it's not that bad!"

As he adjusts his glasses, he replies, "Madam, may I convey to you, 'Happy shopping,' and I'll see you later."

Just as the professor is about to leave, Doctor Lasara notices an exceptionally tall and oddly looking individual who seems to have been intensely interested in her conversation with the professor. Looking at him directly, Lasara notices that he abruptly turns away and moves quickly into the crowd of mall shoppers. Concerned, she remains motionless for a moment as her thoughts turn to apprehension, which may have many undesirable consequences. She says, "Wait, Professor! Did you see that tall man staring at us?"

The professor takes a moment before leaving and looks around before answering, "No, I'm sorry, I did not notice anyone."

Suddenly, she hears a voice of redemption call out to her, "Lasara! I'm so glad I found you! Can you and the pròfessor please give Eleanor and me a hand with all these boxes?"

As Reanna struggles to avoid dropping any packages, Doctor

Lasara says, "Reanna, how did you and Eleanor manage to carry all these packages through the mall?"

Reanna replies, "Well, I don't get a chance to come into Star Port City that often."

As Doctor Lasara and the professor take several packages from Reanna and Eleanor,

Reanna replies, "Oh, thank you!"

As she lets out a breath of relief, Reanna and Lasara stop for a moment and laugh at their silly dilemma. Eleanor then says to Lasara, "I thought she would never stop shopping today!"

Reanna says, "I would have had all these packages delivered, but you know..."—she lowers her voice— "the safehouse."

Lasara agrees, "Yes, now, Reanna, let's get out of here. Come on, professor." Curiously, Reanna asks, "Why, Lasara, is something wrong?"

"Yes, I think so! I'll tell you later."

Upon returning to the hotel, they meet up with Trikan and LamBrute as Lasara tells Trikan about the incident of the individual who was staring at her in the mall. She continues, "When I made eye contact with him, he abruptly turned away and disappeared into the crowd!"

Later that evening, Doctor Lasara receives a notification on her computer that the court appearance for Captain Johnathan Shawnwood is scheduled for 10 am tomorrow. They will be picked up by a government court transport and taken to the Security Council. There, they will meet the seven justices, and Captain Johnathan will have counsel support from his chosen attorneys, who will represent him in the government charges. The seven justices will hear the case, and their decisions will be in accordance with all government charters, including those of all governmental agencies and military department officials.

Early the next morning, before they enter the government transport, Lasara tells LamBrute, "When we get to the court complex, there's no need for you to stay with us. Take my flightcraft, and you, Reanna, and Eleanor can go back to the safehouse." Smiling, she states, "The professor has been asking about Cen-Ton quite often!"

The professor jokingly interjects, "Finally, someone is listening to me. Thank you, Lasara." LamBrute smiles as he acknowledges, "We will see you back at the safehouse."

A short time later, they arrive outside the main gates of the Department of Justice facility. Councilwoman Lasara and the professor are then greeted by the Authority Rank Officer-Escort Minister, who says to them, "Good morning, councilwoman, good morning, professor, and good morning to you, Captain! Councilwoman, expect a large crowd when you enter the main gates of the court building."

Smiling, Aunt Lasara says, "I'm fully aware of what to expect since this official government hearing has received a lot of publicity, ever since the fair and open government trial law was passed." Nudging the professor, she smiles and says, "Doesn't that make you feel good, professor?"

Looking at her for a moment, he rolls his eyes and says, "I'll let you know how I feel when it's all over."

As they exit the transport, they are surrounded by spectators who recognize the captain on the way to the court complex, and they begin shouting, "LET HIM GO! HE'S INNOCENT! HE'S DONE NOTHING WRONG!"

As Trikan and Aunt Lasara push their way through the crowd, they enter through the iron gates into the court building, and she says, "I did not expect such a large crowd!"

As the court official closes the entrance to the complex, some of the spectators push to keep it open. Aunt Lasara looks at the professor and notices a look of concern on his face. At the same time, the escort minister is completely bewildered and becomes apologetic that no security measures would have prevented that unruly situation. Looking at the professor and smiling, Aunt Lasara tells him, "Professor, why didn't you try talking to the crowd? Perhaps you could have helped the escort minister control the situation."

As the cheering continues in the background, the professor replies, "Yes... Yes, thank you, Lasara, next time, I will!"

Councilwoman Lasara is well-versed in court proceedings. They enter a turbo-lift that takes them up to the third floor and into a comfortable, ornately designed waiting room, where they can relax before entering the council court chamber.

The court escort officer says to Councilwoman Lasara and Captain Trikan, "I wish both of you good luck!"

Upon leaving, they thank him, and Aunt Lasara tells the professor, "Well, professor, we might as well make ourselves comfortable; we don't know how long this will take."

Minutes later, a court orderly knocks on the antechamber door and opens it halfway. He then says, "Councilwoman Doctor Lasara and Captain Shawnwood, will you please enter the court? Your attorneys have already taken their place before the Supreme Council."

Doctor Lasara and Trikan enter the courtroom, take their places beside their attorneys, and engage in a quiet conversation. Most of the spectators in the courtroom are government colleagues of Doctor Lasara from various departments throughout the large governmental administrations. Doctor Lasara makes it a point not to pay attention to anyone she is familiar with. Her focus remains professional and honorable in the court proceedings. The appointed Supreme Court clerk calls out the usual start, "This hearing is now in session."

Before announcing their legal intentions, the seven Supreme Court judges turn off their audio device speakers and call for a recess. Councilwoman Lasara and Professor Zola are approached by a court aide, who informs them that a special meeting with Supreme Justice Calandra has been granted through her attorneys, allowing them to be escorted into her private chambers.

Trikan and his attorneys leave the courtroom and decide to wait outside in the crowded main lobby, where reporters and other court officials join them.

Trikan reads some of the brief statements handed to him by his attorneys as a well-dressed, tall individual hurriedly pushes his way through the crowd, stops for a moment, and forcefully shoves Captain Trikan, almost knocking him to the marble floor. Trikan then looks at the individual, and before he can say anything, receives an apology, "Oh! Excuse me, it was my fault!"

As he helps Trikan pick up some of the papers he dropped, he quickly walks away, leaving his court attaché case on the ground. Trikan calls out to him, "You're forgetting something!"

The tall individual hesitates for a moment, then stares strangely at Trikan and says, "Oh yes!" He quickly returns, picks up the attaché case, and leaves.

Aunt Lasara and the professor arrive to see the tall individual turn away and suddenly exit down the hallway in the opposite direction, carrying his briefcase. Aunt Lasara asks, "What was that all about, Johnathan?"

"I don't know. But I don't think it was just accidental." She then begins to realize that she has seen him before! Turning to the professor, she asks, "Professor... Do you remember what I told you in the mall, about that person staring at us, who seemed very interested in our conversation? Well, it was HIM, Professor! Right now, he's somewhere in this courthouse!"

Trikan interrupts, "What is this all about, Aunt Lasara?" He then turns to the professor and asks, "Professor?"

Lasara then tells him, "Johnathan, I feel that this incident was not just by chance! I am sure it was the same individual who took an interest in my conversation with the professor at the mall. Johnathan, if you see him again, be careful!"

"Yes, of course."

Aunt Lasara activates her Dial-Date and notifies the in-house security personnel of the incident that occurred outside the courtroom.

Professor Zola says to her, "Lasara, they're back in session." Looking into the courtroom, Lasara notices that the seven supreme judges are about to take their place, and the trial will be called into session at any moment. "Professor, you'd better leave now; there's no point in staying here. We'll meet you back at the hotel."

The professor replies, "Very good, Doctor Lasara. Captain, good luck!"

The professor leaves as the command sergeant of court security approaches Councilwoman Lasara and Trikan.

Supreme Justice Calandra becomes aware of a disturbance outside the main doors of the courtroom, involving Councilwoman Lasara and the command sergeant of court security. One of the other justices that is sitting next to her says, "Justice Calandra, do you want us to start the trial roll call again?"

As she is transfixed on the conversation taking place outside the courtroom, she replies, "No, not yet! Not until we can find out what is going on with Councilwoman Lasara and security!"

As she patiently waits and tries to make sense out of the partial statements that she was able to hear, security leaves, and Lasara and Trikan enter the courtroom, allowing Justice Calandra to question Lasara after she takes her place next to Captain Trikan. Justice Calandra addresses her old friend, "Councilwoman Lasara, can you tell me what was taking place outside my courtroom? Please, don't bother telling me every detail, or we will never get on with the court proceedings today."

Standing, Lasara replies, "I will be happy to answer the court, Your Honor, and be as brief as I can."

Justice Calandra then responds, "Thank you, Councilwoman Lasara; you may begin."

Lasara continues, "I made a report about an incident that I felt could have a harmful and direct impact on disrupting the proceedings of this honorable court and giving the impression that Captain Johnathan Shawnwood was part of a well-contrived conspiracy. A conspiracy to disrupt and destroy the integrity of a fair court hearing by the action of an individual carrying a certified court security case and intentionally pushing his way through the crowded court entranceway. Most of the witnesses, including Captain Johnathan, perceived this incident as harmless, believing the individual was just in a hurry. I then realized that I had seen this individual somewhere before and became very suspicious about his intentions. That is when I notified security and gave them the description of the tall individual.

Your Honor, the command security official ran a photo identification of all personnel, including the attorneys that are present, with their clients, and we received no positive match, not even the slightest identifying feature with the individual that was recorded on the court security cameras."

Acknowledging, Justice Calandra replies, "Thank you, Doctor Lasara, for your help."

The judicial assistant announces, "This court is now in session, trial case number 7398."

Justice Calandra announces to the attorneys of the accused that they should submit their summations and plea statements to the court's computerized repositories, and that there will be a short delay while the statements are processed. The verdict evaluation will be available for viewing on the court's telescreens, including the decisions brought forth by the Supreme Justice.

The courtroom remains silent as if no one is present until the seven judges reveal their verdict on the telescreen. As Justice Calandra observes the seven telescreen images, she announces, "Now, this court can see the verdict has NOT justified the charges of case number 7398. Captain Johnathan Shawnwood is not guilty, with one stipulation! Four of the seven supreme judges announced their decision to dismiss all charges against Captain Johnathan Shawnwood and an agreement that he must abide by. He must follow the instructions recommended by this court's decision to return to his military responsibilities.

He is now assigned to a military air flight base, where he will perform his duties as a captain. He must also participate in recommended supervised rehabilitation during his stay. This court is now adjourned!"

As Aunt Lasara and Trikan leave the courtroom and exit the government complex, they thank their attorneys before stepping into the government transport that will take them back across Star Port City to their hotel. Trikan remains silent, knowing that the governmental authorities may be monitoring his words, while Aunt Lasara engages in a brief conversation with the government transport driver.

After they arrive, Aunt Lasara, Trikan, and the professor go into the restaurant's lounge to have a late lunch. Lasara spends a couple of moments as she opens her pocketbook and takes out a small lipstick case. She then removes the cover and applies a small amount to her lips, placing the cover on the opposite side of the case. She then sends a coded message to LamBrute, instructing him to turn on her office computer screen.

Several moments later, a coded message from LamBrute appears, confirming her request and sending her holographic images of the incident in the mall and outside the courtroom hallway. She observes the matching hologram of the individual and then says to Trikan, "Does he look familiar, Johnathan?"

Trikan observes the holographic image on her arm computer and says, "Yes, that's him all right, Aunt Lasara!" She then sends LamBrute a coded message, "Thank you, LamBrute; everything is good. Now come and pick us up."

Chapter 16:

The Holographic Code

Later that evening, after a successful flight mission, LamBrute pilots Lasara's flightcraft to the safehouse as he jettisons the last of the tracking devices and continues on course over a mountain range to the small community enclave of mansion estates, half a world away from Star Port City. Trikan says, "Good work, LamBrute!"

He responds, "When I landed at the hotel, Captain, I just knew they would put tracking devices on our flightcraft."

In the dark mountains of Alphanian pines, Lasara's flight transport descends and hovers for a short period over the mansion estate; moments later, it slowly comes to a soft landing. The exit door opens, and its four passengers disembark and are greeted by Reanna and Chef Eleanor in the windswept night with the cold mountain air. The professor then activates the recently installed invisibility device on Doctor Lasara's craft as the ship disappears on the tarmac.

As Doctor Lasara approaches the coded, sealed, domed entrance, the zone facial modulators confirm her facial features to an exact coded copy of her identity. It activates the roll-up exit door to the tarmac, allowing them to enter the safehouse.

The telescreens switch off outside broadcast monitoring and then turn on again, allowing only interior security viewing.

Later that evening, after dinner, Reanna and Eleanor begin to unpack the gifts they had bought, while the professor and LamBrute engage in a quiet conversation. After unpacking the last of the gifts, Lasara says, "Well, professor, now all we have to do is wait for Johnathan to receive his orders to report to the air flight base."

The professor seems to be deep in thought about something as he stares into the fireplace. Receiving no response, she ignores him for the moment and then says to LamBrute, who is standing by the large table studying a land graph,

"LamBrute, where is Johnathan?"

"The captain is out back, chopping Alphanian timber logs for the fireplace."

Immediately, Lasara says in disbelief, "You have to be kidding! He must be frozen by now."

Reanna adds, "Lasara, hasn't it always been that way? He needs this time to be alone. Ever since he was a young child, he would go out there for a long period, and when we asked him, he would always say that he needed time to think about things, and the physical work would help him make up his mind!"

Lasara agrees with her, "You're right, Reanna, I don't know why I forgot that. Now let's go out and find him and tell him to come back in."

As Lasara and Reanna go out into the cold, windy night, they can make out a figure a reasonable distance beyond the clearing, where a thick forest of Alphanian trees grows wild in the winter season. As they call out to him, Trikan stops for a moment, the sound of their voices taking him back to a time when he sees himself as a young child, with blurred images of the past, entering into the adventure of future experiences with his only friend at his side, Pup.

He calls back, "Yes, I'm coming in! It's too cold out here anyway!"

Chef Eleanor and LamBrute are setting the living room table for honey tea and a special dessert that she baked. The professor then asks Lasara, "Where is the captain?"

As Trikan walks into the living room, he answers, "Right here, Professor!"

The professor says, "I was in deep thought about something that I would like to discuss with you, Captain."

Aunt Lasara adds, "We're a long way from Star Port City; I suggest that we refrain from discussing the past events and move on with the present."

The professor tells Aunt Lasara, "It's not about the past or the present. It's about our future."

Lasara smiles. "However, we're in a farmland county where life is much simpler. So, let us all enjoy this evening with one of Eleanor's special dessert recipes that she has prepared for us!" Aunt Lasara looks at Trikan and smiles. "We are going to have a lot to do, I imagine, when the professor has his discussion with you, Johnathan."

Smiling, he tells her, "Don't worry, Aunt Lasara, I'll behave myself!"

After their evening of tea and dessert, Chef Eleanor removes the trays from the table. On her way to the kitchen, Reanna and Lasara give her a hand and remain in the kitchen area to prepare for an early morning breakfast. The professor remains silent as he sits in a comfortable chair in front of the fireplace, while LamBrute and Trikan go over to the table that holds the large architectural design document of the Central Detention facility. LamBrute then says, "How do you propose to get into Central Detention, Captain? This place is a fortress. One way in and one way out!"

For a moment, Trikan studies the entrance that leads to the tramway that delivers food and other supplies to the prison. "That's a good question, LamBrute. The other problem is, I don't know of anyone who was there who could guide me and tell me something about the place inside, other than this architectural maze that was designed before its construction."

The professor then says, "I can!"

"Professor, I thought you were asleep?"

"Captain, I wish I were, and that my experience inside Central Detention was just a dream!"

He begins to think back to the first time in his life when he was in court, answering charges brought against him by the military.

"Captain, I was found guilty along with several other higher-ranking governmental scientists on the charges of genetic replication. We all received life sentences in Central Detention, and after a short period, we were given a choice of staying incarcerated in Central Detention or exile! They intended to remove us from public view. The locations were secretly selected, and I accepted exile in an old, abandoned science lab in the Old City, where it was desolate, and I was alone."

He remains silent for several moments, thinking back again, ... *"There I was, in the prison flightcraft, listening to some of the other passengers' stories about why they were on their way to Central Detention. I was asked by one of the prisoners who was sitting across from me, 'What did you do, old man, that you're on your way to Central Detention?'*

The noise of the flightcraft engines made it difficult to hear, and I was in no mood to shout or express my true feelings and engage in a conversation with anyone. As I leaned forward to the inmate sitting across from me, I expressed myself as loudly as my voice would allow, 'If you don't mind... I don't want to talk about it, as well as think about it!'

Some of the other prisoners heard my response and agreed with me, as one of them shouted out, 'He's right! Leave him alone! It's best not to think about it. Where we're going, we will have plenty of time to think about the same thing over and over again!'

Before I closed my eyes, I whispered to myself, until we lost our minds... The rest of the prisoners remained silent as they endured the journey to the place where they would wait for time to pass before they saw freedom again.

The flightcraft slowed down, and the passengers experienced a sudden jolt as the prison tractor beam connected with the transport tower. The massive Banishean doors opened onto a gantry platform high above ground level, allowing the tractor beam to absorb the flying craft and swallow its beleaguered prisoners into the dark hollow of the mysterious monster known as Central Detention.

Once inside, the prisoners were made to change into drab grey uniforms in a large room like a dormitory and then placed in their cells..."

As his thoughts return to present-day reality, he leaves his comfortable chair, walks over to the table, and remarks, "There are several ways in and out of Central Detention, Captain; you just have to pick the right location among them."

Trikan asks, "I had no idea you were a prisoner in Central Detention, professor?"

"That was the past, Captain. Let's concentrate on the future!" Pointing to the blueprint, he continues, "There are several observation towers on the roof to observe and destroy an intrusion from any area around the prison complex. The roof section also contains a landing platform below the dome, and you must get inside the energy dome before your ship is destroyed. The dome is part of the energy source that operates the entire prison; unfortunately, there's no information on where the power plant is located, nor any indication of the power feedline connections.

Inside the large energy dome, the multitudes could hold little hope of ever escaping; no flightcraft could land to rescue anyone or help someone escape while the power was on. The flightcraft would be destroyed instantly!

Sentry robots have the main elevated entry port into Central Detention, well-guarded, and the inmates are never allowed into the elevation lifts that take you up to the towers.

Once inside the visiting center, located on the main floor, visitors enter and exit through the main ground-level entrance. The entire facility is equipped with robot-controlled scanning eyes that relay every expression and movement made by visitors.

The paranoia that created this system undoubtedly created the same mind entity that observes the visitors through the telescreen. I became familiar with the entire process of Central Detention during my entire stay; I did not receive any visitors. Just before completing a half-term sentence, I was transferred to one of the many caves in the Old City, and there I was put into exile!

Despite all the security measures that were enforced at the prison, inmates were allowed to keep their modified arm-cuff computers because they facilitated smooth prison operations due to the large prison population. The primary purpose was to enable direct communication between the warden and the inmates, informing them that their cells would be opened at mealtime.

They would also be allowed to walk down to the main floor, where their meals were prepared and served, without the supervision of a sentry robot.

Additionally, the modified Dial-Dates were used solely to receive messages from the Central Detention superintendent, informing them that an inmate may leave their cell and proceed to the visitors' section upon the arrival of a visitor.

Captain, the time I spent in isolation allowed me to remove the inoperable visual screen in my arm-cuff computer and modify its molecular structure at the subatomic level. Using my Dial-Date disc component, I was able to adjust the electronic frequency installed by the prison authorities and restore it to its original state with my added modifications. The frequency change I made could not be detected outside my cell or by any other in-house arm-cuff computers. Using an algorithm of exclusive number sequences, I was able to receive holographic images of the entire prison cell complex, including the roof's landing flight platform and towers."

Trikan responds, "So, your experience gave you the missing parts that are unaccounted for on the architect's blueprints?"

As the professor stares at the fireplace, he says, "Precisely, Captain!" A slight pause, and he then says, "Captain, we need some more of your chopped timber logs; the flames are about to go out." LamBrute tells the captain, "I will take care of that, Captain."

Aunt Lasara enters the room at that moment and asks, "When you return, LamBrute, would you like a cup of hot rum tea and a fresh honey croissant that Chef Eleanor baked for anyone who might desire a late-night snack?"

LamBrute replies, "Thank you, that would be very kind of you and Chef Eleanor."

As Trikan and the professor continue their discussion of the architecturally designed blueprint for Central Detention, LamBrute returns, throws several large timber logs into the fireplace, and then joins the conversation at the table. The professor then continues,

"Captain, most of my secret inquiries from my arm-cuff computer gave me the routine of everyday life and also the administrative program of prison staff members, with one high-ranking officer's routine. I witnessed an unusual view that repeated itself just before the landing of an air-flight food supply craft. When this occurred, I observed the prison official approach the tower, which was several yards away from the landing platform. Upon entering, he stepped up onto an oval platform disc and then walked to the center, where he stood for a moment.

Energy rays began to emanate from the center of the disc, and a hologram appeared all around him, depicting ionic and neutron energy combined with strange markings within the energy field. He then performed an action with his Dial-Date computer, and the platform disc slowly moved as he stepped off. He then walked over to a keyboard screen and typed in a code in front of a large steel door, and it opened. When the door was fully opened, he entered a large communication frame room that contained some slotted units of malfunctioning communication *Magnite* plates, which were in the process of failing.

He removed the defective plates of *Magnite* and replaced the units with new radioactive sensors. Just before he replaced the last damaged sensor, he seemed to be preoccupied for a moment with the door beginning to close. He then quickly left the room.

Captain, another thing that puzzled me was that there were no tribar handles on the inside of the door to allow anyone to exit the room once the door was closed. Another thing, Captain, what made the holograph disc move, and where did he get the entrance code from to enter the room?"

Trikan replies, "That's an incredible story, Professor!"

The professor continues, "That's only half of the story, Captain.

That room controls all the exterior entrance and exit doors to the entire prison and the landing flightcraft hangar bays, which is the electronic energy design that's missing from the blueprint. As you can see, the entire map of the prison contains no electronic outlines! The only time the tower is used is when the prison receives deliveries of supplies."

As Aunt Lasara enters the room, she asks, "Professor, would you mind if I took Johnathan away from you for a moment?"

The professor looks up and replies, "Not at all. Perhaps, some time away from this manuscript,"—he begins to roll up the blueprint and continues— "will give me the answer I'm looking for!"

Aunt Lasara looks at the code frequency indicator on her arm computer and says to Johnathan, "I just received a teller-coded message from military command. In twenty-one sequence solar days, you will be notified of your base location, Johnathan."

The professor then says, "I think we will call it an evening! I'm ready to retire."

Trikan looks over at LamBrute, who is sound asleep, sitting in what was the professor's chair. Trikan smiles. "Professor, I think LamBrute has already taken your advice. Good night, Aunt Lasara, Professor."

They leave, and Trikan walks over to the jagged stone fireplace, places his hands on the large mantel above the hearth, and spends moments of reflection. As he looks into the open flames, he sees the burning embers of the past, and for a moment, he feels the presence of Elisa.

Morning breakfast begins with the absence of one guest, and the cordial conversation continues with the usual reference to complementing Chef Eleanor's breakfast creations.

Professor Zola says, "This is a splendid breakfast, Chef Eleanor! I only wish that the captain were here to enjoy it. Where is he this morning? I want to speak to him, and don't tell me that he is outside chopping firewood again!"

Turning to Reanna, Lasara asks, "Do you have any idea where Johnathan is this morning?" Putting her cup of tea down, she says, "Lasara, I don't have the slightest idea where Johnathan is. Now, don't pick on him. This isn't the first time he hasn't shown up for breakfast."

Lasara agrees, "You're right, I won't until he gets here."

The professor states, "But I do need his presence down in the flight hangar!"

Aunt Lasara tells Cen-Ton, "Cen-Ton, why don't you go and wake up the captain and tell him that the professor needs him, and I forgive him this time for not showing up for breakfast!"

As Cen-Ton goes up to the captain's room, he knocks on the door and waits for a couple of moments, but there is no response. He then enters the room, and Trikan is still asleep. "... CAPTAIN, WAKE UP..."

He replies, "Yes, Cen-Ton, what is it?"

"... IT'S TIME TO GET UP, CAPTAIN... I HAVE TWO MESSAGES FOR YOU... THE PROFESSOR WANTS TO TALK WITH YOU... AND YOUR AUNT LASARA SAYS THAT SHE FORGIVES YOU FOR NOT SHOWING UP FOR BREAKFAST..."

Trikan smiles. "Now, where is the professor?"

"... I RECALL HIM SAYING, CAPTAIN, THAT HE WILL BE DOWN IN THE UNDERGROUND FLIGHT HANGAR..."

Trikan says, "Thank you, Cen-Ton. I'll go and talk to him."

"... YOU'RE VERY WELCOME, CAPTAIN..."

Once downstairs in the air flight hangar, Trikan fails to see the professor. He calls out to him and receives no immediate reply. He calls out again, "Professor... Professor Zola?"

A second later, the professor calls back to him, "Over here, Captain! In the flightcraft."

Trikan walks over to the open escape hatch, looks in at the empty hull of the ship, and says, "Professor... What are you doing under the substructure of this old wreck?"

Dropping a tool, the professor emerges from beneath the floor structure, wipes his hands, and says, "Give me a hand, Captain, please!" I wanted to complete the work on the antique that you purchased, and I won't ask you how many credits you paid for it. This job is almost completed, and it will be when LamBrute returns with the invisibility device. It will fly as well as any invisible flightcraft if you know what I mean.

Trikan smiles. "You're quite a genius, Professor!"

As the professor wipes his hands again with a clean cloth, he replies, "Please, no compliments! Not until after the mission is successful. Your transportation is almost completed. This ship can now take you to Central Detention. The invisibility factor will be one hundred percent operational!"

As the professor presses the combination sequence on the engine's starting device, the flightcraft is automatically activated with the subatomic engine running in a low-frequency mode. While holding the device up in front of Trikan, he says, "I'll keep this in a safe place until the day of the mission. Now, when LamBrute returns with the invisibility of atom-transfer protons, this craft will stay invisible until you deactivate the proton enhancer. Oh, and Captain, after the mission is successfully over, try to get your purchase credits back from that merchant. I won't charge him for the improvements I made!"

They both begin to laugh as LamBrute returns and asks, "Did I just miss something?"

Trikan replies, "Yes, the professor wants me to get my purchase credits back!"

Lambrute's eyes widen. "Oh, that again? Not likely, Captain, that merchant is too clever!"

Several days pass, and a coded message is transferred to Councilwoman Lasara's personally privileged government Dial-Date account. Across the screen, the coded message reads:

> *"Captain Shawnwood is now hereby assigned to Doctor J. Torry of the Clinical Psychology Department.*
>
> *He will engage in a period of rehabilitation and report his progress to this court.*
>
> *After successful treatment, he may, by choice, return*

> *to his military obligations as a full Captain in Flight Group Command.*
>
> *The date of the first appointment will be five sequence days from this report. The captain will be present at Scout Command Air Flight Base LK-11-North Zone, nineteen hundred kilometers northwest of Star Port City, in the Sclerean Mountain Range.*
>
> *Once he arrives, he will report to Doctor Torry, located in the Clinical Psychology Department, on the Base in section A-1-A-Eleven.*
>
> *A copy of this report shall be given to the said captain by court order, under the directive of Councilwoman Lasara."*

Aunt Lasara removes the transcript copy, calls Johnathan over the intercom, and tells him, "Johnathan, I just received your command orders on my office computer. When you're finished down there with the professor, I'll fill you in on the details!"

Looking at the professor, Trikan says, "Well, professor, I guess you're on your own until we get this thing over with. Whatever you do, don't lose those architectural documents. Professor, there's something that I have been wanting to ask you. Do you have any idea...?" He pauses and then continues, "You know what, professor, we'll let it go for another time."

The professor replies, "No, I know what you want to ask me, Captain. The answer is yes, I do know where Elisa is being held. She's in the women's section of Central Detention, and we're going to do our best to get her out of there!"

"Thank you, Professor!"

"Now go, captain, and get this thing over with! Don't worry, LamBrute is a good assistant too. I could not ask for anyone better!"

As Trikan takes the hydro-lift up to Aunt Lasara's office, he asks her, "Good news or bad news, Aunt Lasara?"

"Well, it all depends upon you, Johnathan, and what you do when you get there. Here, this is the transcript that I received."

Trikan reads the transcript for several moments and replies, "It says here, Doctor Torry is the top-rated psychiatrist, and he also gives group seminars on the inner workings of the mind and has a one hundred percent success rating with the patients."

Lasara replies, "No, it's not he; it's she, and you have to report within four days to the Air Flight Base at 0800 hours."

According to the transcript, you report directly to her office upon your arrival. Jonathan, when you arrive at the base, I suggest you wear your full-rank uniform. We do not want you to get involved with the sentry robots. They have a long history of reacting with force before listening to any explanations, especially to anyone who is not dressed in their full rank uniform on the base camp, and—" Trikan interjects, "And I will behave myself, Aunt Lasara, that's a promise!" She says, "Good, now you're beginning to think along my lines! Oh, by the way, Jonathan, there's a call waiting for you on my computer from Officer Reynolds, requesting contact.

"Reynolds! I'll call him back immediately; thank you, Aunt Lasara!"

Trikan activates the military code sequence program on Lasara's computer, and a moment later, Officer Reynolds appears on the screen, "Captain Shawnwood... I heard the good news this morning and was given your flight time. Welcome back, Captain, report zero-eight hundred!"

"Thanks, Reynolds, it will be good to be back!"

Aunt Lasara asks, "Who is this Reynolds, Johnathan?"

"Flight Lieutenant Reynolds, a friend from the academy."

She smiles and says, "It's good to have friends, Johnathan."

Every night after dinner, the professor goes over and reviews the details of the blueprinted document of Central Detention until the captain and LamBrute can almost anticipate what the professor will say next about the prison fortress. This is the routine up to the last evening before Captain Trikan leaves for the air base.

The following morning, Professor Zola wishes him good luck and a safe flight. He then says, "LamBrute, I advise you to be careful and avoid any altercations with Security Central Robots when you land at the camp."

LamBrute acknowledges, "Yes, professor, I will."

Aunt Lasara says, "Oh, Johnathan, before you leave, I meant to tell you last night that I'm working with some of my colleagues in the council to get that young woman of yours some type of early release from Central Detention if possible." Speechless for a moment, he says, "Aunt Lasara, you are the best!"

Reanna then says, "Johnathan, take care of yourself and please come back to us when all this rehabilitation nonsense is over with!"

Trikan smiles. "Not to worry, Mom, I will!"

Trikan makes his way across the windswept landing platform with LamBrute, and they board the hydro-craft. LamBrute activates the high-gear turbo thrusters and begins to lift the craft off the tarmac. The captain seals the pressurized entrance hatch cover as the craft's computer begins to navigate the craft into a high-speed flight form trajectory.

Trikan takes his place beside LamBrute in the copilot's control console as LamBrute turns towards the captain. "Well, captain, you're on your way." Smiling, he agrees, "Yes, LamBrute, it certainly looks that way."

LamBrute then flies the craft over the safehouse, flashing all the exterior landing lights on and off as a gesture of safe departure and safe return. They then head southwest, avoiding Star Port City as they continue their journey to the A-1-A Military Base.

Smiling, Trikan says, "LamBrute, I was just thinking about what the professor said to me last night. He's been right before!" Trikan remains silent, then LamBrute asks, "Right before what, Captain?"

While leaning back and adjusting his seat to get comfortable, Trikan replies, "About going to the military camp. He felt that there might be some danger involved."

LamBrute asks, "Danger, captain?"

Closing his eyes and becoming comfortable again in the copilot's seat, he says, "Well, they did try to get rid of me, LamBrute. Who's to say they may not try again?"

Chapter 17:
Therapeutic Prognosis

The large body of water below the flightcraft, with its canal tributaries, divides the northern continent from the southern hemisphere, which accounts for most of the flight time until they reach the large military air base just before the early morning military roll call.

Trikans' flightcraft D-729 lands outside the camp's main gates on the large landing field after it receives clearance from the military air tower control specialist. LamBrute cuts the main engines to Aunt Lasara's luxury flight transport, knowing full well that the flightcraft will be inspected after landing. Aunt Lasara took the precaution of having Professor Zola remove the invisibility device he had installed on the craft. She also had the professor delete all previous conversations from her onboard flight computer, as well as identity photos from the computer's view screen. The air base scan found nothing preventing Captain Trikans' clearance, along with his classification code rated: *"1-A Certified Unit Officer."*

After entering the scout camp compound, Captain Trikan and LamBrute are scanned for weapons and asked to take identity photos on a computer view screen that will match their facial likenesses to a pre-approved order clearance to enter the camp. Captain Trikans' clearance classification code is automatically scanned, and he is to be in proper uniform and on restricted duty. Next is the Trikinian, LamBrute, who is issued a temporary clearance code. *"1-W: Work Unit, Captain's Pilot: Private rating; Nonmilitary personnel."* His base camp clearance may accompany the captain until his services are no longer required.

Minutes later, a scout land support vehicle operated by a robot driver arrives at the main gate.

"... CAPTAIN... WELCOME TO THE SCOUT AIR BASE... MY ORDERS ARE TO TAKE YOU TO CAMP SECTION DOME ELEVEN, WHERE DOCTOR JEAN TORRY IS EXPECTING YOU AND YOUR AIDE...."

Trikan looks at LamBrute. "How do you like the service?"

LamBrute looks up at the clear skies over the camp and replies, "Let's get this over with, Captain!"

Trikan smiles and says, "At least you get to leave in a little while!"

LamBrute looks around, and all he sees are multitudes of scout troops training in some

combat field activities, while others are servicing armed flight attack vehicles. He then replies, "I hope you're right, Captain!"

Trikan and LamBrute enter the domed complex through a double-door foyer, where a computer console screen activates as the outer doors close and lock. The voice from the screen activates a questioning monologue, identical to the camp's entrance security program.

"...Welcome, captain... Please wait as we routinely verify your previous security analysis performed at the base entrance..."

Instantaneously, pulsating light signals announce the subjects: "... Captain Trikan and a Trikinian scout named LamBrute are accepted into our parallel code information identification clearance. The subjects may gain entrance into the main lobby and report to the hostess secretary at the main security counter..."

Dressed in a military uniform, the female receptionist greets Trikan and LamBrute.

"Welcome, gentlemen. Captain, Doctor Torry is expecting you.

Your clearance is in order, gentlemen. You can take the hydro-lift directly to Department C-Fifteen and her office complex.

Upon exiting, you will be in the patient's lounge section.

Please make yourself comfortable; complimentary refreshments are available. Thank you, and enjoy your appointment."

While walking down the corridor to the hydro-lift section, Trikan asks LamBrute, "Did you hear what she said, LamBrute?"

LamBrute immediately answers, "We get to eat?"

Smiling, Trikan replies, "Yes, LamBrute, if you like military packaged food. Don't bother reading the life expectancy on the label; it will probably outlive us!"

As they exit the hydro-lift, the captain and LamBrute enter a spacious lounge area illuminated by soft blue lighting. A robotic voice comes over the speakers in the nutritional section of the lounge, where an automatic beverage dispenser is located: "Welcome to Doctor Torry's Office Complex. A beverage display is available with soft drinks and a variety of snacks. Please help yourself."

Trikan and LamBrute take their beverages into the lounge section and place them on one of the small sectional tables. An attractive female enters the lounge area and greets the captain and LamBrute. "Good morning, gentlemen. I see that you are enjoying your beverages. I am Doctor Jean Torry, a cognitive psychiatrist, and you, Captain? You must be Captain Shawnwood?" He smiles as he is about to stand up, but she states, "Relax, Captain... There's no reason to be formal." Looking at the clipboard again, she turns to LamBrute. "And you are the Trikinian scout?" He responds, "My name is LamBrute." She smiles and says, "It's nice to meet you, LamBrute."

Doctor Torry then writes LamBrute's name down on a referral entrance document, which she will later submit to her computer files to generate a detailed dossier on her new patients, Captain Trikan and his escort LamBrute. "I'll leave you two gentlemen alone for a while.

As she looks at the captain, she smiles. "I have to go back to my office to get your schedule for your stay at the camp, Captain."

Walking towards her office, she stops and turns. "LamBrute... You have a twenty-four-hour standard visitor pass. After that, I'm afraid you'll have to leave. I am sorry, but it is the rules."

LamBrute replies, "Yes, doctor... I understand."

She then proceeds to her office and returns shortly thereafter. "Captain, this is your camp itinerary schedule."

Handing it to Trikan, she gives him time to review it before telling him, "As you can see, you have access and privilege clearance to any place within the compound of the camp. However, you may not participate in any training programs or share barracks with any personnel. You have been given private quarters as a captain due to your rank, which I am sure you already know is quite admirable, and if I may emphasize the No List:

You will not engage any of the scout troops in conversation other than returning a respectable salute after receiving their required one. You will not engage in group conversations, nor will you engage in discussions with anyone holding a higher rank. Also, you will not engage or answer questions with anyone of the same rank as Captain. You will only answer questions to higher-ranking officers with a simple 'Yes' or 'No', sir.

This program calls for strict discipline, Captain! I will ask you questions, and you may answer them as you see fit. Additionally, I have an assistant, Doctor Jeffery. If you are willing to sign this document, it will grant him the same privileges I have to converse with you. You do so by your own free will."

Taking Doctor Torry's agreement, Trikan agrees to let her assistant participate in his rehabilitation program.

Handing her back the document, he pauses for a moment. "Here you go. When do the sessions start?"

"Tomorrow morning, Captain. I expect to see you in my office at zero-eight hundred. At that time, I will introduce you to my assistant, Doctor Jeffery."

The following day, a little before Trikans' therapy appointment at 0800 with Doctor Torry, he walks across the hydro-field with LamBrute to the flight transport. "Well, captain, this is it... I'll see you when this is all over."

Trikan agrees, "I'm looking forward to it, LamBrute. I just hope that I don't get thrown any more surprises?"

LamBrute smiles and agrees. "I know what you mean, Captain. I've seen the way you were looking at her!"

Trikan smiles back. "Was it that noticeable?"

"I think so, captain, and I am sure she was aware of it too!"

"Have a good trip, LamBrute, and tell everyone that everything is good here."

"Will do, Captain!" LamBrute salutes Trikan and boards the flight transport. Trikan then steps away before the hydro engines kick in and then walks back out of harm's way to the camp entrance hall.

As LamBrute engages the turbo lift, the flightcraft pauses for a moment and then receives the all-clear signal from the flight control tower, allowing it to proceed with full takeoff. It only takes a few moments, and the flightcraft is in full flight mode and disappears over the mountain camp compound.

On the way back, Trikan notices the landing of a military flight transport, and as the recruits begin to disembark, they assemble into a typical military formation. They are then put under a military inspection protocol, and for several moments, Trikan experiences the memory of the first day he arrived at Air Base Command. A smile appears on his face down the long hallway as he thinks back to when it all started.

Before entering the canteen, he stops, tries to focus on reality, but is quickly drawn back to the past, plagued by feelings of uncertainty. Suddenly, he gets a flashback and thinks," *I wonder what happened to Sergeant Larsen?"*

He trained himself a long time ago to a condition where he practiced a set of rules to never dwell upon the past. What was done cannot be changed; he could not take the blame for things that happened in his past; he never intentionally harmed anyone. When did this all become part of his life's journey? This was not the first time he had been drawn back to the past, with feelings of hurt and distress. This was the moment of the long walk down the corridor of life. His thoughts will continue and become focused once again on reality. The time was the present, and he would live by and deal with the conditions placed before him to free Elisa.

As he enters the canteen, he picks up a typical military-prepared breakfast from a dispenser. A voice calls from behind the counter, "Captain, you don't want that! Let me give you a freshly packaged breakfast just prepared this morning."

"Thank you!"

As he checks the time on his wrist computer, he refocuses on reality, realizing he is late for his scheduled appointment.

A short time later, he opens the door to Doctor Torry's office and is not greeted warmly. "You're late, Captain! Did you not read the conditions that we posted on your sentence therapy? That you would show up on time for your therapy program! Look at this, Captain!"

She points to the telescreen on the wall. "You have a habit of being late! Look how many times you were late for classes at the military academy. I don't know why they kept you!" Looking at Trikan, she asks, "What are you thinking about?"

Smiling, he says, "I'm thinking about eating my breakfast. Would you care for some?"

Staring at him, she replies, "No... No... Go ahead, Captain! Have your breakfast! She pauses and then asks, "Captain, would I disrupt your breakfast if I invited my assistant to come in and meet you?"

"No, go right ahead. I want to meet your assistant."

As she exits the office, Trikan thinks to himself: *"How did I ever get into this situation?"*

He was determined to keep his part of the court's agreement and remain free. If he stepped too far over the line, he could find himself as an inmate in Central Detention and not on the mission to free Elisa.

The door to the office opens, and Doctor Torry walks in with her assistant. "Captain, this is my assistant, Doctor Jeffery." Correcting herself and trying to take control over her annoyance with the captain's less-than-professional behavior, she restates her introduction, "Excuse me... Doctor Jeffery, this is Captain Trikan. Oh, excuse me once again; this is Captain Johnathan Shawnwood."

Looking at the captain, Doctor Torry's assistant salutes and says, "It's a pleasure to meet you, Captain!"

Stopping his breakfast, Trikan suddenly looks around for something to wipe his hands with. Sitting across from the captain at her desk, Doctor Torry says to him, "Is this what you're looking for, Captain?"

As she hands him a facial tissue from her desk, he takes it, and she abruptly gives him another one while saying, "Just help yourself to anything you see, captain. Be my guest!"

Trikan smiles at her as he wipes his hands and then returns Doctor Jeffery's salute. The captain and Doctor Jeffery are having a cordial conversation as Doctor Torry looks at her schedule for the interview and announces, "I don't mean to interrupt, but your time's up, Captain; I have to run an errand; I have to leave."

Trikan and Jeffery stay engaged in conversation relating to subjects other than the immediate circumstances that have placed them at this moment in their careers.

Upon Doctor Torry's return, she waits outside her office and listens to the conversation between the captain and her assistant. She hesitates several times as she attempts to enter the room and then stops again—each time, Jeffery and the captain are engaged in laughter. Their conversational content varies across different periods, from their early school days to their graduation from the military academy. She finds none of their conversation and subject matter important as she deactivates her code sequence and enters the office. "Well, gentlemen... I have a feeling that I wasn't missed!"

Jeffery smiles. "Oh, don't be silly, Doctor! You are always missed when you are not around!" Trikan then adds, "Yes, I agree."

She looks at him for a moment and then says, "Doctor Jeffery... I have a new friend! Well, my new friend, Captain, your session is over! You may leave and go and do whatever captains like to do, and be back here tomorrow morning on time!"

"Okay, doctor, until tomorrow!" Jeffery interjects, "Captain, it was a pleasure meeting you!"

"The same here, Jeffery!"

Trikan turns back to Doctor Torry before leaving, and cordially, he says, "Doctor..." She stops and stares at her desk. "Are you forgetting something, captain?"

As she looks directly at him, he says, "Oh, sorry about that!"

He proceeds to remove his breakfast tray from her desk, and as he is about to exit her office, she says to him, "Captain... I just got a great idea! It's all right for you to be late tomorrow if you have breakfast in the cafeteria!" Trikan stops, looks back at her, and smiles before he leaves. She then says, "Well, Jeffery... What do you think?"

"I like him. He is very nice, Doctor!"

"I'm glad you like him, Jeffery. Now, is there anything about him that you can tell me, besides the fact that he's a nice guy and you like him? By the book, Jeffery!"

"Well, he has many sides to his personality, and that would be part one! Second, I think he can be anyone's best friend if they want him to be their friend. What about you, Doctor Torry? What do you think of the captain?"

She pauses momentarily before answering, "It's too short a time; you have me at a disadvantage, Jeffery. You spend more time with him. I can't tell you."

She was about to say something further, but then stopped and remained silent. Jeffery then says, "Yes, I understand, Doctor Torry. If I may say something, by the book again, I think most people, after they get to know him, will conclude that they can trust him!"

After that, Trikan would have breakfast in the Mess Hall Cafeteria every morning, obeying Doctor Torry's every word. It did not take long for the entire air flight group to get to know him. For the outpost unit, breakfast became a high point of their morning with the celebrity captain.

In a short amount of time, the order came down from the High Command that Captain Johnathan Shawnwood was on restricted duty. He would no longer be allowed to have breakfast in the cafeteria due to his popularity with the unit command personnel. As he has been officially informed, he must now have his breakfast in Doctor Torry's office.

Early the next day, Trikan will follow the higher command order that instructed him to take his breakfast in Doctor Torry's office. As she walks in, she is surprised. "What are you doing here in my office, Captain?"

He replies, "Having breakfast, doctor."

"I thought we had an agreement! I see now that I have to put you on report!"

He says to her, "Don't do it!"

"What did you say?"

"Doctor Torry, did you read the memo yesterday?"

"No, I wasn't here... I was off the base, visiting a friend, and there were no client appointments yesterday!"

"Then you'd better check your computer for staff orders, doctor."

She checks her computer for the updated staff orders and says in a low voice, "Oh no... OH NO!" Looking at him, she asks, "How did you arrange this?" She sits silently for several moments, looking at him, and then says, "Okay, captain, you win!"

Trikan tells her, "Hey, I had nothing to do with it!" Staring up from her desk, she says, "Go on, captain, have your breakfast!"

Several weeks have passed, and the captain's popularity is not diminishing. Many of the command troops ask permission to come into her office and engage in a conversation with him. Doctor Torry allows the troop personnel to go into her office to talk with the captain by appointment only. The calls come in more frequently to her office, to the point where it becomes an everyday occurrence, and most of her time is spent scheduling appointments for the captain, which takes away from her programs.

The constructed time for the captain's rehabilitation program becomes less of the daily work regimen, and she finds herself making reports on his progress and documenting rehabilitation sessions that don't exist. Doctor Torry has become a prisoner in her workplace by allowing the unit's personnel to meet with the captain in her office. She realizes that she has given in to a Captain Trikan fan club. She blames part of this problem on herself and never gives a time limit on their visits.

She then gets the idea of taking her work with the captain out of the camp, to places as far away as possible, and not letting anyone know where he is, except for her assistant, Jeffery. She is free to conduct treatments for her patients and is unrestricted within the camp compounds.

A resort area is a reasonable distance from the camp, offering an environment of seclusion from military personnel that would be more conducive to the captain's rehabilitation. According to his case history, he never took any time off from his career, and according to the files, he is a workaholic and possibly someone who did not have a very social life. After making her decision, she will treat her new patient off the base. That afternoon, when the fan club decided to leave, she was finally given the chance to speak with the captain alone and return to the rehabilitation program to which he had been assigned.

"Captain, before you go..." She reads his profile report without looking at him and then says, "Captain, tomorrow, the program calls for us to continue your rehabilitation treatments outside the influence of military protocol. As of tomorrow, you will be out of uniform and will wear civilian attire. After breakfast, we will take my hydrocopter to a small resort town. I think you will enjoy this part of the program, Captain?"

He says to her, "Okay, that sounds great, Doctor!" The captain is about to leave her office, and she calls out to him, "Oh, Johnathan... Do you know where the civilian hydrocopter field is on the base?"

He stops and replies, "Of course, yes!" She shouts out to him, "Good! Don't be late!"

After the captain leaves, she waits until her office door closes and then contacts her assistant, Jeffery, on her telescreen. "Yes, Doctor Torry, may I help you?"

"Yes, Jeffery, I have something to tell you... I did it!"

"You did what, doctor?"

"I finally got them out of my office!"

"Got who out of your office?"

She replies, "The captain's fan club!" Finding her statement a little amusing, he says, "Oh... Right, doctor. How did you manage that?"

"Well, it was quite easy, and I don't know why I didn't think of it sooner! This is their last meeting here! Tomorrow, my office will be closed. We're leaving in the morning for the Summerville Mountain Resort, where we'll spend several days. Then, we'll head up to my cabin to assess its condition; I haven't visited my cabin retreat in a while. As of tomorrow, the captain will be receiving his court-ordered rehabilitation away from the camp and his admirers."

"That sounds good, doctor. Is there anything you would like me to do while you're gone?"

She replies, "I have no appointments for the next several weeks! Jeffrey, you can come up whenever you'd like. Just contact me, and I'll let you know where we are and if we're staying in the cabin. I want to see what the captain suggests when we get there. So, I can evaluate what goes on in his mind when he's away from the base."

"Yes, doctor... I understand that a preference of choice is very informative! It will help you with the complete profile analysis without asking the subject too many questions."

"Yes, Jeffery, I know that he is a very popular captain, and I am sure as his popularity spreads, he has taken on a psychological profile within his mind that the whole world around him is either for him or against him. I don't blame him for that. Unfortunately, it comes with the territory!"

"Yes, I do agree... Thank you, Doctor Torry; I look forward to visiting you and the captain. I think the captain may become a textbook subject that you will use to teach your students how to distinguish and become aware of what happens to an individual when he achieves notoriety and celebrity status!"

Doctor Torry smiles as she replies, "When I start teaching in the Fall semester at the university, it won't take long for my students to realize that this Captain Trikan is going to be nothing more than a myth!"

The long summer days at the Mountain Lake Resort are filled with sightseeing excursions and sailing of hydro-crafts on the lake. Doctor Torry and the captain dine at quaint mountain resort restaurants and spend the evenings visiting a carnival site in the area. The more time Doctor Torry spends with the captain, the more her reports about him begin to take a less critical prognosis of his mind. She includes less contradictory feedback about her patient in her reports.

She feels good about that and about her work, achieving the goal she so desires: her client's honest opinion.

After several weeks at the resort, Doctor Torry is now becoming less interested in writing her daily reports after spending time with the captain. She has also become somewhat neglectful of her professional conversations with him. More than once, she finds herself quietly listening to his past experiences while not responding to his official title of Captain Shawnwood. Instead, she responds to him with, "I don't believe they did that to you, Johnathan!"

As they begin to get to know each other better, on an outing one afternoon, Doctor Torry tells him that her job was to win him over to the government and persuade him to behave himself and forget all about his past experiences.

Smiling, he says to her, "Did it work? Or did you put down that I'm a hopeless case?" Immediately, she replies, "Johnathan, don't say that. My work is to help! I never put it in my reports that anyone is a hopeless case. If I did that, I could not live with that thought! Everyone is different. Some of my patients take a little longer." Looking directly at her, he says,

"Okay... Please stop, forgive me. I was wrong to say that."

She then says to him, "You see, you're becoming much more thoughtful than you were before. We can all change a little at a time, but for some of us, it may take a little longer." Sitting back, he says, "You're right, Doctor Torry. Every day is an adventure in the good things that our lives have to offer." She takes his hand. "I agree with you, Captain! Every moment is to be enjoyed. Johnathan, if you think you're in danger, then I am in danger, too!"

Looking into the reflection of her blue eyes, he says, "No one can tell what the government has in mind. They tried to eliminate me before."

She smiles caringly and says, "I can tell you this, Captain, there are no government plans to harm you. My mission, as assigned by the council, is to get you back. As we speak, the council program is in full cooperation with the military to determine the location of your scout troops and what happened to them. I understand you, Captain, and I agree with you on many things." Trikan affirms, "So much of what you are saying is like you're reading my mind." Smiling, she asks, "Does that embarrass you, Captain?"

"No..."—smiling, he adds— "No, no, of course not!" She laughs. "You're such a liar, Captain!" As she looks at him, she tries not to think about the fact that this assignment will end.

The next day, Doctor Torry submits her report on the captain to her assistant, Jeffery, to be filed in her office. He then engages in a conversation with her on the telescreen.

"May I ask you something, Doctor Torry? How are the two of you getting along?"

She replies, "By the book, Jeffery... I agree with your opinion; he has many sides to his personality, and I think he can be anyone's best friend if they want him to be. Jeffery, have you read my reports on the captain? Jeffery, I'm waiting, and you're too quiet."

While filing papers in her office, he turns and looks back at the telescreen. "Okay... I will say it! I always liked the captain from the moment you introduced me."

He remains silent again, and she says, "Jeffery, you're too quiet again. What else, Jeffery? I'm waiting." He smiles. "Your reports are excellent, Doctor. You've made a lot of progress with the captain."

"And what else, Jeffery?"

Looking at the screen, he remains silent before replying, "I think you have fallen in love with the captain!" She asks, "Would that be a bad thing, Jeffery?"

He says back to her, "No... As a matter of fact, I am very happy for you!"

She smiles and replies, "Thank you, Jeffery. I am incredibly fortunate to have you as both my assistant and my friend. Are you going to come up and visit us? I'm sure he would enjoy your company also, and it may help take his mind off some of the things he's been through that we talked about in his past."

Jeffery agrees, "Okay, great! I'll finish up here and see you this weekend!"

Looking into the telescreen, she says, "Okay, good, Jeffery, this is our plan. The captain and I are leaving the lake resort area after dinner this evening. Then, we will drive up to my mountaintop cabin, where we will spend the rest of our time. When you come, you will stay at the cabin with us, and I will make reservations to have dinner at the very popular Pine View Restaurant down in the lake area, where they have entertainment of mountain folk music and dances wearing traditional mountain costumes."

Smiling, Jeffery replies, "I will be looking forward to it!"

As the telescreen automatically turns off and her conversation ends, she orders breakfast. She then quietly walked into the balcony suite bedroom, where she had opened the terrace doors to let in the cool morning mountain lake air. After breakfast arrives, she slowly walks out onto the terrace and places the breakfast tray on a glass table. Without making any noise, she moves the two comfortable terrace chairs next to the table and then places down a small vase of fresh-cut flowers that the hotel furnishes.

Doctor Torry then looks back into the bedroom to see if Johnathan is still asleep. She then walks quietly and is about to wake him, but stops. Looking at him for several moments, she gently touches his shoulder and says, "Johnathan... Are you awake?"

She gets no response but smiles and says, "Come on, captain... Breakfast is waiting."

With his eyes open, he smiles and says, "Good morning, Doctor Torry."

She smiles back as she repeats his words, "And a good morning to you, too, Captain! Breakfast is served on the terrace with the compliments of your doctor! Oh, I spoke to Jeffery this morning and invited him to come and spend this weekend with us at the cabin. I am going to make reservations at the same restaurant where we will have dinner tonight. It's the Pine View Restaurant in the Lower Lake area. Is that all right with you?"

He agrees, "Yes, I like Doctor Jeffery, and it's nice that you invited him up for the weekend. He deserves a break, especially since he's doing all your work for you back at the office!"

Smiling, she pushes him and says, "Oh, come on, you're so mean to me."

The two of them begin to laugh, and after breakfast, Trikan and Doctor Torry spend the rest of the day shopping for souvenirs in the quaint little shops around the lake. Doctor Torry never had it in her mind to stay at her cabin when she came up with the idea of taking her work with the captain away from the busy military base and his new friends.

That evening at the Pine View Restaurant, they spoke about the enjoyable times they had since arriving at the resort. Doctor Torry then receives a text on her arm-cuff computer from Doctor Jeffery and says, "Johnathan, it's from Jeffery. He said that he is coming up this weekend. He also said that all the work is completed, and there is nothing on the schedule for the next couple of weeks. He will see us soon and say hello to the captain for him. His last message was, 'Happy to spend the weekend with the two of you!' Johnathan, we'll leave first thing in the morning, which will give us the time to clean up the cabin before Jeffery arrives!"

As their dining room waiter places their drinks on the table, Doctor Torry asks, "Why is that person staring at us?"

Trikan looks over for a moment and observes someone he thinks he has seen before standing at the crowded restaurant entrance. The individual then abruptly turns and exits through the entrance doors as the dining room waiter at the table turns and says,

"Oh, that's the tall, quiet one; he's new and was hired recently. He always does that and leaves us all the extra work!"

As Trikan looks back again at the entrance, he continues his conversation with Doctor Torry while ignoring the incident.

The following morning, they rent a *Turbo Fusion Road Sedan* and drive up through the farm country to Doctor Torry's ten-acre mountain cabin. Pulling onto the property, Trikan smiles as he comments, "So, this is your small mountain cabin?"

She replies, "It's not exactly small, but it's quite comfortable inside." As they enter the cabin, she asks, "So, what do you think, captain?" Smiling, he turns towards her, "It's very nice!"

She says, "It will be after we get it cleaned up!"

As he looks up, the tall wooden beam column construction runs parallel to the staircase that leads to a loft area of the cabin with an outside terrace. The downstairs rooms are furnished in a country style, and a large fireplace is directly across from the dining area. Doctor Torry asks, "So, what do you think, Captain? Can we clean it all up before Jeffery arrives?" Smiling, he turns towards her. "Yes, I like it, and it says so much about you."

"Okay, then you can take the upper level and clean it while I take care of it down here!"

They spend most of the day cleaning up the cabin and then have dinner, and stay up late to talk in front of the warmth of the fireplace until the early morning hours.

The next day, after breakfast, Doctor Torry spends most of the early morning hours cleaning out the flower beds from falling leaves around the front of the cabin porch. At the same time, Captain Trikan rides on a self-propelled grass and weed cutter, cutting out weeds and high grass from around the driveway approaching the front of the cabin.

Then, that evening, they drive down to the small farm town and have dinner in an old barn converted into a restaurant. They speak to many friendly residents who live there and work on the farms. Before returning to the cabin, they stop at the local town market and purchase food supplies for several days that they will need while staying at the cabin. Before leaving, Doctor Torry orders several large bundles of chopped firewood for the fireplace to heat the cabin. The proprietor tells her that he does not have any on hand, but the earliest he can arrange delivery would be about two days from now, and he will deliver it to her cabin. She tells him, "That's fine. We have enough to last us until then."

They arrive back at the cabin, and after putting the food supplies away, they go up to the loft terrace to enjoy the cool night's country air and share conversation while they have a glass of wine. They discuss the dinner and the new friends they have just made with the residents of this small-town farm community. Trikan agrees with her as she holds up her glass and says, "A toast to our friendship; may it be long-lasting!" As the two glasses touch, he says to her, "Lasting... Forever." Standing at the edge of the dark balcony, Trikan listens to the sounds of the wild night owls calling out in the dark areas of the forest, where no moonlight can find them. Occasionally, a winged creature can be seen in a moment of flight, as it answers the call in the secret language of its species, in this mysterious world that will last until the light of dawn. Trikan stands transfixed, looking up at the night sky, and in the fields below the cabin, tall pine trees block out the moonlight across the areas of woodlands but fail to stop every pathway of light that reaches the cabin's terrace.

As the moonlight casts a silhouette of the Captain and Doctor Torry, it's as if they were in a theater standing together on a stage, at another time and life; two great performers that don't exist in the present, performing for an audience that's hidden away in the shadows of the night. She looks at him, and he becomes part of the moonlight's silhouette of a mysterious performer on the stage of life that she has fallen in love with. She softly asks, "Captain, why are you looking up at the night sky? What are you looking for out there?"

He says to her, "I'm just thinking about something I had read in a cave in the Trikinian Mountains. It was written on the base of an ancient statue: *"Take a voyage on the ocean of stars and let the solar wind fill your sails, which can only be seen in a midnight dream. Sail across the midnight hour to a planet beyond the sunrise, where you will find new life in the sunlight of a new day."*

She looks at him, remains silent for several moments, and then says, "Johnathan, do you really think there are other worlds out there past the two outer planets?"

He does not answer, remains silent for a moment, and then says, "Will we ever know?"

She replies, "Perhaps, Captain, someday we will!"

In the fields below the terrace, the moon has risen and now fills the open woodlands, its light cutting new pathways to the open fields beyond the cabin. Doctor Torry falls as if into a dream that she cannot awaken from. It is as if she is a new star who cannot stay too long in a universe of uncertain mysteries. She has fallen like so many stars before her, not resisting how she feels about the captain; she looks at him with the moonlight reflecting in his eyes and says, "I would like to take that voyage with you, captain." He looks at her for a moment, and they kiss.

The next morning, the drive outside the city's highway to the mountain retreats is empty of other vehicles: this is not unusual at this early morning hour. Jeffery's ground transport travels at a slightly higher speed of over one hundred miles per hour, with automatic slowdown sequences along the highway's magnetic ground-post stanchions that automatically slow down the vehicles in hazardous topographic areas. He will arrive at the cabin within the next hour and a half if he maintains his current speed.

Before entering the ridgeline of Mount Overlook, an emergency roadblock section has been set up. The electronic speed post system that protects the entire highway has been turned off in sections due to construction services.

Jeffery's luxury motorized ground transport slows down automatically as it approaches a security roadblock. A highway unit security Sentry Patrol Mountain Ranger walks up to Jeffery's vehicle and says, "Driver... State your purpose and destination zone."

Jeffery replies, "Hello, officer, why is the road closed?"

The officer responds briefly as he hands Jeffery an electronic computer tablet with a map screen displaying the mountain region. "I'll tell you after you show me your vehicle identification tag and destination."

Jeffery logs in to his destination and vehicle identification code, and as he hands the computer tablet back, he tells the officer where he is going. "I'm heading to Mount Overlook, officer, to Doctor Torry's lovely residence!"

The officer replies, "Oh yes! Doctor Torry's place on Overlook Drive! Well, I'm sorry, Doctor Jeffery, you won't be able to get up there by this main highway."

As he reads the identification information on the tablet, he continues, "There's a mountain rockslide blocking the highway several miles ahead! You're going to have to turn around and go back to Old Forge Road and take road one-fourteen, up to Old Country Road, and then head north to Doctor Torry's place."

As Jeffrey turns his vehicle around, he thanks the officer. He heads a quarter of a mile south and then turns onto road one-fourteen. Once on Old Country Road, he calls Doctor Torry's cabin.

As the telescreen computer console automatically comes on, Doctor Torry picks up the receiver, sees Jeffery on the screen, and calls out, "Captain, it's Jeffery! Good morning, Jeffery... I'm glad that you decided to come up early. You can now join us for breakfast!"

He replies, "Okay, that will be great; I'm going to be a little delayed! I had to turn off the main highway due to a rockslide. Right now, I'm on Old Country Road, the long way around the mountain up to your place!" She says, "That's fine, Jeffery... Breakfast can wait until you get here. I have to go back to the kitchen." She then calls out to Trikan, "Captain... Can you come over here and talk to Jeffery?"

Trikan talks into the monitor below the console screen, "Hello, Doctor Jeffery... I've heard that you'll be a little late. That's okay. You picked a good time to come up, and the weather is going to be great all weekend!"

As he talks to Jeffrey, the door entrance chimes begin to play a musical tune that can be heard throughout the main floor of the cabin. Doctor Torry enters the living room, tells Trikan that she will get it, and to continue his conversation with Jeffery. As she walks into the hallway of the main entrance to her cabin, she remarks, "That's funny... He said we wouldn't get the firewood delivery for two days."

Trikan hears Doctor Torry's surprising remark and immediately stops talking to Doctor Jeffery as if in a state of panic, suddenly realizing something is wrong with her statement. Instantly, he yells out to her, "JEAN... NO, WAIT! THE DOOR!"

His response is too late; as she opens the door, a massive explosion sends furniture and glass debris flying through the cabin from the blast in the vestibule. Trikan rushes over to her, picks her up, and carries her out, away from the smoke and burning embers of what is left of the front entrance of the cabin. He holds her in his arms and says to her, "Jean... Jean, talk to me!"

"Trikan...What happened?" She then slowly closes her eyes and remains silent.

At that moment, Jeffrey pulls up to the front entrance of the property and immediately gets out of his transport, leaving the door open and the engine running. He rushes over to Trikan, who is holding Jean in his arms, and asks, "Captain, is she all right?"

As Trikan looks up at Doctor Jeffery, he replies, "No, she's not! CALL EMERGENCY SERVICES, JEFFERY; DO IT NOW!"

Still holding her in his arms, he says, "Listen to me, Jean... You're going to be okay! Help is on its way!"

Jeffery says, "They received my call and sent an affirmative, Captain! They're on their way!"

"Jeffery, stay with her; I have to take care of something!" As Trikan looks at his Dial-Date computer, and he receives a global satellite overview of the mountain area. He sees an individual running out of the woods, getting into a light-grey luxury sedan, and driving south on the main highway. Trikan then uses the face recognition identification on his Dial-Date, and a photo ID appears with only code letters: **M... A... R... UNSPECIFIED...**

Trikan then gets into Jeffery's hydro-craft and slams the door while putting the transmission into its highest gear level. The hydro sedan's traction fails to obtain level ground stability, so it lunges forward as Trikan turns the transport around and heads south on Old Country Road. Jeffery yells out to him, "Captain, you'll never catch up to him on Old Country Road! You're too far away from the main highway!"

As Trikan drives, he realizes that the speed columns will prevent him from catching up to whoever was responsible for what happened to Jean. To the left of him are acres upon acres of cornfields. Trikans' quick reflexes turn the vehicle sharply to the left at high speed, causing it to crash through the farm fence and onto the cornfields; he is now heading east towards the main highway.

Hitting high speeds, his vehicle begins to shake and rock over the uneven ground as it pushes aside cornstalks for several miles. Trikan then crashes through the far east farm fence onto the main highway heading north. Not satisfied with the speed of the transport, he strikes the dashboard console with his weapon several times, smashing the performance monitor that governs the maximum speed at which the vehicle can travel.

Now, the miles-per-hour monitor can only show the vehicle's speed as it heads north at 180 miles per hour on a collision course with the assassin's vehicle.

Trikans' speed causes a glitch in the highway's magnetic radar speed-monitoring system, as Trikans' vehicle crashes through the antimagnetic radar shield, preventing a head-on collision with Marcus's vehicle.

The high speed of Trikans' transport allows a force of energy to sideswipe each vehicle, tearing off the Driver's side door and windshield of the assassin's vehicle. Sending it off the highway and crashing down the mountain, it explodes a second after Marcus is thrown from his vehicle. Now, in a much calmer state of mind, Trikan contacts Jeffery, "Jeffery, how is Jean?"

Doctor Jeffery replies, "The emergency services took her a short time after you left. Just before you called, I received a message saying they had stabilized her condition. Captain, I think she's going to make it."

Trikan replies, "I hope so, Jeffery!"

Captain Trikan and Doctor Jeffery spend most of the day until nightfall, cleaning up the debris from the damaged entranceway of the cabin, and gathering some of Jean's personal belongings and assignment reports on her case work with the captain.

The following day, Jeffery gets on Doctor Torry's computer, contacts a local construction company, and arranges for repairs to the cabin. Trikan attends to his equipment and replaces the fire cartridge in his laser weapon. The captain then asks Jeffery, "So, what do you think? Did we take care of everything?"

"Yes, we did everything necessary. The repair company will arrive later. They will also install a new security system upon completion of the work. They have already given me the confirmation codes, and I'll give them to Doctor Torry when she's well enough to understand what has happened."

Trikan says, "Very good. We're out of here! We'll use Doctor Torry's flight hydrocopter."

As they walk over to the flight hangar, Doctor Jeffery remains silent. He focuses on his arm-cuff computer screen and pays little attention to what Captain Trikan says. Trikan asks, "Did you hear what I said, Jeffery?"

Still focused on his arm computer screen, Jeffery says, "Oh no, captain, I'm so sorry! Captain, it's about you! They are blaming you for what happened to Jean. They just issued a military warrant for your arrest!"

Stopping for a moment, Trikan states, "Here we go again!" Looking back at Jeffery, he adds, "First thing I have to do is get you back to the camp. I don't want to get you involved in this. There's a small marine transfer station forty miles out to the coast. I'll drop you off there, and you'll have no trouble getting on one of the tourist bus transports that go to the camp repeatedly."

Jeffery replies, "That will work, Captain, but what about you?"

Trikan tells him, "After I drop you off... I'll think about it. Now, let's get out of here before some sentry robots show up looking for me!"

After dropping Doctor Jeffery off, Trikan sets the hydrocopter's flight computer to a direct course to the safehouse.

Chapter 18:

Central Detention

After being unconscious for several hours, Marcus waits until nightfall before climbing up through the rocky mountain forest terrain onto the highway, making his way to the lake resort area, and then contacting an auto cab service.

A little while later, Marcus spots the small vehicle, steps onto the roadway, and motions for the cab operator to slow down and stop. The robotic auto driver leans out of the driver's window and says to Marcus, "... ARE YOU MY PASSENGER THAT CALLED FOR A PICKUP...?"

As Marcus gets into the cab, he responds, "Yes."

The driver asks, "... WHAT IS YOUR DESTINATION... ARE YOU GOING SOMEWHERE IN THE LAKE AREA? IF YOU KNOW THE ADDRESS... YOU MAY TYPE IT IN..."

Marcus replies, "No, Star Port City!"

The driver turns around and says, "... STAR PORT CITY...? THAT'S QUITE A WAY..." Staring, Marcus points his laser weapon at him and says, "Do you have a problem with that, driver?"

As the driver's eyes widen, he responds, "... NO, SIR... NO PROBLEM AT ALL..." Marcus states, "Then just turn around and drive!"

The next day, Marcus enters the medical complex of **Pro-Genesis Labs** in Star Port City.

He purposely did not return to his headquarters assignment division, for he would not have an explanation for his appearance.

Instead, he decides to contact Doctor Stanford.

His idea was to arrive as early as possible to avoid being seen by anyone who recognized him; he took the elevator to the lab center of the Androidian DNA research facility.

As the doors open and he steps off the lift platform, he heads directly to Doctor Stanford's office. Pushing the door open, he walks into a large reception area and immediately asks, "Is Stanford in?"

Somewhat startled, the doctor's secretary looks up at Marcus and hesitates for a moment before asking, "Do you have an appointment?"

Raising his voice, Marcus answered back, "I asked you... Is Doctor Stanford in his office?"

Remaining quiet for a moment, she answers him, "I'll tell you again, you can't see the doctor without an appointment!"

Marcus then raises his voice once more and tells the secretary, "I Won't Tell You Again... I Want to See Stanford!"

Hearing the disturbance outside his office, Doctor Stanford opens his office door and asks, "What's going on out here?" Looking directly at Marcus, he tells his secretary, "Cancel all my appointments for the rest of the day."

Doctor Stanford then says, "Please, come in, Marcus."

As they enter his office, Doctor Stanford closes the door. As Stanford sits down behind his desk, he looks up at Marcus.

"What are you doing here, Marcus?"

"I need your help, Doctor!"

Acknowledging, Stanford replies, "I can see that, Marcus; what happened to you?"

"I was in a turbo-craft accident!"

Stanford asks, "Were there any fatalities?"

"No... No one else was involved."

"Where exactly did this accident happen, Marcus?"

Becoming agitated, he says, "Doctor Stanford, are all these questions necessary?"

"Well, let's see, Marcus."

Opening his desk file, he removes a folder labeled **"MARCUS: RAS-7000"** next to a laser weapon with its safety off. He then spends a few moments reading the contents and then asks,

"Did this have anything to do with your assignment?"

"I don't know what my assignment has to do with my accident, Doctor Stanford!"

After putting the folder away, he looked at Marcus and said, "Okay, Marcus, let's get you fixed up!"

As Doctor Stanford attends to several of Marcus's injuries, he tells him, "You're going to have some scar tissue on this facial wound, and it can be removed at a later date."

Stanford then goes back to his desk and says, "Marcus, I'm going to give you something in case you experience some discomfort." He opens his drawer, takes out a packet of pills that reduce the elevated states of anger, and then instructs him, "Marcus, I want you to take these several times a day!"

Marcus responds, "I am fine, doctor; I don't need your medication."

"Okay, Marcus, have it your way. Oh, Marcus, never come to my office again without contacting me first. Do You Understand, Marcus? You're not one of my patients, and from now on, all of our communications will go through your control administrator, Doctor Evans!"

As Stanford places his hand on his laser weapon, he continues, "Do you understand me, Marcus?"

Marcus remains silent for a couple of moments and then says, "I understand you, doctor; I will keep that in mind!"

He then leaves Doctor Stanford's office.

Doctor Evans starts his daily routine of checking his security telescreen, and on the screen, it states: "... ONE MOMENT PLEASE... YOUR SECURITY CLEARANCE IS IN PROGRESS... RELEASE POSITIVE ACCESS CONFIRMED..."

The computer's modulation sequencing becomes activated and begins to speak, "... **REPORT DOCUMENT GOVERNMENT INVESTIGATION MC-J7 GOVERNMENT INQUIRY HAS CONCLUDED ITS INVESTIGATION OF THE INCIDENT INVOLVING CAPTAIN JOHNATHAN SHAWNWOOD. ARREST WARRANTS ARE ISSUED FOR THE INDIVIDUAL INVOLVED IN THE DELIBERATE ATTACK ON DOCTOR JEAN TORRY... THIS INDIVIDUAL HAS NOT BEEN APPREHENDED AS OF YET...**"

What Doctor Evans sees on the telescreen is shocking news. ...CASE NUMBER MC-J7 WILL REMAIN OPEN INDEFINITELY UNTIL IT IS SOLVED... Doctor Evans turns off his telescreen and hastily calls Doctor Stanford's office.

An automated robotic receiver replies: "**... GOOD MORNING... MAY I HELP YOU...?**"

Doctor Evans answers, "Yes, may I speak to Doctor Stanford?"

The automated robotic receiver replies again, "**... I AM SORRY... DOCTOR STANDFORD IS NOT AVAILABLE AND WILL NOT BE IN THE OFFICE TODAY. WOULD YOU LIKE TO MAKE AN APPOINTMENT...?**"

Doctor Evans becomes slightly agitated and says, "No appointment! I must speak to him; it's important!"

The robotic receiver responds, "**... AT THE SIGNAL, PLEASE LEAVE YOUR MESSAGE, AND THE DOCTOR WILL GET BACK TO YOU IN THE ORDER IT WAS RECEIVED. THANK YOU...**"

Doctor Evans leaves his message: "Doctor Stanford, call my office; it's important!"

He then leans back in his chair, distressed, as he thinks about the emergency teleview that he observed just a short time ago on the government's report, and he whispers to himself, *"What's next, Marcus?"* He then checks the time on the office clock and realizes he must leave his office to attend the department supervisor's daily briefing and take his place at the conference table. He will have to wait to speak to Dr. Stanford to get his opinion on the incident.

Early the following day, Doctor Evans arrives in his office and observes the communication channel on his telescreen. As it comes into view, it's the call he has been waiting for: Doctor Stanford. "Doctor Evans... how are you?"

"Good to talk to you, Rex! I think we have a problem on our hands."

Stanford replies, "Go ahead, Doctor Evans, there is no one in the office with me."

Evans continues, "It's about the government report on the code channel."

"Go ahead, Evans, I'm listening."

"Well, it's about the incident that took place at the cabin!"

Stanford responds, "Yes, I know... It's about Jean. It was no accident! You know what I'm talking about. You're his Control; just be careful! I'm not blaming you, Doctor Evans, for what took place. When he was programmed, I was against his encoded use of explosives, and the military program director overruled me with orders that came down from higher up! As you know, yesterday I was not in my office and was involved in a meeting about our assignment for several hours. I have been advised to touch base with you and relay their message with the strictest confidence. It's about the assignment, Evans; play it any way you like. Just tell him the project is on hold for now, and he should take an extended vacation. That means no contact with anyone, and I have instructed him to never come to my office again without an appointment; all communication will go through you at an unspecified time. Be safe, Doctor!"

Across the bottom of the telescreen, it reads: "... MESSAGE DELETED... NO BACK-UP ON FILE..." Suddenly, his thoughts are interrupted as he looks at the blinking indicator on the telescreen outside his office.

For a moment, the feeling of uneasiness becomes part of the message relayed to him by Doctor Stanford when he sees Marcus standing outside his office door.

Doctor Evans releases the entrance lock to his office, and the door opens as Marcus walks in. Doctor Evans greets him, "Come in, Marcus... It's good to see you again!"

"Yes, Doctor. I am sure it is for you."

"Come in, Marcus, sit down!"

Marcus takes a chair and positions it directly across the doctor's desk. Doctor Evans says,

"So, Marcus, what can I do for you? You didn't keep last month's appointment, but that's okay, Marcus; I'm sure you were very busy! So now, how can I help you?"

Marcus listens and replies, "Do I look any different to you, doctor?"

"Yes, as a matter of fact, you do! I was just going to ask you what happened."

"So, I guess you haven't spoken to Doctor Stanford?"

"Oh, Doctor Stanford? No, why?"

"I had a minor accident, and he's the doctor who took care of me. Maybe I should have come here first? Doctor Stanford did not have much to say; he seemed somewhat agitated and told me in no uncertain terms that in the future, I have to contact you before I can see him!"

"Yes, I understand that, Marcus." He hesitates, remains quiet, and then says, "Yes, after all, I am your Control!"

Marcus looks directly at Doctor Evans and says, "I have a feeling, and if you don't mind my saying so, that something is going wrong with our mission. You know, doctor, I was always interested in completing our program successfully, and I still have confidence that the mission will be completed as planned!"

Trying not to show his uneasiness, Doctor Evans says, "Yes, Marcus, I understand how you feel about the events that have taken place recently, and for now, it seems that the assignment has to be put on hold. You know what, Marcus? Why don't you take a long vacation and make no contact with anyone? Let's just say the assignment is on hold for now! We will contact you and bring you back when we're ready to continue; don't come to my office for any reason until I contact you first. Do you understand, Marcus?"

Marcus says, "That sounds familiar, Doctor Evans. Are you sure you haven't been talking with Doctor Stanford recently?"

Somewhat nervous, Doctor Evans says, "No! Marcus, I was not happy with your assignment from the very beginning! I voted to find an alternative way to remove the captain. I said, let the government do whatever it takes to find another way, but the committee overruled me!"

"Well, doctor... It is your right to have an opinion! I'm happy you told me, and I see you are a government official who plays by the game's rules."

Marcus looks at a trident spear with spring-loaded cylinders on a display plaque mounted on the office wall. These types of weapons were used by seafaring fishermen back in ancient times. Marcus asks, "So you like to fish in the oceans, doctor?"

As Doctor Evans is preoccupied typing a report on his computer, he pays no attention to Marcus, who has removed one of the cylinder tridents from the display. As Evans finally pays attention to what Marcus is doing, he says, "Be careful with that! They're antiques!"

Marcus stares at Evans, "Yes, Doctor, I know, and dangerous

too!" As he releases the safety on the trident weapon, he fires it directly at Doctor Evans, killing him instantly.

Doctor J. P. Granite, the Chief Department Administrator of Androidian Medicine, leads a team of medical specialists, including a high-ranking military officer, into Doctor Torry's room. Doctor Torry's nurse has instructed them not to engage in conversations with one another while they are in her room.

Doctor Torry's nurse quietly approaches her bed as Doctor Granite asks, "Can I talk to her?" The nurse tells him, "I'm afraid it won't do any good, doctor; she can't hear you. She's still in a comatose state, and we're hoping for the best."

Looking at Doctor Torry, he turns to the other officials. "I guess we might as well leave and file our reports." Looking back at the nurse, he says, "Let us know immediately if there's any change in her condition."

"Yes, doctor, I will."

As she walks them out of the ICU, she dims the lights to a soft setting, and it could hardly be noticed that someone has been left in the room if it were not for the life support unit that Jean's survival depends upon. The blue detection screen that monitors her existence bathes Jean in color contrast, reflecting off her temperature-controlled blanket and covering her in a transparent blue haze as if transcending her into another dimension.

A short time later, the telescreen in the room becomes activated, and a moment in time becomes a familiar voice calling out to her, "Jean... Jean, can you hear me? Doctor Torry, wake up!" Moments of silence pass, and the voice calls out again, "Jean, wake up! It's important. I need to talk to you, Jean!"

Suddenly, Doctor Torry slowly opens her eyes and says, "Captain... Is that you? I cannot see you..." In a weak voice, she says, "Where are you, Johnathan?"

"Yes, Jean, it's me, over here on the telescreen! Can you see me now?"

As she gathers her inner strength, she turns her head slightly and can see the telescreen, and in a faint voice, she says, "I can see you now, Captain. Are you alright?"

"Yes, Jean, I'm fine. Everything is good now. Jean, listen to me, I need you to get better, do you understand me, Jean?"

"Yes, captain... I need to get better..." In a faint voice, she asks, "Where is Jeffery? Is he with you?"

"Jeffery is on his way to visit you, Jean. Try to get some rest now."

"I will."

As her eyes close, she falls into a restful sleep, and he says, "Get better, Jean, I'll see you soon." Trikan contacts Doctor Jeffery. "Jeffery, I just spoke with Jean. Go to the hospital as soon as possible and see what you can do. Take care of her, Jeffery. I'll get back to you again when the time is right."

Trikan receives a message from Jeffery, "Good news, Captain, thank you! I'm on my way!"

Arriving just before dark, the landing field lights go on the flight deck above the craft hangar as the hydrocopter lands. Feeling safe again in Aunt Lasara's domain, Trikan is greeted first by his friend, LamBrute, who says, "I won't ask you how you are, captain." Raising his voice to be heard over the spinning blades of the hydro-craft, he adds, "They have been waiting all day to hear from you, Captain. They will be glad to see you!"

On their way into the safehouse, Trikan tells LamBrute, "Doctor Torry's ship must be put below ground in the hangar. They probably will realize it's missing."

"I will do that immediately, Captain."

Trikan enters the house and is greeted by the professor. "Good to see you again, Captain, regardless of the circumstances! They are waiting for you in the dining room. I know it is a bit too early to ask you what led to this devious act. But as long as you are all right, that is what counts the most. The report on Doctor Torry is that she remains in an unconscious state. They don't expect to be able to get a statement from her for quite some time, but she will be okay!" Trikan states, "Good... Whoever is behind this has failed again!" He pauses for a moment before he says, "Jean... If only I could have stopped her!"

Looking at Trikan, the professor replies, "It's not your fault, Captain. She felt safe that you were there with her."

As they enter the dining room, Aunt Lasara greets Trikan. "Johnathan... There are no words to describe how bad I feel about what happened. What can I say? No one will talk to me! The council members refuse to answer my calls; it is as if I don't exist! But that is enough about me." Trikan says, "I'm the one who caused all of this, Aunt Lasara, and I'm the one who has to fix it!" Aunt Lasara adds, "Well then, Johnathan, you cannot stay here; it is not safe! I can no longer tell you who we can trust outside of this room. I can see now that the trial meant nothing. I no longer have confidence in justice. I can only go by their actions. They failed at the War Games and will not stop until they accomplish what was supposed to happen there! You were not supposed to survive! In the morning, Johnathan, you are going to leave for Trikinia. You will be safe there. LamBrute and Cen-Ton will accompany you. Alden is awaiting your arrival; the professor has already contacted him. You will take my flightcraft first thing in the morning."

Reanna then says, "Johnathan, we're going to miss you again! Please, stay safe!"

Trikan smiles, "I will miss you as well."

Reanna then hugs the man she raised as a child, as LamBrute walks into the dining room and declares, "Captain... Cen-Ton and I will accompany you to Trikinia. It will be good to go home again. Captain, I put your scout duffel bag in your transport for an early departure tomorrow morning. When I was doing so, this rehabilitation report fell out."

He hands it to him, and Trikan reads it out loud, "It's from Doctor Torry:

> *'There are no more reports that require transfer communications about the subject, Captain Johnathan Shawnwood. His rehabilitation is complete. This concludes the treatment report; he is an individual who possesses both the strength of mind and the strength of will. My recommendations for the captain are to put himself in the place of his dreams, a trust he must keep with his family and friends, looking towards the sunlight, a new beginning for a new day... The military should be proud of his integrity and loyalty... Diagnosis complete.'* "

Looking up from the report, he says, "She must have placed this in my supply pack the night before." He hesitates, and LamBrute says, "Before the morning attempt on your life! Come on, Captain!"

As Trikan, LamBrute, and the professor spend the rest of the evening discussing their morning departure, Professor Zola removes the documents from a walled cabinet they had previously studied in the mammoth government structural fortress known as Central Detention.

He tells Trikan, "Take this with you. This is everything we discussed and reviewed together. Captain, everything you need has been placed in your ship for the assault on the prison! Your extreme heat-resistant flight suits are already on board. Your craft is equipped with a delta-quad invisible shielding, and your ship's cryptograph sequence entrance has already been accepted into territorial airspace above the high-fusion energy dome above the prison."

LamBrute then says, "May the eagles of Trikinia watch over us and keep us safe when we go on our mission!"

Trikan says, "Professor, there's something I must take care of before we leave!"

The night before their mission, they all gather in the large living room, forming a consensus on how they will get Elisa out of Central Detention.

The professor looks at the blueprint on the table for the last time and remarks, "After we get through the energy dome, we have to find our way to the warden's office. According to my calculations, the prison cells are opened by his command. Bear that in mind: the control of the chambers must be located somewhere in his office. It would be foolish to think otherwise!" The line goes to the tower, where I observed the official when the gantry gates would open to accept supply deliveries to the prison. Captain, it's all beginning to make sense now!"

Trikan listens intently to the professor. "According to the plans, there is a similar crossover design, similar to the electronic diagrams throughout the blueprint inside the panel room, that has no identification! It must be how you deactivate the deadly energy dome above the prison. It's the only described return energy source in the blueprints that contains an exact duplicate of the primary power facility that operates the prison. It bears no explanation why it should be part of this document."

The professor then adds, "Look over here, captain, there are no electric lead lines throughout the complex within the entire fourteen levels of the prison! That being said, four of the fourteen are sub-chambers below the foundation of the prison with no entrance or exterior exit emergency ramps."

Trikan asks, "How do the cellblocks open and close, then, professor?"

"Look, Captain, everything is here except the prison warden's control center that operates the prisoner cellblocks. No documentation indicates the existence of a control headquarters within the prison complex. It was deliberately omitted from the diagram. So, it is obvious that these cells can only be opened and closed by a direct line to the warden's office. Do you see what I mean, Captain?"

Trikan remarks, "Hidden in plain sight!"

Looking at Trikan, he says, "You're correct, Captain! The warden's office is the key to the solution!"

The next morning, the doors begin to open, and the merchant's flightcraft is elevated to the surface, ground-level landing field tarmac. Chef Eleanor is serving breakfast to the adventurers who will make their flight across the mountains to Central Detention to free Elisa.

During breakfast, the family gathered together and shared moments in their conversation about the past, present, and future. The professor tells Trikan, "About our flight, captain, remember, we can't leave the old flightcraft in its invisibility mode; we'll only use it when necessary. Only a short time ago, Captain, I was thinking—" Trikan stops him. "Professor, I know exactly what you're going to say! It's all beginning again, and it's not a bad dream, Professor. I wish it were! Elisa has waited long enough, and I will help her regain her freedom and her life!"

The professor smiles as he grabs Trikans' arm and tells him, "I will join you when you complete your mission in the tower and turn off the energy dome. It is about time that Elisa regains her freedom!"

Aunt Lasara suddenly adds, "Johnathan, I know you and LamBrute will succeed!" LamBrute then says, "Doctor Lasara... I am proud to be going with the captain! We're stronger together than apart!"

"Thank you, LamBrute! I will keep Alden informed."

Chef Eleanor then says, "Let me get back into my kitchen. I don't want Johnathan to see me get teary-eyed."

As she leaves, she looks at Johnathan and says, "Come back to us safe, Johnathan!"

As the autopilot engines activate, Trikan, LamBrute, and the professor walk out to the ship and join their pilot, Cen-Ton, who is already aboard the flightcraft. As they board, Lasara and Reanna wait at the hangar elevator entrance of the landing bay tarmac, and before closing the heavy flightcraft's door, Trikan waves one last time as Aunt Lasara calls out to them, "Good luck, and come back safe!" Standing next to Lasara, Reanna shouts, "Rescue her, Johnathan, and may the 'Eagles of Trikinia' watch over all of you!"

As Trikan takes the copilot's seat, he tells LamBrute, "Our flight course will take us over the Trikinian territory where the new construction towers are being installed for the climate-controlled heat shields."

"Yes, captain, you're correct."

Trikan adds, "We will have to take a higher orbital flight trajectory to avoid the lower elevation of the heat shields. As you know, the new shields take time to be put into their orbital flight positions; the newer types have been known to malfunction, blocking one hundred thousand orbital space quadrants. Am I correct, Cen-Ton?"

"... AFFIRMATIVE, CAPTAIN... I AM ALREADY PROGRAMMED TO AVOID A FATAL ENCOUNTER WITH THE HEAT SHIELDS..."

The professor then says, "Excellent thinking, Captain! The flight over the heat shields will give you the advantage of stealth flight from ground-based detection, just in case we are detected by government agents who wish to collect the reward for your capture."

Trikan acknowledges, "Thank you, professor, for reminding me that I'm a wanted man!"

The professor smiles, and the bond they all share will never be broken as they continue to rescue Elisa. The professor then tells the captain, "Everything you need has been put on the ship, including your fire-resistant flight suits with the standard hydro-rocket packs. Your velocity helmets are equipped with night vision and ground-to-ship communication. Your arm computer will be in a non-operational state for a short time until you land on the roof. I'll tell you the rest when we get there."

Trikan asks, "Professor, tell me about the security post tower room again."

"That will have to wait, Captain, until you are inside. There will be changes and possibilities. It will all depend on you. There must be an ingenious way of opening the steel door at the room's far end. Right now, our only clue is the large disc at the center of the chamber."

"Okay, professor, once inside, I will disengage the main relay feed from the antimatter fusion dome if it's in there."

The professor agrees, "Yes, captain, there has to be a lever exchange device of high-voltage electrical current because the dome is canceled out when the prison receives its supply ships that land on the raised tarmac platform near the tower room. Also, the exterior doors of the prison will become unlocked and automatically open throughout the entire complex after you destroy the power cartridges. Remember, there's no time to waste; you must leave that room immediately! You are locked in there when that steel door closes, and your life ends within seconds!"

Trikan then says, "Professor, you failed to mention how I am going to get down onto the roof?" The professor explains, "Oh, did I? How foolish of me! This old merchant ship is now equipped with several anti-fusion drone projectiles. Once fired, they will explode upon impact, causing a high-energy field change that will rupture a section of the dome. This will remain in an open, reverse-polarity state for several seconds, allowing you to pass through and land on the roof. You will still experience a high-energy field as if you have just passed too close to the sun. We are going to do something that has never been done before—an assault on the prison fortress!"

Looking at the professor, the captain replies, "We're not going to fail, Professor!"

Looking at his Dial-Date, the captain says, "When we arrive at Central Detention, we will arrive at the prison during a shift change, as planned. There will be less activity compared to the earlier hours when the prisoners are allowed out of their cells, requiring additional sentry robots to be on duty!"

LamBrute adds, "Captain, professor, I am going to ensure all the failsafe units are in the proper order."

The professor announces, "Thank you, LamBrute. Now, I suggest we get suited up; we don't have much time!" The professor continues, "Let us get back to how we will get both of you through the energy shield dome. Each of the fusion cylinders I added to this flightcraft has a neutron fusion projectile, which I will refer to as an antimatter missile. After turning on our invisibility shield, our flightcraft will be undetected. When we approach our target, we will fire one of the projectiles that will implode, creating an opening in the energy shield dome. Captain, you will follow it and gain access to the energy field. I estimate the missile will cause a breach in the dome's electronic power field, and I will open it for several seconds to allow you to enter with your flight-to-ground rocket pack and land safely on the roof. You will experience an extreme rise in temperature from the combustion rays that send the projectile through the dome. After you are safely inside the blast area of the energy shield, it will close again. LamBrute will follow behind you, Captain, in the same procedure; however, he will gain additional entrance time due to the weakened state of the energy field."

Trikan then asks, "Professor, why didn't you tell me all of this before?"

The professor replies, "I didn't want to upset you!"

Looking at LamBrute, Trikan asks, "LamBrute, did you just hear what the professor said?"

"Yes, he said he didn't want to upset you!"

Trikan responds again, "I didn't mean that, LamBrute; I meant the whole missile thing." LamBrute answers, "I never liked missiles, Captain, but I'll do it anyway."

Smiling, Trikan states, "Did you hear that, professor? He said that he would do it anyway. So, I guess we're going to do it, professor!"

Closing the visor luminous on his helmet, Trikan speaks into the voice modulator, "LamBrute, do you copy?"

LamBrutes' response is heard, "Affirmative, Captain!"

The professor states, "Cen-Ton will pilot the craft until you can turn the energy dome off completely. He will then land the flightcraft on the roof that adjoins the control tower, and I will leave Cen-Ton and join you while the invisibility screen remains activated until we return to the craft."

The professor then hands the captain an informational regulator clip and instructs him to insert it into his helmet's visual system. "Insert this into your helmet, captain. It contains much more detail than we discussed, and you will experience the same holographic imagery I witnessed inside the tower complex. It will help both of us access the entrance into the frame room!"

Reaffirming, Trikan says, "I will be in constant contact with you, professor, with every move I make!"

The professor continues, "It's the hologram with the prison official that we talked about. As you will see, upon entering, he stood in the center of a large steel disc for a short time, and suddenly, the whole room appeared as a three-dimensional hologram. The entire room became very bright, then translucent colors appeared. The hologram remained as he stepped off the platform and adjusted his Dial-Date, and the platform disc began to turn. When it stopped its slow rotation, the steel door to the room opened, and I could see that it was an electronic program frame room. Its contents held some slotted units of malfunctioning communication *Magnite* plates. They were in the process of failing with their sensory communication relays; he removed the defective plates of *Magnite* and replaced the units with new radioactive sensors. Just before he replaced the last damaged sensor, he seemed preoccupied with the door as it began to close; then, the hologram started to move again and changed its position. That is when I could see no more! The explosive energy field at the center of the hologram appeared as bright as our sun! That is when he quickly left the chamber. Captain, one thing that puzzled me was the lack of an exit tribar handle on the interior of the door. But now I can assure you, the room will also hold and destroy an intruder once the door is closed!"

Trikan asks the professor, "What made the holograph appear?"

"I don't know, Captain, you're going to have to be there to have that knowledge!"

"Professor, he must have used some type of code with his Dial-Date to gain access to the frame room. Where did he get them from, professor?"

"There's only one way to find out, Captain, what happened when he stood at the center of the platform disc? What did he do, Captain?"

At that moment, the ship's magnetic elevation warning beacons activate, and a voice modulation announces: "**... STRUCTURAL PLATFORMS... FLIGHT OBSTRUCTION... CHANGE ELEVATION COURSE... EMERGENCY COURSE CHANGE...**"

Sitting in the copilot's seat next to Cen-Ton, Trikan asks, "Can we pass through, Cen-Ton?"

"... YES, CAPTAIN... I'M REDUCING OUR COURSE SPEED, WHICH WILL DECREASE OUR CHANCES OF A COLLISION WITH THE HEAT SHIELDS... OUR FLIGHT ELEVATION COMPUTER COURSE IS ACTIVATED... WE WILL BE OVER THE HEAT SHIELDS IN SEVENTEEN SECONDS IN QUARTER SEQUENCE..."

As LamBrute moves to the front command console and joins the professor, he looks out through the craft's heat-resistant aviation glass. The professor then remarks, "It's magnificent, LamBrute! Look how many there are out there! Each platform, thousands of square miles of heat-resistant Banishean steel absorbing all of the deadly sun's rays that turn forests into deserts!"

As the cabin remains silent for several moments, they look outside into orbital space, gazing southeast at the planet's southern hemisphere. They observe a multitude of heat shields ablaze, absorbing the destructive energy of the sun's new day. The fusion energy is then deflected back across the new horizon, as the tower observatories are the planet's grid system that controls the functions of the heat shields.

As he observes the new sunrise, the professor remarks again, "What a magnificent achievement, isn't it?"

LamBrute says, "The new tower construction project in Trikinia will add to the future stability of the orbital platforms."

The onboard computer audio relay then announces: "**WE ARE NOW APPROACHING THREE-QUARTER SEQUENCE TIME REFERENCE COORDINATES... ENGINES ARE OFF, AND WE ARE NOW IN ORBITAL SPACE ZONES APPROACHING CENTRAL DETENTION.**" Professor Zola retains the knowledge to cause a delay in the power grid that operates the antimatter protection field above the prison dome. The opening can last for no more than a tenth of a quarter sequence; the exact timing is vital.

The professor explains the procedure one last time to the captain and LamBrute before they exit the ship, "Remember, when you leave the ship, captain, to penetrate the zone, you will need to maintain your speed of fifteen hundred quad sequences behind the projectile, to pass through the death shield portal before it closes. It will last only for that sequence of time. So, you must enter when the fired projectile explodes and creates a subatomic breach in the dome shield; otherwise, if the portal closes before you enter, your rocket packs will explode, and you will be vaporized instantly! Your touchdown will place you several yards from the landing platform. After removing your flight suits, you will go directly to the end of the prison control tower, and there, you will use your laser weapons in full-blast mode and destroy the entrance door. LamBrute will remain on guard outside as you enter the control chamber, Captain."

Cen-Ton interrupts, "... WE'RE APPROACHING ZERO POINT DESTINATION... THE FLIGHT SHIP IS IN ORBIT CONTROL OVER TARGET... INVISIBILITY SHIELD ACTIVATED...

HOLDING OVER TARGET CODE ZERO..."

Trikan then says, "That's us, LamBrute, and right on target!"

As they strap their military velocity rockets to the harness rack of their flight suits and secure their helmets, they activate their voice modulation power packs.

"Can you hear me, LamBrute?"

"Loud and clear, Captain!"

"Cen-Ton, do you hear me?"

"...YES, CAPTAIN... LOUD AND CLEAR..."

Trikan then activates his helmet's visor, which displays a luminous vision screen offering both close-up and distant peripheral vision. He then says, "Okay, LamBrute, this is it!"

LamBrute replies, "I know the drill, Captain, I'll be right behind you! One point two sequence seconds, your blast opens the energy dome, and you will be in flight with your rocket pack. A moment later, after you are safely within the dome, the blast area of the energy will close. By the time you touch down, I will follow the second neutron-fusion projectile that will blast open the energy dome again."

Looking at his Dial-Date, he continues, "The time sequence has been calculated... I'll be able to enter through the blast opening approximately three-and-one-half sequence seconds behind you, Captain!"

The professor then shouts out over the noise of the open exit hatch, "Captain, as a reminder..."

"Yes, professor, what is it?"

"Let me remind you, Captain, when the blast turns off the energy field over the prison, an alarm may go off, and sentry robots will be on their way up to the tower section. Time is not to be wasted; every moment will have value in determining whether the mission succeeds or fails. LamBrute will need your help if he encounters any problems. At that time, Cen-Ton will land the flightcraft near the tower and maintain the craft's invisibility shield for the entire duration of the mission. I will be able to join you, and the three of us will make our way through the maze of tunnels and blocked corridors until we reach the level complex center. There, we will find the hydro-lifts that service the entire prison complex, allowing us to reach any level of the prison that we so desire. Level ten is where the warden's office is! That is our chosen location. I believe that is where the code room is, and we will find the Scanner disk that contains all the codes to open every cell in the entire prison, including the women's dormitory section."

Cen-Ton alerts the captain, "... CAPTAIN, WE ARE STILL OVER TARGET... CONFIRMATION IN COUNTDOWN MODE... TWENTY-SECOND SEQUENCE... NINETEEN SECONDS... FIFTEEN-SECOND SEQUENCE... FOURTEEN SECONDS... TEST TARGET DRONE MISSILE FIRED...."

As the test missile is launched from the transport, the professor tells Trikan, "There it goes, Captain!"

The high-velocity projectile strikes the energy shield above the prison and implodes, creating a fusion tear in its subatomic structural energy field that immediately closes. Cen-Ton adjusts the console radar-visual screen with the ground-to-ship magnification and turns around, "... PROFESSOR... CAPTAIN... THE IMPLOSION OF THE ENERGY SHIELD WAS EXACTLY AS CALCULATED... THERE ARE NO GROUND ALERT SURVEILLANCE SIGNALS DETECTED... ALL OUR ONBOARD INSTRUMENTATION DETECTION IS NEGATIVE..."

Trikan shouts to the professor, "Well, professor, your plan is working so far!"

"Thank you, Captain. Are you ready?" Trikan replies, "As ready as I'll ever be, Professor!"

The captain turns to LamBrute and says, "LamBrute, are you ready to go?"

"I'm as ready as a Trikinian eagle. Good luck, Captain!"

Standing next to the open escape velocity hatch, Professor Zola strikes an emergency release lock on the exterior platform. At the same time, the countdown begins with the release of the first neutron fusion projectile. The ship's alarm signals that the emergency release platform is in place.

Trikan steps out onto the safety exit angle ramp and fires his rocket backpack. Following the blast trail of the fired neutron projectile, Trikan travels through the sub-atmosphere over the energy sky dome while maintaining a safe flight distance behind the subatomic ballistic missile.

As it strikes the electric vortex of the energy shield dome, it blasts open an entry field, allowing the captain to enter through and safely land on the roof. Following the captain, LamBrute steps out onto the safety exit angle ramp. Professor Zola stands next to the emergency release lock on the hatch door and looks towards LamBrute. LamBrute speaks into his helmet, saying, "I am ready!" The professor replies, "Cen-Ton, start the count for the second projectile release!"

"... AFFIRMATIVE, PROFESSOR... THREE SEQUENCE SECONDS... TWO SECONDS... RELEASE SEQUENCE... THE SECOND PROJECTILE IS NOW ON TARGET..."

Suddenly, LamBrute blasts free from the transport before the energy field closes again from the second projectile blast that will allow him to enter the dome.

Once through, he lands several yards safely away from Trikan. He then calls out to the captain through his helmet's audio communicator, "Captain, there's some type of illumination crawling up along your rocket pack!"

The captain responds, "I copy that, LamBrute! I can feel the heat!"

Immediately, LamBrute removes his fire-resistant canister and sprays the captain's smoldering suit. LamBrute then remarks, "That was a close one, Captain! Let's get that suit off!"

Trikan adds, "No doubt it's from the portal entrance blast residue! When you went through the vortex, it remained open longer, just like the professor said it would, and it didn't affect you. My entire suit is covered with hot fusion residue!"

As he is helping the captain remove his flight suit, Trikan tells the professor, "Your calculations were excellent, professor. We're right on target!"

The professor's coded response is transmitted back to the captain's helmet receiver unit. "You know what the next procedure is, Captain?"

The captain communicates in a coded message, "Seven, Five, Fourteen, Twenty-One." The professor responds, "Affirmative, Captain!"

In the **Android Security Control Center,** located one level below the roof complex, a new technician identifies three glitches on the energy shield dome and immediately reports them to his supervisor in the control room. He moves to the monitor screen, and the supervisor says, "What do you have there?"

The technician says, "A moment ago, I received a scope-screen anomaly on my monitor! It happened again, and then my screen went back online!"

The supervisor then asks, "Play it back; let me see it!"

As the supervisor studies the screen briefly, he tells his newly assigned assistant, "Oh, you will get used to this when you get more experience at this security post. You will understand many more of these power surges—most of them come from those damn raven hawks! Most of them get vaporized once they hit the energy dome. But you will be surprised, now and then, one of them gets through the screen, burns up on the way down, and ends up on the roof!"

Adjusting the security cameras to a picture scan of the gantry roof area zone where he received the anomalies, the technician says, "Look at this. So, what do I do now?"

The supervisor looks at the screen and remarks, "I'll be damned! They must have been raven hawks, and one did get through, and it burned up on the gantry roof! Well, now we need a report on it... Send sentry robots to put out that smoldering before it gets worse and give us a location report on any damage."

Before Trikan can enter the tower, he receives a signal alert on his visor helmet's view screen. The captain says, "Wait a minute, LamBrute, we have company!"

Looking through his telescopic view scope on the inside of his visor luminous, the distance display readout scanned two light movements on an entity scale with weapon capacity.

The captain says, "LamBrute, do you copy?"

"Affirmative, Captain, two sentry robots are headed in our direction! They just landed on the roof with their rocket packs."

"Okay, let's wait and see. They're undoubtedly out here and preoccupied with the smoldering EVA suit fire!"

"Captain, I suggest we get to the tower and keep monitoring their presence."

"My thoughts exactly, LamBrute!"

Suddenly, the professor contacts the captain, "Captain... What's going on down there?"

"Just a little distraction, professor... Now let's get into the tower, LamBrute!"

The captain and LamBrute activate their rocket packs to a low-frequency sound lift above the prison roof and travel a short distance to the tower complex. Trikan adjusts his laser weapon and points it toward the roof tower doors, which burn off the electronic locks and slowly open.

Trikan enters the tower room as LamBrute takes his position in the doorway. "I'll wait here, captain, just in case we get another visit by sentry robots!"

Once inside, he sees for the first time what the professor referred to when he spoke about the tower room and the hologram he had seen in the chamber above the large, steel platform disc. It was not the same as the professor had described, and Trikan communicates back, "Look at this, professor, there are some forms of coded inscriptions along the outer edge of the large, steel disc. Do you have any idea what this platform is for?"

The professor responds, "No, captain, I'm afraid not! The bright fusion light of the hologram obstructed my detailed analysis of the platformed disc!"

Trikan then asks, "Professor, did you at any time have the ability to see above the hologram?"

"No, captain. Why do you ask?"

"Because I'm looking up, and it seems that the ceiling is equipped with some sort of domed security device that has projectiles extending out from the center of it."

A slight pause from the professor, and he then asks, "Are you talking about some type of danger, Captain?"

"Exactly, Professor! Steel-tipped pike spears are waiting to be released onto the center of the platform. Do you have any suggestions?"

The professor pauses momentarily and then replies, "I'm afraid not, Captain. The only way we will find the answer to your question is for you to immediately transfer the code unit frequency on the platform to your Dial-Date. It may produce the same hologram of the prison official that I recorded. Captain, the point system of your Dial-Date should be facing the steel door."

Moments later, Trikan replies, "Okay, professor... I entered the code, and nothing is happening!"

The professor pauses for a moment, then says, "It's obvious, Captain, you have to be standing in the center of the platform when you enter the code!"

LamBrute calls out, "Captain, do you know what you are doing?"

Not answering LamBrute, Trikan answers back, "Okay, professor... I'm standing in the center of the disc now and reentering the code."

"Captain, there's no recourse if you get the code wrong!" Looking up at the pike spears, he says, "Yes, professor, I'm aware of that!"

The professor asks, "Has anything changed above you since you entered the code, Captain?" Looking up, Trikan answers, "No... Wait, Professor! Yes, there is a change! There is a red glow in the center of the dome, and I believe there was a slight movement in the pike spears!"

The professor answers, "Captain, when you entered the code, you somehow lost time symmetry. Reenter the code again quickly, and do not hesitate before the completion!"

Trikan immediately enters the code sequence into his Dial-Date again and then says, "Okay, professor, now there's something else happening that you're not going to believe! I'm standing in the middle of our solar system, and you're right, professor, it's a hologram!"

Excited, the professor exclaims, "That's incredible, Captain! I was not able to see that before! Has anything else changed that you can make out?"

"No, not that I can tell, Professor!"

"Look at your Dial-Date. Have the code numbers changed, Captain?"

"Yes, professor, they have!"

Urgently, the professor replies, "Change the code quickly,

Captain! Align the code numbers with the universal alignment change of the planets in our solar system."

Instantly, Trikan aligns his Dial-Date computer with the astrological alignment of the planets in their star systems, and the planets' holograms remain in place.

"Right now, Captain, I can't see you, so you must describe any change you are aware of to me. I will do my best to help you. Can you explain to me if there is anything else happening with the planets pertaining to their orbits?"

As Trikan looks at the hologram of the solar system, he says, "No... Wait, Professor! Something is happening! There is a slight movement of the platform disc!"

The professor says, "That can only mean a diversion in the orbital time sequence. Captain, your Dial-Date computer is a metric algorithm code finder! Set the dial to the planetary orbital time program analysis, and you should receive higher-dimensional analogs about the geometrical design of our planet's orbital changes, giving you slightly more time to complete your mission. The inscriptions, Captain, on the disc platform, can you make them out?"

"Yes, Professor!"

"Well, captain, you're standing on a large metal disc which is a representation of our solar system! Each carved symbol is a microsecond in our star system, and the symmetry of time cannot be altered as our planets move. Simply put, Captain, you are looking at a giant Dial-Date! A calculus of the movement of every planet and moon in our solar system. Each microsecond is registered with the value of the triangular markings on the disc. Remember... The vortex of time change can only work in a forward direction. What you are looking at is the detection of matter in time, quartz symmetry! That's what the codes represent!"

Following the professor's instructions, the steel door automatically opens and slides into the interior construction of the chamber wall.

"The room is open, professor... It worked! There's someone in there, and it's a hologram of the uniformed prison official, just like you said!"

The professor then says, "Yes, that's very good, Captain! Every time the code sequence matches the planetary orbits, the hologram will reappear in the time continuum portal. What you are doing right now is looking into the past! Don't let it distract you!"

"Wait a minute, professor, you're not going to believe this; the prison official is not there anymore. There's someone else in the frame room!" The captain is shocked at what he sees as he observes something that confuses him, and his mind gives in to what he is experiencing. "Professor... I don't know how, but I'm now inside the frame room and don't know how I got here."

A slight pause before Trikan can collect his thoughts. The professor then calls out, "Captain, you're looking at the symmetry of the future! You must not stay where you are... You are still standing in the center of the platform disc! You must leave the center of the disc and step off immediately at the exit of the triangular point system!"

The captain follows the professor's instructions and steps off the platform quickly. Just before entering the frame room, the shank rods suddenly fall and strike the center of the large steel disc. As each shank rod hits the platform, it explodes into brilliant fusion spheres of energy, causing the hologram's center to continue displaying planets that now orbit around the center of a bright sun. Trikan says, "Professor, I'm inside the frame room and now disengaging the power dome."

The professor continues, "As you can see, Captain, the frame room contains cartridges of Magnite communication plates that I described to you, the ones the official was replacing that failed. They control all the prison's exterior doors and gantry ramps! Once the *Magnite* cartridges are destroyed, all the exit and exterior gantry bay ramps will remain open and be impossible to close."

Trikan replies, "Affirmative, Professor!" Stepping back from the power source relay of the sky-energy dome, Trikan turns and fires his laser weapon, destroying the trunk lines that operate the current field to the dome. Walking several feet towards the steel door, he remarks to the professor, "You were right about the inside construction of the steel door, Professor. It contains no tri-bar handles! Once the door is closed, it is impossible to exit the room! Another one of their traps to eliminate an intruder!"

"Yes, Captain, and you have exactly eighteen seconds to destroy all of the *Magnite* cartridges and exit the tower!"

The captain immediately reacts to the professor's statement and fires his laser weapon at full blast, destroying the large, frame-walled units containing the *Magnite* control plates and setting the room on fire. Trikan steps back out from the steel door with no time to spare as it closes and leaves the tower chamber, and the massive explosion destroys the entire frame room. LamBrute and Trikan distance themselves from the tower. LamBrute says, "Well done, Captain!"

As the two friends look back for a moment, they see the sun rising above the tower in the center of a four-dimensional universe.

The onboard computer's voice modulation activates: "... **FLIGHT CAPTAIN REPORTING... LANDING RESTRICTIONS HAVE BEEN REMOVED FROM QUADRANT TEN SEVENTY-ONE... THERE ARE NO LINEAR MILE RESTRICTIONS...**"

Cen-Ton turns and looks at the professor. The professor pauses momentarily and then says, "It's your ship, Cen-Ton!"

Cen-Ton speaks to the onboard computer as he looks at the readout of the planned drop-off of the tower mission. He gives the coordinates to the onboard computer: "... LANDING SITE Q-261720..."

The computer responds: "... **AFFIRMATIVE Q-261720... NO OBSTRUCTIONS... LANDING IN PROGRESS...**"

The professor calls down to Trikan, "Captain, do you copy? We are about to land."

"I copy, professor."

"Captain, stand clear of area Q-261720; we are coming down!"

"You're clear for landing, professor; nothing is happening here. Below us is another story; they never had anything like this happen before!"

As the invisible flightcraft touches down on the prison roof, the passenger hatch opens, and the professor climbs down the short distance on the automatic safety ramp. "Captain, you and LamBrute have done a great job! However, we must act quickly before they realize what is happening. As I have stated, we must enter the warden's office as soon as possible and avoid detection. Cen-Ton will remain with the flightcraft for a prompt departure!"

"Affirmative, Professor! Now, let's finish the job that we came here for!"

LamBrute adds, "I'm with you, Captain!"

The professor then tells Trikan, "Follow me, captain. There is a hydro-lift on the other side of the fortress tower, and this unit is used for work repairs on the tower when needed. It goes down to the maintenance department on level twelve, where we will find maintenance uniforms and indoor transportation magnetic electro-pods. Every floor has them for the security guards to use; without them, the guards would be unable to navigate and maintain order. When we get the electro-pod, we can travel throughout the complex until we arrive at the Central Command Center in the middle of the prison, where multiple hydro-lifts service the entire fourteen levels."

After putting on their maintenance uniforms and communication helmets, they board one of the electro-pods to travel throughout the vast prison complex, which contains all the administrative offices of various departments within the military prison. The professor says, "Our objective will be level ten, the warden's office."

As the captain, Professor Zola, and LamBrute are on their way down to the warden's office, they hear the security speakers for the first time: "**...MALFUNCTION, MALFUNCTION...**" repeatedly. The message continues throughout Central Detention. "**... ALL ROOF DOORS ARE NOW OPEN! LANDING RAMPS ARE MALFUNCTIONING! SENTRY ROBOTS' ATTENTION... REPORT TO LEVEL THREE... YOUR CENTRAL COMMAND OFFICER WILL INSTRUCT YOU ON YOUR NEW ASSIGNMENT POSTS...**"

Above the main prison complex in the warden's office, the warden, in an agitated state, is yelling at his top command officers, "Don't tell me that you don't know what's going on! Go and find out what is happening, and don't come back without answers! I don't want the government council to ask me about this unless I can tell them it's been taken care of. Do you hear me?"

The command officers leave the warden's office, and a moment later, the telescreen comes on from **Central Council Security Control-Star Port City.**

"Warden Tollon, what is going on over there? Everyone in the council is talking about it. You're experiencing some internal communication breakdowns. We also understand that all of your exterior ramp and gantry landing facilities are now open?"

The warden responds, "Yes, Security Control, we're experiencing some type of glitch in our electronic gamma fields! I assure you that the problem does not affect our security or prison population! As we speak, I'm looking at the complete cell facilities of the prison on my screen, and all the prisoners are secured in their cells!"

"So, what you're telling me, Warden Tollon, when I report back to the generals of Central Command, I will inform them that you have the situation under total control?"

"Yes, that is correct!" Sitting back in his chair, Warden Tollon feels that the problem will be taken care of shortly by the in-house security maintenance department that shares the functions of running the vast facility with sentry robots.

As Trikan, the professor, and LamBrute step off the hydro-lift and make their way to the Warden's office, Trikan says, "Professor, I hope you're right that the controls of the prison cells are in the warden's office?"

The professor then replies, "Where else can they be, Captain?"

Trikan acknowledges, "Okay, Professor!"

The professor's conversation is interrupted again by a further announcement from the Warden, demanding that the problem be solved before daylight tomorrow morning. Before the captain, professor, and LamBrute can take one of the available hydro-pods, they must stand aside as several sentry robots run down the corridor, board one of the hydro-pods, and leave for an emergency call.

"Captain, they did not even notice us!"

"You're right, LamBrute! Thanks to the professor for advising us to wear these maintenance uniforms over our flight suits."

Boarding a passenger's hydro-pod, they travel down the long corridors of constant directional change, lacking any explanation of a comprehensive destination. Without Professor Zola's unique knowledge of the prison complex, it would be almost impossible for the captain and LamBrute to find their way to the central building facility and the warden's office.

After traveling through the pre-planned maze of the prison's construction, they pass many well-conceived cell blocks that house the prisoner population. Before reaching their destination, they pass some sections on the hydro-pod. Professor Zola recognizes some inmates in their lockup cells from when he was a prisoner in Central Detention. After their daring escape through the prison cellblocks, avoiding sentry robots, they arrive at the central lobby, which features the main level of the hydro-lifts that service all the levels in the prison.

The captain, professor, and LamBrute step into one of the hydro-lifts in the crowded main lobby, where no one pays particular attention to the three helmeted individuals in maintenance uniforms. This busy main lobby accommodates service workers, prison medical staff, and food delivery services daily throughout three shifts, maintaining a rhythm of continuous movement within this prison complex. The professor presses the indicator level ten, and as the doors close, the captain says, "Let's see, Professor, if we can get the warden to help us open the prison cells!"

LamBrute adds, "If he says no, captain, I'll help him change his mind!"

As the captain steps off the hydro-lift, he checks his Dial-Date viewfinder for the location of the warden's office. He says to the professor, "Hallway C-Ten-Seventeen. Is that right, professor?" The professor glances at his Dial-Date indicator and replies, "Correct, captain."

On the way, the captain picks up a utility tool kit that an emergency service worker carelessly left in the hallway when the alert was announced throughout the prison due to the power failure. He says, "This should help us, Professor. Now, who can tell we're not emergency service workers?"

As they walk down the corridor to the warden's office, they see a company of sentry robots carrying laser weapons coming towards them in the opposite direction as they follow their commander. As they approached one another, Trikan, LamBrute, and the professor engaged in a loud conversation about the repair duties that they had been assigned.

At that moment, as they occupied the same space in the hallway where they would pass, the captain, LamBrute, and the professor gave the commander a respectful military salute. The commander's response is returned to them instantly. After they pass, LamBrute tells Trikan, "That was a close one, Captain!" Trikan turns to look back at the sentry robots as they enter the hydro-lift.

As the doors close, he says to the professor, "Let me see what's in this utility toolbox that I'm carrying around." He places it down, opens it, and looks through some of the contents, which include basic repair tools. He then says. "These tools were hardly ever cleaned?"

Pausing for a moment as he looks at a can of heavy utility grease with no cover on it, he says, "No wonder. What a mess!" Looking up at the professor, he says, "Professor, how would you like to be our prisoner?"

Looking at the captain, the professor replies, "Captain, would you mind explaining that in more detail?"

"Sure, here's the plan..."

The captain picks up the can of grease and tells the professor. "First, we'll dirty your maintenance uniform with this utility grease." As he wipes the professor's uniform with a dirty rag that he dipped into the can of grease, he says, "There now... How does he look, LamBrute?"

"Like a mess, captain."

The professor states, "I still don't know your plan, Captain."

"It's very simple, professor. Two vigilant maintenance workers found you hiding in the locker room during the emergency announcement period, and we're taking you to the warden's office as our prisoner. Then, we will deal with him!"

The professor concludes, "I see your plan now, Captain! It is a creative way to access the Warden's office. However, when we stand on the electronic entrance plate in front of the Warden's door, the entrance view screen will automatically turn on. He will be able to observe us on his telescreen to decide whether to allow us to enter his office."

Smiling, he says, "I like your plan, Captain!" Trikan replies, "Good, now let me remove your helmet."

The captain then continues to give the professor's face an untidy look with the greasy cloth. When they approach the warden's office, they step upon the electronic entrance plate while LamBrute and the captain firmly hold onto the professor's arms. Suddenly, the view screen activates, and the warden observes two helmeted maintenance workers holding a disheveled individual wearing a dirty maintenance uniform, without a helmet.

The warden is about to say something and is abruptly interrupted by Trikan, who forcefully says, "Warden Tollon... We found this intruder in our maintenance locker."

Raising his voice again, Trikan says, "When he saw us, he tried to escape!"

As Trikan pushes the professor forward in anger, he continues, "We trapped him as he tried to get away! We are on our way to take him down to Central Security, but I thought you might want to know about the incident first."

"Yes! Take him to Central Security!"

The warden changes his mind a moment later, "No, no, wait! Let me question him first!"

Warden Tollon releases the auto-lock on his reinforced office door, and as it begins to open, he calls out, "Bring him in!"

The captain and LamBrute walk the professor into the warden's office. As the warden gets up from behind his desk, he directs them to sit the intruder in a chair in the center of the room, several feet from his desk. As he slowly circles the professor, he stays silent for a couple of moments. He then says, "Who are you? How did you get into the maintenance room?"

The professor remains quiet, and the warden continues, "Are you one of my prisoners? You must be responsible for what is going on! Your silence says that you are GUILTY! You know all the gantry bay doors are open, right? Your silence is a complete confirmation of your guilt! I could destroy you now, but not before I find out how many are working with you. Do you understand what I'm saying?"

Walking back to his desk, he smiles and sits across from the professor. "I'm putting you in one of our cells, and I'm going to enjoy questioning you later! When we get through with you, you will tell us everything we want to know!"

Turning on his intercom and removing an electronic cell-lock signaling device, he activates a hidden electronic web circuit board in his office, which is part of the ceiling above them. Using the handheld signaling device, he sends an electric finder code impulse throughout the entire ceiling board system until he finds an open cell.

During the process, Captain Trikan observes a continuous, faint pulsation of blue indicator lights within the ceiling complex until the warden finds an open cell. A faint red glow appears; he then stops his probe and announces over the intercom to security that a prisoner will be arriving on level five and will be placed in cell block 5289.

For the moment, Warden Tollon does not notice the laser weapon that is pointed at him until Trikan informs him. "Don't put it back on your desk, Warden! The cell-lock device! Hand it over!"

The warden becomes confused. "WHAT ARE YOU TALKING ABOUT? Who Are You?"

Professor Zola then stands up, approaches the desk, and says, "Are you still interested in knowing who I am? My name is Professor Zola, and I was one of your prisoners! Do as you are told, and no one will get hurt!"

The warden replies, "Ah... Yes, now I remember who you are; you were one of my worst prisoners!" The professor says, "Do as you're told and hand it over!"

As the warden hands the professor the cell lock-code key, he sits behind his desk and reaches for a weapon.

At that moment, LamBrute shouts out, "CAPTAIN!"

Immediately, Trikan fires his laser weapon, destroying the Warden instantly. The professor then says to the captain, "Well, captain... Now, to get this thing to work and open all the cells." Looking at his Dial-Date, Trikan tells the professor, "We don't have time for that! The blast from my weapon set off the silent alarms! They know exactly that it's in the Warden's office!" The professor then asks, "Well, how will we open all the cells?"

Ignoring the professor momentarily, Trikan tells LamBrute, "LamBrute, put your weapon on full blast, and let's get out into the hallway. Come on, Professor!"

They move a reasonable distance from the office, and Trikan says, "It worked in the frame room, and it's got to work here!"

As they fire their weapons on full blast into the ceiling of the warden's office, they destroy the entire communications center and the electronics, allowing all the prison cells to open automatically. The captain then tells the professor, "LamBrute and I will escort you back to the hydro-flight ship. You will wait for us there, and then we will proceed to the women's dormitory prison complex to locate Elisa. When we find her, I will signal you to start the flight sequence engines onboard the transport. When we return with Elisa, you will take off immediately; you have a long flight back to the safehouse."

Before they enter a hydro-lift to the tower roof, prisoners are already on the prison complex's outer grounds, preparing to leave for their freedom.

Once the professor is safely within the invisible flightcraft, Captain Trikan and LamBrute make their way to the women's dormitory prison section.

Chapter 19:
Shields Of Destruction

As the morning sun sends its light across the quadrant, the prison security guards realize that the mass exodus is impossible to stop.

After speaking with President Clarkston at Star Port City, prison officials notified the government council and explained the situation. President Clarkston is observing the prison situation in his office on his telescreen. As his Aide opens the double doors to his office and allows several council members to enter, they approach him and find him in a somber mood.

The council members remain silent as he finally turns away from the screen and looks at them. He then talks into the telescreen's two-way close-circuit audio security speaker and says, "NO, General... There is nothing that we can do at this time! Tell all the prison guards and sentry robots to stand down! Let them all go! We will have plenty of time after we capture the person responsible for this and anyone else involved. Yes, General, I understand! Issue a national military alert!"

He pauses and then says, "I don't know, but I can assure you that we will track them all down, and they will be the first to go back into Central Detention with the rest of the escapees once the system is back online. As it stands, we have more questions than answers. We do not know how the prison's security codes were breached. It has to be the work of a superior mind that was able to obtain restricted information!"

He then looks at the council members and says, "Or do we have a traitor within our government council?"

He gets up, walks towards a large window, and looks out across the government plaza. Without turning around to look at the council members, he says, "You are all under suspicion until this matter is cleared up. Dismissed!"

As most leave without saying a word, several stay back and close the Council President's office doors. Their presence takes President Clarkston aback, and he becomes concerned about why they did not leave with the others. He says to them, "What is it? Didn't I make myself clear? Did I leave something out that you didn't understand?"

One of the council members tells him, "Ray, you know exactly why we're here! When will you face reality? We respectfully appreciate your friendship with the highly respected Councilwoman Doctor Lasara." There is a short pause, and the council member continues, "This Captain is a problem for us and your position as president of the government. Captain Shawnwood is dangerous to you, and so is Councilwoman Lasara. When you became a member of the Pteranodon, you were given the votes to lead and become the council president of the government! Now, you must earn your position, and it is time to repay the privilege our society has given you. Again, I'll ask you, what will YOU do about this, Captain, Mister President?"

Staring directly at the council member, he says, "He's NOT my problem! The military trained him, and he belongs to them, so let them solve the problem! There's nothing that I can do! Now, get out of my office! Or do I have to call security?"

As he motions to his Aide to open the double doors of his office, he says, "The doors are open, Councilmen. Have a good day!"

The lead councilman says, "Are you serious?"

President Clarkston looks at him and says, "Yes... Very serious. Now get out!"

The councilmen turn and leave the office with the others without saying a word. Halfway down the long hallway, the lead council member remarks to the others, "The president will regret this day!"

As his Aide closes the double doors, President Clarkston says to him, "From now on, my office is off-limits to them without an appointment!"

The drama of the prison emergency continues as the event has taken on a life of its own. Angry individuals who have experienced extended periods of incarceration begin to take out their anger and destroy the area around them by knocking over computer modules, smashing window portals, and knocking over sentry security identification unit screens. As they enter the hydro-lifts that transport them to the main lobby, they compose their anger and behave as they walk through, past the sentry robots stationed out front, managing the steady flow of large ground passenger transports that will take them to Star Port City.

The women's dormitory section is also in a state of confusion as they take overcrowded hydro-lifts down to the main floor lobby. The captain and LamBrute take one of the hydro-lifts to the women's dormitory prison complex, and as the doors to the hydro-lift open, they are confronted by a frenzied group of female inmates fleeing.

Upon seeing the two helmeted figures in prison maintenance uniforms, the female inmates panic and push back as they crowd the corridor leading to their open cells. Trikan says to LamBrute, "LamBrute, I think it was a bad idea to keep these helmets on. I think we'd better get rid of them!" Removing them quickly, LamBrute adds, "My thoughts exactly, Captain!"

Several women in the crowd, who had intended to use the hydro-lift to escape, are frightened and push back from the open doors as the two tall figures in maintenance suits are about to step off the hydro-lift platform. The crowd in front of them, who are still frightened, remain silent until they hear from the one with the long hair, the Trikinian. LamBrute tells them, "Ladies... Calm down, and let me introduce you to Captain Trikan!"

Remaining silent, they do not believe what they're hearing. LamBrute continues, "Yes... It's him, Captain Trikan, it's him! He's here to help you get out of this place! He also needs your help to find someone here with you!"

Trikan then says to the crowd, "Does anyone know where I can find a young woman named Elisa?"

Before answering him, one woman responded, "I don't believe it! It's Captain Trikan!"

Another woman turned around and asked several others in the crowd, "Can someone help him find Elisa? You know Elisa?"

Several women in the back of the group call out, "We know where she is! We'll take you there, Captain!" Her statement is repeated down the corridor to the cell areas, where some of the female inmates are packing last-minute personal items.

They stop, step out of their cells in disbelief, and yell, "We're going to be free! It's going to happen!"

Trikan calls out to them, "All the prison gates are open! You are free to go!" LamBrute stays back for a moment and helps some of the inmates carrying large bundles of personal belongings as the captain continues through the crowd, telling them, "The guards have been ordered to stand down and will assist you in leaving the prison in an orderly manner!" They all cheer as some grab onto him momentarily, saying, "Thank you, Captain!" while others yell, "You're great, Trikan!" Many in the crowd reach out to touch him.

As he continues down the corridor, the ladies in the back call out, "Captain, we'll show you where she is!" Another woman yells, "Are you going to marry her, Captain?"

Smiling, he tells the helpful group, "Tell me where she is, and I'll find her."

A voice in the crowd yells, "She's in West Section Five!" He shouts back, "Thank you for your help! Ladies, be safe, board the transports, and go home to your families!"

A chorus of "thank you" and words of gratitude fill the hydro-lift corridor, including the voice modulators that have been automatically turned on again in the hydro-lifts to broadcast a courtesy message to all the passengers: "Watch your step when entering the hydro-lifts! If you do not indicate a floor preference, you may exit at the lobby at the front entrance of the exit ramp, where you will find ground transport buses that will take you to the military airbase flight transports. There, you will get air flight transportation back to Star Port City, where Maglev transits will then take you to your desired locations."

    Trikan stops momentarily as the last recorded words from the hydro-lift can be heard. He asks LamBrute, who finally made his way through the crowd, "LamBrute, did you hear that?"

    "I heard it, Captain." He then adds, "Captain, that's a sweet sound!"

    Agreeing, Trikan smiles. "Yes, LamBrute, the sweet sound of Freedom! Now, let's find Elisa!"

    Making their way to West Section Five, they pass several dorm cells still occupied by some of the last remaining inmates, who are about to experience their freedom. As they pass, the Captain and LamBrute receive looks of surprise from some of the last inmates, who do not quite understand what is happening. For them, it has not yet come to the realization that they are at the end of their incarceration.

    Trikan stops as he looks down at the long corridor lined with open cell doors and observes the last woman's dorm occupant leaving her cell. It's Elisa!

    A moment in time becomes another world, a place of adventure and the experience of falling in love. He is back at the beginning, where he experienced real life and found meaning in looking across the high mountains of Trikinia, which brought him back memories of the rainforest and Elisa. While dropping the travel luggage bag of her belongings, Elisa calls out when she sees him, "Hey! Don't I know you?"

Smiling, he answers, "No, I don't think so..."

"Yes, I know you, you're Trikan, and everyone is looking for you!" "So, is that a good or bad thing, Elisa?"

Smiling, she says, "It's a bad thing for them! Because they can't have you; you belong to me!" She then runs to him, throwing her arms around him, and says, "I missed you, Trikan!" Instantly, they kiss, and he tells her, "That's why I'm here! Now, let's get out of this place; the Professor's waiting for us!"

As LamBrute approaches, he tells her, "I have your travel luggage bag, Elisa."

Smiling, Elisa answers, "Thank you, LamBrute! The captain said that the professor is waiting for us!" Trikan then asks Elisa, "You know LamBrute?"

She smiles again while looking at LamBrute and replies, "Everyone knows LamBrute! He's one of Alden's special guards! LamBrute, have you seen any of the Trikinian warriors you recognized as they were leaving the prison?"

He replies, "No... That can't be right! That's against the law! There's a treaty against that—no Trikinian shall ever be imprisoned in Central Detention! They are supposed to be turned over to their diplomatic Trikinian authorities."

Elisa answered back, "Oh yeah? Look at me! And besides, I don't know anything about treaties! All I know is what I heard; they are in the underground section of the military lockup! A few days after being brought here, I observed air personnel troops being marched in by armed sentry robots! They also were locked up in the underground cell chambers with the Trikinian prisoners!"

Trikan then says, "So, what are you saying is that all this happened right after the rainforest?"

Elias nods, "Yes! It happened just after I arrived here."

As if speaking to himself, he says in a low voice, "That makes sense, what Sergeant Larsen told me about the scout troops that night at the camp; when he went into the mess hall for dinner, no one was there. These are my guys! It makes perfect sense! This was their revenge against my troopers for sending the survival pod down! Come on, Elisa... Let's get you on board the transport and get you out of here!"

The captain then tells LamBrute, "Let's find us an empty hydro-lift that will take us up to the transport!"

As the captain, Elisa, and LamBrute return to the main lobby, they find it deserted. No one is around, and they have their choice of several of the empty hydro-lifts. They enter one and give a voice command destination to the top level of Central Detention, and in a few moments, they exit the hydro-lift.

Upon entering the center of the lobby on level fourteen, which contains a circular, glass-enclosed security complex, they find the entire facility empty. They push open the unlocked glass doors through the security center and enter the office complex. It allows them to use the office's interior hydro-lift elevator, which takes them to the roof. As they reach the invisible transport's landing site, Elisa asks, "Where is the transport?"

Trikan tells her, "You can't see it because it's invisible."

She replies, "Invisible? Are you kidding me? How did that happen?"

Trikan says, "Ask the professor. He's very clever!"

Elisa smiles. "Yes, he is."

Using his Dial-Date, Trikan sends a text message to the Professor, stating that Elisa is with them and that she is safe; he can now begin the flight sequence engines. Inside the flight transport at the helm, Cen-Ton tells the Professor, "... PROFESSOR... THEY ARE ON THEIR WAY... AND ELISA IS WITH THEM..."

"Very good, Cen-Ton; now turn down the magnetic program invisibility shield to twenty percent so they can see the faint outline of the ship and stand by to activate flight sequence engines." When they arrive at the transport, the professor opens the flight passenger hatch and sees Elisa for the first time since she was taken to Central Detention. Reaching down to her, he helps her climb up the passenger ramp leading into the ship.

The professor then extends his hand to the captain, who yells up to him over the engine noise. "No, professor, I'm not going with you. I'll see you back at the safehouse! LamBrute and I have to take care of a few more things!"

LamBrute hands Trikan Elisa's bag, and he throws it up to the professor. "Now, get out of here, Professor! Safe trip!"

Elisa calls out from the transport, "Trikan... Stay safe!" As she throws him a kiss, the Professor closes the passenger hatch and tells Cen-Ton, "Cen-Ton, full invisibility screen and take off immediately; course destination... Safe Zone Quadrant!"

Captain Trikan and LamBrute step back several feet from the flightcraft as the thruster engines blast-lift energy elevates the craft off the prison tower roof. Trikan looks up and sees Elisa waving to him from one of the exterior view portals, and moments later, the craft becomes invisible. LamBrute says to the captain, "Well, captain, they're on their way!"

Trikan, still looking up, whispers, "Safe journey!"

The professor sends a coded message informing Aunt Lasara: "They have rescued Elisa and are on their flight back, and everything is good!"

Aunt Lasara sends a coded request: "Professor, may I speak to the captain?" Professor Zola replies: "He's not on board... The captain and LamBrute have some important unfinished business to take care of."

Aunt Lasara replies: "Well, I hope they stay safe, Professor. I'll see you when you get back."

The captain and LamBrute go to the glass-enclosed security

center and are not surprised to find it vacant, like most of the prison complex. With no prisoners, there are no security patrols to worry about. The captain tells LamBrute, "We have plenty of time to find out where the underground prison complex is."

    Sitting down at one of the security computer centers, Trikan turns on the screen and receives a comprehensive photo display of the prison sections. Working floor by floor, he searches the entire fourteen levels of Central Detention and finds all the unit floors empty. He tells LamBrute, "Look at this, LamBrute..."

    He brings back the photo of the prison complex, which reveals underground sub-chambered cell sections. He leans back to allow LamBrute to get a good look at the monitor and the contents of sections below ground, underneath the first-floor lobby.

    LamBrute says, "Captain, you found sub-section prison cells and an arms room!"

    "Yes, LamBrute! Now, let's go find our guys!"

    As he types the words into the keyboard: Military Complex ... *Central Detention... Sub-Chamber Lockup Cells... Access!* The screen displays information on the entrances and exits of the sub-chamber cells.

    "Here we go, LamBrute!"

    "Nice job, Captain!"

    "Who would ever think the sub-chamber cells would be right under the main floor of the huge entrance hall lobby to the prison?"

    LamBrute agrees, "Hidden in plain sight!"

    Smiling, Trikan replies, "Exactly! Especially when the prison has fourteen levels. Come on! Let's get our guys out of there!"

    Pressing the issue key, Trikan receives a submap of the tunnel complex, granting him access to and an exit from the entire sub-tunnel complex of the military lockup below. As they enter the turbo lift, they look at the familiar floor display panel. The captain remarks, "This lift unit will only go to the lobby."

LamBrute asks, "What is that locked unit alongside the display panel?"

Trikan looks at LamBrute, "Well, let's find out."

Taking his laser weapon out of his side holster, he breaks open the locked cover of the duplicate display of floor units, which are identical except for the addition of unit buttons at the bottom of the display panel labeled "**SUBFLOOR**." "There it is, LamBrute!"

The captain presses the subfloor chamber button that takes the elevator down to the secret military lockup complex. The captain and LamBrute exit the hydro-lift elevator and walk along the well-lit corridors of prison cells. There is no reaction from the inmates. In most cases, they ignore the tall figures wearing prison maintenance uniforms. In a low voice, LamBrute says to the captain, "Captain, these uniforms are a dead giveaway! They think we are prison maintenance workers!"

"Yes, LamBrute, the professor's idea seems to be working again! This time, on the good guys! I think we'd better come clean and tell them who we are!"

Stopping at one of the cell units, the captain asks the occupants on the other side of the prison bars, "Is everyone okay?"

One of the prisoners says, "Do we look like we're okay?"

Trikan answers, "I'm sure you'll be doing much better once we get you out of here!"

The prisoner responds, "Are you kidding me?"

Before the captain can say another word, another Trikinian prisoner calls out, and LamBrute answers, "Yes, we're here to get you out!"

The first prisoner, Trikan, was talking to, stood up, grabbed the cell bars, and asked, "Who are you?"

Trikan tells him, "Forget the maintenance uniforms! Does anyone know how to open these cells?"

A Trikinian prisoner who recognizes LamBrute reaches out through the bars, and LamBrute grabs his arm in the Trikinian warrior's handover wrist unity. The prisoner says to LamBrute, "What's happening, LamBrute?"

LamBrute replies, "As Captain Trikan said... We're here to free you! The prison complex above us is empty!"

Some of the other prisoners repeat, "EMPTY?"

Trikan intercedes, "They lost power throughout the entire prison complex!"

LamBrute adds, "Captain, I guess the complex down here runs on its own power source?"

"I guess Elisa was right, LamBrute. Trikinians are locked outside their country's territory."

He turns around and calls out, "Does anyone have any idea where the room to open the cell units is located?"

A couple of moments of indecision occur among the prisoners as to where they think the central control unit is located. Finally, some agree that it's located in the northwest tunnel passage, near a unit patrol station, where electronic equipment controls all the cell blocks in the sub-chamber. LamBrute says, "How does that sound to you, Captain?"

Trikan replies, "Let's go and check it out and get these cell doors open!"

One of the prisoners says, "Captain, on the way down the tunnel passage, there is a section labeled *'Troop Detention'* with a magnetic indicator on the inside of a dark tunnel that leads to their cell units. It's possible that you would walk right past it without knowing! It's a tunnel pathway on the left, and the entire cell unit is kept in darkness. The only time those scout troops see light is when they're let out to go up to the courtyard!"

Trikan says to LamBrute, "What kind of existence is that?"

"It sounds like they're being punished, Captain, for something they did."

"Yes, LamBrute. Let's go and find out!"

As they follow the prisoner's advice about the scout troops, they proceed down the tunnel, turning their Dial-Dates to the CFL cold fusion light indicator setting. They examine the entranceway to the dark tunnel, and Captain Trikan sees a wall-mounted electrical unit box. He opens the cover and says, "Look at this, LamBrute!"

As he turns on a simple electronic switch, the lights go on for the entire prison section. As they enter the compound unit, they walk past several of the occupied single-unit cells and receive no reaction to their presence. As they continue and pass several more cells, they stop, and Trikan says, "LamBrute, did you say something about them being punished?"

Acknowledging, he says, "Yes, I did, Captain."

"Well, you're looking at the reason! These are my guys; they are my Scout Troops! Let's get these cells open, LamBrute!"

As they leave the cell unit, they are still unnoticed by a couple of the Scout Troops who are still awake. Paying no attention to anything outside their cells, the long and enduring incarceration has taken its toll on their spirits. As Trikan and LamBrute make their way down to the cell block control room, they enter through an unlocked door.

They step into the room, and Trikan turns on the Central Control Sub-Chamber computer. The screen comes on, revealing all the cell sections of the sub-chamber relay complex, which is set to reverse energy field lockup. A blinking sphere pulsates on the screen as it reveals the words:"... **RELEASE TOTAL CELL LOCK MECHANISM...**"

Another section on the screen displays six square-unit sections of the sub-chambers. As Trikan pushes all six square lights on the screen, a keyboard appears, releasing each prison cell. The Northwest and Southeast Sections appear on the computer keyboard screen and suddenly change their color patterns from bright orange to green; the keyword "**OPEN**" appears on each of the six-unit displays.

Trikan then says, "Okay, LamBrute, it's done. Let's get out of here!"

As they leave the control room, Trikan says, "I think I'm forgetting something."

As he stops and turns, he fires a full blast of destructive fusion energy from his handheld laser weapon, destroying the entire computer room. Trikan then says, "LamBrute, go down to the main cell block section; your guys will need someone to tell them what's going on. I will see if that blast woke up the scout troops!"

LamBrute states, "That was 'one hell of a reveille,' Captain!" Trikan smiles in acknowledgment.

When Captain Trikan arrives at the scout troop cell area, he stands before them and says, "You guys want to get up? It's time to go to work; the power of a corrupt military unjustly locked you up! Now, we have a job to do!"

As the scout troops slowly leave their cells, they assemble in front of the captain, and the first sergeant shouts, "You heard the captain! Up and ready!"

When the last trooper takes his place on the line, Captain Trikan says to the first sergeant, "Sergeant... I don't see any of your men with laser rifles."

Smiling, the sergeant replies, "Yes, Sir... I agree with you, Sir! I don't see any laser rifles either, Sir!"

Trikan smiles. "Well, Sergeant, we're going to have to do something about that! Or I will have to put you and your men on report!"

Trikan talks into his Dial-Date, "Commander LamBrute, meet

me at the arms room. I have a bunch of guys here who are itching for a fight. But they don't have anything to fight with."

LamBrute smiles and says, "I hear you, Captain! We're already in the arms room, Captain, and there are more than enough weapons to go around for everyone. Oh, Captain! Besides the weapons, there are field armor uniforms here, too! This section serves not only as an armory but also as a supply room. There are boxes of attack field armor, laser-resistant, electroplated uniforms."

"Commander LamBrute, you just made a whole bunch of my guys happy! Laser-resistant attack uniforms... What else can you ask for?"

Looking at the sergeant, Trikan says, "Well, Sergeant, let's go and help Commander LamBrute and his Trikinian warriors clean out the entire arms room! This way, when the bad guys return, they won't find any weapons!"

As the flightcraft hovers above the luxury safehouse, the transitional stealth fusion leaves the craft as it lands in full view. They are then greeted by Lasara, Reanna, and Eleanor, who give Elisa a warm welcome to the safe house. Aunt Lasara says to her, "This is going to be your new place to live until we can get you back to Trikinia!"

Elisa smiles. "I love it! Thank you..." She looks around and says, "I might not want to go back to Trikinia now. Your place is so beautiful!"

The professor adds, "I don't think your mother, the ambassador, will be too happy with that, Elisa: she's been trying to get you home from that horrible place for the longest time!"

Reanna says, "Perhaps the ambassador would like to come and stay with us too for a while?"

The professor smiles and says, "I will submit the request to her at the appropriate time, Reanna."

Captain Trikan makes code contact with the Professor at the safe house the following day. The Professor replies, "Yes, Captain... We are all okay! When will you get here?"

Looking at his Dial-Date, he focuses on the prison flight air dome, which is twenty-five miles away. Trikan then replies, "Don't wait for me, professor... LamBrute took the last passenger flightcraft back to Trikinia. Some of his guys needed medical attention, and the prison air dome was empty! Everything that could fly is gone. We have combat tractors for transportation. Yes, professor... I am familiar with the air flight squad at Great River, and thank you, Professor. I'll keep in touch."

The coded transmission ends, and Trikan returns to his men in the prison garage, where they complete a final pre-mission checkout of the ground transports. Seeing the captain, each of the five-unit commands calls out to him, "Everything is good, Captain!"

Another unit command shouts, "We have plenty of extra fusion rod fuel on board!"

The captain shouts back, "Good, let's get out of here and see what we can do in Star Port City! They are going to need all the help they can get!" They all shouted out, "YES! Whatever it takes, Captain Trikan!"

As they start their engines, the tank transport begins to exit through the open bay ramp. The large wheel transport crosses the deep, muddy waters outside Central Detention. A battle group of fourteen transports and a full-company squad of scout troops make their way across the desert's dusty terrain, heading for Star Port City.

Captain Trikan is riding up front with the lead battle-ready hydro war tanks. After twenty-two quarter sequences of travel time on the desert road, a red signal light comes on the dashboard computer screen in the lead transport. This signal indicates ground radar interference; a signal transport stop is approximately 2.75 miles ahead of them.

Trikan speaks into the mobile unit intercom above the noise of the track engines on the war tanks. The captain states, "We have trouble ahead! Release lock on all fire weapons, make ready, and load position to fire on command!"

Looking into his viewfinder and speaking into the unit intercom again, the captain says, "Slow speed... Break formation, position left flank... Right flank... Off-road position... Backdrop ten meters, slow speed, steady!"

His tractor driver says, "Captain, tell me when to fire!"

Trikan then orders, "NO, WAIT!"

Still looking into his viewfinder, he says, "We can't win if we fire; we all get wiped out! I'm looking at their new target-to-target desert tanks! When fired upon, they destroy our missiles in flight before we destroy their battle group! We then become their target by our fire trail! Everyone, weapons on safety, continue column formation, maximum forward speed!"

A short time later, the dusty tractor column comes to an abrupt stop. Trikan says to his tank driver, "Let me get out of here. It's time to talk."

As Captain Trikan exits his track vehicle, he begins walking toward a uniformed officer who is on his way down the dusty road toward his lead war tank. Trikan looks at his Dial-Date and identifies the officer as an Android Captain, a Seven-Field Rank decorated Commander, and notes the number of his sixty war troops. Trikan thinks to himself, "*...This Commander has extensive experience... Let's see if I can get him to move his equipment off the main road. Our hydro-war tanks are too heavy for off-road travel. They'll get hung up in the dunes, and we'll never get to Star Port City!*"

When the two commanders reach a distance of several yards apart, they stop and salute each other respectfully. The Android commander says, "Where are you coming from, Captain?"

He receives a quick military response from Trikan, "Central Detention, Senior Captain."

The Android commander responds, "Yeah, I heard the place is a mess! Do you have any idea how it got that way, Captain?"

"I have no idea, Commander; when I arrived with my company squad, the orders were to keep the place under surveillance. I had them check out all the levels when we arrived; the place was deserted! Nothing... No security, no patrol units! I'd be dammed if I knew what was going on."

The Android commander acknowledges, "Okay, Captain, where are your troops headed?" Trikan replies, "We have orders to report to the base for a new assignment. We will be part of a program to round up the freed prisoners."

Acknowledging, the Android commander says, "Okay, captain, you and your combat personnel can camp here until after the storm."

Turning around, the unit commander points to a large, distant sandstorm anomaly coming over the desert mountains. "We lost all communication with headquarters."

As he looks at Trikan with suspicion, he continues, "I'll need to verify your story, and then I will let your company through after the storm."

Trikan then says, "I know about the storm. Most of my guys are new, and I wanted them to experience a sandstorm of this magnitude and continue with their mission. It will be good training for them!"

The Android commander says, "I see your point, Captain, and I agree. I never liked my troops hiding from the elements! I'll let your tank column pass, and you will remain here with me until I can communicate with headquarters and verify your story."

The seven-rank commander gives orders to his sentry robots to remove the roadblock and let the tank column through. As Trikan steps to the side of the road, he hand-signals his lead tank column that they have permission to pass through the blockade.

As the last of the heavy ground hydrofoil tanks passes through, the field commander receives a message from his base command, and again, it is broken up by the static from the approaching storm. The commander speaks into his field communication mobile receiver and remarks about the transmission, which is unclear. "Base Command, can you repeat?" He listens while looking at Trikan momentarily and then responds, "Say again, Base Command... Your message was not clear!"

Trikan is also listening to the broken static transmission. He purposely interrupts the Android commander to distance himself from him, only to receive a clear message that might pertain to Trikan and his troops, who are still seen traveling down the desert road. "Commander, where can I get some fresh water? My throat is as dry as this desert."

The senior commander becomes instantly annoyed at the interruption in his Base Command communication and tells Trikan, "Back at the tent, there's fresh water!"

He then continues to try to receive a clear message from Base Command through the storm. Trikan walks down to the tent, where several war tanks are parked, and climbs into the nearest one. Once inside, he turns on the view screen and the blast energy field multi-rail cannon while observing the commander, who seems momentarily out of touch with reality. The commander finally receives the uninterrupted message despite the storm's interference. As he removes his sidearm laser weapon from his holster, he shouts at his sentry robots while pointing toward the water tent. As they run across the road in an attack formation, Trikan realizes he made the right choice by leaving before the commander receives a clear message, uninterrupted by the storm. Trikan fires a two-thousand five-hundred-degree blast of destructive neutron fusion energy, destroying most of the sentry robots and the unit commander. A second attack by the remaining sentry robots is destroyed, and Trikan fires again as they try to cross the road in his direction.

The silence of the desert has returned as Trikan climbs down off the war tank. He takes out his field distant finder and looks at his tank units that have not stopped moving in the distance. He then signals to them with a message, "Guys, can I get a lift?"

The combat tractor-foils push aside the dust from the desert's sandy wake as they come to a complete stop, and the desert's silence returns. As the desert's sand and dust clear, the end "follow me" tractor-foil is put into reverse and begins to back up to get the captain off the hot desert road. The captain holds an empty water canteen upside down over his head and waves it a couple of times before throwing it off to the side of the road.

As the tractor-foil continues to back up slowly, one of the scout troops jumps off and runs towards Trikan with a full canteen of water. Trikan takes the water canteen, drinks, and quenches his thirst. He pours some water on his head and face, then drinks again until the canteen is empty. The trooper says, "Feel better, Captain?"

"Yes, a lot better!" The trooper then asks, "Captain, what happened back there? We picked up a lot of black smoke and flashes of laser fire on our relay ground scanners!"

"Oh, yes! All I did was ask for some water, and they told me to go and find it myself!"

The trooper smiles and says, "Then, it's a good thing that I brought you out some water, Captain!" As they are near the war tank, both of them start laughing out loud. Captain Trikan has reunited with his unit's command on board the lead tractor-foil and receives a warm welcome back from his troops.

They continue their slow movement with the heavy equipment across the desert in an eastward direction until a fighter war squadron flies overhead, and one of the warcraft fires several explosive fusion projectiles down at them.

The explosions hit alongside the desert road, throwing up sand and debris on several of the slow-moving tanks as the warcraft continued on their way out of the prison zone. Some of the troops become worried that the warcraft will come back. Trikan says, "No way! That pilot is probably one of those new hotshot pilots who just got out of the academy and is showing off. We wouldn't be here right now if he wanted to hit us."

At the **War Council Base Camp** in Trikinia, Alden had a meeting with LamBrute and the freed Trikinian prisoners who were unlawfully being held in Central Detention in violation of the treaty with the Government of Star Port City. He issued an ultimatum through his ambassador and ordered his warriors to prepare for an attack on the Northern Fortress near Trikinian territory. His warriors load large snow sleds with traditional weapons to attack the fort. As Alden walks over to a large map of Trikinia, he says to his warriors, "Look here at these two completed construction sites on our land. We permitted them to build sky observatories that control the heat shield platforms, which are essential to maintaining their climate.

Without them, Star Port City would turn into a desert wasteland in the warmer seasons. By this time tomorrow, if I do not receive an explanation of the entire incident, our ambassador will announce that our two countries are in a state of noncompliance according to our treaties!"

The following day, the Trikinian ambassador was denied permission to land his flightcraft within the city limits and was also not allowed to enter the government building facilities without a prior appointment five days in advance. Star Port City is and will remain under military control until all the released prisoners are apprehended and returned to Central Detention. After an uncomfortable, lengthy ride in an unofficial vehicle with his assistant, the ambassador returns to Trikinia. Alden calls a meeting with his warrior generals and tells them, "They will know by our first action! Their Northern Fortress, a short distance from our territory, will be eliminated!"

The ambassador addresses Alden's war council and explains the situation in Star Port City. He informs them that new restrictions have been implemented and that no *maglev* transport is allowed to leave the city without passing through a designated checkpoint. The primary purpose of this curfew was to stop the mass exodus of escaped prisoners from leaving the city for other parts of the country. The large *Maglev* Transit Terminal has now become the new Central Detention Center, with more than half of the *Maglev* transport offline and remaining in the station's zones. Now controlled by the generals, the government constantly reports transmissions on the public telescreens, justifying their actions.

At the Northern Fortress, a young liaison officer enters the command office and salutes the colonel. For several moments, he remains silent, unable to speak as if to find the right words for what he has just experienced. Looking at the liaison officer, the colonel asks, "What is it? Report!"

The liaison officer says, "Sir! I came in to tell you that we are surrounded!"

The colonel replies, "Surrounded! What do you mean?"

The liaison officer pauses for a moment before answering, "Sir, we are surrounded by Trikinian War Troops!"

The commanding colonel states, "That is impossible! How could that happen?"

Turning on his exterior teleview screens, he cannot quite make out much due to the heavy snowstorm and wind drifts. He gets on his interoffice communicator and speaks to his first command sergeant, "Sergeant, I have our liaison officer in my office; I'd like to know what he's doing here. He told me something that doesn't make sense."

The first command sergeant says, "Colonel, with all due respect, I did not want to leave the situation down here at the main gates; that's why I had sent him to your office. Trikinian war troops surround us, and they demand that we surrender the fortress!"

The colonel says, "That can't be! What happened to our early alert screens?"

Concerned, the first command sergeant states, "They're not functioning, Colonel! Something keeps setting them offline."

Agreeing, the colonel says, "I understand it, Sergeant!"

Sitting back in his chair, he remains silent for several moments and then picks up the telecommunicator again and speaks to the entire Northern Troops within the fortress:

"This is your Commander! Due to circumstances beyond our control, we are surrendering the Northern Fortress to the armed command of the Trikinians. Your weapons are to remain in your quarters, and I expect EVERYONE to be present in the main hangar drill shed! To be present and stand down to a surrender agreement that I will personally sign and hand over to the Trikinians!"

When the government council members hear of the Trikinian's successful mission against the Northern Fortress, they become alarmed and call for a meeting with the president and the generals who took over the government in Star Port City.

Directing their anger to the highest-ranking general of the rebellious group, the council members tell him, "You and the rest of your treasonous officers don't know what they're doing! You must release the president immediately; he is the only one who can bring order back to Star Port City before your actions become a nationwide uprising!"

The general does not say a word; he gets up, walks to the council room's exit, and opens it. He then stops, turns to the council board members, and says, "The president will be released. There is enough bad judgment to go around for everyone, and as for me, I resign! As for the other generals? I will recommend that they resign as well! And if they REFUSE—" Suddenly, another council member calls out to him and says, "And if they refuse, what will you do, General?" Looking at some of the council members, he knows he belongs to the secret Pteranodon Society. He says, "Perhaps that decision should be left to the council." He pauses and then leaves the council chamber.

As the Trikinian assault troops take possession of the fortress, Alden tells his field commanders, "Now, we have one more mission to complete! Destroy the newly constructed observatories that control the heat shields built on our Trikinian land! The treaty has been broken!

There is no legal government in Star Port City. I will not abide by any agreement with a group of renegade generals that have taken over their government!"

Trikinian demolition crews load fusion canisters onto snow sleds, which are harnessed by large Trikinian ice wolves trained to pull the heavy sleds across the snowy terrain as they head toward the two control observatories in the high mountains of Trikinia.

Before nightfall, two large explosions are detected by ground force radar-seismograph monitors throughout the planet's northern hemisphere. Several of the immense heat shields that are in orbital space over Star Port City break formation and begin to descend after being released from their orbital controls. The shields take several days to fall over parts of Star Port City in a slow antigravity free-fall motion.

No casualties will occur due to the emergency evacuation plans put into effect immediately when the shields begin their descent. The slow descent of the destructive heat shields does not affect the underground *Maglev*-line transports, where a large portion of the city's population has taken refuge.

Other sections of Star Port City received damaged skyways and ground port terminals, including some government buildings. Justice Calandra makes code contact with Professor Zola using Councilwoman Lasara's code sequence, informing him that the government court complex building is where Doctor Lasara and Reanna are safe. Along with the message, she includes, "Please forward to the captain... To come here to the Government Center when he can."

Upon receiving the transmission, Professor Zola tells Elisa, "I have to let the captain know that they are safe with Justice Calandra!" He immediately sends the coded message to Trikan but receives no response. He waits and sends several more coded messages, and still gets no reply. He then tells Elisa, "I just tried to contact the captain, and I got no response. I suppose the power grids are down, and we are unable to send any transmissions outside the city zones. It looks like we won't be able to contact the captain until the interior city grids are repaired."

Chapter 20:
Star Voyage

By nightfall, they reach the desert mountain town of Oak River, which separates the desert from the mountain regions and has a scout air dome flight base that operates troop replacements to Star Port City.

Trikan says, "This is as far as we go. It's getting dark. The rest of the way, we walk."

One of the troopers says to Trikan, "Captain, it's a long walk to the base!"

Trikan replies, "Right, and we'd better get moving if we are going to take those air flightcrafts before morning reveille. I don't want to fight the *'air flight guys'* in the morning for those hydrocopters!"

Using his night-vision view scope, he remarks, "Look at that... There they are, in the hangars, and they left the rollup doors open for us! What a nice bunch of guys!"

As Trikans' planned strategy was the right move, no one at the outpost camp was aware of anything until they heard the flightcraft engines leave the base in the middle of the night. Several hours into their flight time, Trikan can see that his crew needs some R&R; the journey across the hot desert has taken its toll on them. They still have a 14-hour flight ahead of them before reaching Star Port City.

Trikan gives the orders to land at one of the old mining towns that were abandoned years ago, where they will spend the night.

Trikan had a feeling about the fighter squadron that flew over them in the desert; he thought they might have been given a new assignment to look for the hydrocopters and those who had taken them. Upon landing, he announces, "The radio silence order is still in effect! Nothing goes out, and nothing comes in! I repeat, silence on all receivers, guys... This is a direct order!"

A day and a half later, in the early morning, the sound of the hydrocopter transport engines can once again be heard, giving life throughout the area of the old, abandoned mining town, as the wind machines lift off in the direction of Star Port City. Still concerned about the fighter squadron, Trikan gives orders to his flight crew to set their navigational guidance systems to the **A-1A ARMY AVIATION** landing facility two hundred kilometers outside of Star Port City.

There, they will land at the Army Hydrocopter Flight Base, which would be the last place that the fighter squadron would look for them. Trikan says, "I think it's safe now to break radio silence! There's nothing around that could catch up with us before we land at the base. I'm going to send a message to the safe house."

A few moments pass, and Chef Eleanor answers the message, "Johnathan! I'm happy you finally contacted us; we were beginning to worry. The professor tried—" Trikan interrupts her, "Thank you, Eleanor, for being concerned; I did not need to make contact with the Professor at any time."

She replies, "Yes, I understand. All communications were disrupted due to the heat shields. We just got back online this morning from the damage they did, and I spoke to the professor!" Trikan then asks, "Did you say heat shields? Eleanor, can I please speak with him?" Her response is immediate, "No, you can't, he's not here. The professor and Elisa visited Doctor Lasara and Reanna in Star Port City! Oh, captain, as it turned out, after they landed on the roof of the court building, they weren't able to come back! When the roof was hit by debris from the heat shields, it damaged the upper floors of the court building and destroyed your flightcraft. I'm afraid they have no way of getting back, Johnathan!"

Trikan pauses momentarily and then says, "Eleanor...?" She continues, "Parts of the city are also destroyed! There were no casualties, and everyone left the city before the storm arrived. It took nearly all day for it to happen, and everyone was allowed to go!"

Trikan hesitates again and replies, "You're the best, Eleanor. I'm on my way to get them out of there!"

The Army Flight Base is just north of Star Port City's significant transit hub, which makes it easy for Trikan and his crew to get into the city undetected.

Most of Star Port City remains under the control of the generals, who have a depleted force to maintain order. Desertion has taken its toll on the unit's strength in the city and throughout the outer zones, in protest against the unlawful act of removing civilian authority from government control. Several days have passed since he took on the mission to free Elisa, and his entire world has changed. He is no longer the center of this authoritative society that was out to destroy him.

The captain and his crew arrive at the **A-1A ARMY LANDING AIR DOME,** which is connected by a monorail to the large *Maglev* transportation terminal, which was not destroyed by the fallen heat shields. Military sentry robots patrol the area around the flight terminal, and after the hydrocopter fighter-craft lands, two security robots walk over to the lead flightcraft, carrying laser rifles. Trikan is wearing a flight jacket and a flight helmet bearing the rank of First Captain, and as he slides open the side of the window on the pilot's control cockpit of the fighter aircraft, the security robot asks, **"CAPTAIN... DO YOU HAVE YOUR AIR FLIGHT IDENTIFICATION...?"**

Trikan hesitates momentarily and watches as the last of the fighter hydro-craft lands. He then pulls a metallic identification plate out of the craft's control dash console and hands it to the security robot. The security robot replies, **"... YOU WILL HAVE TO REMAIN IN YOUR FIGHTER CRAFT AND GIVE YOUR MEN A COMMAND NOT TO DISEMBARK FROM THEIR CRAFT UNTIL YOU RECEIVE YOUR CLEARANCE IDENTIFICATION..."**

As the command security robot leaves with the ID plate, Trikan looks at the other security robot standing outside the craft, his laser rifle pointed directly at Trian's hydro-craft, ready to fire. Trikan slowly releases the safety lock on his laser weapon, and he does not take his eyes off the command security officer as he enters the airbase control terminal.

Once in the compound, Trikan tells his crew in code sequence, "Sit tight! Don't attempt to leave your flightcraft until I tell you. You all know where the terminal is; keep watch, downrange!"

Each fighter-craft personnel loads their weaponry with small explosive cartridges designed for low-frequency, rapid-fire rotation to destroy many small moving targets. Before Trikan can continue his coded conversation with his crew, the hangar bay doors open, and a security battle group of sentry robots comes out firing their laser weapons at several of the fighter-crafts. Their attack destroys one of the fighter-crafts while damaging two others on the field. They then receive a surge of high-velocity fusion fire back from Trikans' command, eliminating the entire battle group of robots. Before the sentry robot, standing guard outside Trikans' fighter craft, can take evasive action against him, he is destroyed by a sudden blast from the captain's laser weapon.

Moments later, Trikan gives another command to fire again. This time, the fighter craft sends neutron missiles that travel across the field and hit the air control tower building, destroying the entire airbase control facility and adding further destruction to the general's authoritative rule over Star Port City.

Most of the government buildings that have endured for centuries are now covered in crushed rubble by the massive heat shields, with the exception of the court complex building and the government counsel chamber, which was spared; it is here that Aunt Lasara and Reanna have taken refuge with Justice Calandra in her private quarters. Governmental court security guards maintain order, while President Tollon calls an emergency session for all council members.

In the proceedings before the council, the president announces that several high-ranking command generals have been placed under house arrest and ordered to appear immediately before the full council to explain their role in the disaster.

As the generals arrive and enter the council chamber, President Tollon tells them, "Do you realize what you have done? You have destroyed our city and also destroyed the confidence in a free government! We will immediately begin negotiating a peace treaty with the Trikinians. We need them for whatever help they are willing to give to restore order! The new president, Justice Calandra, will address the population regarding a proposed peace treaty with the Trikinians. She will broadcast this message to every citizen as soon as she contacts the Trikinian ambassador when our telescreen communications are repaired."

The top floor of the old government building, with its marble columns still intact, has a damaged roof above five marble floors that showcase the building's antique history. The professor and his daughter, Elisa, along with several of Trikans' company troops who were assigned to him but did not participate in the rainforest operation, await news from outside these hastily constructed barracks. Elisa nervously paces back and forth while holding a military communication field telescreen to her ear. Impatiently, she gestures with her hands, "When will the power come back on?"

The professor replies, "Did you try the telescreen, Elisa?"

"All dead! We lost everything since yesterday, and today we still have nothing!"

The professor tries in vain to calm Elisa down, but nothing he says makes the slightest difference. "My dear Elisa... I'm afraid it's up to..." He pauses and then remains silent for a few moments. "I regret to say it may take several more days before we have communication back!"

Elisa continues with a worrisome outburst, "Did we win? Did we lose? Is it over for us?"

Her outburst is interrupted by a noise from below the building lobby entrance. The scout troops sitting in the room with Elisa and the professor instantly respond to the noise. They all take defensive positions around the room, expecting an attack, as one of the troopers runs towards the entrance and puts his ear against the door with his weapon in a ready-to-fire position. Some of the other scout troops speak in hushed voices. The one who has taken a position by the doors turns and motions, "Don't anyone move, I hear voices."

The other scout troops sit quietly in the rubble of the broken marble columns from the ceiling debris; their weapons pointed toward the doors in a fixed position. The lead scout troop reaches up, unlocks the doors, and slowly moves back from his forward position with his weapon ready to fire.

At first, the voices outside cannot be identified. Captain Trikan and his group of scouts had made their way to the top-floor lobby. Their voices have now become familiar and echo down the marble corridors. Elisa, standing by the professor, immediately reacts when she recognizes Trikans' voice. "It's the Captain!"

As she runs toward the double doors, she pushes them open and, without hesitation, enters the lobby. Two of Trikans' command troops are startled and turn their weapons on Elisa.

Instantly, they realize she is one of them and lower their weapons. One of the scouts shakes his head in disbelief as Elisa ignores them, runs a short distance, and throws herself into Captain Trikans' arms.

Trikan says to her, "I guess you missed me?" Smiling, she replies, "You know I did!"

A moment later, the power comes back on, and the massive ornate chandeliers illuminate the once forbidding dark corridors of this old government building complex. The large telescreens are also back online, broadcasting the president and the council's leadership as they address the general population. They reassure them that contact has been made with the Trikinian ambassador and that peace negotiations will begin immediately.

Trikan and Elisa are about to follow his troops into the room when suddenly Trikan stops and tells Elisa, "I hear something down the corridor!"

As he placed his laser rifle and field pack in the doorway, he told Elisa to wait. He then walks down the hall, checks several open rooms, and realizes that the sounds he heard came farther down the hallway. As he continues, he opens the doors to several more office facilities until he comes to the last room with the door open and the lights on. He walks in and realizes the sound he heard came from a telescreen left on before the power outage.

He walks over to turn the telescreen off and hears, "Remember me, Captain?"

Trikan turns around and says, "Oh, it's you again, Marcus! Did you enjoy your trip down the mountain?" Marcus replies, "Your sense of humor doesn't amuse me, Captain! I had my chance to get rid of you in court that day. It was a mistake, I should have! Then you had your chance, captain! You should have followed me down the mountain. Now it's too late for you to destroy me, Captain!"

As Marcus has his laser weapon pointed directly at the captain and is about to fire, Trikan instantly activates his invisibility screen and disappears as Marcus's laser blast strikes across the room. Suddenly, he hears a voice behind him. "Maybe he can't destroy you. BUT I CAN!"

As he turns, Elisa says, "This is for Jean!" She then fires Trikans' laser rifle, instantly destroying the assassin, Marcus.

Trikan reappears and says to Elisa, "You did it again!"

Elisa replies, "You mean saved your life?" She smiles. "You owe me, Captain!"

Smiling back, he says, "I wouldn't have it any other way!"

Elisa and Trikan return to the big room and join the scout troops on the terrace with the professor. They look down at the cheering crowds that have heard the announcements of a new peace treaty with the Trikinians and the appointment of Justice Calandra as the new president. They then notice the uniformed personnel on the balcony with Captain Trikan, who helped fight and secure their freedom.

They start waving and calling up to them as many in the crowd begin to chant Trikan's name. Elisa raises her voice above the cheering crowds and shouts, "Professor, can we make it back to Trikinia?" The professor replies, "No, I'm afraid not. With the damage that was caused by the heat shields, it's going to take a while before we can get back to Trikinia."

As the crowd continues to celebrate, the captain calls out to the professor, "We're NOT going to Trikinia, and we're NOT staying here. We're going to the Asteroid!"

Elisa automatically remarks, "The Asteroid?"

Trikan then states, "Yes! How can I find Earth if I stay here?"

The professor looks at the captain with an expression of disbelief, "You're serious, Captain?"

"Yes, professor, there must be some information on that old wreck, something we can use to find Earth?"

Trikan turns and makes his way through the crowded balcony of scout troops and receives their congratulatory praise for a job well done. Before entering back into the large lobby on his way to the hydro lift with the professor following him, he spots Sergeant Larsen coming out of one of the hydro lifts with some newly arrived scout troops. Larsen calls out, "Captain!"

As Trikan makes his way through the crowd, he says to Sergeant Larsen, "Good to see you!"

"Same here, Captain!"

"Your arm is all fixed up?"

"Yes, Captain, it's all good now. Thank you, Sir!"

"So, you're back with your command unit, Sergeant?"

"Yes, Sir, Captain!"

Trikan acknowledges, "It's all going to be good now, Sergeant."

"Yes, Sir, I agree!"

Trikan and the professor work through the crowd until they find an available hydro lift. As Elisa is still engaged in a conversation with several female unit scouts, she realizes that she must catch up to Trikan and the professor before they leave. She ends the conversation pleasantly and runs through the crowd after Trikan and the professor, shouting, "Hey... Wait for me!"

Before Elisa makes it to the hydro lift, the professor tells Trikan, "If you are going to the asteroid, Captain, you'll need a flight transport. This is a government facility, Captain; we may be able to find one for you."

Elisa reacts urgently, not a moment too soon, as she runs into Trikans' arms and says to him, "You're still trying to get away from me? I told you, it's not going to happen!

" As the doors to the lift begin to close, Trikan smiles at her and replies in a comforting voice, "That is exactly what I was trying to do."

Smiling, she says, "You're a big liar!"

Seconds later, before any more words can be spoken, the doors to the retro lift open at the sub-level, revealing several official government flightcraft. Standing there are Aunt Lasara, Reanna, and the new President, Calandra.

Smiling, Aunt Lasara says, "Are you looking for a flightcraft, Johnathan? We were just about to go upstairs and celebrate with you. President Calandra insisted that we come up and see you!" The professor says, "That's quite remarkable, if I may say so myself. Coincidence and reality, a perfect balance on the scale! How extraordinary!"

As the new president extends her hand to Trikan, she says, "Thank you, Captain, for the help you gave to give us back our freedom that we so well deserve!"

As President Calandra hands the code plate of her flightcraft to Trikan, she says, "I was about to give this to your Aunt Lasara to give to you, as a gift from me! As long as you are here, I want to say good luck, Captain! It's your ship now; I thank you again!"

Trikan remains silent momentarily and then says, "I don't know what to say."

President Calandra says to him, "Be well, Captain, and my best wishes for both of you!"

Aunt Lasara and Reanna walk Trikan, Elisa, and the professor across the gantry landing bay to the president's flight transport, spending a couple of moments embracing and wishing Trikan and Elisa a safe journey.

Elisa gets on board first, followed by the professor and the captain. Taking his place in the control com, the captain activates the module's flight power systems. As the large passenger flight transport begins its antimagnetic surface lift across the gantry, it exits the government building.

Once it reaches orbital space, it goes into free flight at hypersonic speed towards the asteroid belt. During that period, Elisa spent her time selecting the emergency-exit flight oxygen suits for when they landed on the asteroid. She attaches the oxygen-breathing helmets necessary for their extravehicular activity of the interior inspection of the crashed ship *Andromeda*, which now offers no onboard sealed unit sections containing oxygen.

The automatic preprogrammed flight plan to the asteroid crash site stays on course as Trikan receives a message from Alden, wishing him a safe voyage and reminding him that the Trikinian people will always welcome him back. He then says, "Commander LamBrute would also like to say a few words to you, Captain!"

"Captain... Stay well, my friend!"

Trikan smiles as he replies, "We will always be on a mission together, LamBrute, when we fight for our freedom. May the Eagles of Trikinia watch over us, my friend!"

Suddenly, the destination alarm signal comes on throughout the ship as it approaches the asteroid field. Ground radar-computer electronics disengage the thrust engines, while onboard robotics scan the asteroid for suitable topographic landing sites near the crashed ship. Danger-screen landing lights illuminate the exterior of the huge, ill-fated *Andromeda,* as combination screen cameras send eerie close-up photo scans to the onboard computer and to the captain, Elisa, and the professor. The onboard computer makes final adjustments for a smooth landing on the asteroid terrain, a short distance from the ship, *Andromeda.*

On its final landing approach, the thrust engines dislodge the landing field beneath the ship, which is composed of stones and burnt asteroid material, triggering a vast dust storm. The touchdown seemed uneventful until the underside cameras revealed a large fissure splitting a section of the asteroid. Standing behind the captain, Elisa is almost thrown to the floor as the craft rocks back and forth, then stabilizes and comes to a landing.

Several moments later, as the dust settles outside the craft, clear pictures appear on several view screens inside the control cabin of the flight transport. Trikan works the keyboard beneath the large telescreen for a close-up view of the destruction of the ill-fated *Andromeda.* After the activation of the aerial cameras, the craft's communication-information relay becomes activated, and a metallic voice speaks out from the viewscreen:

"THIS IS YOUR AUTOMATIC CRAFT PILOT... YOUR DIRECTIONAL FIELD FINDER IS NOT NECESSARY... YOU ARE WITHIN WALKING DISTANCE OF YOUR DESTINATION... THE AREA THAT YOU SELECTED DOES NOT CONTAIN ATMOSPHERIC CONDITIONS THAT CAN SUPPORT LIFE ENTITIES... YOU WILL NEED LIFE SUPPORT UNITS TO LEAVE THE SHIP AND DESCEND TO THE SURFACE OF THE CLASSIFICATION READOUT PERTAINING TO THE HOSTILE ENVIRONMENT OF THE

PLANETOID, COMMONLY REFERRED TO AS AN ASTEROID... OUTSIDE TEMPERATURE RANGES FROM ONE HUNDRED AND TEN DEGREES TO TWO HUNDRED AND EIGHTY DEGREES, WHICH VARIES UNSPECIFIED, DUE TO FREQUENT SOLAR WINDS THAT REMAIN CONSTANT THROUGHOUT THE ASTEROID FIELD... BEFORE LEAVING THE SHIP... YOU MUST SUIT UP AND TEST YOUR OXYGEN-PRODUCING EVA-EQUIPMENT... DEADLY GASES EMANATE FROM BENEATH THE POROUS COMPOUNDS THAT MAKE UP MOST OF THE ASTEROID'S SURFACE..."

Before Elisa takes her eyes off the viewscreen, which shows a close-up of the damaged control com of the *Andromeda*, including a tear of twisted metal down the port side of the ship, she remarks, "How did any of them survive the initial impact?"

The professor responds, "In fact, Elisa, most of them did not! The exception was a young child and his nurse, who lived long enough to give him life and send out an emergency distress signal to orbital communication satellites that were in place at that time, due to mining operations in the asteroid belt. Unfortunately, by the time help came, the child's nurse could not be saved." Trikan remains silent as he turns off the telescreen and says, "We'd better suit up, Professor!" Before any conversation can continue, the ship's automatic pressurized exit door opens, and an elevation platform lowers several folding steps that continue until they touch the ground of the asteroid. As they exit the transport, they stop for several moments and stand before the wreckage of the enormous spaceship *Andromeda* without saying a word. The professor then remarks, "It was magnificent, Captain!"

"I agree, Professor."

Trikan pauses for several moments and then says in a low voice, "I wonder how many passengers were on board?"

As they approach the large opening of the *Andromeda*, debris blocks a clear path to enter the ship. Trikan clears away several damaged heavy exterior panels that are blocking their entry into the hull. Its burnt interior and other destroyed compartments throughout the communication area of this once spacious luxury transport no longer exist.

The dark interior is illuminated by the bright spectral beam lights on their helmets as they walk through the cluttered entryways from the control bridge to the ship's interior. Damaged compartments lead to the ship's operational central command, which contains a hangar dome resembling a dispatch center for smaller flight crafts.

A section level above the high ceiling at the center of the ship features two escalator units: one that carries passengers to the upper level and the other that descends, returning to the main midway hangar area. Professor Zola becomes interested in what appears to be a hangar command dispatch center, featuring a large screen at the back of the control modules for seating personnel. These modules resemble flight release coordination commonly used in spaceport hangar centers. On closer examination, the professor shines his light on the substantial walled telescreen in the back of the flight operations center, and he says, "Look at this, Captain! Behind the poly-glass screen is a star map of a universal star system that, to my knowledge, does not exist."

He says softly, "It's a place in the universe called the gateway to the Constellation Orion."

Trikan takes a photocopy of the map with his Dial-Date computer. Elisa then calls out to Trikan, who has wandered off on her own, "Trikan..." A little more excited, she calls out a second time, "Captain, come down here and look at this! It's a banquet hall!"

Trikan asks the professor to check his Dial-Date photo of the star map and submit it to memory storage on his arm computer. "I'll be right back."

When the captain reaches the open archway that leads into a fashionably decorated dining room, he is presented with large murals of scenes from a period with which he is unacquainted.

Trikan spends moments of interest as he observes the murals of an astronaut stepping off a Lunar Module and touching the moon's surface for the first time. Then, another large mural of a circular space station orbiting a blue planet in the distant background.

Standing for a moment and looking at the banquet table and the rest of the large banquet room, he realized that this section of the ship was not affected by the impact of the *Andromeda* crashing into the asteroid.

Trikan then calls Elisa, "Elisa, do you hear me?"

Elisa answers, "I'm down the hallway... I am in a medical center... No, it's a nursery!"

Trikan leaves the dining room and walks down the passage corridor to Elisa, following her helmet's bright beacon lights.

As he walks into the nursery, he feels like he's been here before. Elisa is puzzled by his silence and says, "What's wrong, Trikan? Are you alright?"

In a low voice, he replies, "This seems somewhat familiar to me, and I don't know why."

He says, "Come on, Elisa, let's go find the Professor!"

When they arrive back at where the professor is, they remain quiet, daring not to take his attention away from the work he was able to achieve in reactivating some of *Andromeda's* computer time and space navigational coordinates. Trikan looks up at the large screen above the computer center, to a full-wall projection screen of space and time. As a star chart of a galaxy appears, it is identified as the Milky

Way.

During this segment, the ship's memory relay charts appear at the bottom of the screen, showing the exact location of nine planets near the Alpha Centauri Star System. The professor's wrist-computer Dial-Date has collected the information, and as he hands it to the captain, he says, "This is going to be very valuable to you, Captain. It seems the ship's computers have been communicating with each other after being away on a long journey, in another dimension of time." Elisa then adds, "How strange is that?"

Turning to her, he responds, "It's not strange at all, my dear. There are many dimensions in time and many secrets in the universe! The computers are now back online after the ship was destroyed. When it crashed here, on the asteroid... I do not have the answer for you, but somehow the ship's computers could continue communicating in a time continuum mystery that I cannot explain."

Captain Trikan stares at the screen momentarily and tells the professor, "According to your Dial-Date and the ship's computer read-out log, the *Andromeda* traveled two and a half years at light speed!"

The professor then says, "Captain, if you are about to say what I'm thinking, repairing this ship would be a major task and not necessary. If you do indeed want to travel to this place called Earth," Elisa interrupts the professor and says, "Professor, I'm going with him!"

Smiling, the professor tells her, "Yes, I know, and I will miss both of you." Trikan then asks, "Professor, the tiny gold bracelet that I asked you to hold for me before I left Trikinia... May I have it?"

"The gold bracelet, Captain?"

The professor pauses for several moments and then says, "The gold bracelet...? Perhaps I lost it, Captain. I am sorry!"

Trikan replies, "That's all right, Professor, it's not that important."

The professor then continues, "Getting back to your decision, Captain, if you recall, when we were on our way to Trikinia, we entered the cavern wall behind the statue of the warrior. We were in a large observatory, surrounded by ancient books. When we looked up, there was a telescope for studying the universe, and the interior walls were lined with volumes of ancient textbooks. None of it was real, Captain! The interior structure was just a hologram."

The crashing sounds of broken debris hit the devastated hull of the *Andromeda* as the professor raises his voice. "We didn't know then that we were in some ancient flightcraft hidden inside the mountains of Trikinia! Had I not satisfied my curiosity, Captain, and removed the old manuscripts that were stored beneath the shelves of books, I would not have discovered that they contained writings from the ancient scribes. After reading these manuscripts, I realized they were star charts that do not exist in our star quadrant, Captain! This was testimony that this mountain was indeed a spaceport for a spaceship of interstellar travel. It all took place as it was written according to the documents, a very long time ago!"

Their conversation is interrupted by ominous sounds outside the ill-fated *Andromeda*. The professor immediately recognizes the sounds as the asteroid breaking apart!

Trikan tells him, "I'd better go and remove our equipment." Elisa adds, "I will go with you, Trikan!" The professor then says, "I'll see what other information I can get from this computer."

As the professor approaches the computer display console, he activates a sequence of commands to Trikinia. Moments later, the large double-domed roof hatches open, while beacon indicators flash inside the hollow mountain construction silo, which begins to ignite its hydro-fusion energy blast field.

As the professor continues to type in the ship's voyage command, along with the crash site location of the *Andromeda* on the asteroid, the blast engines ignite and lift the ship from the hangar port in the mountain, while sending topographic anomalies throughout the mountain regions of Trikinia.

The engines then engage in a full-stage velocity blast, and like a giant life force of mysterious creation, the ship rises and leaves the mountain silo as it passes over on its flight to the asteroid. The large ship blocks out the starlit sky as it continues its automatic, preprogrammed flight.

Trikan and Elisa exit the transport craft that brought them to the asteroid, and after removing some supplies they'll need, their departure isn't too soon. The craft they used to reach the asteroid falls through a fissure into open space as that section of the asteroid breaks apart. Trikan and Elisa make their way back to the Andromeda and climb aboard through the torn, damaged hull of the ship to join the professor.

As the intensity of the asteroid's solar wind increases in velocity, it carries debris past the ship's portal view windows and continuously strikes the hull of the *Andromeda*. Breaking through some exterior vision port windows, Trikan, Elisa, and the professor try to find a safe place inside the ship, away from the damaged open section of the forward com area.

The professor says, "Captain, the ship inside the mountain is a *Time Craft*, and it's on its way! The ship is capable of bending space and time during its flight. Do you still want to find Earth, Captain?"

"Yes, Professor!"

Looking at Elisa, the professor says, "And you, my dearest daughter Elisa, your mother, and I will miss you. Keep her well, Captain!" Looking at Elisa, Trikan smiles as he replies, "I will, professor… I will!"

The professor leaves them and goes to the torn-out, damaged port section, looking out into the storm. "Your ship is landing, Captain!"

As he looks out again into the turbulent winds of the Asteroid Belt, being hit by wind and particles of asteroid debris, he says, "Hurry... before it's too late!" He then calls back to the captain, "Captain, you and Elisa must leave now!"

Trikan grabs Elisa by the arm, and the two of them begin to climb down onto the broken debris of the *Andromeda*. Elisa yells back, "Professor, we can't leave you here! Why are you staying?" The professor shouts down to her, "Don't worry about me! There's a rescue ship coming for me! Now GO, if you want to survive!"

Trikan is about to call back to the professor, but before he can say anything, the professor raises his voice over the strong asteroid winds and says, "Captain, the ship can only provide several moments to board! Do not worry about me; now GO!"

Captain Trikan and Elisa ran towards the passenger lift platform and were immediately picked up into the spacecraft. The emergency relay controls sound for passengers to follow flight instructions at alarmed sequences, to strap themselves into flight-controlled passenger seats after the unit-controlled craft enters an orbital flight.

An instant later, the ship's massive engines lift the craft off the asteroid, causing more destructive damage to the asteroid as the ship leaves its landing site.

The ship's voice control modulation announces:
"ATTENTION ... ATTENTION... ONCE IN ORBITAL SPACE, WE WILL APPROACH LIGHT SPEED IN TEN-QUARTER-SEQUENCES OF TIME... ALL PERSONNEL MUST ENTER HIBERNATION UNITS BEFORE THE END OF THE FIRST QUARTER SEQUENCE..."

As they stand in the control room, a teary-eyed Elisa grabs the captain's hand and says, "Trikan, do you think my father will be rescued and taken off that asteroid in time?"

"Yes, Elisa, I think the professor will be just fine."

As Trikan looks at the ship's telescreens, he observes the entire asteroid breaking up, with the *Andromeda* and its contents being carried away in the intense solar winds to become part of the universe's ancient memory. Trikan and Elisa kiss moments before entering the hibernation units as the ship begins to enter the high-velocity time sequence.

Cen-Ton is pouring a cup of tea for Ambassador Annora, and she says, "Thank you, Cen-Ton. Please take the tea kettle to the professor and tell him not to stay up too late." As Cen-Ton opens the door to a dimly lit room cluttered with antiquated experimental devices and shelves lined with old books and manuscripts, the professor reads a book on his desk under a single-lit lamp. Cen-Ton enters carrying the tray, and as he approaches the professor, he asks, "... PROFESSOR, WOULD YOU LIKE A CUP OF TEA...?"

The professor puts down the book he is reading and answers, "Oh, yes, thank you, Cen-ton. That would be nice."

The robot places the tray on the professor's cluttered desk and pours the tea into his cup. He then places the kettle back onto the tray and turns to leave the room. "... PROFESSOR... AMBASSADOR ANNORA SAID TO TELL YOU NOT TO STAY UP TOO LATE..."

"Yes, thank you, Cen-Ton!"

Stopping a few feet from the desk, Cen-Ton picks up a small gold bracelet and turns to the professor. "... PROFESSOR... I BELIEVE YOU DROPPED THIS...?"

Again, the professor's attention is taken away from his book as the robot hands him the bracelet. The professor takes it from him and, for a moment, reads the inscription inside the bracelet: ***Johnathan Shawnwood – Scotland Earth.*** He pauses for a couple of moments before placing it into his vest pocket. He then replies, "Thank you, Cen-Ton."

The robot is about to leave the professor's study when he stops, turns, and asks, "... PROFESSOR... DO YOU THINK THE CAPTAIN AND ELISA WILL FIND THEIR DESTINY...?"

Professor Zola suddenly stops reading, places his book on his desk, and says, "I believe they already have!"

Cen-Ton replies, "...I WILL MISS THEM, PROFESSOR..."

"Yes... We will all miss them, Cen-Ton."

www.ingramcontent.com/pod-product-compliance
Lightning Source LLC
LaVergne TN
LVHW021753060526
838201LV00058B/3081